One Classic Latin Lover, Please

MARCIA LYNN McCLURE

Published by Distractions Ink
P.O. Box 15971
Rio Rancho, NM 87174

Published by Distractions Ink
©Copyright 2012 by M. Meyers
A.K.A. Marcia Lynn McClure
Cover Photography by ©Somakram/Dreamstime.com and
©Geotrac/Dreamstime.com
Cover Design and Interior Graphics by Sandy Ann Allred/Timeless Allure

First Printed Edition: December 2012

All character names and personalities in this work of fiction are entirely
fictional, created solely in the imagination of the author.
Any resemblance to any person living or dead is coincidental.

McClure, Marcia Lynn, 1965—
One Classic Latin Lover, Please: a novel/by Marcia Lynn McClure.

ISBN: 978-0-9884276-4-8

Library of Congress Control Number: 2012951958

Printed in the United States of America

To a Cast of Characters Who Inspire Me…
To Ricardo Montalbán and Gene Tierney.
To my college roommate and forever-friend, Sandy.
To my children, Sandy, Mitch, and Trent—who love the positive,
upbeat, danceable music of the '80s almost as much as their dad and
I do. (They also know that there is no substitute for Steve Perry!)
To Rob Pilatus (who now rests in peace) and Fabrice Morvan—
I don't care what the music industry, history, or anybody else says.
Rob and Fab rocked the big shoulder pads and long braids! They
sang one of my favorite songs ("Girl, You Know It's True") and will
always be the real Milli Vanilli to me!
And finally, to anyone who has ever inspired me in any regard,
whether in my writing or in life.
Thank you!

CHAPTER ONE

Tierney O'Brien faked a grateful smile as she thanked Maisey Buchanon for the red satin and lace baby-doll nightie. She smiled, blushed when everyone made the expected "Wooo-whooo!" exclamation, and said, "Thank you so much, Maisey! I'm sure Dillon will love it!"

But Tierney's stomach churned with a slight nausea at the thought of wearing something so scandalous and revealing it in front of Dillon Hawthorne on their wedding night—on *any* night, for that matter. Sure, she was engaged to Dillon. She'd been engaged to him for nearly six months—dated him for six months before that. And Tierney was fond enough of Dillon. But since the moment he'd asked her to marry him and she'd said yes, Tierney O'Brien had owned the sinking, almost sickening feeling that she'd made a mistake. And as her wedding day inched closer and closer, the seemingly permanent nausea that had taken up residence in her stomach the instant Dillon had slipped the three-carat solitaire onto her finger grew stronger and stronger.

As Bethany Howard handed another bridal shower gift to Tierney, she could almost hear her brother's voice echoing through her head. *Don't marry this guy just because Dad and Mom picked him out and pushed you together, Tierney,* Alec had told her over and over again. *Hold out for someone you're really, really in love with!*

As the bridal shower guests watched Tierney begin to open the gift wrapped in silver and white, Tierney's stomach spasmed with anxiety. One more week and it would be too late to cancel the wedding! One more week and it would be done: she'd be Mrs. Dillon Hawthorne. But

Tierney gritted her teeth and tore open the paper to reveal yet another lingerie box with the Victoria's Secret logo on it.

"Oh, wow!" she exclaimed with false excitement.

"You will *love* this one, Tiern!" Aubrey Fairchild exclaimed.

"You mean *Dillon* will love it!" Aubrey's twin sister, Tiffany, added with an insinuative giggle.

Again Tierney felt her cheeks pink up as she drew the elegant yet very sexy red satin and black lace out of its box. Naturally the expected catcalls erupted from the guests, and Tierney's stomach, already sore with churning and nausea, tied itself into knots of anxiety.

"I hope you've been tanning, Tierney," Blair Sinclair commented. "Otherwise the red will totally wash you out!"

"Blair!" Aubrey scolded. "It will not! Everyone looks fabulous in red. Especially Tierney."

"You guys…thank you so, so much!" Tierney announced, studying the ridiculously large mountain of opened bridal gifts, most of which were sexy lingerie. She wondered for a moment what ever happened to people giving brides-to-be things like Crock-Pots, toasters, and spatulas. Yet glancing around the circle of friends in attendance, she could see that not one of her pampered and wealthy friends ever spent a moment in the kitchen.

Tierney sighed, realizing that when she went shopping for Aubrey Fairchild's bridal shower—for Aubrey was to be married exactly one month after Tierney—she certainly wouldn't be buying a Crock-Pot for Aubrey. Nope. Aubrey was definitely a Victoria's Secret kind of girl.

Again Tierney's anxiety welled as she thought of her impending wedding night with Dillon. She wouldn't even feel comfortable wearing her red-and-black plaid flannel Christmas pajamas in front of him, let alone the silky, sexy nightgown the Fairchild twins had just given her. And shouldn't a woman feel at least somewhat comfortable in anticipating intimacy with the man she was married to? Shouldn't she be actually looking forward to it?

Yet Tierney's mother had told her that she hadn't been comfortable with Tierney's father for a couple of years after they were married, assuring Tierney that all the anxiety she was feeling about marrying Dillon was absolutely normal.

Alec, on the other hand, vehemently disagreed. When Tierney had called her older brother and only sibling to tell him she'd accepted Dillon's proposal, she thought for a moment that Alec O'Brien was going to reach through the phone and strangle her! In fact, Alec had spent nearly two hours trying to talk Tierney into calling Dillon that very night and breaking up with him—not just telling him she'd changed her mind about marrying him but breaking up with him altogether.

But Tierney was confused, scared, and frustrated. She wasn't strong like Alec was—strong enough to respectfully stand up to her parents the way Alec had. Furthermore, what if Dillon was the one she was meant to be with? After all, a guy didn't propose marriage to a girl if he weren't serious about building a life with her—a family—right?

"Now apparently your brother has a shower gift for you, Tierney," Tierney's mother said, snapping her attention back to the festivities at hand.

"What?" Tierney asked.

Glynnis O'Brien sighed with exasperation at Tierney's inattentiveness. "Alec," she explained. "He's sent some silly gift for you to open here."

But Tierney smiled. She loved her brother more than anything or anyone. She knew he was disappointed in the fact she was marrying Dillon, but she also knew he loved her unconditionally. Alec had always been her strength, and she'd missed him so much since he'd moved to Washington State. She'd often wondered whether, had Alec still been living at home when Tierney had begun getting into a more serious relationship with Dillon, Alec could have given her the courage to walk away—no matter what consequences their parents exacted on Tierney.

"What is it?" Tierney asked with sudden excitement and less despair. "What did Alec send, Mom?"

But Glynnis rolled her eyes and shrugged. "Well, I don't know, Tierney," she whined. "Probably one of his stupid—"

"When should we bring in the stripper, Mrs. O'Brien?" Tierney heard Blair whisper to her mother.

"Later, later," Glynnis whispered, waving with one hand in a gesture of dismissal. "We'll get Alec's gift out of the way first."

Instantly, the momentary zeal Tierney had experienced over learning Alec had sent a gift for her evaporated. Oh, how she loathed the male strippers the mothers of her friends always hired to perform at their daughters' bridal showers. Oh sure, they were always good-looking, incredibly buff professionals. Madison Waverly's mother had even managed to hire a real Chippendale stripper for Madison's bridal shower. But acting like a bunch of idiots over some stranger stripping off his shirt and pants to stand there dancing around in his way-too-small underwear just wasn't Tierney's idea of entertainment.

Of course, Tierney realized her ideas of entertainment varied greatly from the norm—from the norm of the new century anyway. While the friends in Tierney's social circle enjoyed Broadway, lavish parties, endless shopping, and being slathered with jewelry, exotic trips, and other gifts from men attempting to win them, Tierney enjoyed community theater, quiet evenings at home in front of the fire, volunteering at the local orphanages and rest homes, and watching old MGM musicals.

In fact, it was more often than not that both Tierney and her brother, Alec, joked about having been switched at birth with children of normal, middle-class families they each wished they belonged to—for even Alec had tastes that leaned more toward cheeseburgers than shrimp cocktail.

Tierney smiled as she thought of her brother, Alec. He'd been her confidant, her protector, the only person in all the world who truly knew who Tierney was—knew the true desires of her heart. She giggled a little as she thought of Ricardo then. Even Ricardo had come from Alec. He'd been a gift for Tierney's fourteenth birthday, and Tierney O'Brien would never forget the first moment she'd walked into her bedroom to find the life-sized cardboard cutout of a young Ricardo Montalbán standing in her room beside her bed.

The fact was Tierney had fallen in love with Ricardo Montalbán when she'd been no more than eight years old. Left to her own devices one night by her nanny while her parents had been out to a New Year's Eve party and Alec had been sick in bed with the flu, Tierney had settled down and begun flipping satellite channels. Suddenly, something caught her attention—a young and handsome, very dashing, very romantic Ricardo Montalbán, waltzing with a youthful, shy, and innocently lovely Jane Powell. It was Tierney's first mid-twentieth-century MGM musical and would always remain her favorite. And in that moment, it had contributed to defining her.

From that night on, Tierney O'Brien seemed to come to know herself through vintage movies of the twentieth century and nostalgia of all sorts. Tierney found that she loved not only the happy endings of the old 1950s musicals (realistic or not) but also the "Latin lover" ideal of the time period. In fact, her love for the old movie Latin lover concept prompted her to do her research as well. Certainly, Ricardo Montalbán reigned as her favorite of the old Latin lovers, but she also studied and enjoyed the performances of the very first cinematic Latin lover Rudolph Valentino (though he was, in fact, Italian and not Latin). Although Tierney did not find Valentino to be nearly as handsome or attractive as Ricardo Montalbán, she was pleasantly taken with Valentino's manner of kissing a woman. It had always been Tierney's opinion that Valentino's popularity with women had more to do with the fact that he kissed a woman the way all women of the silent movie era dreamed of being kissed—dramatically, passionately, and, above all, thoroughly! Even considering the modern times in which Tierney lived, she had never been kissed the way Valentino kissed Nita Naldi in his 1925 film *Cobra*. Even the manner in which Rudolph Valentino merely kissed a woman's hand made Tierney's heart leap more than any kiss she'd ever experienced.

The only modern-day actor Tierney had ever added to her list of ideal Latin lovers was Antonio Banderas. Until the day she'd seen his performance with Catherine Zeta Jones in the mid-1990s version of *The Mask of Zorro*, even Antonio had not made Tierney's list. Yet as Zorro he finally had.

It wasn't that Tierney lived in a fantasy world, avoiding reality and believing nonsense. She knew the cinematic Latin lovers of the early to mid-twentieth century were purely daydreams—learned early on to admire the actors' performances and not the actors themselves. With the exception of her beloved Ricardo Montalbán—a devoutly loyal husband to his wife, Georgiana, for sixty-three years, Georgiana's unexpected death being the only thing to separate them in the end—most Latin lover actors led scandalous lives when not on screen.

Therefore, though Tierney enjoyed the movie performances of Valentino, his successor Ramón Novarro, and Ricardo Montalbán's comrade in Latin lovers arms Fernando Lamas (and an occasional Antonio Banderas performance), she did not get lost in the rationalizing infatuation that women of the generations upon generations before her had. She simply adored the characters they played.

Yet through it all, the man born November 25, 1920, in Mexico City as Ricardo Gonzalo Pedro Montalbán y Merino remained Tierney O'Brien's ideal dream-man. And every morning since the day she turned fourteen, Tierney awoke with a smile as the image of Ricardo Montalbán greeted her from the life-sized cardboard cutout Alec had lovingly gifted her years before.

It was one of the many regrets Tierney had about accepting Dillon's proposal and her upcoming wedding. She'd have to leave Ricardo Montalbán behind! No man would want a life-sized cardboard cutout of Ricardo Montalbán lingering in their bedroom—and it bothered Tierney that she regretted leaving Ricardo behind. It seemed to her that she should be glad to give up Alec's gift, but she wasn't.

"Just roll it in here," Glynnis O'Brien said, snapping Tierney's attention back to the bridal shower at hand. "Let's get this over with so we can continue with the party." Tierney was further aggravated with her mother's attitude as she heard her mumble, "Alec and his asinine gifts…they drive me crazy sometimes."

Yet as all the guests began whispering, giggling, and speculating, Tierney smiled as she saw Aubrey and Tiffany pushing a very large box toward her. The box was on a roller platform and was wrapped in red shiny paper and embellished with wide black velvet ribbon and a large black velvet bow. The box looked to be about seven feet tall and four feet wide, and Tierney giggled again, wondering what Alec could have sent her.

"There's a card with it," Tiffany said, offering a red envelope to Tierney.

Accepting the card, Tierney felt the first sincere smile of the evening spread across her face. Alec knew her. Alec loved her, and she knew his gift would be individual—something only she and he understood. No doubt it would be humorous as well, for Alec was nothing if not clever, and he truly enjoyed making people smile and laugh.

Quickly Tierney opened the envelope and removed the card.

"Read it out loud," Aubrey suggested.

Tierney's smile broadened as she read the front of the card aloud. "*A special day demands a special gift…a gift sent with loving intent. Therefore, for you on your special day, I present to you…*" Tierney paused long enough to open the card and then read, "*One Classic Latin Lover with a very special message. I love you, baby sister. Alec.*"

As Tierney began to giggle, the younger women at the party began to press her to open the box.

"What could possibly be in there?" Madison asked.

"It's the stripper for sure," Blair suggested, giggling with excitement.

As fast as she could, Tierney tore the wrapping paper on the front of the tall package to reveal a plastic handle attached to the box with the words, *Pull this*, written nearby. Tierney wondered if Alec had found a way to make her cardboard cutout of Ricardo Montalbán into something more lasting than just cardboard.

Pulling on the handle, however, Tierney gasped as the front of the box broke away to reveal Alec's gift—one classic Latin lover!

There inside the large box stood a man—not a cardboard cutout man but a real man. And, oh, what a man it was! Tierney's mouth hung agape as she studied the man standing in the box. He was literally tall, dark, and incredibly, incredibly handsome! Dressed in a high-end white shirt, black tuxedo, and black bow tie, the man owned black, loosely swept back, Antonio Banderas hair that gave him both the short-cropped look of a refined gentleman and yet the "just raked my fingers through my hair" appearance of a man who could seduce a woman with simply a smile. His short, dark whisker growth was perfectly manicured—a goatee and mustache, with a not-too-thin and not-too-thick beard line that followed his perfect square jaw from his goateed chin to his sideburns. His eyes were dark and smoldering—the perfect complement to his Latin complexion. His cheekbones were set high, and his nose was as straight a nose as Tierney had ever seen. Broad shoulders, long legs—the man was gorgeous!

As Tierney began to regain her senses, her first thought was a delighted, *Where did Alec find this guy?* Her next thought, however, had to do with how plain Jane and dowdy she must look to him. Brown hair with caramel highlights, green eyes, the plainest brown dress she owned, she probably looked like something the cat had just dragged in.

The man stepped from the box to stand right in front of her. He was so close to her, so close she could smell the faint scent of him—of some masculine shower gel or cologne—and it was overwhelming to Tierney's senses. She began to take a step back, but the man reached out, taking hold of her arm, pulling her close to him and into ballroom dance position.

"I hear you tango," he said. His voice was low and smooth like crème brûlée and sent goose bumps popping up all over Tierney's arms.

Tierney nodded and managed to whisper, "A little."

The man smiled, his perfect lips perfectly accenting his perfectly white teeth. "Well then," he said, and from somewhere the music began.

Tierney couldn't help but grin as she heard the strains of one of her favorite tango compositions, John Powell's "Assassin's Tango," wafting through the highfalutin reception hall her mother had rented for Tierney's bridal shower. Alec had thought of everything, and Tierney's grin widened to smile. Oh, how she loved her brother—and his clever ideas.

Tierney giggled as the classic Latin lover her brother had sent to her began to lead her in the tango. Oh, it wasn't a difficult tango by any means, but it was purely provocative and delicious! As they danced, Tierney couldn't keep from smiling up at her partner. He was so perfect! And although it was obvious he was not a professional ballroom dancer (much to Tierney's relief), he did own exceptional rhythm, style, and strength. Yep, this guy was oozing masculinity, virility, and power.

"Where *did* Alec find you?" Tierney asked as they continued to dance—as goose bumps continued to erupt over her arms and legs, her neck, her back.

"Silencio, querida ama," the man breathed, however—gazing into her eyes with an expression of desire. "We dance now. We'll make love after."

Tierney giggled as the Latin lover Alec had sent to her reached down, taking hold of the back of her right knee with his hand. Tugging until she bent her leg, the Latin lover then slowly pulled her knee to his waist and leaned her back into a dramatic dip as he softly blew his warm breath over her throat and neck.

Tierney was simultaneously thrilled to the tips of her toes and amused at her brother's very thoughtful, very clever gift. She tried to ignore the lingering goose bumps on her body and the deepening regret that Dillon had never thrilled her the way this stranger was thrilling her at that moment.

"Now see here, young man!" Tierney heard her mother begin. But she didn't finish her interruption of Tierney's dream tango with Alec's gift. For at that very moment, the doors leading to an adjoining reception hall opened, revealing a troupe of twenty or more handsome, tuxedo-clad men.

"Ladies…your Latin lovers have arrived!" one man announced. "Please join us for the tango!"

Tierney watched, smiling as the men then invaded the room—each taking the arm of one or two bridal shower guests and leading them into the other reception area. "Assassin's Tango" began once more, and all the bridal shower guests were then so caught up in either tangoing with a would-be Latin lover man or waiting their turn to tango that Tierney and Alec's classic Latin lover gift were completely forgotten—left all alone.

"I do have a message from Alec," Tierney's Latin-fantasy-come-true began once the doors to the adjoining room had been closed to ensure privacy.

Tierney looked up into the classically handsome face of Alec's gift, smiled, and said, "I'm sure you do…but I just have to thank you first." The man grinned as she continued. "I don't know how Alec talked you into this, or how much he paid you or whatever. But thank you. You truly did put a very bright spot in what has otherwise been an awfully dark day for me."

The classic Latin lover smiled, gently caressing Tierney's cheek with the back of his hand. "Well, I hope so," he said. He brushed a strand of hair from her forehead and began to slowly sway with her again. "Will you dance with me once more…before I deliver Alec's message?"

Tierney smiled. "Of course," she giggled as he pulled her against him and began to dance a much simpler tango. After all, what woman in her right mind would ever refuse to dance with this man?

The classic Latin lover danced with Tierney for quite some time, holding her close against his warm, muscular body. Tierney felt an odd euphoria wash over her, an elation that seemed to numb her fears—all her worries, regrets, and concerns—until all that remained to her consciousness was the sense of protection she felt while being held in the strong arms of the handsome stranger. The moments seemed timeless—unhurried—and Tierney wished it could last forever, that she could remain dancing with her classic Latin lover, remain in his arms, and never have to leave, never have to marry Dillon.

"So," the Latin lover began, however, "first of all, let me assure you that I'm a close friend of Alec's…not some stranger he hired."

Tierney looked up at him then, wondering how long her eyes had been closed, her head resting against his firm pectoral muscle. "Oh, well, that actually makes me feel better…that he knows you, I mean." She smiled up at him and grinned.

"I'm glad," he said. "It's important to Alec that you know he didn't send a stranger to deliver his message." He paused and frowned a little, adding, "And it's important to me that you know it."

"Okay," Tierney said. Anxiety was beginning to rise in her—for she already sensed what message Alec meant to convey.

"Run, Tierney," the man said. "Alec just wants you to run. Don't marry this guy. You're not in love with him and—"

Tierney stopped dancing and attempted to push herself out of the Latin lover's arms. But the man tightened his grip at her hand and waist.

"Wait for the man you want…the man you need," the stranger said. He was frowning, his expression entirely serious.

"Alec knows the pressure I'm under from my mother and—" she began.

"It's your life, Tierney. It should be your choice who you marry," he continued, however. "Don't be forced into making the most important decision you'll ever make by your mom, who just wants you to marry this guy because his family is wealthy and well connected."

"But he p-proposed to me," Tierney stammered. "Dillon proposed to me, and he wouldn't have if…I can't just blow that, can I?"

"Yeah, you can," the Latin lover assured her.

She was going to ask him why Alec hadn't come himself to deliver his message—the message she already knew. Tierney and Alec had spent hours on the phone, Alec trying to persuade Tierney not to marry for simply practical reasons.

"Alec says to remind you that you're a passionate girl," the Latin lover said, interrupting Tierney's thoughts. "He says that this Dillon guy is a dud…wouldn't know passion if it jumped up and bit him in the—"

"I know what Alec thinks of Dillon," Tierney interrupted. "He's told me a million times."

The Latin lover exhaled a breath of frustration. He was growing impatient with delivering Alec's message—or perhaps he was growing impatient with wasting his time with Tierney.

Almost frantically, for she did not want to inconvenience him any further, Tierney tried once more to push herself from his arms. This time he let her go.

"Are you in love with this guy?" the Latin lover asked.

"He's a very kind man," Tierney answered, folding her arms across her chest. She was rattled, confused, and utterly undone.

"I didn't ask you if he's a nice guy. I asked you if you're in love with him," the Latin lover stipulated.

Tierney paused—felt tears welling in her eyes. "My parents have already spent so much money on this wedding…on the invitations, the travel arrangements. My mother would burst in to flames if I didn't…if I didn't…"

"The fact that you even mentioned the money and your mother's reaction tell me that you've already been considering—"

"I can't just…I can't just walk away!" Tierney exclaimed as a sudden desperation to escape enveloped. It was indeed a desperation to escape she was feeling—but not a desperation to escape Alec's bridal shower gift of a classic Latin lover. Suddenly all Tierney could think about was running from her mother, from Dillon, and from the only home and life she'd ever known.

"No, you can't," the Latin lover said. Reaching out, he took hold of her arms—held her firmly as he stared down at her. "That's why Alec told me to tell you to run."

"B-But…I…"

"He's waiting for you," the Latin lover said. When Tierney frowned with confusion (for so many emotions and thoughts were racing through her, she was finding it difficult to focus on anything but the Latin lover's gorgeous face), he continued, "At the McDonald's you guys used to sneak off to in high school. Alec is waiting there to meet you…and he's got everything worked out. So run, Tierney. Just run."

Tierney shook her head. "It's not as easy as you think."

The handsome man looked toward the closed doors that led to the other reception room. "Those guys will keep your mom and all your friends in there for at least thirty minutes. That's plenty of time for you to get out of here, call your soon-to-be ex-fiancé, and break it off…and get to the McDonald's to meet your brother."

"It's not that easy," Tierney whispered.

"It is that easy," the Latin lover assured her.

"But what if Dillon…what if…I mean, he proposed to me," Tierney stammered. "What if he's the one I'm supposed to marry…or the only one that ever wants to marry me?"

"He's not the one you're supposed to marry," he answered. "Alec knows it, and you know it." He smiled and shook his head, adding, "Hell, I don't even know you, and *I* know it!"

Tierney studied the man a moment. Oh, he was too beautiful to be true! Surely he wasn't just a friend of Alec's. He *had* to be an actor or something.

"You must think I'm the biggest idiot," Tierney whispered, suddenly very embarrassed by everything Alec had obviously told his friend. "Alec can be such a creep sometimes," she mumbled as she blushed with humiliation and looked away from Alec's messenger.

Tierney looked up, however, when she felt the man's grip tighten on her arms—felt him pulling her body toward his again.

"No," he said. "I think you're a people-pleaser…and that maybe you need a little bit more to convince you than just Alec's stupid idea of sending a message."

Unexpectedly, Tierney was rendered breathless as the Latin lover reached out with one hand, taking hold of her chin as his free arm wrapped around her body, pulling it flush with his own.

She should slap him! She should totally slap him! But instead, all Tierney could do was watch as the most incredibly sexy pair of lips she'd ever seen moved closer and closer to hers—until the Latin lover's face was so close to hers that she had to close her eyes.

The gentle beginning of the kiss rendered Tierney weak in the Latin lover's arms. But the manner in which the kiss erupted into an intense, fiery barter of passion took her breath away! Burning, moist, and driven like no kiss Tierney had ever experienced, Alec's friend—a total stranger—evoked more positive emotion, more strength in determination, and more physical desire in Tierney than she'd ever imagined she possessed!

In that instant, as the handsome Latin lover bathed her in euphoria, Tierney realized that Alec was right. She realized that *she* was right! To settle for poor, sweet Dillon when such a pent-up need for true love, affection, and attraction was simmering inside her would be not only wrong for herself but utterly unfair to Dillon.

As the Latin lover Alec had sent to her ground one last wet, fevered kiss to Tierney's accepting mouth, one word echoed in her mind. *Run!*

Pushing herself from the Latin lover's arms and brushing tears from her cheeks, tears of mingled joy and fear, Tierney stood staring at the man—stunned at what it had taken for her to see into her own soul.

Then, as if nothing had happened between them—the sultry tango, the exchange of information from Alec, or the sweltering, scandalous kiss—the purely gorgeous man sent to be her classic Latin lover for one sweet, bliss-filled half an hour simply said, "Run."

Yet Tierney paused—not for wondering whether calling off her wedding to Dillon were the right thing to do but because of him. She paused, wanting to take in the very last vision she would ever have of the mysterious Latin lover her brother had sent to her. She could still sense the taste of his kiss on her tongue; her lips still tingled with the feel of his pressed to them.

"Run, Tierney," he repeated. "Now!"

And then, with the haunting strains of the violin in "Assassin's Tango" echoing through the reception hall, Tierney O'Brien turned and ran.

CHAPTER TWO

If there were one thing in all her life Tierney O'Brien would never forget, it was the classic Latin lover her older brother, Alec, had sent to her bridal shower. The nameless, tormentingly handsome, tuxedo-donning Latin lover had indeed done the job Alec had sent him to do: he'd convinced Tierney to bring her wedding to Dillon Hawthorne to a stiff and unalterable halt. If there were another thing Tierney O'Brien would never forget, it was the near nuclear fallout that followed.

Oh, she'd escaped well enough. Tierney had taken the gorgeous Latin lover's advice (that is, Alec's advice) and hightailed it out of the reception hall where her bridal shower was being held. Racing to her car, she didn't stop—simply drove to Dillon's office and explained that she couldn't marry him and why. Tierney hadn't waited for Dillon to argue but rather forced the three-carat diamond solitaire engagement ring he'd given her into the palm of his hand, turned, and fled.

The very instant she was out of Dillon's office and driving toward the McDonald's she and Alec haunted as teenagers, Tierney began to feel the magnificent wave of relief one feels when a good and right decision has been made.

However, just as Alec had warned as he'd sat with Tierney enjoying a fine McDonald's supersized number one, good and correct decisions didn't always come with complementary good and correct consequences. And though Tierney had expected her mother's shrieking in anger, her father's silent sighs of wishing her mother weren't shrieking with anger, and the questioning from every venue she could imagine, she hadn't expected the cruel ostracizing from her friends and associates.

No one understood why Tierney had called off the wedding and broken up with Dillon—no one (save Alec, of course). Tierney's so-called "friends" played at the pretense of understanding, for nearly two weeks. But quickly Tierney recognized that the fact she'd chosen to follow her heart instead of a trail of money, position, and social expectation was simply not acceptable to Glynnis O'Brien and her arrogant, money-grubbing circle of contacts.

Still, Tierney had endeavored to stick it out. She'd immediately moved into the apartment Alec had secured for her on a month-to-month lease basis. She'd quit her job at the country club and gone to work for a lesser-known florist downtown. Yet it seemed everywhere she turned or looked or stepped, Tierney bumped into someone who knew she'd "left Dillon Hawthorne standing at the altar"—someone who would instantly erupt into berating her and telling her she would never amount to anything without Dillon or her parents' money and social position.

Even the strongest self-esteemed person could never have endured under such circumstances—perpetual criticism and negativity and urgings to remain dependent on parents or a wealthy husband—to live a life of lavish luxury instead of lingering as a hard-working, middle-class nobody.

And so, almost a year later, on the last full weekend of October, Tierney found herself sitting on an airplane, gazing out the window as the pilot announced that Mount Rainier was visible through the windows of her side of the plane. She was running, and maybe she was a coward for running, but not according to the feelings in her heart—and not according to Alec. Alec had left home (run—sprinted, actually) two years earlier and hadn't regretted it for a moment. He'd done his research before running (just as he'd encouraged Tierney to) and settled in what he claimed was the most beautiful spot in the whole wide US of A—Leavenworth, Washington.

It hadn't taken Alec long to build up his snow removal business in Leavenworth, and he'd been very successful. Far more important was the fact that he'd been very happy. Oh, it hadn't been easy. Alec had explained to Tierney at length the struggles he'd faced—both financially and personally—but he was truly satisfied with the life he'd literally plowed out for himself. Thus, he'd encouraged Tierney to move to Leavenworth as well, admitting that the biggest reason he wanted her there was his own selfish desire to have his little sister live close to him. But he'd also explained that Leavenworth was a friendly, wonderful, almost dreamlike place to live, even for the fact that tourism was the driving force of the city's economic health. A small population, beautiful landscape, and the entire town center's being modeled after a Bavarian village were all reasons Alec had fallen in love with the place—all reasons he promised Tierney would fall in love with it too.

As the airplane circled the Sea-Tac airport in preparation for landing, Tierney smiled, admiring the marvelous colors below—Seattle in autumn. Crimson-, gold-, orange-, and even purple-leafed trees were everywhere, often mingled with the perpetually green pines that were likewise everywhere. Although the scenery was very beautiful in its prolific colors and Pacific shores mingling, the visibility of the thick humidity hanging over the landscape reminded Tierney that she was glad she would be traveling a bit east of the coastline. Leavenworth wasn't quite so moist and gloomy all year. Yet no one in all the world would argue with the beauty of the Emerald City—of not just the trees but the vines that lined buildings, bridges, and walls along the interstate, all having changed their leaves to flaming oranges or brilliant vermilion. It was truly stunning.

As the plane landed and taxied to the gate, Tierney's anxieties lessened a little. Soon she'd be with Alec, and then all would be well. Alec would take care of her—if she needed taking care of, that was. Alec owned wisdom and experience, and Tierney trusted him unconditionally. Still, as she stepped through the door of the gate and into the Sea-Tac terminal airport, Tierney tried to gulp down the lump of self-doubt gathering in her throat. What if she couldn't land the job with the florist Alec knew in Leavenworth? What if she hated the weather? After all, the only snow she'd ever known was the kind at the ski lodges her family frequented in the winter months—the ski lodges filled with waitresses and waiters, masseurs and manicurists, and all the other people who labored to ensure the comfort of the lodge patrons.

Shaking her head in an effort to dispel her self-doubt, however, Tierney looked up to be guided by the signs indicating the direction to the baggage claim and hurried onward. There would be no looking back—only looking forward. That's what Tierney had promised herself when her mother had told her that if Tierney chose to leave Monterey and go to Alec, then she was on her own. There would be no financial assistance from her parents—not ever—no matter what.

Tierney had quickly responded by telling her mother that money was not everything in life and that her mother would regret ignoring that timeless truth one day. Then, having taken only the things she'd purchased with her own money or gifts she'd received from others, Tierney turned and walked out of her parents' home.

A wave of relief washed over Tierney as she saw Alec waiting for her at the baggage claim. He smiled, spread his arms wide, and called, "You're free!"

Throwing herself into the strong security of her brother's protective embrace, Tierney giggled and tried to keep her tears of mingled joy and trepidation from escaping her eyes.

"I can't believe I'm here with you!" she exclaimed, holding tight to Alec. "I can't believe I had the guts to do it!"

"I can," Alec reassured her. "And life is going to begin for you now, Tiers," he said. Ending their loving hug, he held her away from him a moment as he studied her. He smiled, nodded, and said, "You look good. No worse for the stress Mom put on you at all."

"I'm wearing a lot of makeup," Tierney giggled. She sighed and linked her arm through Alec's. "I feel so much better now. Just seeing you helps so much."

Gazing into her brother's bright green eyes a moment, Tierney giggled, reached up, and tousled his chestnut hair. "I want that," she said.

"What?" Alec asked, smiling.

"That look you have in your eyes," she explained. "That 'life is good' look you have."

"Oh, you'll have it soon enough," Alec chuckled, putting an arm around Tierney's shoulders and pulling her snug against his side. "Don't you worry. I promise you that you're going to love it here, Tiers." He nodded his reassurance once more and sighed, "Now, let's get your bags and start home."

"How long of a drive is it?" Tierney asked—though she'd never minded long drives in Alec's company. In fact, she relished them—for the conversation was always, always wonderful.

"Just a couple of hours," Alec answered. "I figure we'll be home just in time for dinner at my favorite restaurant, Von Bomburst's."

"Uh oh," Tierney giggled. "Sounds eccentric." She wrinkled her brow.

Alec smiled. "Oh, you'll love the food, Tiers! Very Bavarian. And I think it has the best bratwurst in town."

Tierney shook her head. "You're already trying to socialize me, aren't you? Like those skittish, messed-up dogs they rescue on that animal police show we used to watch when Mom and Dad weren't home?"

"Naw," Alec denied. "I just want to make sure you have a good dinner your first night here."

"Mm-hmm," Tierney hummed with suspicion. "Dinner in a public venue…with people and everything."

Alec laughed. "People do inhabit the earth, Tiers, and not all of them are arrogant snobs like Mom's friends. The people in Leavenworth, they're, like…normal. You'll love it. And Von Bomburst's really does have the best brats in town…in my opinion anyway."

Tierney laughed—smiled with sudden comfort, contentment, and hope as she watched Alec retrieve her luggage from the baggage conveyer. She did feel free—free and hopeful and almost truly happy.

The drive through the magnificent Cascade Mountains toward Leavenworth was awe-inspiring! In truth, Tierney couldn't decide whether she had never seen such beautiful mountain scenery or if her newly acquired sense of freedom simply made her more able to appreciate it. She couldn't believe she'd left Monterey and that she was moving to a small town in Washington State—actually moving there to live.

Here and there as Alec drove them toward what would be Tierney's new home, her stomach would begin to churn with anxiety—miserable anticipation at the job interview Alec had set up for her with the only floral shop owner in town. If she didn't land the job with the florist, she had no idea what she'd do for employment.

Alec had suggested Tierney could work for him if she didn't bag the job with the florist. He'd explained he'd just buy another pickup and put a snowplow on it, teach Tierney how to plow, and let her have at it. There was plenty of plowing to go around. But though Tierney wasn't averse to the hard work and midnight hours required by Alec's business, she wasn't sure she could hack it—at least not for long. It was a demanding job, and in truth, Tierney wasn't all that big on the idea of being out in a blizzard in the middle of the night all by herself. She figured she could work for Alec in the summer months well enough—landscape maintenance like mowing, weed whacking, and watering. But the snowplowing—the very idea caused an enormous dread and apprehension to well in her. Still, she figured Alec had been teasing anyway about her driving a truck for him. At least, he'd been *mostly* teasing.

However, during the drive from Seattle to Leavenworth, each time Tierney's nervous anxiety would begin to get the best of her, Alec would engage her in some trivial, lighthearted conversation—something to calm Tierney and help wave her worries away for the moment. It was just further proof that her brother knew Tierney better than anybody— knew her thoroughly, to her very core. Alec had known her heart better than even *she'd* known it at the time, and he knew how to break through her fear, feelings of obligation, and simple knuckling under to her mother's demands. It's why he'd sent his friend—the mysterious, nameless, sexy Latin lover guy—to her bridal shower all those months before. Alec had recognized that the one thing that could turn Tierney's head and really get her attention was a classic Latin lover type—and it had worked.

In truth, not a day had gone by that Tierney didn't think of the classic Latin lover Alec had sent to rescue her. In the stressful, crazy days following her breakup with Dillon, Tierney had considered asking Alec just who the most beautiful man she'd ever seen was, and how Alec was acquainted with him. But she knew how stupid it would be to press for information. The guy had simply done Alec a huge favor, that's all. What good would it do Tierney to find out anything about him? So she'd decided just to cling to the fabulousness of what had happened—the sudden, unexpected appearance of the better looking than Antonio Banderas, smooth, suave, and very attractive in every sense of the word Latin lover who had danced with her, kissed her, and managed to convince her she would be doing the wrong thing in marrying Dillon. It had been like a dream, and Tierney would always think of it that way.

"I'll have to bring you back out to this candy store," Alec said, drawing Tierney's thoughts back to him. "It's got the best saltwater taffy I've ever had…and so many flavors it will totally spin your brain."

"I love saltwater taffy," Tierney said as she gazed out the window to the small but well-advertised candy store.

"Oh, I know it," Alec chuckled. "I was lucky if there was ever one piece left in my Christmas stocking by Christmas night."

"Yeah, but it was only fair after the way you were always stealing my Almond Roca," Tierney countered.

Alec nodded. "You gotta give that to Dad. He knew how to fill a Christmas stocking, right?"

"Totally!" Tierney giggled. And it was true. Though their mother had little or nothing to do with purchasing gifts for Alec and Tierney at Christmas and on birthdays, their father had always made sure Santa left their favorite candy and toys in their Christmas stockings on Christmas Eve and that there were plenty of thoughtful, well-planned gifts waiting under the tree for them on Christmas morning—both from Santa and their parents.

"Why do you think he stays with her?" Tierney heard herself ask. She looked to Alec to see his expression had changed to that of worry and frustration. "Why doesn't he just leave her? She doesn't love him anymore. She treats him like a dog…treats us like employees or something."

But Alec shook his head. "I don't know," he answered. "Maybe he's just too trapped to get out. Or maybe he doesn't want to go through the legal fight over everything."

Tierney sighed with discouragement and nodded. "I felt like I was leaving an abused puppy by the side of the road when I left," she mumbled.

"Me too," Alec admitted. He shook his head. "But we can't do anything about it, Tiers. Dad would have to empower himself somehow. We can't help him unless he realizes he needs help." He paused and then added, "He told me to leave, you know."

"What?" Tierney exclaimed. "What do you mean? He kicked you out?"

But again Alec shook his head. "No, of course not. Just…that day I decided to leave and had that big argument with Mom…as I was packing my stuff, Dad came in and told me I'd never live a normal life, never be able to make my own decisions or know true happiness, unless I left…moved as far away from him and Mom and all their crap as I could."

"Wow," Tierney breathed, still astonished. "I didn't know that."

"I didn't have time to tell you, not with all the drama going on," Alec admitted. He smiled and laughed a little. "I thought Mom's head was going to blow right off that day." He looked to Tierney and winked. "Don't think badly of me for this, Tiers, but you'll never know how satisfying it was for me to turn around and leave with Mom standing there looking like a screaming Roman candle on the Fourth of July."

But Tierney didn't think badly of her brother at all. In fact, she smiled.

"Well, don't think badly of me," she said, "but I felt the same way."

Alec laughed. "Isn't it awful? The fact that we both enjoyed escaping to the tune of Mom's hysterics?"

Tierney laughed too. "Yeah. It is awful!"

"But here we are now—beautiful, isolated Leavenworth," Alec said, gesturing with one hand that Tierney should look ahead of them.

At once Tierney gasped with instantaneous delight. The scene before her seemed almost as dreamy as the Latin lover Alec had sent to her bridal shower! Nestled amidst a smattering of beautiful Alpine hills, the center of Leavenworth appeared just as if Tierney had stepped out of the real world and into the perfect little Bavarian village. Every building was Bavarian-style. It seemed every window was dressed with a perfectly quaint flower box and autumn-colored mums and greenery. She half expected to see Heidi and her lederhosen-bedecked grandfather walking along the street—half expected the sinister child-catcher from *Chitty Chitty Bang Bang* to appear from just around the corner! She could almost hear an alpenhorn—imagined it being blown by standing on top of a hill.

As Tierney glanced over to one lovely, grass-covered hill, she smiled when Alec said, "I know, right? You half expect to see Julie Andrews twirling around singing 'The Sound of Music.'"

"Why didn't you tell me how gorgeous it was here?" Tierney asked.

"I did!" Alec answered, shaking his head with amusement.

"I mean, look at the color of these leaves. It's surreal!" she exclaimed. "It's like Vermont in autumn, only different. Reds, golds…oh, look at that orange! What kind of tree is that?"

"'It's like Vermont in autumn…only different,'" Alec mimicked in a high-pitched voice. "I see you have lost your way with words, Tiers."

"Shut up," Tierney giggled. "You know what I mean."

"I do," Alec admitted. "You mean it's beautiful, and I've been telling you that for two years."

"But you didn't tell me it was like *this*!"

"And here we are at Von Bomburst's," Alec sighed as he parked in front of a white-and-brown, Bavarian-style building that stood a bit off the beaten path of the main street. "You've got to have a brat with sauerkraut here. They are the best in town!" As he turned the key in the ignition, the loud rumble of the diesel engine of his pickup died, and he added, "I mean, every restaurant that serves bratwurst here claims to serve the best, but this place really does have the best."

Tierney smiled. "Sounds delicious. I'm kind of starving, actually."

"Well, come on then," Alec said. "I'll get your door."

Tierney sighed as she watched Alec hurry around the front of the pickup to the passenger's side. She was feeling better and better—more and more hopeful. After all, though she was fiercely determined to be financially independent and self-reliant, she knew Alec would never let her starve or go without shelter. Furthermore, his company had always been comforting and joyous. Life would be better now. She'd be able to make her own decisions.

Tierney's smile faded a little, however, as she thought of her father—still trapped in Monterey with her arrogant, controlling mother. Yet as Alec opened the pickup door for her, Tierney knew Alec had been right. No one could help their father until he wanted to help himself.

"Are you ready for some awesome food?" Alec asked, taking Tierney's hand and hurrying her toward the restaurant entrance.

"I'm always ready for some awesome food. You know that," she answered, smiling at him. He was a good brother—a supreme brother—and she loved him to the very depth of her soul. Tierney knew she'd never be able to repay Alec for his help, support, and encouragement—for sending that gorgeous man to her bridal shower to screw her head on right for her. But she could be loving and kind to him—supportive, encouraging, and everything else she should be anyway.

As they stepped into Von Bomburst's, Tierney couldn't help but giggle. It was definitely a themed restaurant—and very well done!

She leaned over to Alec and whispered, "I feel like you should be wearing lederhosen."

"Tierney," he said, looking at her with a scowl, "I love it here…but you will never see me in a pair of lederhosen."

Tierney laughed, imagining that, whether or not Alec thought lederhosen were cool, he would look awfully cute in them.

"But you'd get to wear knee socks and stuff," she added.

Alec rolled his eyes with feigned exasperation. "Do you want me to feed you or not?" he teased as a hostess approached. Tierney smiled, for the girl was dressed in a traditional Bavarian outfit as well. She looked exactly like Truly Scrumptious turning around on a music box.

"Von Bomburst's!" she exclaimed then.

Alec smiled. "I was wondering when you would figure that out."

Tierney continued to smile with amused delight as Alec spoke to the pretty hostess and she showed them to their table. Baron Bomburst—the idiot, childlike ruler of Vulgaria who wants to possess the magical flying car Chitty Chitty Bang Bang. Tierney could see that not only was the restaurant named after the villain of Ian Fleming's novel but also the interior was decorated as the reader might imagine Baron Bomburst's kitchens to look like. It was adorable! Cozy, wildly atmospheric—perfect!

"Oh, I love this!" Tierney whispered as the hostess left her and Alec alone at their table. "It's wonderful!"

Alec was smiling from ear to ear. "I knew you'd like it. And they really do have the best brats in town."

Tierney picked up the menu the hostess had left. "So are you saying I don't even get to look at the menu?"

"Oh, you can look at it…but I really want you to try the bratwurst tonight, okay?" Alec nearly begged.

Tierney giggled. "You can order the bratwurst and sauerkraut for me, Alec, but I still want to look at the menu—you know, for next time."

"Okay," Alec agreed. "And thanks for trying it for me."

"It's the least I can do, considering everything," Tierney said as she began to look over the menu. "Mmmm!" she hummed. "Look at all this stuff I can't pronounce. I love that!"

"Hey, man!" Tierney heard a man's voice exclaim. She looked up over the top of her menu, expecting to see their waiter greeting Alec. She gasped, however—gulped and nearly choked on her astonishment as she saw none other than her gorgeous, dream-borne Latin lover of all those months before standing at their table shaking hands with Alec.

Quickly, for her blush was already the color of radishes, Tierney raised her menu in order to hide her entire face.

"What're you doing here?" she heard Alec ask. "Are your mom and dad shorthanded again? And where's your lederhosen?"

"Dude, shut up…or I'll shove some lederhosen down your throat, man," the Latin lover warned. "Yeah, two waiters quit this morning. So I'm filling in." There was silence for a moment, and then Tierney heard the Latin lover lower his voice and ask Alec, "Is it the girl from the Christmas Shoppe?"

"No way, man!" Alec answered. "Do you think I suddenly grew an extra set of guts or what?"

"Well, then who is it?" the Latin lover asked.

The moment was upon her. Tierney knew she could either continue to be a coward or simply find the extra set of guts Alec had just mentioned and man-up.

Therefore, from behind her menu, she said, "I'll have one classic Latin lover, please." Slowly then she lowered her menu—radish-red–faced and all—and forced a friendly grin as the gorgeous, handsome, delicious, illegally attractive man smiled at her with recognition.

"Hey! It's you!" he exclaimed. "Alec told me you were coming out here." He glanced to Alec a moment, adding, "But he didn't say when."

"You remember Rome, don't you, Tierney?" Alec asked.

Tierney glared at him a moment—miffed at his not warning her that the Latin lover would be in Leavenworth. "Of course," Tierney said, attempting to appear unrattled. "How could I ever forget?"

"I don't think we've officially met," the Latin lover said, offering a hand to Tierney.

"Not officially, no," Tierney agreed, accepting his offered hand.

"I'm Rome Novak," the man introduced himself. "I work with Alec in the snowplow business." He grinned with a mischievous expression and added, "When I'm not moonlighting as a potential home-wrecker, that is." He paused and arched his handsome, dark eyebrows, continuing, "Or a waiter at my parents' restaurant."

"Well, it's nice to meet you officially," Tierney said as he released her hand. The warm, tingling sensation his touch had caused to travel up her arm lingered, however. "I'm Tierney O'Brien, Alec's sister…when I'm not moonlighting as a parasitical sibling, that is."

"No way," Rome Novak kindly argued. "Alec has been bouncing off the walls ever since he talked you into moving out here. You'll be good for him." He lowered his voice and leaned closer to Tierney. "And maybe you can talk him into asking out that little blonde he's so crushed on over at the Christmas Shoppe. I can't get him to move on that."

Tierney smiled at her brother. "Hmmm. A little blonde in a Christmas Shoppe, is it?"

"Rome!" Alec scolded. "Man, don't go telling my sister stuff like that. You know how women are all match-makey and stuff."

However, Rome leaned closer to Tierney—close enough that his breath on her cheek caused goose bumps to erupt over the back of her neck.

"Her name is Heidi…if you can believe it," he whispered. "Heidi Svensson."

"Heidi Svensson, is it?" Tierney asked, winking teasingly at her brother.

"Dude!" Alec scolded his friend. "Man, just put in two orders of brats with sauerkraut and be gone, garçon." Alec waved his hand in a dismissive gesture.

Rome Novak smiled, winked at Tierney, and mouthed, *Heidi Svensson at the Christmas Shoppe*, and then said, "Yes, sir. Will that be all, sir?"

"That and some lederhosen on our waiter," Alec teased.

"Two brats with sauerkraut. Got it," Rome repeated, ignoring Alec's lederhosen remark. "We'll have that right out for you." He paused, smiled at Tierney, and added, "And it's good to finally meet you, officially, Tierney."

"You too," she managed in response.

She sighed as she watched Rome Novak walk away, noticing the way every other woman in the restaurant watched him walk away as well.

Then, turning to her far-too-secretive brother, Tierney exclaimed, "He works with you?" in a reprimanding whisper. "You could've warned me that I was about to come face-to-face with…with…with…"

"Your dream lover?" Alec chuckled.

"Shut up!" Tierney scolded between gritted teeth. "I about passed out when I looked up and saw him standing there! How embarrassing!"

But Alec merely shrugged. "Why? He's my friend…and he did me a big favor. Actually, he did you a big favor. So just let it go. He's cool about it. He's cool about everything. So you just be cool too."

"Easy for you to say," Tierney grumbled. She frowned when Alec laughed to himself. "What now? What is so funny to you about all this?"

"You," he answered. "'I'll have one classic Latin lover, please,'" he repeated, mimicking Tierney's voice. "Great intro, Tiers. I'll give you that one. *Great* intro."

Tierney sighed with mingled exasperation and amusement at her brother's antics. She shook her head as she studied him a moment.

"You're a total brat, you know," she told him. "And I'm just glad Mr. Novak there told me about your little Christmas Shoppe girl."

Instantly Alec leveled an index finger at Tierney. "Don't go there, Tiers. Rome was just trying to get me back because of the lederhosen thing."

"Heidi," Tierney sighed with triumph, however. "Heidi Svensson. And she works at the Christmas Shoppe. How perfect!"

"I'll show you a perfect knuckle sandwich if you keep it up, girl," Alec playfully threatened.

Tierney frowned a moment then, thoughtful. "Rome Novak?" she asked. "Where does a guy get a name like that?"

"His parents' last name is Novak," her smart-aleck brother responded.

"Yes, I can figure that much out, Smart Alec," she mumbled. "But he just doesn't look like a Novak. He looks more like a…like a…"

"Like a Montalbán?" Alec teased.

"Well, yeah…if you want to know the truth," Tierney admitted. "That dark hair…his skin is, like, perfectly…like…so naturally tan and—"

"Oh, give me a break," Alec interrupted. "This sounds like a makeup demonstration at Dillard's." Shaking his head and lowering his voice, he said, "Rome and his sister are adopted. Rome was born in Mexico City, and his sister was born in Cuba. His parents couldn't have kids biologically, so they adopted Rome and Celeste when they were babies." Alec sighed and sat back in his chair. "Yep, Mr. and Mrs. Novak are just plain old white people. Rome and Celeste, however…both of them are totally stunning. I mean, Celeste has these green eyes that can look right through you. It's freaky-gorgeous."

"Freaky-gorgeous," Tierney repeated. "Now there's a phrase I like. It's very descriptive."

Alec nodded, and then silence hung between them for a moment.

"When's your interview at the florist?" he asked.

"Day after tomorrow," Tierney answered as anxiety began to well in her. "I'm so nervous, Alec. I feel like…like I was never prepared for stuff like this."

"That's because you weren't," Alec affirmed. "Mom tried to raise you to be a trophy wife…like all those old biddies she hangs with. Someone to shop all day, hang out at the country club, and look down their nose at other people."

Alec studied Tierney for a long moment. She could see the emotion in his eyes—his brother's love for her and his joy that he'd managed to help her escape.

"You'll like it here in the real world, Tierney," he said then. "People are nice…friendly. Even the mean ones aren't as mean as some people in Mom's circle. I'm so glad you're here. I need you."

Tierney felt the tears welling in her eyes—tears of joy in knowing Alec loved her as much as she loved him—tears of joy in knowing they wouldn't be apart any longer.

Reaching across the table, she took hold of his hand and squeezed it with tender affection. "I'm glad I'm here too, Alec. And I need you too. Thank you for rescuing me."

But Alec's smile of mischief returned. "Don't you mean thank you for sending Rome to bust up your wedding?"

Tierney rolled her eyes, shaking her head with amused exasperation. "Well, that too, I suppose."

"Hey…I forgot to ask you guys what you want to drink."

Tierney startled a little in her seat at the sound of Rome Novak's voice behind her. In the next moment, he was standing right next to her, asking, "Water or something else? Or both?"

"I-I'll just have water, thanks," Tierney answered.

"Me too," Alec answered.

"I'll bring them out then," Rome said. Tierney looked up when she heard him add, "Hey, Tierney."

"Yeah?" she asked, looking up at him—then wishing she hadn't, because just looking at him caused her stomach to fill with butterflies.

Quietly he whispered, "Heidi Svensson…at the Christmas Shoppe."

Tierney smiled, giggled a little, and whispered, "Got it!"

"Man! I am gonna take you out," Alec grumbled.

"I'll get those waters," Rome chuckled.

Again Tierney watched Rome walk across the restaurant toward the kitchen—watched every other woman of any age watch him walk as well.

"So I guess he's quite the ladies' man, huh?" she asked Alec.

"Oh, they all wish he were," Alec answered. "But Rome is kind of stupid when it comes to women. He doesn't see them gawking at him and stuff. He's just a regular guy. It's one reason I like him. He's just normal, you know?"

Normal? Tierney thought, however. There was nothing normal about Rome Novak! Not where looks were concerned, anyway.

Yet Tierney tried not to think about the fact that she would now reside in the same city as the man who had showed up in a tuxedo, tangoed with her, kissed her, and changed her life. He was just a guy, after all—Alec's friend and business associate. Tierney knew she'd have to let go of the memory of the mysterious Latin lover that had snapped her brain to attention all those months ago. But the realization deeply saddened her, for it had been such a wonderful memory to cling to. Those moments in Rome Novak's arms—those moments she was able to live the dream of being held the way he'd held her and kissed the way he'd kissed her—they'd carried her through, changed her life, and it would be difficult to ignore it all.

Exhaling a heavy sigh, Tierney smiled at Alec and asked, "So…when do you usually start having to plow snow?"

"Any day now," Alec answered. He smiled at her, leaned forward on the table, and said, "And, Tiers, I cannot wait for you to see Christmas in this place! If you think the leaves of autumn are pretty, you'll freak when you see the Christmas lights…especially when it's snowing."

Tierney smiled again. "It sounds like a dream!" she said.

"Oh, it looks like a dream," Alec assured her.

Tierney was hopeful then. Christmas in such a dreamy setting—she could imagine it would be wonderful. And maybe it would help her to let go of the dream she'd been dreaming for so long. Maybe the excitement of Christmas, and the joy of finally getting to share it with Alec again, would lessen her disappointment in having to accept that Rome Novak had only been playing the part Alec had asked him to when he'd appeared at her doomed bridal shower.

But when Rome returned to the table with two glasses of water, Tierney knew that nothing would ever soothe that disappointment—the disappointment in knowing Rome Novak would never just suddenly appear again and whisk Tierney away on wings of her ultimate dream come true and the unexpected, and instant, passion that had accompanied it.

CHAPTER THREE

Tierney brushed the tears from her cheeks with the back of her hand. As she watched John Wayne's and Gail Russell's ghosts sailing together on a ship of clouds, she sniffled—wishing the old black-and-white movie would've ended differently.

"Another unhappy ending," she mumbled as she put a check mark on the list of movies she had sitting on the end of the ironing board. "And a frowny face," she whispered as she drew a frowny face following the checkmark. Sure, she'd had good cry when Gail Russell had died in John Wayne's arms, but even a good cry was no excuse for an unhappy ending.

Tierney propped the iron back safely on its haunches and sat down on the couch to rifle through the other DVDs piled there. The fact of the matter was Tierney was incredibly stressed out! Her interview with the florist in town was later that very afternoon, and Tierney had woken up in such a bundle of nerves that she'd known right away there was only one thing to do—ironing.

Ironing was Tierney's coping mechanism. She couldn't really remember when she'd discovered that the act of ironing calmed her down, but it was before the age of twelve—she knew that much. Shirts, pillowcases, her grandfather's handkerchiefs, or her grandmother's quilting fabric—it hadn't matter what it was she was allowed to iron, but by the age of twelve, Tierney had discovered that ironing soothed her. At first it was just the rhythmic motion of ironing she found relaxed her. Then it was the sound of the steam the iron exhaled each time she lifted it. By the time Tierney was eighteen, she'd discovered that if she simultaneously watched old movies while she ironed, she could distract her mind from worrisome events that were upcoming.

Thus, now she found herself having just watched a rather disappointing old John Wayne and Gail Russell movie in an attempt to distract her thoughts from her upcoming job interview. Naturally, she couldn't end on a sad note. Therefore, choosing an old and familiarly safe musical starring Esther Williams and her ever-beloved Ricardo Montalbán, Tierney pushed play on the DVD player and retrieved one of Alec's T-shirts from the pile she'd found in the basket of clean laundry on top of the dryer.

The opening credits and music began to roll, and Tierney sighed with satisfaction. No matter how many times she watched *Neptune's Daughter*, it always ended the same happy way—and Esther Williams and Ricardo Montalbán never ended up swimming in the clouds of heaven together in it.

The doorbell rang, and Tierney frowned. She didn't feel like talking to some desperate solicitor, so she ignored the first ring and the second. But when whomever it was began hammering on the door like aliens were landing in Leavenworth to turn citizens into pod people, Tierney sighed, set the iron on its haunches, and went to the door.

"Okay, okay! Where's the fire?" she asked as she opened the door. She gasped, however, breathing, "Oh," as she saw none other that Rome Novak standing at the threshold.

"Hi, Tierney," Rome greeted. "Where's your brother? I just scored the best…" His voice trailed off as a frown puckered his handsome, handsome brow. "Are you okay?" he asked, studying her face.

"Oh! Oh yeah!" Tierney assured him, remembering that she'd been crying only moments before. "I-I was just—"

"Are you sure?" Rome asked, stepping into the house and closing the door behind him. He was holding a package in one hand but reached up with his free one, cupping her cheek and brushing a tear away with his thumb.

The gesture was entirely thrilling to every physical sense Tierney owned, and she tried to ignore the quiver of delight that traveled up her spine.

"Yeah. I-I was just watching one of my ironing movies, and it had a sad ending, you know?" she awkwardly explained.

Rome's frown lingered, however, even as he asked, "Ironing movies?"

"Yeah," Tierney affirmed, tucking a strand of loose hair behind her ear. "I like to iron when I'm stressed out. And I've got that interview today, so I just put a movie in and was ironing…and it ended really badly and—"

"You iron when you're stressed out?" he more stated than asked. His frown disappeared, and he smiled again, obviously amused at her confession.

As Rome quickly studied Tierney from head to toe, his smile broadening as he did so, Tierney remembered exactly what she was wearing: the oldest pair of baggy pajama bottoms she owned—pink with the word *bootylicious* stamped across the rear end—and an old brown T-shirt she'd owned since high school that had a picture of 'N Sync screen-printed on the front.

"I-I, um…I was just kind of lounging around waiting until it was time to get ready for that interview and…" she stammered.

"And ironing and watching movies," Rome finished for her.

"Yeah," she admitted, blushing crimson.

Rome was still smiling at her—still looking her up and down as if she were a funny sort of museum display.

"Is Alec here?" he asked. "I've been trying to call him, and he's not answering."

"I think he forgot his phone," Tierney answered. "I tried to call him too and got his voicemail. He went out to get a few things at the store."

"Man," Rome breathed with disappointment. "I scored big, and he's gotta see this." He paused a moment and then asked, "Do you care if I wait for him? It's for the party tomorrow night." He held up the package in his hand. "He's gonna love these! They're perfect for our thing for my mom."

"Your thing for your mom?" Tierney asked. She had no idea what Rome was talking about, though she did truly love watching his lips move when he talked—his perfectly shaped, entirely manly lips that had once been pressed to hers.

"Didn't Alec tell you?" he asked. "I mean, you've gotta be there too. You're not going to want to miss it. And besides, it's Halloween. What else are you gonna do?" He looked around a moment. "Looks like you've got all the ironing done, so there's no excuse not to come tomorrow night."

"Come where?" Tierney asked.

"To my family's Halloween party, of course," Rome answered as if he'd expected her to know all about it. "We have it every year, and this year Alec and I have a special surprise for my mom. She's going to love it. I can't wait to see her face."

He moved past Tierney, plopped down on the sofa behind her, and tossed the package he'd been holding to one side. Tierney heard him chuckle and immediately knew why. Attempting to cover her bum with her hands, she spun around and faced him.

"Bootylicious, huh?" he teased. Winking at her, he said, "Well, I wholeheartedly concur."

"Sorry. It's just a pair of my old...I wasn't expecting anyone and..." Tierney sputtered, still blushing.

"Oh, but don't mind me," Rome said with a gesture that she should continue ironing. "You go on and iron away." Grinning at her, he continued, "In fact, why don't you do me a little favor here?"

Tierney didn't know what to do or where to run as Rome stood once more and began unbuttoning the black button-up shirt he was wearing.

"Since I'm going to my mom's house in a little while, I know she's going to give me a hard time for the condition of my collar." Stripping off his shirt to reveal the most perfectly formed torso Tierney had ever seen on a man in real life, Rome held his shirt out to her. "Would you mind pressing it out for me? Just the collar, I mean? If you have time."

"Oh...s-sure," Tierney said, accepting the shirt Rome held toward her. It was still warm from the heat of his body, and Tierney caught a whiff of a reminiscently familiar scent—the same scent he'd carried months ago while dancing with her.

"You sure you just want the collar pressed?" she asked as she positioned the shirt on the ironing board.

"Yeah," he assured her. "It's always what Mom seems to notice."

"Okay," Tierney said. Yet as she started to iron, she heard Rome sit back down on the couch—began to worry if her bum was moving around too much and attracting his attention to the stupid "bootylicious" written across it. It was mortifying, being caught in such a state of sloppy self-indulgence. He'd think she were a lazy, whiny baby. She couldn't believe she'd told him about her ironing thing— about the sappy movies too.

"You know," Rome said from behind her, "I've never seen anybody swim like that before…and to music even."

Tierney glanced up to see Esther Williams gracefully dive off a rock formation, enter the water like an elegant swan, and begin to swim.

"Yeah, it's a corny '50s musical," she explained. "I love them."

"I know what a musical is," Rome lightheartedly defended himself. "I have a mom, you know."

Tierney smiled. She figured she might like Rome's mom.

Just then, the front door opened, and Alec stepped in. He took one look at Tierney, another look at Rome, and laughed.

"Well, isn't this domestic?" he teased.

"Tierney's ironing my collar," Rome explained.

Alec nodded. "She's gonna save you from another nagging from your mom, huh?"

"Yeah," Rome affirmed. "But, dude, wait until you see what I just picked up at the post office."

"You mean they got here?" Alec asked, suddenly very exuberant.

"They did," Rome answered. "And they are perfect, dude! We will totally rock the house tomorrow night at my parents' party."

"Well, let's see them!" Alec ordered. "Break them out, Romeo, and let's try them on."

"Do *not* call me Romeo," Tierney heard Rome correct her brother. "And we can't try them on in front of Tierney. She might be a spy."

"I'm not a spy," Tierney defended herself as she stripped Rome's shirt off the ironing board and turned to hand it to him.

"But you're stressed," Alec said. "I can see that by the ironing." Alec reached out and took a cookie out of the tin of sugar-coated shortbread cookies Tierney had sitting on the free end of the ironing board with her movie list. "And by these," he added, popping the cookie into his mouth. "I should've hidden my stash better." Alec winked at her, however.

"What…is this a family thing?" Rome asked, taking two cookies from Tierney's tin. "What's with you and your sister and—"

"Hey, man, at least you don't see me ironing and watching musicals when I'm stressed," Alec noted.

"Good point," Rome mumbled as he reached out and accepted his shirt from Tierney.

"Don't knock it until you've tried it, Alec," Tierney said, suddenly realizing she'd been staring directly at Rome's broad, bronze, muscular chest as he'd buttoned up his shirt. "B-but I suppose I should start preparing for that interview."

"You'll do great, Tiers," Alec said. "There's no reason she won't hire you. I know she needs the help, and no one else is as qualified as you."

"And besides," Rome interjected, "if you decide not to take the job, me and Alec will teach you how to plow snow with us." He grinned. "We could get you a pink four-by-four and have 'bootylicious' painted on the tailgate." He looked to Alec and asked, "Right?"

"Of course," Alec agreed with a chuckle.

"Watch it, Mr. Latin Lover Boy," Tierney said, wagging an index finger at Rome. "Or else I'll tell your mama that you didn't iron your own collar after all."

Rome frowned and playfully said, "Oooo! Your sister plays hardball, Alec."

Alec laughed and then said, "Come on, man. Let me see the…the stuff."

Rome retrieved the package he'd been carrying from where he'd tossed it on the sofa. "See you later, Tierney," he said, smiling at her. Then looking to Alec, he scolded, "Dude…when were you going to tell her she has to come tomorrow night?"

"Oh yeah," Alec mumbled. Looking to Tierney, he said, "By the way, Tiers, tomorrow is Halloween, and I promised the Novaks we'd both be at their party. Okay?"

"Whatever you say, Alec," Tierney said, shaking her head. "But do I have to dress up as anything? Are you dressing up?"

Alec and Rome both smiled.

"Hell yes, we're dressing up!" Alec exclaimed.

"But you don't have to wear a costume, Tierney," Rome said, obviously sensing her discomfort. "It's about half and half. Some wear costumes, some don't. No pressure."

"I-I might pass on wearing anything then…if that's okay," Tierney said. "I mean, I'm not prepared with anything."

"Oh, you don't have to wear anything," Rome said. "But my mom might think it's a little scandalous if you don't."

Tierney blushed deep red, even though she knew Rome was only teasing her. "I meant I might pass on wearing a costume of any sort, Mr. Novak."

Rome looked to Alec. "Dude, she keeps calling me Mr. Novak…like I'm her high school biology teacher or something."

Alec nodded. "Yeah…she does that when she's been ironing."

"Okay, okay!" Tierney exclaimed. "You guys are like toddlers when you're together. Go off and open your package and do whatever you're doing. I've got to get ready for that interview."

"All right, all right," Alec said, taking his sister's hand and squeezing it with reassurance. "We'll lay off. But you need to not worry, Tiers. Everything will work out. I promise."

"Yeah, it will," Rome added. "And if you decide you don't want the flower thing job, I know a Bavarian restaurant looking for bootylicious waitresses, okay?"

Tierney rolled her eyes, even though Rome was amusing. "Okay. Now you boys run along and do your…whatever it is you're doing."

Alec bent and kissed the top of Tierney's head. "You'll be fine, Tiers. Really."

Tierney nodded and tried to keep tears from welling in her eyes. But she was frightened and insecure—even for all Alec and Rome's encouragement.

"Good luck, Tierney," Rome added. He grinned with sympathetic understanding. "And I'll see you tomorrow night, okay? Whether or not you decide to wear anything."

He laughed, and so did Alec—and even Tierney couldn't help but giggle.

It took every ounce of self-control she had not to gawk after Rome as he left the room—as jaw-dropped as all the women in the restaurant had gawked at him the night she arrived. She raised her hands to her face. Yep—she could still smell the scent of him that had clung to his shirt. It was masculine, woodsy, and comforting somehow.

Turning to unplug the iron and turn off the movie, Tierney thought to herself that there was no other option. She had to land the job at the florist's. She truly could not imagine herself being able to plow snow—not for extended periods of time, anyway. Furthermore, the thought of waitressing scared her to death for some reason. She wondered for a moment if it were the thought of waitressing that scared her or the thought of working for Rome's parents. What if she did go to work for them and failed at being good at her job? Then what would Rome think of her?

Tierney shook her head—growled at herself under her breath for having such ridiculous thoughts. Rome was Alec's friend, not hers. He was drop-dead gorgeous and probably on the top of every woman's dream-man list in Leavenworth. Furthermore, Tierney had to get her own life together before she allowed herself to dream again—to dream of anything to do with romance, a man, love, or anything in the deep emotional category.

Besides, she knew her lingering (albeit powerful) attractions to Rome was simply whatever that syndrome was called when a woman fell head over heels into infatuation with the man who'd rescued her somehow—and Rome had certainly rescued her. Tierney couldn't even imagine what her life would have been if she'd actually married Dillon.

"Dude, there's some cardboard cutout guy in here," Tierney heard Rome call out to Alec.

"Oh, that's just Tierney's lover, man. No worries," Alec answered.

Tierney blushed to the tips of her toes even for the fact that she was in the room alone. "I'll have you know that his name is Ricardo!" she called out.

She giggled and rolled her eyes as she listened to Rome and Alec exchanging sarcasms about her cardboard lover as she headed toward her room. They were funny together. In fact, Tierney was suddenly overwhelmed with gratitude and understanding—a gratitude that Alec had found a true friend when he'd moved to Leavenworth and understanding of what a wonderful thing it was. She hoped she'd find a friend like Rome was to Alec. She remembered what Alec had said about Rome's sister, Celeste. Maybe she'd find Celeste would be a friend to her.

"Are you bringing this guy to my parents' party tomorrow, Tierney?" Rome called from one of the bedrooms. "Because if he can't make it, I could hook you up with a date who has skin."

"Open your package and mind your own business, Romeo," she called in return.

"Hey, lady! You call him Dr. Jones!" Alec scolded from the back room.

Tierney laughed as she heard Rome chuckle, "Good one, man! I loved that movie."

Life certainly would be different living in Leavenworth with Alec. And suddenly the reiterated realization calmed Tierney's frazzled nerves. Alec loved her. He wouldn't let anything happen to her—she knew that. Even if she had trouble finding a job, Alec would take care of her. And all at once, Tierney O'Brien felt more secure and safe than she could remember being since she was a little girl.

"Well," Tierney said, closing the door behind her, "she's going to give me a chance, at least. Only three days a week, but it's better than nothing, right?"

"It's awesome, Tiers!" Alec exclaimed from his place lounging on the couch. His smile was broad and sincere, and Tierney felt better at just the sight of it.

The truth was that when Mrs. Potts had explained she wanted to hire Tierney on a contingency basis (until she was more certain she could afford to hire her, as well as that Tierney could really do what she claimed where arranging was concerned), Tierney had felt utterly defeated. A mere twenty-fours hours a week wouldn't come close to making her financially self-reliant, even at the higher wage Mrs. Potts had offered.

Yet the moment she walked into Alec's warm, inviting home, the moment she saw him lounging on the couch with the TV remote in hand, she'd begun to feel better. His smile—the sincere pride she saw in it—further boosted her confidence, and Tierney owned the sense that this was just the first stepping-stone—that more would follow.

"What's she going to pay you?" he asked.

"Twelve-fifty an hour…at first anyway," Tierney answered. "If it works out, she'll bump me up to a lot more and full-time."

"See?" Alec asked. "Things are coming together. I told you they would."

"Well...yeah, I guess. But...but I'll still have to live with you for quite a while, Alec. I was hoping to give you your privacy back pretty quickly."

Alec got up from the couch, strode to Tierney, and gathered her into a warm, affectionate embrace. "I don't want you moving out. Not until it's necessary or both of us are really ready. I want you here for as long as I can have you. Okay?"

Tierney smiled, returned her brother's embrace, and sighed, "Okay."

"Now," Alec said, releasing her, "I picked us up some dinner...and there's a Hitchcock marathon on that old movie channel you like tonight. I figure we can grab some pizza and some popcorn and settle in. What do you say?"

Tierney sighed again, for the feeling of loving security she'd missed for so long was washing over her like a warm summer rain.

"I say perfect!" She smiled, tossed her purse in the corner, and added, "Let me just put some jammies on so I can be more comfortable, and we'll start." However, when Alec smiled and chuckled to himself, she frowned and asked, "What?"

"Nothing," Alec lied.

"Tell me," Tierney demanded. "What is so funny all of a sudden?"

Alec shrugged. "Just that...well, anytime we talked about you today after Rome was over here, he just called you my 'bootylicious sister.'" Alec shook his head. "You don't know Rome the way I do. You'll never hear the end of it."

"Oh, great," Tierney sighed. The last thing on earth that she'd ever wanted was for Rome Novak to associate her with something so ridiculous.

"It's funny though," Alec said then.

"What else is funny?" Tierney asked, rolling her eyes with embarrassment and exasperation.

"The fact that Rome never said a word about that stupid 'N Sync T-shirt you were wearing," Alec answered. He grinned his naughty, smart-aleck grin and added, "I guess he was too intrigued with your...well, your apparently bootylicious booty to notice Justin Timberlake smeared all over your chest."

"Oh, great," Tierney sighed. Then, desperate to change the subject, Tierney teased, "Did you see your *Christmas Shoppe* girl today, darling brother? And when do I get to meet her?"

"No and never," Alec answered. Shrugging his shoulders, he added, "Besides, Heidi Svensson is all hot after Rome. He's just too dense to notice it. And any man who went up against Rome Novak for a girl's attention would have to be a total fool."

Tierney didn't like the uncomfortable, unhappy feeling that was knotting up in her chest. The girl Alec was interested in was only interested in Rome?

"Well, does Rome have a girlfriend?" Tierney heard herself ask. She was astonished in that moment—for it wasn't the question she'd intended to ask. She'd intended to ask Alec how he planned to handle the situation, but it wasn't the question she heard come out of her own mouth.

An understanding grin began to spread across Alec's face then. "Ah ha! You did fall in love with him when I sent him to bust up your wedding," he exclaimed.

"What?" Tierney nearly shrieked. "No! No! Not at all! Would you be serious for a minute?" Yet she wondered in the same instant why she was so defensive. "I just meant to ask if this Heidi chick has a reason to think she might be able to get her claws into Rome. And I want to know what you're feeling about it all. I mean, if you like her—"

"Rome thinks I like her," Alec interrupted. "But I have my eye on someone else."

"You do?" Tierney asked, nearly giddy with hope. "Who?"

But again Alec shrugged. "The proverbial perfect woman that every man wants who's completely out of my league…and reach."

"Tell me!" Tierney begged. "I have to know. And anyway, maybe I can help."

"Nope. It's not worth mentioning, Tiers," Alec said. He exhaled a heavy sigh. "But…if you admit to me that my pal Rome rang your bell when he showed up at that damn shower Mom was throwing for you, I might give you a hint as to who the woman is that rings mine."

"I can't admit something that didn't happen, Alec," Tierney fibbed. "I'll just wait, I guess…keep my eye on you and wait. I'll figure out who this mystery woman of yours is, one way or the other."

"He rang your bell, Tiers," Alec said, smiling at her. "I know he did. I can read you like a book when no one else in all the world can."

But Tierney simply straightened her posture and said, "I'm going to go put on my stupid bootylicious pants now, Alec. So cue up an Alfred H. movie—preferably something with Cary Grant—and I'll be right back."

Yet all night long—during every Hitchcock movie they watched, during every bowl of over-buttered popcorn Tierney shared with her brother—Rome Novak kept popping into her thoughts. He'd been popping into her thoughts constantly since she'd officially met him such a short time ago in his parents' restaurant. And Tierney had been constantly trying to drive him out of her thoughts since. In truth, it was wearing her out.

But as she thought about what Alec had told her—that even Heidi Svensson was "hot after" Rome—Tierney felt more and more discouraged somehow. Even for her success in getting her foot in the door with Mrs. Potts, Tierney felt discouraged, and she knew it was because of Rome.

Part of her even wished for a brief moment that Alec had never sent that perfectly gorgeous man dressed as a perfectly gorgeous Latin lover to her bridal shower to convince her not to marry Dillon. Yet if Alec hadn't sent Rome, Tierney was pretty sure she would've married Dillon—and that would've been a disaster.

"Man, what I wouldn't give to make out with Ingrid Bergman back then," Alec commented as he watched the last scene in Hitchcock's famous *Notorious*. "She was a real beauty, if you ask me. All, like, natural, you know."

"Yep…she was," Tierney said.

Tierney looked at her brother—studied him for a moment. How hard would it be to like a girl who only had eyes for your best friend? Tierney imagined it would be miserable. And yet it was obvious Alec valued Rome's friendship enough to let the matter slide.

Alec O'Brien was a good man—in spite of their mother's best efforts. Tierney admired him for so many reasons, and now she had another. Alec was a true and loyal friend to Rome Novak. She wondered if Rome were as true and loyal to Alec. But then she remembered his flying out to Monterey, dressing up like the classic

Latin lover Tierney had always dreamed of, and braving a mob of women to do what he'd done to help her. Yep, Rome Novak was a true and loyal friend to Alec as well—not to mention handsome, built like the archetypal muscular male, suave, clever, playful, an excellent dancer, a perfect kisser…

"What are you thinking about?" Alec asked, jogging Tierney's thoughts back to the movie. "Your face is all red."

"Oh, nothing," Tierney fibbed again. "I think I'm just a little overheated." Tossing aside the blanket she'd had on her lap, she smiled at Alec and asked, "Which movie next?"

CHAPTER FOUR

"But they won't expect *me* to do anything, right?" Tierney asked as she watched Alec adjust his wig. "I mean, the lip-synching thing…it's totally voluntary, isn't it?"

"Oh yeah," Alec assured her. "Rome's parents just have anybody who wants to do one let them know a week or so before the party." Alec smiled and nodded with triumphant pride as he studied himself in the mirror. "And this year, me and Rome…we're gonna blow his mom's mind with this." He turned around, struck a pose, and asked Tierney, "So? What do you think?"

Tierney's smile was so wide it almost hurt. Alec looked incredible! She couldn't wait to see the lip sync he and Rome had prepared— couldn't wait to see Rome's mother's reaction.

"So she was a real fan, huh?" she asked.

"Oh yeah!" Alec assured her as he turned back to the mirror and adjusted a wayward cornrow braid. "I guess she cried for a week when…whichever one was considered the best looking died."

"Yeah. Rob Pilatus," Tierney sighed. "He *was* gorgeous. I think he died in, like, 1998. That whole scandal and mess they went through…I guess he really never got over it."

Alec stopped, turned, and looked at Tierney with a puzzled expression. "You know which one was supposed to be the good-looking one? You know when he died?" he asked in obvious astonishment.

Tierney smiled. "Of course I know about him," she giggled. "After all, he was a pretty, pretty man." She shrugged. "And anyway, I loved that song…and the old music video. And I don't care if they were lip-synching. They did a good job of it."

Alec shook his head. "Your knowledge of Hollywood trivia and crap just amazes me sometimes."

"It sticks with me for some reason," Tierney admitted.

"So anyway," Alec continued, "I suggested that Rome be the good-looking one…since his mom will be the one who enjoys it most. Plus, he's a better dancer."

"And you'll be Fab and do most of the lip-synching," Tierney filled in for herself.

"Fab?" Alec asked, a look of utter disgust puckering his brow.

Tierney laughed. "Yeah! Fabrice Morvan, the other Milli Vanilli guy…the one that sang the most in 'Girl, You Know It's True.' Dude! Didn't you do your homework?"

"Of course I did my homework!" Alec exclaimed in defense of himself. "Do you know how hard it was to get these wigs? Perfect cornrows with long, perfect braids? And Doc Martens ain't cheap, sista! And I had to have this girl we know make these ugly, shoulder-padded '80s jacket things…and I'm wearing women's leggings. So yeah! I did my homework!"

Tierney giggled—for the truth of the matter was that Alec looked hysterical standing there dressed like one-half of the famous (and infamous) singing duo Milli Vanilli. Still, it was a perfect costume! The cornrows and braids wig was phenomenal, and whoever the girl who'd made the wide-shoulder-padded jacket, tapered down to fit Alec's hips, she'd done a great job. The black leggings that stopped at midcalf, black socks, and black Doc Martens shoes were perfect. And the spray of baby red roses made into a boutonnière he had pinned high on his left lapel was the perfect finishing touch! She wondered if Rome's costume would be as authentic looking—wondered if he'd actually managed to find a large double coin brooch to wear on his Rob Pilatus jacket.

The thought of Rome dressed up like Rob Pilatus caused Tierney's heart and stomach to flip inside her. Rome was so incredibly good-looking already, and she was dying to see how hot he looked dressed up like the prettiest member of Milli Vanilli.

Tierney wished she could quit thinking about Rome Novak. It seemed to her that she thought of nothing else. Still, at least thinking of

Rome distracted her here and there from stressing about starting her job at the florist the following week.

"Wait until you see it, Tierney," Alec chuckled then. "It will crack you up. We've been practicing for a month. We're so stupid."

"I think it's wonderful...all the work you guys have put into this for Rome's mom," Tierney assured him. "You guys will be great."

There was a knock on the door, and Alec said, "Okay, that's gotta be Rome. Will you let him in? We want you to take some pictures before we leave for the party, okay? Do you mind?"

Tierney's smile returned as she studied her brother once more. "Not at all! You guys are crazy!"

Hurrying to the door, Tierney literally gasped when she opened the door to see Rome dressed as Alec's Milli Vanilli counterpart. He was gorgeous—even with a wig and dressed like he'd just stepped out of an old 1989 music video.

In fact, Tierney squealed with delight as he stepped into the room, clapped her hands with approval, and looked Rome up and down over and over and over.

"I love it!" she giggled. "I cannot believe how good you look...how good you both look!" She paused a moment, still smiling as she studied Rome. "Of course, your legs aren't skinny enough, and you're way, way bigger than Rob Pilatus was—and better looking, of course—but *wow*! It's perfect!"

"Rob who?" Rome asked.

"Dude!" Alec exclaimed as he entered from the other room. "My sister is such a Hollywood history nerd. She knows their names."

"But I thought they were just Milli Vanilli," Rome teased.

Tierney reached out to feel the fabric of Rome's broad-shouldered, tapered red jacket. "It's perfect!" she giggled again. She just couldn't seem to hide her delight and amusement—especially as she looked from Rome to Alec and back. Their costumes were just plain phenomenal! "Gee, I feel like such a loser now, not having a costume," Tierney teased.

"*You* feel like a loser?" Alec asked. He looked to Rome and said, "She just told me my name is Fabrice, dude."

"Dude!" Rome exclaimed, frowning with sympathy.

47

"Whatever," Alec sighed. "Let's just get some pictures. Then we can go. We don't want to be late to your mom and dad's soiree."

"No, we do not," Rome said. Tierney giggled as she watched him struggle to pull his phone from the pocket of the jacket that was fit so snuggly at his hips. He touched the screen a couple of times and then handed the phone to Tierney. "Here. Just touch the camera icon, and it'll take."

Tierney was still smiling as Rome and Alec positioned themselves in front of the bare wall behind the door.

"Okay, Rob and Fab...now strike a pose," she instructed. Tierney couldn't help but laugh when Rome and Alec did exactly what she'd told them to—struck a pose that she'd seen on old Milli Vanilli posters online. "Oh, this is *so* awesome!" she exclaimed as she took several photos.

"Here," Alec said, handing his own phone to Rome. "Take some of me and Tierney, okay?"

"Sure," Rome said, shaking his head to cause the long braids of his wig to fall back from his face.

Tierney posed with Alec, delighted that she would have photos to remember the event by. She reminded herself to use the camera she always carried in her purse. Maybe she hadn't had many great photo ops over the past year, but this was one she could not forget to record.

"Okay, now take one of me and Tierney," Rome unexpectedly said then. Reaching out, Rome took hold of Tierney's hand and pulled her to stand with him in front of the blank wall.

"Oh, here," Tierney said, handing Rome's phone to Alec.

She looked up to Rome, and he smiled at her. "Okay, try to look like a groupie...like you're all excited to meet me," he requested.

"I can do that," Tierney agreed. Goose bumps broke over her as Rome settled one strong, muscular arm across her shoulders.

"Okay," Alec said, directing Rome's phone screen at them. "Smile and say, 'Milli Vanilli,' Tiers."

Tierney made the exaggerated expression of a fan caught in the arms of her favorite movie star—a big toothy grin—as she clung to Rome's jacket.

"You guys have to text these to me," Tierney said as Alec handed Rome's phone to him.

"Tell me your number, and I'll text them right now," Rome said, smiling at her.

As Tierney told Rome her cell number, Alec exclaimed, "Dude! We look awesome!" as he caught a glimpse of his and Rome's reflection in the sliding glass door across the room. "We are going to own the women at your mom and dad's party."

"Thanks," Rome said as he saved Tierney's number to the contacts on his phone. "I'll text them to you now."

Tierney felt a bit foolish when her heart leapt a little in her chest at the realization she was about to receive a text message from Rome Novak. She decided to pretend that, now that her phone number was saved in his phone, she and Rome were more intimately acquainted somehow. Tierney wondered for a moment if women ever really got over the delightful thrill that rose within in them each time a good-looking man stared at them, smiled at them, or flirted with them. She wondered if, when she was fifty and came across some handsome Rome Novak sort, she would still be secretly enchanted by his attention as she was in that moment. She figured she would—that any woman would—at any age.

"Come on," Alec said. "Let's go. I can't wait to see your mom's face when we walk in, dude!"

Tierney giggled with amusement as Rome quickly ran in place for a moment, mimicking one of the dance moves Milli Vanilli had performed in their old music video.

"Me neither!" he agreed, bumping fists with Alec. "Mom is going to freak when she sees us."

Putting an arm across Tierney's back, Alec said, "Come on, baby sister. You can be that chick in the 'Girl, You Know It's True' video."

"In the slinky, blue elastic dress thing?" Tierney exclaimed.

"Yeah," Rome chuckled. He put his arm around her waist, sending goose bumps racing over her. "But you look way, way better in your fuzzy little sweater here," he added, stroking the sleeve of Tierney's brown sweater.

"Oh, I'm sure," Tierney mumbled with sarcasm.

"Come on," Alec said. "You're about to have the time of your life, Tiers."

Both men removed their arms from around her, and Tierney tried not to be nervous as they left the house. New people? A party? It was everything that had secretly begun to frighten Tierney since the day she'd broken up with Dillon. Yet as she watched Alec and Rome exaggerate their swaggers and flip their braids this way and that, she giggled. How could it *not* be the time of her life—with Milli Vanilli as her escorts?

"You guys look awesome!" Celeste Novak laughed as she opened the door to see Milli Vanilli standing on the front porch. Covering her mouth as she continued to laugh, Celeste shook her head. "Seriously! Mom is going to freak!"

Tierney, however, could only stand on the porch next to Alec in flabbergasted astonishment as she stared at Celeste Novak. For a split second, Tierney wasn't sure if she were staring at a younger version of Salma Hayek dressed as Carmen Miranda (complete with a scarf wrapped around her head and a tropical fruit hat) or if the beautiful young woman standing at the open door were really Rome's sister.

"Do you dig the hair, Celeste?" Rome asked, moving his head back and forth to make the long cornrow braids of his wig swing this way and that.

"It's perfect!" Celeste exclaimed, clapping her hands together. The Latin-born beauty looked to Alec then—and Tierney did not miss the blush that rose to Celeste's beautiful cheeks as she said, "Oooo, Alec! What an awesome brooch!"

"I know," Alec laughed (almost nervously). "It's totally legit, right?"

"It is! Mom is going to die!" Celeste exclaimed.

Tierney studied her brother for a moment—observing the way his cheeks seemed a little rosier than a moment before, his body language a little stiffer.

"What?" he mumbled, glaring at Tierney.

"Nothing," Tierney said as understanding washed over her. Rome's sister! It was Rome's sister Alec had a thing for!

"Come on in," Celeste said, stepping aside. "But wait until I go ahead of you so I can see Mom's reaction!"

As Rome and Alec stepped aside to allow Tierney to enter the house first, Celeste offered a hand to Tierney.

"I'm Celeste Novak," she said. "Alec has been so excited for you to get here!"

Taking Celeste's hand, Tierney shook it and said, "I hope I don't drive him nuts too quickly. It's nice to meet you, Celeste."

Then Celeste (the Latin goddess of beauty) giggled. "What's with all this hand-shaking, right?" Pulling Tierney into her arms, Celeste offered a comfortable, welcoming hug. "Welcome to Leavenworth, Tierney…*and* to our party!"

Alec and Rome entered then, closing the door behind them.

"Where's Mom?" Rome asked.

"Out on the back porch," Celeste answered, laughing again as she studied her brother from head to toe. "How much did you guys spend on these costumes?"

"Probably not as much as you spent on yours, so shut up," Rome told his sister as he pretended he was going to pluck a banana from her fruit hat.

"You do look really great, Celeste," Alec offered. "I mean…more than great. You look…look…like…you know…wow!"

Celeste blushed again and almost sighed, "Thanks, Alec."

Tierney was convinced then. It was *Celeste* Alec liked—and she was fairly certain the feeling was mutual. Furthermore, Tierney entirely understood why Alec thought Celeste was out of his reach. Celeste Novak was astonishingly beautiful! Dark, almost black eyes and the longest eyelashes Tierney had ever seen—well, the longest lashes she'd ever seen that weren't false, anyway. Celeste had the perfect hourglass shape too—buxom yet slender, curvy hips but not too large. She was wearing a lime-and-white striped sarong and matching rumba-sleeved halter-top. She even had a classic beauty mark to the left of her lower lip! It was like she'd walked out of a stereotypical role in some old Hollywood movie about a Latin supernatural being.

As if her looks weren't enough to capture Alec's attention, Celeste seemed so nice and so normal—like she didn't know how gorgeous she was. Tierney studied Rome a moment, thinking he had the same quality—an ignorance to how lethally good-looking and attractive he was.

"Come on, Tierney," Rome said, unexpectedly taking Tierney's hand and almost yanking her farther into the house. "You need to meet my mom and dad."

"Wait, wait, wait!" Celeste said, however. "Let me go ahead of you. I want to see Mom's face when she sees you guys."

Tierney giggled as she observed her brother watching Celeste hurry away. The platform shoes Celeste was wearing as part of her costume made her hips sway more exaggeratedly than they probably normally would have, and Alec O'Brien was thoroughly entranced.

Leaning closer to Alec, Tierney whispered, "Wipe the drool off your chin, Alec…before you give yourself away."

Alec glared at Tierney and quietly snapped, "Shut up, Tiers."

But Tierney was amused—delighted, excited, and hopeful! Alec had his eye on someone, at last! The incident with Valerie Gilland years before had scarred him for life—that was for certain. He'd never trusted another woman since, and though he'd dated several girls over the past couple of years, it was always very casual, and none of them had made Alec nervous and blushy the way Celeste Novak obviously did.

"Come on, bootylicious," Rome said, tugging at Tierney's hand once more. "Let's get this party started, hmmm?"

"Yeah…come on, bootylicious," Alec laughed, looking to Tierney. He winked at her then as if to say, *Touché!*

The Novak home was warm and cozy in both atmosphere and decor. Lamps, shelves, and furniture were slathered in fake cobwebs and assorted black and orange Halloween decorations; jack-o'-lanterns and pumpkins were tucked seemingly everywhere. As Rome led Tierney through the house and toward a sliding glass door leading to a covered porch, she tried to soak it all in—the scents of the homemade root beer she saw bubbling in a cast iron caldron that obviously had dry ice in it, of pumpkin lids cooking because of the candles in the jack-o'-lanterns, of salty chips and ranch-flavored dip.

As they reached the patio, Rome released Tierney's hand, turned to Alec, and said, "I suppose we should, like, make an entrance for my mom's sake, right?"

"Absolutely," Alec agreed with a nod. Alec looked to Tierney and asked, "Wanna go in first? Or after us?"

"Definitely after," Tierney assured him with a giggle. She had no desire to walk out onto a porch full of people she didn't know and have them stare at her in wondering who the heck she was.

"Okay then," Rome said, inhaling a deep breath. "Kiss us for luck, okay, bootylicious?"

Tierney's eyebrows arched in surprise. Was he kidding?

Alec leaned toward her, tapping his cheek with one index finger, however, and Tierney placed a quick kiss there.

"Me next," Rome said, leaning down a bit.

But instead of offering Tierney his cheek, he reached out and took hold of her chin, planting a quick, warm kiss to her lips.

"Dude," Alec chuckled, frowning even as he smiled at Rome, "quit pervin' my sister, man."

"What?" Rome said, releasing Tierney's chin and shrugging as if he hadn't done anything out of the ordinary. "For luck…like in *Star Wars* when Princess Leia kisses Luke for luck before they swing out over that chasm thing and—"

But Alec shook his head, mumbling, "Shut up, man."

Rome grinned, winked at Tierney, and then followed Alec in stepping out onto the Novaks' covered patio.

The reaction of the guests to the sudden appearance of Milli Vanilli was quite audible, to say the least. Everyone erupted into clapping and catcalls, and Tierney figured it was Rome's mother who (dressed like a very familiar character from the Harry Potter books, Professor Trelawney) squealed with delight and flung her arms around Alec and Rome as she jumped up and down and laughed with joyous amusement.

But Tierney found she couldn't move to join the others out onto the patio. She stood completely immobile—still reeling from the fact that Rome had kissed her on the lips for luck, instead of allowing her to kiss his cheek the way she'd done with her brother. He'd kissed her—right on the lips! He'd actually reached out, taken hold of her chin (in very much the same way he had at her bridal shower all those months ago), and kissed her!

It wasn't until Celeste appeared, linking arms with her and saying, "Come on out, Tierney. Mom and Dad are dying to meet you," that Tierney finally snapped out of the awed trance that had rendered her immobile.

"Hey, Mom," Celeste called as she escorted Tierney out onto the patio. "This is Alec's sister, Tierney."

The woman dressed as the kooky divination teacher clapped her hands together and squealed with excitement. Tierney was amazed at how perfectly perfect Mrs. Novak's Professor Trelawney costume was—right down to the frizzy long hair and pop-bottle-bottom glasses.

"Tierney!" Mrs. Novak exclaimed, throwing her arms around Tierney's neck and embracing her tightly. "We are so happy you're finally here! Alec has been chattering on and on about you for weeks!"

Mrs. Novak unwound her arms from around Tierney and, keeping hold of her shoulders, drew back from her and studied her for a moment. Then, calling over her shoulder, "Edward! Get over here and meet Alec's little sister! She's just adorable," Mrs. Novak actually reached up and gently pinched Tierney's cheek.

The gesture made Tierney giggle. She suddenly felt far more comfortable—even warmer than she had a moment before.

A tall man dressed like Captain America stepped up, smiled at Tierney, and then wrapped his long, strong arms around her as he said, "Well, hello at last! My ears are sore from hearing so much about you from Alec." The man chuckled, put one arm around Mrs. Novak's shoulders, and said, "I'm Edward Novak, Nikki's husband, Rome and Celeste's father." Mr. Novak raised his free arm, flexing his bicep and adding, "And Captain America, of course."

"Wow!" Tierney breathed. "I've never met a real-live super hero before!"

Mr. Novak was pleased. It was obvious by the way his grin spread into a delighted, rather cheesy smile.

"Oh, I like you already, Tierney O'Brien," he said. "And flattery will get you everywhere with me."

"Welcome to our home, Tierney," Mrs. Novak said, "and to our party. Call me Nikki, by the way, and I promise that you're going to have so much fun tonight. There's tons of food, tons of people to meet and talk to. Oh! And what do you think or Rome's idea for the snack table, hmm?"

Taking Tierney's hand, Mrs. Novak led her to the long refreshment table. The table was draped in black cloth and skirting and simply piled with Halloween-themed goodies. There were breadsticks embellished with green food coloring and Parmesan cheese and sliced to look like witch fingers, shrimp (and what looked like cocktail sauce) molded to look like a brain and served with crackers, and a few rubber roaches for decoration. There was a cheese ball decorated to look like a giant, bloodshot eyeball, barbequed chicken wings stretched to look like bat wings, and little hot dogs wrapped with some kind of dough to look like little mummies with tiny mustard-made faces. A bowl of dip had five crooked, long, peeled carrots stick out of it, causing the dip to look like the palm of a hand and the carrots to look like fingers. There were casseroles that looked like entrails, a vegetable pizza appetizer that had crackers standing in it to mimic a graveyard scene. And at the center of the table sat a jack-o'-lantern that had been carved with a round, open mouth, from whence a fat river of guacamole originated to then spread out over a thick covering of parchment paper. The guacamole was lined on either side with tortilla chips.

"You see?" Nikki said, shaking her head and pointing to the guacamole-vomiting jack-o'-lantern. "Do you see the kind of mind my son has?" Yet the woman laughed the next moment, her face erupting into a wide smile and expression of pride. "Don't you *love* it?" she asked with exuberance.

Tierney laughed as well, nodded, and answered, "It's awesome. Gross…but way awesome!"

"I know, right?" Nikki agreed. Then taking Tierney's arm once more, she said, "Let's toss you out of the frying pan and into the fire, shall we? You need to start meeting everyone."

And meet everyone she did! For the next forty-five minutes, between Rome's mother, father, and Celeste, Tierney met every guest at the party. Occasionally Alec would track her down to check on her—ask if she were okay and having fun. Much to Tierney's surprise, she was always able to answer, "Yes," and was glad.

The Novaks were a wonderful, friendly, and obviously very caring family, and Tierney found herself thinking she'd never been in such a wonderful atmosphere before—not in all her life. Still, as she found her attention constantly drawn to Rome—wondering what he was doing and who he was talking with—a touch of anxiety did creep into her mind here and there. She liked Rome—liked him far more than she had any right to—and it worried her, deeply.

The back covered patio of the Novaks' house was very large, spanning the entire length of the house and at least thirty feet wide. Being the focal point for the entertainment of the evening—lip syncs performed by some of the guests and apparently dancing later, as Alec informed Tierney—everyone lingered near the patio or just inside the house in the kitchen and adjoining family room.

As the evening progressed, the party guests would be summoned to congregate on the patio to enjoy a lip sync that someone had prepared. Tierney had never experienced anything quite like watching friends and neighbors perform in this manner, and she found it wildly intriguing as well as superbly entertaining.

One middle-aged couple performed a hysterical lip sync as Sonny and Cher singing "I Got You, Babe"—with the six foot four inch husband being dressed up and performing as Cher and the five foot nothing wife dressed as Sony Bono and performing his parts. Tierney found herself having laughed so hard that a lower backache ensued for several minutes afterward. There was an elderly woman who did a marvelous job of impersonating Christina Aguilera, a friend of Rome's who lip-synched to a Michael Bublé number, and a group of women in their thirties (one of whom was eight months pregnant) who performed to a Spice Girls' song.

It was obvious to Tierney that each and every lip sync had taken a lot of time and effort to prepare, and she was amazed that the Novaks' friends had put so much of themselves into it—just for a Halloween party.

Still, each time Mr. Novak would announce another lip sync was about to be performed, Tierney's heart would leap in her chest—evidence of her excitement at seeing just how prepared Alec and Rome would be. Of course, it became evident quite quickly that Celeste (being the one in charge of the order in which people performed) had saved her brother and Alec for last.

Yet at nine o'clock sharp—as Tierney stood talking with Alec about how entirely different Rome and Celeste's upbringing must have been from their own—Celeste stepped up onto the impromptu stage Mr. Novak had built just a little ways beyond the patio and announced that the last lip sync of the evening was about to begin.

"We'll start the dancing after this last lip sync," Celeste added. "So the fun isn't over yet. But I do have a feeling that this last lip sync will be very entertaining indeed."

"Oh, great. It's time," Alec mumbled.

Tierney looked to him. "But I thought you were stoked about this," she said.

"I was," Alec admitted. "Until right now. Everybody is going to be watching."

"And by everybody you mean…" Tierney began, meaning to imply that Celeste was the one Alec was worried about performing in front of.

"By everyone, I mean everyone," Alec interrupted, however.

"Ladies and gentlemen—" Celeste began to introduce.

"Come on, man!" Rome exclaimed, suddenly appearing behind Tierney and Alec. "Let's go! Get your game face on, dude."

Alec inhaled a deep breath, puffing it out forcefully. "Okay…let's do this thing, bro," he said.

"Please help me welcome to the Novak Halloween stage…" Celeste continued, "give it up for Milli Vanilli!"

Tierney laughed and whispered to herself, "And the crowd went wild!" as everyone in the room began to applaud and whistle as Rome and Alec, long black braids swinging, hurried up onto the stage.

As the music began—the instrumental intro to Milli Vanilli's most famous song, "Girl, You Know It's True"—and Rome and Alec began to dance, every woman of every age in the room squealed with delight, including Tierney!

"Oh my gosh!" Celeste giggled as she hurried down from the stage and stopped to stand beside Tierney. "They look *so* awesome, right?"

"Totally awesome!" Tierney giggled as the energy in the room carried her away to a carefree feeling of joy.

"I mean, look at their hair!" Celeste laughed.

Tierney laughed too as she watched both Rome and Alec twirling around in order to make their cornrow braids swirl out. As she and Celeste laughed together, Tierney was again overwhelmed by not only a backache but also tears of mirth that were now filling her eyes.

"They kill me!" Celeste gasped between laughs.

Everyone in the room was still clapping as the vocal part of the song began. Quickly the crowd quieted down, however, and Tierney watched with awed admiration as Alec and Rome began to lip-synch.

Both men's mouths and dance moves were perfectly in sync with not only the song but also each other. It was truly an incredible performance. In fact, it was such an incredible performance that the crowd began chanting "Encore!" before the final few bars of the song were even finished.

As Rome and Alec finished their performance, both looking a little like they were ready to suck wind, Rome nodded, pointed to his father, and said, "Okay…one more time, Dad."

The crowd went wild again, and Tierney was glad Rome and Alec were going to repeat the performance. She'd been laughing and crying so much with joy that she'd missed half of it.

As "Girl, You Know It's True" began for the second time, the crowd was just as excited and began singing along and moving to the rhythm as they watched Rome and Alec. But of all the people at the Novak Halloween party, it was obvious that Rome's mom was more euphoric than anyone over the guys' performance. As Tierney watched Nikki Novak singing and dancing along with Rome and Alec as she watched them, she tried to imagine her own mother ever enjoying anything so thoroughly. She knew she wouldn't be able to envision Glynnis O'Brien ever being so carefree and happy, and she was disappointed.

How much of life her mother and father were missing! How much of life she and Alec had missed! She understood now why Alec was so very happy—how he'd managed to find contentment and joy in leaving home and building his own business and circle of friends in Leavenworth. This—the type of thing Tierney was experiencing for the very first time thanks to the Novaks, thanks to Rome, who had convinced her not to marry Dillon—this was living life to its fullest! No amount of money or things, travel to exotic places, or hobnobbing and name-dropping could ever match the feelings of pure joy, mirth, comfort, and contentment that Tierney was experiencing at that moment!

As the long black braids swung on the makeshift stage, as the Novaks' guests reveled in amusement and pumpkin-barfed guacamole,

Tierney O'Brien experienced the first epiphany of her life—an assurance that she'd absolutely done the right thing in breaking up with Dillon and finding the courage to leave Monterey the way Alec had. Certainly things may be harder, such as making a living for herself, but she saw the proof before her and all around her not only that life was meant to be lived for more than that—but that it *could* be!

•

CHAPTER FIVE

"It's incredible, isn't it?" Alec asked as he and Tierney stood watching some of the Novaks' guests beginning to dance. "Who knew life could be so challenging and yet thoroughly enjoyable at the same time, right?"

Tierney smiled and shook her head. "I didn't," she admitted. "I mean, I spent my whole life hiding in my room from Mom—at least when I wasn't hanging out with you somewhere on one of our afternoons of trying to escape. I watched old movies, listened to music, and spent probably years on the Internet, if you added all the time up, just researching history, the past, nostalgia. And now I realize, I was just looking for something that was missing in life." She held one hand out, gesturing to where Rome's Captain America father and Harry Potter professor mother were slow dancing on the patio. "And tonight I realize…for the first time, I realize that *this* is exactly what I was looking for," she said. "The normal, everyday life…the kind of life Dad used to describe to us before he withdrew from the world. Dad grew up like this, in just a normal, happy, middle-class family where people laughed and talked and hugged and kissed and drank homemade root beer." Tierney looked to Alec, trying to ignore the tears welling in her eyes. "Why didn't he stand up to Mom more? Why didn't he try to bring her into his world instead of getting dragged into hers?"

Alec sighed and put an arm around Tierney's shoulders. "I think…I think stress and pressure—the demands to maintain the lifestyle Mom wanted, the one he thought he wanted when he started really making big money—I think it just wore him out. It was all he could do to make the money. He didn't have anything left in him to stand up to Mom."

Tierney choked back the tears and said, "I always try to think of him that way, you know? As a farm kid…branding cattle, riding horses, bucking bales, and eating Grandma's stew."

"Mmmm! Grandma's stew!" Alec hummed. "That was always my favorite meal."

"Mine too," Tierney agreed. "And I try to think of Dad that way—happy, hard-working, instead of so hard-stressing."

"You know, he did change after Grandma and Grandpa died," Alec offered, "kind of like maybe he felt his last link to the good life was gone."

"He did, didn't he?" Tierney agreed. In fact, she'd never really realized it before—realized that part of her father had seemed to die when his parents were killed in the fire that had consumed their home late one night. Her father had never been the same after that. He'd withdrawn—seemed perpetually sad.

"So?" Rome asked as he and Celeste stepped between Alec, Tierney, and the dance area then. "Are you guys having fun?"

"Dude, are you kidding? This is awesome!" Alec assured his friend. "Even better than last year, I think."

"And you and Rome," Celeste began, blushing as she gazed at Alec, "you guys were unreal! I loved it!"

"And what did Miss Bootylicious think, hmm?" Rome asked as he stepped closer to Tierney. "Did we do okay?"

Tierney blushed as well—but from the sudden warmth that engulfed her at Rome's being so close rather than the bashfulness Celeste was obviously feeling. How could she keep from smiling at Rome when he looked so perfectly gorgeous in his braided wig and '80s jacket? She thought to herself that Rome Novak would've owned any decade he'd been born in; any time in history, he would rule as the archetypal male.

"It was so awesome!" Tierney managed to answer at last. "Honestly," she added, glancing to Alec a moment. "You guys were seriously dangerous up there!"

Rome's smile broadened as he muttered, "Must've been that good luck kiss."

"Must've been what?" Celeste asked.

out of the way just in time to avoid the spray of root beer that shot out of his mouth.

Alec was laughing as well, entirely overcome with mirth. And although Tierney was giggling, she felt sorry for Celeste when the beautiful young woman blushed as she realized that she'd entirely misunderstood what Alec was explaining.

"Shut up, Rome," Celeste pouted as her pretty brows puckered into a frown. "He said he used to fly from Seattle to Bellingham. Anybody would think that."

"That my arms must get awfully tired?" Alec laughed, slapping Rome on the back as they enjoyed a good chortle at Celeste's expense.

"You guys are poops, and I'm not talking to either one of you for the rest of the night," Celeste said, stomping one platform-shoed foot.

"Oh, come on, Celeste," Rome said. Tierney smiled as she saw Rome's obvious compassion for his sister's feelings. "It was funny. Don't be mad. It was really, really funny."

Celeste sighed, nodded, and forced a slight grin. "My feet hurt," she said, reaching down to take off her shoes. Tierney was surprised at how very short Celeste really was. The platform shoes she'd been wearing must've added five or six inches to her height, for once she removed them, she barely stood as high as Rome and Alec's shoulders—at least two inches shorter than Tierney.

Tossing the shoes under a nearby chair, Celeste sighed. "And I'm tired of this hat. It's kind of heavier than I thought it would be." She paused a moment, grinned, and added, "Maybe that's why I sound like such a ditz. Maybe the hat was cutting off the circulation to my brain."

In the next moment, Celeste pulled the hat and scarf from her head, running her fingers through the long, long, long raven-black hair that tumbled out from under it to cascade over her back and shoulders. Tierney felt as if she were witnessing the filming of a high-end shampoo commercial. Celeste's hair was magnificent! Standing there short, curvaceous, and swimming in hair so beautiful a mermaid would envy it, Celeste Novak looked simply ethereal.

The music changed, the song "Truly Madly Deeply" beginning to play.

"Well, now that you've stripped down to your old self," Alec began, taking hold of Celeste's arm, "wanna dance with me?"

Tierney grinned, entirely elated as she watched Celeste's face light up. "Yeah," the Latin beauty said, smiling at Alec as he took her hand and began to lead his barefoot, secret crush to the patio dance floor.

"Sorry I almost got you with that root beer, Tierney," Rome said, tossing his empty cup into a garbage can located in one corner. He shook his head and chuckled. "I love when she does that. She cracks me up."

"She's beautiful too," Tierney said.

"Yeah, she is," Rome agreed as he turned to watch Alec and Celeste begin to slow dance.

"It kind of makes me want to crawl into a hole," Tierney mumbled, smiling as she watched her brother's face, so lit up with excitement.

Rome looked back to her, a puzzled expression wrinkling his dark brows. "Why?" he asked. "With a bootylicious booty like yours?" he teased then.

Tierney rolled her eyes with feigned exasperation. "Oh, you really are a piece of work, huh?" She shook her head. "I'll say this much though. If you and Alec are as good at snow removal and landscaping as you are at sarcasm and lip-synching, you must make big bucks."

Rome smiled. "I'll take that as a compliment," he said. Then frowning once more, he added, "I think."

Tierney laughed. "No, seriously. You guys were awesome."

"Naw, you're just saying that because somehow I always show up dressed as one of your teenage fantasy men," he teased. "First some Latin lover type and now…" He paused, moving closer to her again. "Now it's Milli or Vanilli, whichever one I am, right? It's the hair, right?"

Tierney quietly gasped and held her breath as Rome's hands settled at her waist—as he leaned forward, causing the long black braids of his wig to surround her face.

"Yep," she managed to breathe. "That's it. Without the wig, I wouldn't even be interested," she teased in a desperate effort to match his mischievousness and appear as unaffected as she could.

"Really?" Rome asked, frowning at her.

Tierney giggled. He seemed sincerely concerned.

"No, silly," she said, playfully slapping him on the chest. "But if you're going to tease me, then prepare to be teased right back."

Rome straightened his posture, grinning as if he were pleased with her willingness to banter with him. "Want some more of my pumpkin puke before it's all gone?" he asked.

Tierney's smile broadened, and she answered, "It's really good guacamole, you know."

"Yeah, we like it. It's my mom's recipe," Rome said. "Come on." He took hold of her arm. "I know that what Mom just put out is all that was left in the fridge, and I'm starving."

"Starving?" Tierney squeaked. "I've been watching you eat all night long."

"You've been watching me all night long?" Rome flirted.

Tierney rolled her eyes and repeated, "I've been watching you *eat* all night long."

"So you've been watching me all night long then. You admit it."

Tierney shook her head as she followed Rome to the refreshment table. "You're as impossible as Alec."

"Oh, I'm way more impossible than Alec, I'm sure," he chuckled.

As Tierney stood next to Rome while he downed what was left of the guacamole, she watched Alec dancing with Celeste. Alec's face was simply beaming with pleasure, and Celeste's expression was just as euphoric.

"He likes her, you know," Rome mumbled with a mouth full of chips and guacamole.

Tierney quickly looked to him. "You know? You mean he's told you?"

"Hell no!" Rome exclaimed. "It's just obvious, that's all—at least to me."

"Does…does Celeste like him back, do you think?" Tierney ventured.

Rome looked at her with one eyebrow arched in sarcastic disbelief. "Do pigeons dive-bomb statues and clean cars?"

"Really?" Tierney asked with hope and excitement.

"Yeah, really," Rome answered. "I swear, she doesn't talk about anything else but Alec."

Tierney sighed with overwhelming hope in Alec's future happiness. She wanted Celeste to like Alec—wanted her to love him—wanted Alec to finally move beyond the nightmare Valerie had been.

"Will you dance with me on the next slow song?" Rome unexpectedly asked.

Tierney gulped as both delicious anticipation and anxiety leapt into her throat. And yet she forced a casual smile and answered, "Sure."

"Okay," he said. "I gotta dance with Heidi on this next fast song. But put me on your little dance card for the next slow one."

As the song changed—as Alec and Celeste moved out of each other's arms—Rome dusted the tortilla chip salt from his hands. The song was the Electric Slide, and it seemed everyone in the room joined the dancers on the floor.

"Come on," Rome said, taking hold of Tierney's arm once more. "Everybody has to do the line dances. Otherwise Mom will be dragging you out there if I don't."

The truth was that Tierney loved to dance! She wouldn't have spent all those years in her room watching Internet videos of how to do common line dances if she hadn't. Therefore, as she stepped into line between Rome and his father, Tierney giggled with delight. It was the very first time she'd ever danced the Electric Slide anywhere other than her bedroom and with anyone other than her own reflection.

Everyone was having so much fun, and it was so completely contagious, that soon Tierney was laughing and smiling and feeling more liberated than she ever had. As she danced between Rome and his dad—laughing to herself at the idea that she was sandwiched between a Milli Vanilli and Captain America—Tierney glanced around to see that everyone at the party was smiling. Some people were terrible dancers, some were mediocre, and some were good. But one in particular, Rome, was so cool and smooth that Tierney actually felt her body bust out in goose bumps as she watched him for a moment. She bit her lip to keep from giggling as a strange sort of shivering pleasure raced up her spine.

Suddenly, during one of the backward steps, Tierney gasped when she felt Rome's hands at her waist—felt his breath on her neck as he said, "So…you're a closet dancer, huh? And here I almost bought that bashful act."

It was time to turn then, and when Rome released her, Tierney thought she would've back-stepped forever if it meant Rome would keep touching her and talking into her ear so that she could feel the warmth of his breath on her neck and in her hair.

All too soon, the Electric Slide ended, and as if someone had held up a cue card in her direction, Heidi stepped right up to Rome and asked, "Ready, Rome?"

Rome smiled at Heidi and said, "Of course," as he took her hand and led her to the middle of the floor.

"She is so in love with Rome," Celeste grumbled as she stepped up beside Tierney. "It drives me nuts."

Tierney, who always tried to be the nice person in the room wherever she was, shrugged and insincerely offered, "She seems nice."

"Oh, she's nice enough," Celeste admitted. "But she's not for Rome."

Tierney looked to Alec when he chuckled.

"What's so funny?" Celeste asked him, frowning.

"You," he answered. "You watch over Rome like a mother hen."

Celeste straightened her short posture and said, "Well…he's vulnerable."

Again Alec laughed. "What?"

"He is!" Celeste argued. "He's just a piece of beefcake to most to girls, I think. I don't think many of them appreciate the whole…you know…the whole *him*." Celeste looked to Tierney and began, "You know what I mean, don't you? He's so much more than a handsome face and big muscles…just like Alec."

Tierney's eyebrows shot into arches over her eyes as sweet, innocent Celeste walked right into it next by reaching out to wrap her hands around one of Alec's biceps and saying, "I mean, Alec is the same way—all muscley and handsome. But those of us who really know him know that he's kind, sexy, works hard, has a great sense of humor, and has a lot more to offer than just the obvious carnal thrill. Right?"

As Celeste looked to the dance floor, watching her brother dance with Heidi, Tierney shook her head as Alec smiled and mouthed, *Sexy?*

Mouthing *shhh* to Alec, Tierney then agreed with Celeste with a firm, "Exactly."

"I just want someone to love him for *him*," Celeste sighed. "Not just because he's pretty."

Celeste frowned, and Tierney immediately understood that there was more to Celeste's worries about Rome being truly loved than she was telling. She studied the Latin goddess for a moment and then exchanged understanding glances with Alec.

"Well, he looks out for you just the same way, doesn't he?" Alec offered with a kind smile.

Celeste sighed and smiled again. "He does…though I don't know what he sees in you." She shrugged. "But there must be something he trusts about you…because he never worries about me when I'm in your company."

"Probably because he knows he could take me if I ever stepped out of line," Alec joked.

"Oh, right," Celeste mumbled as she turned her attention back to the dance floor. "Like you'd ever be tempted to step out of line with me." She shook her head. "You're funny, Alec."

Tierney's lower jaw nearly dropped to the floor. Could Celeste really believe that Alec wasn't interested in her romantically?

"Come on, Alec," Celeste said, suddenly turning and taking Alec's hands in hers as she began to swivel her shapely hips as she moved backwards out onto the dance floor. "Let's go see if we can hear what they're talking about, okay?"

"Whatever you say, Celeste," Alec mumbled—and Tierney could see by the look on his face that Alec O'Brien would do anything and everything the Latin beauty ever asked him to.

The feeling of joy in seeing her brother so happy was nearly overpowering! They'd had such a difficult childhood. Oh, Tierney and Alec had never wanted for any*thing*, but they'd certainly done without a lot emotionally. That fact had never been more obvious to Tierney than on that very night. But as she watched Alec dancing with Celeste—as she could almost *see* the wanting, tortuous secret he was holding back where Celeste was concerned—she began to think that, at least for Alec, maybe the pain of emotional neglect would be healed soon, something he only thought of when he was choosing how *not* to raise his own children.

Not wanting to spend another moment watching Rome dancing with Heidi, Tierney concentrated on watching Carmen Miranda and her own Milli Vanilli, Captain America and his own Professor Trelawney. It was all so fun, so real, and she was thankful to be witness to it—to be a part of it.

The fast song ended, and Tierney smiled as Celeste began to leave the dance floor but was halted as Alec reached out, taking hold of her waist and pulling her to him in slow dance position. She gulped when her attention was drawn to Rome. He was striding toward her, smiling, and it seemed like slow motion as he reached her—for instantly he put one hand at her waist, pulled her against him, and held her other hand in his in dance position as he led her onto the dance floor.

Breathe was singing "Hands to Heaven," and Tierney gazed up into Rome's handsome face, wondering if maybe she actually were in heaven instead of still on the planet Earth.

"What?" Rome asked, grinning down at her.

"What do you mean?" Tierney asked, reveling in the feel of his warm body against hers.

"You're smiling at me like you know something," he answered.

Naturally, Tierney knew she was smiling simply for the fact that even looking at Rome made her feel blissful. But she hid her reason for smiling well by countering, "Well, Alec just received verbal confirmation that your sister thinks he's hot."

"He did?" Rome asked with obvious approval.

"Yep," Tierney answered. "Of course, Celeste doesn't *realize* she just confirmed it for him. But I believe—now how did she put it?—I believe she said he has more to offer than the obvious carnal thrill."

"What?" Rome exclaimed so loudly that several other couples looked at him for a moment.

"Shhh!" Tierney giggled.

Rome shook his head, amused. "Poor Celeste," he mumbled. "She never seems to think about what she's saying before she says it."

"And it's part of her charm, right?" Tierney offered.

"Definitely," Rome agreed.

They didn't speak for a little while, and Tierney felt sort of dizzy and breathless as Rome rested his chin on the top of her head as they danced. She simply loved the way it felt to be in his arms. She loved the fact that he was such a good dancer—with perfect rhythm and an astounding feel for the music. She was tempted to close her eyes, to allow herself to be lost in the moment, but she was afraid that if she did allow herself to dream—to inhale the masculine, rather woodsy scent of Rome's skin, to concentrate on the way his throat brushed her forehead now and again—she was afraid she'd plummet into the depths of despair when it was over.

"Ooo, don't look now…but they seem mighty cozy over there," Rome whispered.

"Who?" Tierney asked, having entirely forgotten about Alec and Celeste. She started to look to her right, but Rome lowered his head, placing his cheek against hers to stop her from looking.

"What do you think 'don't look now' means anyway?" he laughed. "Do you want them to see us staring at them and ruin their moment?"

"They're having a moment?" Tierney exclaimed in a whisper.

"Mmm-hmmm," Rome hummed, the low rumble in his throat reverberating through Tierney's body.

In truth, Rome had no idea if Celeste and Alec were "having a moment." All he knew was that he and Tierney *were*—whether or not she realized it. The feeling that he shouldn't drag his feet too long in letting Tierney O'Brien know he was interested in her (profoundly interested in her) had been eating at him since the day she'd arrived. Of course, he'd been interested in her from the moment he'd stepped out of that stupid box dressed like a stupid Latin lover. But any idiot would've known that a woman's bridal shower, being thrown when she was perched on the precipice of marrying another man, wasn't the place to hit on her. And still, Rome had hit on Tierney as much as he could under the circumstances—and managed to talk her into breaking up with the idiot she was going to marry.

But afterward, all he could do was wait—wait and see if the pretty girl he'd decided he'd wanted to get to know better would heal a bit, move beyond all that had happened with that rich guy. Rome had waited and waited, and then when Alec had told him that he'd finally managed to talk Tierney into moving to Leavenworth, something deep inside Rome Novak had begun to whisper to him that he shouldn't drag his feet in laying claim to her—even if sensibility shouted otherwise.

And so, there he was, slow dancing with Tierney—with the woman he'd had some sort of crazy and immediate attraction to months before. There he was slow dancing with her, and making up all kinds of crap just to be closer to her. Rome comforted his conscience by silently reminding himself that Alec and Celeste really *could* be having a moment.

Meanwhile, the voice in his head was urging him to step things up, and though it was entirely against his nature to move so quickly, a plan began to formulate in him mind—and he would follow it no matter the consequences.

"So," Rome began, "what do you think of the way my parents go all out for Halloween?"

Tierney, still distracted by wondering what kind of "a moment" Celeste and Alec were having, asked, "What?"

Rome stood straighter then, looking down at her and repeating, "What do you think of the way my parents do Halloween?"

Tierney smiled up at him and said, "I honestly have never seen anything like this," she answered. "And...and it's so personal, you know?"

"Personal?" Rome asked.

Tierney was suddenly more aware of how close Rome was holding her—right up against him—so blissfully right up against him. The paradise of it weakened her knees a little.

"I mean...it's personal," she tried to explain. "They know everyone here. The food is fun and homemade, not catered. They thought it out and obviously put a lot of work into it. The decorations are just too...just perfect—all the jack-o'-lanterns and spiderwebs and stuff. I love it! I mean, homemade root beer served out of a cauldron with dry ice to make it look like a witch's brew? I love it!"

Rome simultaneously grinned and frowned. "I'm thinking you don't usually get out much on Halloween, right?"

Tierney laughed a little and shrugged. "Not to something that isn't a fundraiser or put on just to impress. This party...it's meant to entertain friends and family. That's the pure purpose of it. It's like a gift, from your parents to their friends and stuff. When I think of the time they must have spent, the money, the effort—it's a sacrifice for them, I'm sure, and they do it all for other people." She paused a moment, glancing away from him and to where Alec was dancing with Celeste nearby. "It's just wonderful, that's all."

"Even with the jack-o'-lantern that barfed guacamole?" Rome chuckled.

"Especially because of the jack-o'-lantern that barfed guacamole!" she giggled.

Suddenly Rome's hand that had been holding Tierney's in dance position released hers, sliding up the underside of her arm as he directed it to rest on his shoulder as well, before taking her waist tightly between both his strong, capable hands and pulling her even more tightly against him.

In order to avoid looking idiotically awkward, Tierney slid her hands to the back of his neck and laced her fingers together. After all, it was the natural progression leading to a more intimate dance—or at least so Tierney had seen in movies.

"I'm glad you're enjoying yourself," Rome said as he grinned at her. "Mom and Dad…it's their goal for this thing, to make sure everyone has a great time, that they just let go of all their worries and enjoy themselves. Their opinion is that life can be demanding, stressful, and disappointing a lot of the time, but once in a while, you oughta be able to get together with friends and family and just have fun—leave your cares at the door and just eat, talk, eat some more, dance, and most of all laugh. So they'll be very happy to know you're enjoying it…even with the barfing pumpkin."

They danced in silence for a moment again. He was so warm! She smiled, suddenly amused by his swinging braids for some reason.

"What?" Rome asked. "Are my cornrows and braids just too sexy for words or something?"

Tierney giggled and confessed, "Actually, yes." Embarrassed by having openly admitted that she found Rome attractive, she began to backpedal a little by teasing him. "And I've always wanted to slow dance with one of the Milli Vanilli guys."

Rome's smile broadened. "But with which one? Milli or Vanilli?" He quirked one eyebrow and asked, "And which one did you say I am again?"

"Rob," Tierney answered—though Rome Novak was far and away more masculine, more attractive, and much larger than Rob Pilatus had been. "I just still can't believe I'm actually dancing with Milli Vanilli," she answered at last. "I mean, it's like a dream come true!"

Rome's smile broadened to display his movie-star white teeth. "So it's always been a fantasy of yours, has it? To have a special moment with one of the Milli Vanillis?" he frowned a little. "Rob, is it?"

"Yes," she affirmed. Lowering her voice to a whisper and lifting herself on her tiptoes, she added, "The best looking one."

Rome smiled. "And this Milli Vanilli fantasy of yours…always involved what? Just dancing?" A spark of roguishness leapt into his mesmerizing eyes as he continued, "Or was it maybe a little more like this?"

Tierney gasped a bit as Rome promptly ended their dance, keeping hold of her hand as he began to lead her from the dance floor and back into the house. Before Tierney could even think to ask what their intended destination was, they had apparently arrived at it—the hallway that led to the bottom-floor bedrooms.

Her heart began to beat faster as Rome then pushed her up against the wall and, in a lowered voice that had the same intoxicating effect on Tierney as she imagined alcohol would, asked, "Or was it more like this? Having either Milli or Vanilli shove you up against the wall and…" Pushing Tierney's hands up against the wall above her head, Rome held them with one hand as his other took hold of her chin. He grinned a purely seductive grin and said, "After all…we both know that I'm just the guy to fulfill all your fantasies, right?"

Is he kidding? Tierney had just enough time to think before Rome's mouth pressed against hers in a firm but testing-the-waters sort of kiss.

"Right?" he mumbled before kissing her again.

"A-apparently so," Tierney managed to stammer in a whisper.

Rome grinned with pleased triumph and released his grip on her hands in order to take her face between his.

"You're a really good sport," he said. "Do you know that?"

He didn't allow even a moment for Tierney to respond—just pressed his mouth to hers again in another firm but almost cautious kiss. Yet as Tierney's arms slid down the wall, her hands coming to rest at Rome's wrists as he held her face, she did allow herself to be lost in his kiss—and in kissing him back.

Without breaking the seal of their kiss, Rome directed her hands to rest at the back of his neck. Tierney was rendered breathless as he then put his hands at her waist, pulling her against him, as his mouth ground to hers in a more demanding kiss—moist, heated, and entirely knee-weakening.

"Rome Novak—let that girl breathe a minute and get out here and help your father move the refreshment table so we can have more room for people to dance!"

Tierney felt her face blush crimson at the sound of Mrs. Novak's voice. Even as Rome broke the seal of their mouths, grinned at her, and tweaked her nose, her blush intensified. She was entirely humiliated! A guest in Mr. and Mrs. Novak's home—a first-time guest, in fact—and there she stood kissing their son!

"Mom!" Rome scolded, however, turning to face his mother. "I'm kissing a girl right now."

"I can see that," Mrs. Novak said, smiling and winking at Tierney with understanding. "But your father needs help. You can get back to it after you've helped him move the table."

Rome shook his head as he released Tierney and turned to face her mother. "Oh, sure, Mom…like she's ever going to let me get her alone again after knowing that my *mother* is just gonna to walk up and—"

Mrs. Novak smiled and laughed, however—kissed Rome on the cheek and patted his butt as if he were a naughty toddler as she reached out to take Tierney's hand. "Run along, Romeo," she giggled. "I haven't had a chance to talk to Tierney all night." Smiling at Tierney, she added, "Until now."

"Oh, all right," Rome grumbled. Wagging an index finger at his mother, however, he added, "But don't tell her about any of my bad qualities or go showing her my naked baby pictures or anything. Do you hear me?"

"Run along, puppy," Mrs. Novak said, whacking Rome on the seat again. "Your dad's waiting for you."

Rome frowned, tossed his head a bit to throw his braids back away from his face, and grumbled, "See you later, Tierney. It seems I haven't finished my *chores.*"

As he sauntered away, his Milli Vanilli braids swinging back and forth in perfect rhythm with his sexy swagger, Tierney's smile returned. After all, how could she hold back a smile with such a perfect vision in front of her?

"He's a good boy, you know…even for his tendency to pout a little here and there," Mrs. Novak said, looking to Tierney with a happy smile.

Tierney nodded, returned Mrs. Novak's smile, and hoped her blush was fading a bit.

"We met briefly, Tierney, but I'm afraid with all this hoo-ha, I haven't had a chance to visit with you much," Mrs. Novak began as she began to walk back toward the part of the house where the party was being held, still holding Tierney's hand in leading her. "But we think the world of Alec, and I'm sure you're just as wonderful as he is. How are you liking Leavenworth?"

"Oh! It's…it's beautiful," Tierney answered in full honesty. "And Alec swears it's even gorgeous in the wintertime."

"Oh, good! I'm so glad to hear that." Mrs. Novak then turned, taking Tierney's free hand in her free one. "Well, I suppose I should officially introduce myself again. It was so chaotic before. I'm Nikki, Nikki Novak, and we're so glad you agreed to come tonight. Have you been having fun?"

Tierney paused a moment, astonished at the woman's question. Was she kidding? Did Rome's mother really think there was a chance Tierney *wasn't* having fun? After all, the woman had just caught Tierney kissing her son!

Having decided to go the most direct and truthful route with her response, Tierney answered, "Mrs. Novak, this is the most incredible party I've ever been to!" And when Nikki Novak's face lit up like the annual Christmas tree in Rockefeller Center, Tierney knew her answer had pleased the woman. Thus, she decided to ramble on. "I'm not just saying that either. This is wonderful! Everything is so perfectly decorated, and all your friends…well, I've never, never experienced something like this. The lip syncs were…they were awesome! And the food…the dancing…it's all so wonderful." Tierney paused, smiling at the woman with sincere appreciation. "Thank you so much for allowing me to come."

Behind her Professor Trelawney, pop-bottle-bottom glasses, Nikki's eyebrows shot up into an astonished arch. "*Allowing* you to come? Are you kidding? We're so delighted you were able to! Alec has been talking about your moving here nonstop since the moment you agreed to…and we couldn't wait to meet you!" She paused a moment, and Tierney noticed the light of mischief similar to Rome's that leapt to her eyes. "And as soon as Rome gets back from helping his father…you two can get back to what you were doing." She winked at Tierney, and Tierney felt the blush of humiliation return to her cheeks.

"Oh! Oh, that," she began. "Rome was just…actually, he was just teasing me about my thing for Rob Pilatus…you know, just sort of making fun of me."

Nikki gasped, and her hand went to her bosom to cover her heart. "I *loved* Rob Pilatus!" she exclaimed in an almost reverenced sort of breathlessness. "When that song came on tonight…boy, did it take me back." She smiled then and whispered, "I have to admit, I really had a thing for Rob back then. He was gorgeous! And when the boys showed up tonight and did their lip sync…" Nikki paused, shaking her head with admiration. "I mean, wasn't that unreal? I loved it!"

"Me too! It was so incredible," Tierney agreed.

She was thoughtful for a moment. As Nikki Novak looked to where Rome and his father were working to move the refreshment table, Tierney couldn't help but notice the extreme and painfully obvious differences between Rome's mother and her own. Tierney guessed her mother probably didn't even know who Milli Vanilli was.

"Uh-oh," Nikki said, drawing Tierney's attention to where Rome had finished moving the table and was attempting to return to where she and his mother stood. "Uh-oh. Looks like nobody has asked Kimmey Stephens to dance yet. See? Over there, standing against the wall?"

Without pointing, Nikki managed to draw Tierney's attention to a young woman standing up against one wall of the covered patio. At once, Tierney could see the obvious shyness the girl was experiencing. Not only that, but she wasn't the most attractive young woman in the room. Tierney immediately felt bad for thinking such an unkind thing, and her compassion continued to soar.

"Please notice her, Rome," Nikki whispered to herself. "Please, please, please notice her!"

Nikki Novak was the kindest, most thoughtful hostess Tierney had ever met! There she was, no doubt worn near to a frazzle from the preparations for the party and the energy exerted by the party itself, and yet she was still observant and caring enough to notice that one of her guests might not be having fun.

"Come on, Rome baby. Kimmey is right there. Come on," Nikki mumbled as she and Tierney watched Rome stride toward them—approaching the place where Kimmey Stephens stood bashful and awkward against one wall.

Tierney heard Nikki exhale a heavy sigh of relief, and found that she too had been holding her breath in anticipation, as Rome suddenly stopped, looked to the place where Kimmey stood, and smiled at her. Tierney watched as he changed his trajectory, walked to Kimmey, and engaged her in conversation. The girl smiled, the luminance of pure delight pinking up her cheeks.

"That's my boy! Always so thoughtful of widows and wallflowers," Nikki quietly commented. "I'm so proud of him in that. He seems to have some sort of sixth sense with women, you know?" She looked to Tierney quizzically. "It's like Rome has this radar and can always tell when a neglected woman is around. And he's always the one to make sure she's not overlooked…at least by him."

"So he's a real-life hero all the time," Tierney offered. "Not just when a friend asks him to help talk a sister out of marrying the wrong guy, huh?"

Nikki looked to Tierney and giggled. "I really couldn't believe Alec talked him into flying out there and doing that Latin lover thing."

Nikki had confirmed Tierney's suspicions—that Rome's family knew about his flying out to California at Alec's request and attempting to talk Tierney out of marrying Dillon. She blushed with more humiliation, but she wasn't angry, for she liked and admired the fact that the Novak family was so closely knit.

"Believe it or not, he was actually kind of shy as a child, my Rome," Nikki said, returning her attention to where Rome was now leading Kimmey out onto the dance floor. "Alec has really been good for him." She looked to Tierney, adding, "They've been good for each other."

Tierney nodded as she looked back to where Rome was dancing with Kimmey Stephens—to where he was slow dancing with her, smiling down at her, talking to her. Tierney silently scolded herself for the sharp twinge of jealousy it caused to rise in her. It was obvious the girl was in heaven being in the arms of the handsome Rome Novak—

and if anybody knew how she felt, it was Tierney. Besides, she was happy for the girl—though she did secretly hope that Rome didn't somehow fall madly in love with Kimmey as they danced.

"He's such a handsome guy, isn't he?" Nikki asked. "My Rome?"

What could Tierney say? "Yes, he is." She would've looked ridiculous if she'd tried to deny it to the man's mother.

Nikki looked to Tierney and laughed. "Isn't it funny? How handsome Rome is and how beautiful our Celeste is?"

Certainly she knew that both Rome and Celeste weren't Nikki's biological children, but Nikki Novak was very striking in her own way. Maybe not strikingly beautiful at the moment, all decked in her Professor Trelawney garb and glasses. But Tierney had seen Nikki remove her glasses earlier in the evening, and she was a very pretty woman!

"Why is it funny?" Tierney asked.

Nikki giggled, shrugged, and answered, "Because Eddie and I are so plain white and boring." She gestured to Rome. "Rome and Celeste, on the other hand—exotic and unusually attractive."

"There's nothing plain about you, Mrs. Novak. I think you're beautiful," Tierney honestly offered. "And Mr. Novak is very handsome…at least for what I can tell through his Captain America mask and all."

Nikki laughed and suddenly threw her arms around Tierney in an appreciative hug. "Oh, you are a jewel, Tierney! Thanks for coming tonight! And remember to call me Nikki, okay?"

"Thank you, again, for having me," Tierney giggled as Rome's mother released her.

Nikki studied her for a moment. "First Alec and now you," she said. "Our family just doubled its wealth where good friends are concerned. I can already tell."

The music stopped then, and Tierney found she smiled with empathetic joy as she watched Rome thank Kimmey for the dance—even kiss her on the cheek. A man who was always aware and caring of the feelings of "widows and wallflowers" was a rare man indeed.

Then, as the familiar strains of a very familiar song began, Tierney laughed when Rome looked to Alec and shouted, "Dude! It's our song!"

Cupping her hands to her mouth, Nikki called, "Encore! Encore!" as the opening synthesizer solo of "Girl, You Know It's True" continued. Everyone cheered and clapped; Rome and Alec moved to the center of the circle.

Tierney laughed as her brother and his friend started to dance, beginning a repeat performance of their lip sync of Milli Vanilli's infamous video. As she watched the Novaks' guests reveling in being thoroughly entertained—as she observed everyone watching Rome and Alec and singing along to the chorus of the song—such a powerful sense of euphoric happiness rose in Tierney that she wasn't sure whether to laugh or cry.

Truthfully, Tierney had never seen such sincere, carefree joy as she saw on the faces of the Novaks and their guests. She'd never felt the sensation herself before that night and marveled at the profoundly emotional quality of it. Her cares seemed so small and insignificant in that moment. She giggled as she watched Rome's braids swinging back and forth as he danced and Alec mouthed the early rap-style verse. Dang, Rome Novak was gorgeous! It was totally wrong for a man to be that attractive!

"Come on!" Rome hollered. "Everybody!" He motioned for everyone to join them in dancing, but Tierney stepped back instead of forward the way everyone else did.

"No, no, no, you don't!" Alec laughed, however. "She knows this whole thing cold, man!" he told Rome.

As Rome's eyebrows arched in admiration, Tierney shook her head. She had no desire to draw any attention to herself.

"Come on, Tiers!" Alec said as he and Rome strode over, taking her arms and pulling her toward the center of the floor. Alec took Tierney's shoulders between his strong hands, stared down into her eyes, and said, "Let it all go, Tierney. Just have fun. You gotta live for the moment sometimes…and this is one of those times."

"Hey!" Rome shouted, turning toward the guy who was working the sound system. "Start it over, Kyle…would you?"

The guy nodded, and the music stopped for a moment. As the music began again, Tierney watched as Mr. and Mrs. Novak began to dance—as everyone began to dance.

"Come on," Alec said. "Show Rome what you can do."

Standing on either side of her, Rome and Alec began to mimic the steps Milli Vanilli performed in their video.

But when Tierney still paused, Rome leaned down and whispered into her ear, "Oh, come on, Tierney. Are you gonna tell me you can let a complete stranger talk you into busting up your wedding…but you can't dance in public?"

Tierney smiled a little. Rome was right. What did she have to worry about? Everybody else in the room looked like complete idiots, so why shouldn't she join them?

"Fine," she said. As the chorus began, Tierney fell into step with Alec and Rome, performing the simple but iconic dance moves of Milli Vanilli.

Rome clapped with admiration and laughed, "Awesome!"

"Oh, but watch this!" Alec hollered. He looked to Tierney and said, "Freestyle it, Tiers!"

The music had captured her by then—the contagious, carefree fun everyone else was having. So when Alec told her to freestyle it, Tierney did. Breaking into the iconic '80s style of dance made popular by Janet Jackson via Paula Abdul, Tierney let go of any residual inhibitions she was holding onto.

"Damn, girl!" Rome exclaimed as everyone in the room turned and began applauding to a freestyle routine that would've made the King of Pop himself proud.

But Tierney didn't want everyone's attention, so she quickly resorted to just a standard dance step, blushing radish-red as everyone applauded. The crowd then began to repeat the chorus of the song over and over as "Girl, You Know It's True" began to wind down again.

This time, however, Tierney joined in, singing at the top of her lungs along with everyone else. Alec had been right—the Novaks' Halloween party was proving to be the time of her life, and nothing was more wonderful about it than the fact that Rome had spirited her away for an unexpected, but entirely fantastic, stolen moment of "up against the wall" kissing the way she'd only ever before experienced in her dreams.

CHAPTER SIX

As Tierney walked from the florist's shop toward Von Bomburst's to meet Alec for lunch, she frowned. The owner of the shop who had hired Tierney, Jessica Potts, was a kind enough woman. After only three days of working for her, Tierney knew that she and Jessica would work well together.

However, Jessica's husband, Elias Potts, had come into the florist to take his wife out for lunch an hour before Tierney was due to take her break, and the very instant he'd walked into the shop, Tierney's skin had begun to crawl.

For all outward appearances, Elias Potts was a handsome, middle-aged man, with a friendly sort of smile. Yet there was something in his eyes—an almost malicious sort of something. When Elias Potts offered his hand to Tierney and she'd taken it in greeting him, she found it to be very warm and very clammy. She'd wondered for a moment how the man could have such warm and clammy hands when the temperature outside was only forty-two degrees and he wasn't even wearing a coat or gloves. Instantly Tierney knew he was not someone she wanted to linger in the presence of, and she couldn't quite understand why he made her feel so—well, so anxious. Elias hadn't said anything beyond a sociable greeting and that he was glad his wife had another floral designer to help her out in the shop. But Tierney hadn't liked the intonation of his voice and thought to herself that she wished he'd never stepped foot in the door. Elias and Jessica left for lunch hastily, however, and Tierney's sense of disquiet eventually faded.

Tierney began to think over an article she'd read not long before, concerning the fact that there were often mental "red flags" people ignored, especially women. The article explained that these emotional red flags could have saved people not only from pain, misery, and being victims of heinous crimes but also, in one incident, from death. The article focused on several accounts of people who had experienced emotional red flags and ignored them, and this knowledge was permanently added to Tierney's thought processes.

One woman's story featured in the article was particularly horrifying. The woman had glanced out a window and noticed a man coming to her door. A satellite television installation truck was parked at the woman's front curb, and the man was wearing a corresponding uniform. The woman hadn't ordered an installation of anything and therefore was immediately wary. She thought to herself that if the man knocked on the door, she wouldn't answer it, for she didn't feel right about him being there. But even though her first inclination was to "play gone," when the man did knock on her door, the woman's kind nature kicked in. Not wanting to be rude, and thinking that perhaps the man just had the wrong address in his information and was simply trying to do his job, the woman in the article had indeed opened the door to greet him.

The article explained that, upon thinking back on the incident, this woman had experienced at least twenty-three identifiable warning thoughts. It further explained, with affirmation from the woman herself in an interview by the article's author, that if she would've heeded even one of the emotional red flags her sixth sense offered to her, she would have been saved from being a victim of robbery and a profound physical beating.

Tierney was deeply affected by the article. For one thing, she found herself mentally enumerating how many times her mind had screamed at her not to marry Dillon. Hundreds upon hundreds of times, she'd thought she shouldn't marry Dillon Hawthorne. But it wasn't until Alec sent Rome to her bridal shower that she finally listened to her own feelings. Therefore, with the experiences included in the thought-altering article, Tierney had decided she would never ignore the red flags that occasionally popped into her mind—that whether or not she wondered if she were just being paranoid in a situation, she'd rather be safe than sorry. She'd rather offend a satellite installation guy than end up beaten nearly to death—or worse.

As Tierney arrived at Von Bomburst's to find not only Alec waiting for her but Celeste as well, she smiled, letting go of her uneasy feelings where Elias Potts was concerned but also determining she would never linger in his company longer than absolutely necessary.

"Well, baby sister?" Alec greeted as he stood from his seat at their table, kissed her cheek, and assisted her in taking her chair. "How goes work today?"

Tierney shrugged, answering, "Fine. Not too boring."

"Do you like working there?" Celeste asked, smiling at Tierney.

Tierney returned Celeste's friendly smile and said, "Yeah. Jessica is really pretty comfortable to work with."

Celeste nodded, and Tierney tried to ignore the strange trepidation that always rose in her when she was with Celeste.

Ever since meeting Celeste at Mr. and Mrs. Novak's party the week before, Tierney had noticed the way Celeste was trying to become her friend—her good friend. But Tierney was afraid. Because of sweet Celeste's kindness and efforts to befriend her, Tierney had realized that, just as Valerie had damaged Alec where romance was concerned, the experiences Tierney had endured with her supposed friends after she broke up with Dillon had damaged her. She was afraid—afraid to allow herself to truly be friends with Celeste. After all, why would such a happy, obviously beautiful, fun-loving young woman like Celeste Novak want to be friends with Tierney? Surely there had to be some underlying reason—and Tierney figured that the underlying reason was Alec.

Oh, she tried not to be so daytime TV in her thinking, but she couldn't help it. Tierney just didn't trust Celeste to like her for who she was—for who she was other than Alec's sister. And even though Alec had explained that Celeste was an entirely different type of character than the girls Tierney had grown up *thinking* were her friends, Tierney was having a hard time letting go of suspicion and distrust.

In truth, she and Alec and spent hours in conversation on the matter. Alec had confessed his feelings were similar—that he had to fight every day to remember that Valerie Gilland was not the standard for all women, and neither was Tierney and Alec's mother. It was what had stopped him (and still scared him) about pursuing Celeste: he didn't trust women to have hearts.

Still, Alec had assured Tierney that they were wrong in their thinking. Absolutely their experiences with the people they'd grown up with and around had wounded and scarred both of them, but it was something they had to battle through if they hoped to lead happy, loving lives—normal lives.

So Tierney smiled at Celeste—even though she still didn't trust her appearance of sincerity in offering friendship—and asked, "How was work at the Christmas Shoppe today? Did you guys get any new merchandise in that I can't live without?"

Celeste's beautiful face lit up like fireworks over the Statue of Liberty on the Fourth of July. "Oh yes!" she exclaimed. "We got this thing in today, and the moment I saw it, I thought of you and just knew you had to have it!"

Tierney giggled. "What it is?"

But Celeste, eyes twinkling with mischief the same way her mother's did, shook her head, still smiling. "I can't tell you that!" she answered. "It was *so* you that I just *had* to get it for you! You will absolutely die when you see it!" Celeste laughed and then added, "But you have to wait until Christmas. I'm giving it to you as my Christmas gift this year. And anyway, it came in as stock for our gift shop—our non-Christmas section."

Tierney frowned. "Why would you give me a Christmas gift?" she couldn't help asking—for in truth, she was entirely stunned that a woman she'd known only a couple of weeks would find it necessary to give her a Christmas gift.

But Celeste plunked her hands down on the table before her as her mouth dropped open in astonishment.

"Are you kidding me?" she asked. "It's the perfect thing for you! Entirely impractical, of course. But I don't really believe in practical gift. I think gifts should be totally frivolous and fun…and totally individual. So when this little thingy came into the store today, I had to get it for you." Celeste giggled with secret delight. "I'm so excited! I know you'll love it!"

So many thoughts and feelings were racing through Tierney's mind that she couldn't sort them all out right away. Christmas gifts? Celeste had purchased a gift for her? Naturally, the obligatory gift clause her mother had instilled in Tierney began to eat at her mind. Celeste was giving Tierney a gift, and therefore Tierney had to reciprocate. Yet she knew that the usual obligatory gift wouldn't do. Scented candles, day spa gift certificates, fruit baskets—none of them were personal enough. Tierney felt a nervous quiver begin inside her. What in all the world would she get for Celeste Novak as reciprocation for whatever it was Celeste had purchased for her at the Christmas Shoppe gift section?

Tierney was so preoccupied with worry and anxiety about the matter that it wasn't until Celeste said, "Hi, Rome," that she realized Rome had taken hold of the back of the chair next to her and was sitting down.

"Hey, sweetie," Rome greeted his sister, leaning over and placing an affectionate kiss on her cheek. "What's up, man?" he greeted Alec as they bumped fists.

Then Rome looked to Tierney. He grinned at her, and instantly she felt the warmth of a slight blush rise to her cheeks. What was it about the man that had her so alternately delighted and nervous?

"And how's our little bootylicious flower arranger today?" he asked.

"Just fine," Tierney answered, quivering as he actually reached out and brushed a stray strand of hair from her cheek. "How's our classic Latin lover, Milli Vanilli guy today?"

Rome's smile broadened, his brows arching in pleased astonishment. She'd done it! Tierney had done it! She'd managed to meet him with a teasing remark in response.

Ever since the Novaks' Halloween party, Tierney had become more and more aware of how flirtatious and teasing Rome really was. It seemed as if teasing Tierney in a very flirtatious manner had become one of his favorite hobbies or something. Naturally, Tierney loved the fact, but it had thrown her a little off balance as far as how she should react at first. But now—now that she was getting used to it—not only did she love it all the more but she was also learning how to come right back at him. Consequently, every time Rome entered a room or met her and Alec for lunch, Tierney began to blush even before he said a word!

"He ain't *my* Latin lover!" Alec exclaimed. "You're the only one at the table that can claim that, Tiers."

"I don't claim that," Tierney said in a lowered voice. She knew her face was beet-red with embarrassment.

"But you can," Rome said, placing one strong arm along the back of her chair. "After all, you are the only girl I ever…" Rome paused—wrinkled his brows with an expression of puzzlement. "How did I wind up wearing a tuxedo and stuffed in a box to play your Latin lover, anyway?" he asked. "I mean, Alec told me you've always had a thing for old Latin dudes. But I'm thinking it must really be a big *thing*, considering you dumped your fiancé and all, just because I showed up with that message from Alec."

"I don't have a *thing* for old Latin dudes," Tierney playfully argued. "I *had* a thing for Ricardo Montalbán, ever since I was a little girl." She shrugged. "I kind of like all that 'golden age of Hollywood' stuff—the fashions, the movies, the way men were masculine and women were feminine."

"Celeste is into that too," Rome noted. "Right?" he asked, looking at his sister.

"Right," Celeste answered, smiling.

"Really?" Tierney asked Celeste.

Celeste nodded as Rome said, "Thus, the fruit hat lady costume at Halloween."

Tierney smiled. "You mean the Carmen Miranda costume."

"Oh, like I'd ever be able to remember that name," Rome chuckled. "I mean, Celeste has been wearing wax fruit on her head since we were kids, but I can never remember her name."

"Carmen Miranda," Celeste offered with a giggle.

"Yeah, yeah, yeah," Rome said, rolling his eyes. He looked back to Tierney. "When I was younger, I thought Carmen whatever was the Chiquita Banana lady. I didn't even know there was a Carmen Meander or whatever."

Tierney laughed, shaking her head with amusement. "You're funny," she said. "And I totally get Celeste's Carmen Miranda admiration."

"Thank you, Tierney," Celeste said, offering another friendly smile. "We'll have to get together and talk movie stars one day."

Both Rome and Alec groaned and exhaled sighs of exasperation.

"Shut up, Rome," Celeste demanded. "You only wish you were the Latin lover Ricardo Montalbán was."

"He was an actor, Celeste," Rome reminded his sister.

"I will have you know that Ricardo Montalbán was married to the same woman for sixty-three years," Celeste informed her brother.

"To Georgiana Young…Loretta Young's half-sister," Tierney added. "Though I think Georgiana was way more beautiful than Loretta Young."

"Oh, me too!" Celeste agreed.

"Yep," Alec sighed. "That's my sister—in love with a man who was old enough to be her great-grandfather when she was born, mind you." He smiled and winked at Tierney. "I don't know what would've happened to Tiers if you hadn't agreed to go to that damn bridal shower, Rome."

Rome shook his head with amusement. "So old Latin dudes and scandalized lip-synching guys named after ice cream or something. Those are the guys you're attracted to, eh?"

Tierney shrugged. "Some little girls want to grow up to be princesses; some want to grow up to be movie stars. I think girls like me and obviously Celeste…we wish we could just wear all the wonderful fashions of the past, date men that waltzed with you instead of always trying to dirty dance with you. You know?" She sighed with momentary disappointment.

Celeste sighed too, adding, "It's like…men don't swoop women up in their arms anymore."

Tierney nodded. "Yeah. I know what you mean. I always wanted to be wearing some pretty little black dress, retro stockings—the kind with seams up the back—and a pair of black pumps, and have a Ricardo Montalbán type swoop me up in his arms, feel the shoes slip off my silk-stockinged feet and fall to the floor…"

Celeste giggled, adding, "And, when the zipper on the back of your dress gets stuck, have him unzip the back of it with his teeth like Rock Hudson did to Leslie Caron in *A Very Special Favor*?"

"Ooo! I love that movie!" Tierney exclaimed. Looking to Rome, Tierney asked, "Do you know what we mean?"

But Rome grinned and answered, "I'm proud to say, absolutely not. I've never had the desire to have another man swoop me up into his arms, let alone feel a pair of high-heeled pumps slip off my silky feet. *That* I can assure you."

Alec chuckled. "Dude, I'm actually really glad to hear that."

"No, but seriously," Tierney said, placing her hand on Rome's forearm to retrieve his attention. "Do guys ever...don't guys ever wish that women were still glamorous? You know, soft updos, pretty shades of lipstick and makeup, silk stockings, and high heels that make your legs look long instead making you look like you can't walk?" She shrugged. "I guess I'm different...ignorant too. But if you don't know the difference between Ricardo Montalbán and, like, Ben Affleck..."

"Hey, I know the difference," Rome playfully argued. Frowning at his sister a moment, he added, "Celeste has coerced me into sitting through enough corny old black-and-white movies in my lifetime. I've seen Mr. Valentino in action...ol' Rudy, as we call him down at the lodge."

"Down at the lodge?" Tierney giggled.

Rome shrugged. "That's what guys always say in those old movies...that they hang out down at the lodge."

"Ol' Rudy," Tierney repeated. "You're so funny!"

"Oh, am I?" Rome asked. "I'm funny?"

"Really funny," Tierney teased.

"Well, I will have you know that I can be as Chiquita Banana and Ricardo Montalbán-ish as the next guy, lady," he mischievously countered as he leaned toward her.

"Oh, I know," Tierney assured him, delighted as goose bumps erupted over her arms. "I was there, remember?"

"No, I mean now, right here...without the tuxedo," he explained as his head bent toward her shoulder. Rome then reached up, slowly tugging at the collar of Tierney's brown sweater to pull it down so it wasn't as high on her neck. Tierney's face blushed hot, and more goose bumps rippled over her back and neck as she felt his breath on her skin just below her ear.

"Dude, get a room," Alec teased.

Tierney blushed again and, although it was truly the last thing on the face of the earth she wanted to do, playfully pushed Rome away and straightened her sweater collar.

"You guys just don't understand," Celeste sighed as the waiter arrived to take their lunch orders.

But Rome did understand. As he listened the group give the waiter their orders, he studied Tierney for a moment. The fact was she was an old-fashioned girl, living in a world where there was no chivalry, no courtesy, and no true romance. Rome and Celeste were close—always had been—and he knew how Celeste felt, that men were all about sex and nothing else, that women were becoming that way too. And it was a natural way of thinking. After all, in truth, Alec O'Brien was the only guy Rome knew who wasn't always trying to figure out a way to get a girl into bed. And yet he wondered why a lot of women took so long to notice guys like him and Alec—good guys who wanted wives and children and the regular suburban neighborhood lifestyle. Then again, he knew some pretty skanky women too. He exhaled a sigh of discouragement and wondered how the world had gotten so selfish.

He ordered, and he and Alec exchanged an expression—an unspoken understanding that it was time to change the subject. Rome knew he could never live up to Tierney's Ricardo Montalbán fantasy—at least not yet. So he decided he'd have to be satisfied with having been able to touch her sweater and inhale the scent of her skin for the moment.

"Have you been keeping in touch with your friends back in California, Tierney?" Celeste asked.

Tierney wasn't offended by Celeste's question—not in the least. After all, Celeste was a normal girl with a normal family and normal friends, and it was a perfectly normal question.

"Nope," Tierney answered.

"Oh. Well, why not?" Celeste pressed.

Tierney glanced up to Alec to see he wore an expression that conveyed, *Just tell her the truth.*

"You know that old expression…about when things get tough, you find out who your real friends are?" Tierney began.

"Yeah?" Celeste asked.

Tierney shrugged. "Well, after your Latin lover brother here showed up with Alec's message and convinced me to break up with Dillon…I did. And within two weeks, after I'd returned all the bridal shower and wedding gifts, I never heard another word from any of them."

"None of them?" Celeste asked in a squeaky voice of disbelief.

"Nope. Not one," Tierney assured her. "And some of them I'd known since elementary school."

"You're kidding," Rome asked, frowning as he stared at her.

"Nope. Not kidding," Tierney sighed.

Rome shook his head as Celeste sat with her mouth gaping open in obvious horrified astonishment.

"So you're telling us," he began, "that not one of your friends stuck around after you broke up with the Dill?"

Tierney smiled and frowned the same time, curious. "The Dill?" she asked.

"Yeah," Rome affirmed. He nodded toward Alec, who was already downing a dinner roll from the bread plate a waitress had just set in the middle of the table. "Alec showed me your wedding announcement when he got it in the mail…and we started calling your now-ex the Dill."

Tierney laughed, suddenly not so upset at the memory that every one of her friends had quickly abandoned her once she'd broken up with Dillon. "The Dill?" She giggled and then sighed, "I guess he was kind of sour sometimes."

Celeste giggled and didn't look quite so horrified anymore.

"But back to this other thing," Rome continued. "Are you seriously telling me that all those chicks at your bridal shower…they just—"

Tierney nodded and finished, "Ditched me like a bad hairstyle."

"Damn," Rome mumbled to himself.

"Well, you have us now," Celeste stated. Tierney was moved, for she could see the moisture brimming in Celeste's eyes—the compassion. "Right, Rome?" she said to her brother.

"Right," Rome answered, reaching out to retrieve a dinner roll from the bread plate.

"And we're sunny-side-up friends," Celeste continued. "We're friends no matter what."

"You're thinking of eggs, Chiquita Banana lady," Rome said, winking at Tierney with amusement. "I think you mean that we're no fair-weather friends, Celeste."

"Oh yeah," Celeste agreed. "That's what I mean. When the going gets tough…we stick around."

Tierney smiled at Celeste. Maybe she could come to trust the Latin beauty and be her friend—her true friend—her sunny-side-up friend.

"And anyway, everybody has their own emotional baggage," Alec interjected. "Whether it's rotten parents or a history of bad relationships or…or…"

"Or guilt," Celeste offered.

Alec nodded. "Yeah. Whatever it is…everybody's got it."

There was quiet for a moment as everyone was thoughtful—no doubt about the personal baggage they were each carrying as individuals.

"Let's go back to talking about you in silk stockings and me unzipping your dress zipper with my teeth," Rome said, again winking at Tierney. He smiled. "I liked that thread of conversation a lot better."

"Yeah," Alec said. "Although I don't know how warm you girls will be when you hit the plows with us tomorrow night."

"What?" Tierney asked.

"There's a big cold front coming in tomorrow," Alec began to explain. "They're saying it's going to bury us, and sometimes me and Rome like to have someone ride along with us to help keep us from getting bored and sleepy when we're plowing all night long."

"It's actually pretty fun, Tierney," Celeste said. "I went with Rome three or four times last year, and we just talked and listened to music. It's kind of exciting sometimes…in a scary sort of way."

"Yeah," Alec affirmed. "I figure this year, you can go with me and—"

"She can go with *me*," Rome interrupted, however, "and Celeste can go with you. I swear if I have to have Celeste in my truck with me singing "Party in the U.S.A." all night long one more time, I'll lose my mind."

"Oh, that's a great idea!" Celeste exclaimed. Tierney watched the way Celeste's eyes glistened with excitement as she looked to Alec and asked, "Would you mind if I went with you tomorrow night instead of with Rome?"

Alec's smile was as broad as the Mississippi as he answered, "Not at all. I'd love it."

Rome leaned over and whispered into Tierney's ear, "They're having a moment just thinking about it. Imagine the moment they'll have once they're actually together all night plowing."

Tierney smiled, delighted for her brother. Alec was so happy anytime he was in Celeste's company. She could just imagine what a night of isolation with her in a truck cab would do to him.

"And imagine the moment we'll have," Rome added.

Tierney's smile instantly faded—the heat rising to her cheeks, giving her the sensation it was a warm summer day on the beach instead of a late autumn day in Leavenworth, Washington, with a snowstorm on the horizon.

But then she remembered he was only teasing—as he always was. Therefore, inhaling a deep breath of courage, Tierney forced a smile, turned to face him, and said, "*You* imagine it."

Rome chuckled and then turned and thanked the waiter as he set a plate of bratwurst and sauerkraut on the table before him. "Oh, I will, my bootylicious little florist. I certainly will."

As the waiter set Tierney's plate of food on the table in front of her, she gulped with nervous anticipation. Rome was only teasing her—just like always. He was only teasing her.

CHAPTER SEVEN

The cold front predicted to hit did indeed hit—and hard! Tierney could never remember having been so thoroughly chilled. And yet she was happy in being able to wear a sweater all day long. She'd always loved sweaters, but the weather in Monterey had never been cold enough to wear them comfortably, even during the holidays. Therefore, as she stood at Alec's front window watching the snow falling heavy and thick outside, her excitement about going out as Rome's company during his night of plowing grew. She nearly delirious anticipating spending who knew how many hours alone with him, and she'd be able to do it in the soft, cream-colored sweater Alec had gifted her for her birthday.

Tierney thought for a moment about how what she was wearing so thoroughly affected her mood. Standing there in her jeans, snow boots, and cream sweater, waiting for Alec to finish getting ready so they could meet Rome and Celeste to start plowing, Tierney felt calmer, more relaxed somehow. Thoughts of warm mugs filled with hot chocolate, crackling fireplaces, and having Rome's arms around her enveloped her senses, and she couldn't help but smile.

"Are you ready?" Alec asked as he entered the room.

Tierney turned to greet him and smiled when she saw her brother all decked out head to toe in his snowplowing togs—heavy work boots, old jeans, a flannel shirt over long underwear, and a black ski cap. Alec looked purely rugged!

"You look awesome!" she giggled.

Alec smiled. "Manly, huh?"

"Oh, totally manly," Tierney agreed.

"And here come the troops," he said, nodding toward the front window.

Tierney looked back out the front window once more in time to see a big black Dodge Ram Laramie 3500 with a snowplow on the front pull up in front of the house.

The truck's horn sounded, and Alec said, "Grab your coat, Tiers. It's gonna be a long night."

Mingled excitement and anxiety welled up in Tierney's bosom. She was about to spend an undisclosed amount of time in the big black truck cab with Rome—just Rome. It all seemed so romantic, yet she knew it wasn't meant to be that way—that it was work, Alec and Rome's business and financial livelihood. Still, it was a dreamy idea.

As Tierney and Alec stepped out of the house and into the snowy evening, the cold wind sent a chill through Tierney even for her warm clothing.

"It's so cold!" she exclaimed, teeth chattering, as Alec opened the door to the extended cab and helped her in.

"Hi, Tierney!" Celeste greeted excitedly as Tierney settled into her seat and fastened her seatbelt. "This is going to be so fun! You'll love it. Of course, you'll be worn out by the time we get home. But you'll love it!"

Alec scooched in next to Tierney and said, "Hey, Celeste."

"Hi," Celeste responded with a sweet blush of delight.

"You better take your truck home tonight, man," Rome said, looking in his rearview mirror as he talked to Alec. "Otherwise I'm going to end up having to plow your a…butt outta here next time too."

"I know," Alec agreed. "But I needed to put that other plow on and just hadn't done it yet."

Rome switched his attention to Tierney then, winking at her in the mirror. "Hey there, bootylicious sweater babe. You ready for an all-nighter?"

Tierney shrugged—actually, she blushed and shrugged. "As ready as I'll ever be, I guess."

Rome's smile broadened as he said, "Well, then let's head out to the lot to get Alec's truck and get this show on the road, shall we?"

Rome was wearing a black ski cap too, and Tierney experienced a moment of disappointment. She loved his hair—loved staring at it and imagining running her fingers through it. Yet he looked ultra-sexy in his snowplowing clothes too, so her disappointment wasn't too lingering.

As Rome drove them to where Alec stored his other vehicles and equipment, everyone conversed. The energy of being eager filled the truck cab with a sense of excitement and fun, and again Tierney was struck with how much life she'd missed out on having grown up where and how she did.

But she and Alec had discussed at length that regret did nothing to move a person forward or to encourage. And for that reason, Tierney didn't let her thoughts linger too long on what she'd missed but rather focused on enjoying the fact that she wasn't missing it now.

Once Alec and Celeste were in Alec's truck and Tierney was settled into the passenger's seat of Rome's, she watched as Alec drove out of the lot, honking his horn and waving.

"Rome," Alec's voice said over the cell phone walkie-talkies he and Rome used while plowing.

Rome picked up his phone and said, "Yeah."

"Let me call the city and county and see what we've got pending there, and then I'll let you know who's first on the private customer list," Alec said.

"Roger," Rome answered.

"Roger?" Tierney giggled with amusement.

Rome smiled. "Yeah. It's half the fun of the job…using walkie-talkies and acting like we're Special Forces guys on some mission."

Tierney laughed. "You boys are so funny!"

"As opposed to you girls, who want to wear silk stockings and have Rock Hudson unzip your dress?" Rome teased as he shifted into drive and slowly inched through the lot.

Tierney smiled, simply in heaven being with him—alone with him.

Rome stopped the truck and put it in park just outside the lot fence. "And now we wait," he said.

"For Alec to give us our mission orders?" Tierney teased.

"Exactly," he said, grinning and relaxing back against his seat. "We just keep the truck warm and ready to go."

"And how long will that take?" she asked.

"Why? Are you already bored with my company?"

"Not at all," she assured him.

Rome's alluring eyes narrowed, and he asked, "Are you afraid I'll try to take advantage of your bootyliciousness?"

Tierney giggled. "Not at all," she answered. And it was true.

The article concerning "emotional red flags" popped into her mind then. She thought of the way she'd felt when Elias Potts had come into the floral shop—about how many red flags had begun waving in her brain. But with Rome, there wasn't a one. She wasn't nervous in being with him—well, not about her safety anyway, even considering that if he did try to take advantage of her, there was no escape from the truck. She couldn't jump out and run into a near whiteout blizzard, after all—even if she'd wanted to (which she was sure she wouldn't).

Rome studied Tierney a moment—watched her as she glanced around the truck cab, seeming to take inventory.

"This is a pretty fancy ride you have here, Mr. Novak," she said.

"I like it," he responded. "And me and Alec find they do the job fine…until the snow piles up too much and we have to take out the big dogs—the actual snowplows, instead of the pickups with the plows attached to the front."

"Do you like it?" she asked. "The work you and Alec do?"

"Absolutely," Rome answered honestly. "We get to be outside. Usually we can set our own hours, though winter can get to be a drag by the time it's over."

"How long will we all be out tonight?" she asked. "Like, all night?"

Rome smiled. He could see that having to wait was making her nervous.

"Probably," he answered. "But don't worry. We'll talk and plow. And if you get tired, I keep a pillow and blanket in here…because Celeste usually doesn't make it much past two AM."

Tierney puffed a rather breathless laugh. "I couldn't leave you up by yourself," she said. "Alec says I'm supposed to keep you awake and everything. That's why I'm here, right?"

Rome's smile broadened. "You're here to be my eye candy, sugar cookie," he flirted.

"Oh sure," she said, rolling her eyes. She fidgeted in her seat a moment, and Rome enjoyed watching her blush. "Are you hot?" she asked, looking at him as she tugged at the collar of her coat.

"I don't know," Rome answered. "What do you think?"

"Oh my gosh! Are you ever serious?" Tierney giggled as she unzipped her coat.

"I was serious just now," Rome teased. She rolled her beautiful eyes and shook her head. "Go ahead and take off your coat," he said, letting her off the discomfort hook. "I have the heat pretty high in here so I can always jump back into warmth if I have to get out and dig us out or something."

Rome watched as Tierney removed her coat and then gritted his teeth with being far more than merely pleased with the way she looked in her little fluffy, ivory-colored sweater. He'd always had a thing for girls in sweaters, even when he was a kid. Ever since Rome Novak had begun to notice girls, he'd much preferred them in jeans and sweaters than shorts or bathing suits or any other clothing that was more revealing. There was something about Tierney in that sweater that made him wonder if he would actually be able to concentrate on plowing snow.

"Better?" he asked.

She nodded and tucked a strand of long, soft hair behind one ear. She began to fidget again then, and Rome grinned. She wasn't impatient; she was nervous. He hoped the reason she was nervous was because of him—because she liked him. Well, he was already pretty certain she liked him, but he wasn't sure how much she liked him. Was it as much as he liked her? Did she have the same sense of urgency where he was concerned that he did where she was?

Knowing that it would take Alec at least half an hour to work out their routes for the first part of the evening (something he was certain Tierney did not know), Rome decided to step it up—to act on the constant sense of urgency that had been nagging him since the moment he'd stepped out of that damn box dressed like an idiot almost a year before.

The waiting was starting to cause Tierney's nerves to bunch up. What was taking Alec so long? What was she supposed to do with Rome sitting there all casual, staring at her like he was waiting for a movie to start?

Just keep him alert and awake, Alec had instructed Tierney before they'd left. But the problem was Rome looked incredibly alert and awake—incredibly alluring, incredibly handsome, incredibly everything!

Rome must've sensed Tierney's discomfort because suddenly he said, "Here." Reaching for the iPod on the port of the dashboard, he explained, "Maybe this will make the wait less miserable and the night more festive for you."

As Kenny G's instrumental rendition of "I'll Be Home for Christmas" smoothly slid into the air of the pickup cab, Tierney smiled, arched one astonished brow, and giggled, "Festive? Did you just say festive? And you actually have Kenny G on your playlist?"

"Of course," Rome answered, frowning as if offended by the fact she was so surprised. "I mean, if you prefer, like, heavy metal, I've got that too. I could change—"

"Oh no, no, no!" Tierney exclaimed, reaching out to block his hand from touching the iPod. "I just didn't expect it. I thought maybe you plowed to more…energetic music."

Rome smiled. "Oh, by the end of the night, I will definitely be plowing to something else. But while we're waiting, I thought Mr. G would make the snow seem a little less ominous and bit more—"

"Festive?" Tierney teasingly finished.

"Yeah."

"Well, Mr. G does tend to do that," she admitted. "He smooths me out," she added with a sigh as she did indeed begin to relax a bit.

She heard Rome laugh and looked to see him studying her again. "Smooths you out? You mean like when you watch movies and iron stuff? Same kind of thing? Only then you're smoothing out clothes too."

Tierney laughed too. "Yeah…I guess it is similar."

"That's a really good way to put it," he added, thoughtful for a moment. "Kenny G smooths you out." He nodded. "I like that. It sounds a lot better than chilling you out or calming you down. It *smooths* you."

Tierney giggled. "It seems like you're pretty easy to entertain tonight."

"Why? Were you worried about entertaining me?"

Tierney had never been so worried about making sure someone found her interesting instead of boring in all her life. Of course she was worried about entertaining him! She wondered for a moment just how in the world she'd ended up agreeing to go with him in the first place. But though she wondered how it had happened, she knew exactly *why* it had happened. Tierney would do just about anything to spend time alone with Rome Novak.

"Well, kind of," she admitted. "I mean, it must be a bit stressful, all the plowing…especially when you can't see two feet in front of you in this snow!"

Rome, still grinning at her, winked. "Well, you don't have to do much to entertain me, Tierney. You could just sit there all night, and I'd find that interesting enough."

Tierney's heart did several flippy-flips in her chest, as her stomach filled so full of butterflies she felt like she couldn't breathe!

"Ooo! You *are* smooth!" she laughed as she blushed as red as a traffic light at Christmas. "Maybe I should call *you* Mr. G, huh?"

"That's because you smooth me out," he teased.

"Oh, is that so?" she teased in return.

"Yep. You can iron on me anytime, Tierney," he continued to flirt.

Naturally Tierney was delighted nearly beyond endurance. Locked in a warm pickup cab in a snowstorm with Rome Novak? It was ethereal! And as nervous as she was—as jittery at being so secluded and close to him—Tierney knew that she had to hide the fact he caused her to want to bounce around the pickup cab like a rabid squirrel. She needed to appear calm—meet him flirt for flirt like she'd gotten in the habit of doing. She figured *that*, above anything else, might keep him entertained and alert—a witty, flirtatious banter worthy of a drop-dead gorgeous, smart, clever snowplower like Rome Novak.

"I'll remember that next time I'm nervous or stressed out," she said, disappointed when she realized she hadn't left an opening for their flirting to continue.

Rome glanced to the clock on his dash and sighed. "Well, your brother sure is taking his dear sweet time, isn't he?"

He was impatient. Tierney had failed in trying to entertain him.

"Do you usually have to wait like this? This long, I mean?" she asked, attempting to turn the conversation back on—but to a more casual subject.

Rome shrugged. "Sometimes longer. It just depends on the reports and what calls come in and when."

"So you probably usually just, like, read or something, right?" Tierney offered, desperate to keep the dialogue going.

"Nope," he answered, however. "I usually just sit here and think about stuff."

"Like what kind of stuff?" she asked.

Rome looked at her. His eyes narrowed, simmering with an increasingly familiar glow of mischief.

"Well, right now I'm thinking that if this were, like, say 1984—you know, back when my parents were teenagers—I'm thinking that this would be the perfect setup for a full-on N.C.M.O.S."

Tierney frowned. "A what?"

Rome chuckled. "You know, like in high schools now. They called it NickMo at my high school, but my mom says in the '80s, they just used the acronym N.C.M.O.S."

Tierney was still frowning. Shaking her head, she admitted, "I honestly have no idea what you're talking about."

Rome laughed. "Private school, huh?"

"Maybe," Tierney answered coyly, for he'd hit the nail right on the head. She had attended a private school, completely missing out on the fun, misery, and drama of a public high school experience. "So who is Nick Moe? And what is N.C.M.O.S? I assume it's an acronym for something."

Again Rome's eyes dazzled her with an intriguing smolder of amusement. "They're the same, actually. NickMo—it's a nickname for the acronym N.C.M.O. It's actually the same thing as N.C.M.O.S., but I guess our generation is just too lazy to use a five-letter acronym, so they shortened it to four. Personally, I prefer my mom's acronym for—"

"For what?" Tierney interrupted with giggling impatience.

Her giggling stopped cold, however—her smile fading instantly, her heart leaping in her chest—as Rome Novak leaned toward her, saying, "N.C.M.O.S. Noncommittal make-out session, Tierney."

"N-n-noncommittal what?" she asked breathlessly—for certainly he hadn't said what she'd thought he'd said.

"Make-out session," he repeated. "You do know what a make-out session is, don't you? I'm sure they at least had that in private school, right?"

"O-of course," Tierney stammered, feeling suddenly overly warm again. "L-like that party game spin-the-bottle…or post office or whatever," she said, gesturing as if she thought such things were trivial.

"I guess it's similar," Rome admitted. "Did you ever play?"

"Play what?" Tierney asked, feigning ignorance. She didn't want to look stupid in front of him, but his talking about kissing was freaking her out a bit—making her nervous and overheated. All she could think of was kissing him at her bridal shower—in the hallway at Halloween—and it was making her mouth water.

"Spin-the-bottle? Did you ever play?" he asked again.

"Of course," Tierney fibbed. The truth was she'd never played, but Alec had played spin-the-bottle at a party once and had described the experience to her in great detail.

"Well, Tierney, I bet I could spin your bottle like it's never been spun before," he teased.

Thankful he'd returned to his flirtatious teasing instead of continuing to educate her on acronyms, Tierney smiled. The snow outside the pickup had nothing on the flurries of butterflies going on in her stomach. She had to retaliate—return to the teasing tone their conversation demanded.

"You think so?" she asked.

Rome nodded, answering, "Oh, I *know* so."

Arching one eyebrow, Tierney countered, "Maybe I could spin *your* bottle like it's never been spun before. Ever think of that?"

He chuckled. "Actually, yes…I did think of that."

Tierney blushed—tried to steady the pace of her breathing, for it had begun to quicken.

"In fact," Rome continued, "since you did just open the door…I call. Let's me and you have us a noncommittal make-out and see *who* spins *whose* bottle, shall we?"

Instantly Tierney's heart leapt up into her throat—or at least it felt like it did. Was he still kidding? Surely he was. Surely he wasn't suggesting they *really* make out—right there, that very minute, as the engine of his truck rumbled with a low idle and snowflakes the size of daisies continued to bury the streets of the small city.

Yet just in case he wasn't kidding—on the off chance that Rome Novak really meant to do exactly what he'd suggested—Tierney tried to appear unfretted and answered, "You're on. Bring it, bub."

"Bub?" he laughed.

Tierney shrugged. "Would you prefer buster?"

But Rome shook his head. "Nope. Bub will do just fine." He paused a moment, his eyes narrowing as he studied her. "Did you really just say, 'Bring it'?"

"Step up or tap out, playah," she teased.

Again he laughed, and Tierney was pleased in knowing she'd managed to entertain him for a moment.

"Oooo! You're a feisty little thing, ain't you?" he chuckled.

But Tierney smiled and shook her head. "Not really. I just talk a big game."

"Well, I don't," Rome said, leaning over the console toward her.

Tierney gulped as he reached out, taking hold of her chin just the way he had that day at her ill-fated bridal shower—the way he had on dreamy Halloween only a short while before. Leaning over the console further, Rome pressed his left cheek to her right one, and Tierney held her breath.

"Step up or tap out, baby," he whispered in her ear.

Tierney felt every bone in her body begin to dissolve as Rome pressed a long, lingering kiss to her jaw right below her ear. Slowly his mouth caressed her skin as it followed her jawline to her chin. He pressed her lips with his thumb as he continued to softly kiss her chin and jawline. Tierney had never, never, never in all her life been so affected! Well, not since Rome had kissed her the first and last time anyway, but even those blissful previous occasions had been different. This was a teasing sort of windup or something, and it made her want to take his face between her hands and kiss his mouth full on and unreservedly!

Leaning over the console was awkward and uncomfortable, but Tierney's mind silently repeated that she would rather be aching with discomfort than risk interrupting the chance of having Rome kiss her again.

All of a sudden, however, Rome released her chin, and she felt his strong hands slip under her arms and begin to lift her.

"Whoever the idiot was who thought of putting bucket seats and a console in pickups…" he mumbled as he very ably began to pull Tierney over the console and toward him.

Almost before she'd realized what had happened, Tierney found herself sitting in Rome's lap. He grinned at her as he reached down and pushed the button on the side of his seat. The seat slowly slid back as far as it would go, and Rome moved his legs farther apart, causing Tierney's bum to settle down onto his seat between them.

"There now," Rome said, taking Tierney's right arm and placing it around his shoulders and neck. "That's better."

The cold of the pickup's driver-side window felt invigorating against Tierney's shoulders, but not nearly as invigorating as the sensations of pleasure rippling through her body when Rome slipped his left arm under hers that was around his neck, embracing her waist as he again took hold of her chin.

He smiled at her, asking, "Now…what was that you said again? Step up or tap out, playah?"

Tierney blushed at having been so brazen, simultaneously gasping with delight as Rome tipped her head and turned her face from his a bit while pressing a sizzling kiss to her neck.

He was different than any other man who had ever kissed her—far more attractive, of course, but it wasn't just that. It was the way he seemed to be prepping her or something. He hadn't gone right for her mouth, forcing a hard, wet kiss the way other guys had done—even Dillon. It was as if Rome were endeavoring to please her before taking what he might want from her. Tierney smiled as she closed her eyes and allowed herself to enjoy the feel of Rome's kiss on her neck, on her cheek, to her earlobe. It was like he was smoothing her out!

Tierney felt weak, almost intoxicated, as at long, long, *long* last, Rome's hand holding her chin directed her face toward his. Her eyes fluttered open when she sensed he was looking at her—and he was.

"You ready to see if I can really spin your bottle, baby?" he asked, winking and grinning at her.

But Tierney smiled at him and unexpectedly heard herself confess, "I already know you can. You spun it so fast once before that I broke off my wedding. Remember?

Rome's smile broadened. "Is that so?"

"You were there. What do you think?" she whispered.

"It wasn't part of the plan, you know," he said, "me kissing you that day."

"But…but Alec talked you into dressing up and—"

"Alec talked me into dressing up, stepping out of a box like some idiot, and trying to convince you not to marry that dude while we were dancing," he interrupted. "Kissing you…well…" He shrugged. "That was my own idea."

"It was?" Tierney asked as her heart leapt over and over and over again in her chest. Alec hadn't told him to kiss her that first time? Rome had done it of his own volition? Oh, certainly she knew Alec hadn't put Rome up to kissing her on Halloween, but the knowledge that Rome had kissed her of his own choice that day at the bridal shower—it caused her to begin to tremble with a happiness she'd never known before!

"You weren't buying the whole tango, talking thing, right?" Rome began. "And besides…what guy wouldn't want to steal a kiss from you?"

He was too good to be true, too perfect in physical features and the things he said. Tierney didn't know whether to laugh or cry.

"Wow," she breathed. "Do you practice that stuff or what?"

"What stuff?" Rome asked. But Tierney could see he was finished talking. He took hold of her chin as his head descended toward hers—as his arm tightened around her waist. "Now let's get down to some serious making out, okay?"

"O-okay," Tierney breathed.

Rome's warm breath on her lips caused Tierney's entire body to break into goose bumps—caused her to begin to quiver with excitement and desire. His mouth was so close she could almost taste it—and, oh, how desperately she wanted to.

"Hey, Romeo…you warmed up?" Alec's voice interrupted over Rome's phone.

"Or not," Rome growled as he released Tierney's chin and picked up his phone.

"Oh yeah…I'm warmed up all right," Rome responded to Alec, winking at Tierney and causing her to blush.

"Then you and Tierney head out to the city roads East and South and we'll take North and West," Alec instructed. "Then we'll do the ones the county gave us. All right?"

"You got it," Rome answered. "Plowing out now."

"Roger," Alec said. "Keep me posted."

"Roger," Rome said, tossing his phone onto the dashboard.

Alec's interruption had reminded Tierney just how ridiculous she'd been to think she would find herself sitting in Rome's pickup making out with him during a snowstorm. She felt foolish all of a sudden—embarrassed—and she moved to scramble out of his lap.

But Rome's arms stayed around her body. She looked at him, and he grinned at her.

"Shouldn't we get started?" she asked.

The engine of the pickup roared as Rome revved it with a couple of pumps of the gas pedal and shook his head. Tierney tried to wish away her deepening blush, but it was on her cheeks to stay for a while.

"What's a couple more minutes, right?" he asked.

Oh, Tierney *thought* she'd remembered how absolutely delicious Rome's kiss was. She *thought* she'd remembered how perfectly his mouth fit to hers and how magnificent it made her feel, the desire it evoked from her. But clearly she hadn't—for when Rome Novak's lips met hers, Tierney nearly fell apart! She thought for a moment that she would dissolve from the bliss of it—from the nearly painful hammering of her heart!

Over and over again Rome's mouth worked a spell of passion, longing, desire, and pure rapture over Tierney. These kisses were different than the ones she'd been blessed with before. They were almost wanton, driven, and hot and caused her entire body to quiver with pleasure.

He broke the seal of their mouths once, pressing a hot, moist kiss against her throat, and though the sensation was blissful, Tierney knew their time was short. Taking Rome's whiskery face between her hands, she directed his mouth to hers once more, kissing him the way she never imagined she would have the courage to kiss a man.

Tierney sighed when Rome's kisses became even more aggressive then, as he once more stepped into the dominant predator's roll—kissing her with such an impassioned vigor Tierney found she could hardly breathe.

Without warning, Rome suddenly broke from her, lifting her back across the console and plopping her into her seat once more.

Slamming the gearshift into drive, he almost grumbled, "You win. Consider my bottle thoroughly spun."

"But my bottle is still spinning," she ventured. "So doesn't that make you the winner?"

Rome looked at her, exhaling a sigh and smiling once more.

"I'd say we're both winners then," he said, winking at her. As he pulled away from the curb, he said, "I guess next time, we'll have to play post office, right? Give the USPO a real run for their money, huh?"

"Yeah, I guess so," Tierney said, fastening her seatbelt and trying to restore her breathing to some semblance of normalcy. Next time? He'd said next time? Tierney could hardly breathe as it was! She couldn't imagine what would happen to her if there really were a next time.

She watched as Rome reached out and messed with his iPod a minute.

Smiling at her as Bon Jovi's "Lost Highway" began, he said, "I guess we better get down to business now, right? I don't want to get fired for smoochin' with the boss's sister."

Tierney nodded as she watched Rome lower the snowplow blade and hit the gas.

He glanced at her once more, adding, "Of course…then again…maybe the boss is smoochin' with my sister."

"I hope so," Tierney laughed, wondering whether Alec were making the most of his time with Celeste—if he'd been trying to spin Celeste's bottle the way Rome had just spun Tierney's.

CHAPTER EIGHT

As Tierney stood at the floral cart designing a massive table arrangement comprising dark orange Asiatic lilies, burgundy miniature carnations, fuchsia spray roses, bicolored orange roses, peach hypericum berries, and greens, she could almost feel her own happiness seeping into the beauty of the arrangement.

Two nights before—the night she'd spent in Rome's pickup as he plowed the streets of Leavenworth, some of the surrounding county roads, and finally the driveways of private customers he and Alec had procured—had been the most wonderful night of her life! More wonderful even than Halloween, and there had been days when Tierney had been certain nothing would ever top the magic of dancing with Rome and being kissed by him on Halloween. But the night she'd accompanied him plowing—two days later, she still felt as if she could take flight by thinking about it and will her body to do so.

Oh, certainly the kissing—what Rome had teased about being a "noncommittal make-out session," claiming he could spin her bottle like it had never been spun (and he certainly had)—was the wildest, most romantic, and wonderful part of the night! And yet, as Tierney carefully placed an extra lily into the arrangement she was finishing, she stood still awed at how truly wonderful the night had been.

She'd spent ten hours in the truck with Rome—ten glorious hours! And for most of that time, she and Rome had simply talked—shared memories and life experiences—teased, laughed, and even discussed serious matters such as politics and the state of things in the world. It had been an epiphanic sort of night, for Tierney was more certain than ever that she would never, never get over Rome Novak. She knew she wanted him—wanted him all for herself and forever. Of course, she'd known that from the moment she'd met him at her bridal shower—when he'd stepped out of a big box as her classic Latin lover. But after the romantic, insightful, truly bonding night of plowing, she knew she couldn't live without him—at least not happily.

Rome had shared so much about himself—for one, his feelings of knowing he was adopted and the struggles he'd endured as a child and teenager in trying to understand it. But he explained that eventually he began to understand that if his biological mother hadn't given him up, for whatever reason she did—if he'd never been adopted by Edward and Nikki Novak—he would never have known the profound, unconditional love they owned for him. He never would've known Celeste and had the blessing of knowing and loving her, his sister. He never would've met the people he met, been where he'd been and was. He'd winked at Tierney and added that he obviously wouldn't have known Tierney either and told her that knowing her was enough of a reason on its own to be happy that he'd been adopted by his parents.

Naturally, they'd discussed Tierney's past as well—though she was surprised at how much Rome already knew regarding it, via Alec. Rome openly admitted being very happy that she and Alec had "abandoned ship" (as he put it), even though he couldn't imagine how difficult it must've been to make the decision to leave everyone and everything they'd always known.

It seemed as if they'd shared nearly everything about themselves in just that one night, even though Tierney knew they hadn't. They'd done other things as well—sang to whatever song was playing on the iPod when they began to get tired (Tierney giggling when Rome insisted they sing "Jingle Bells" at one point, considering their task as hand) and enjoyed hot chocolate Rome had prepared and poured into a thermos. They'd snacked on ranch-flavored Corn Nuts, laughing about how something so good could make a person's breath smell so bad. And when Rome dropped Tierney off at Alec's house at seven AM, insisting she allow him to exit the pickup and open her door for her, Tierney felt as if she'd already known Rome for years—not just snowplowed with him for ten hours.

Tierney smiled as she thought about the way Rome had walked her to the front door of the house—both of them weary and baggy-eyed from the long night spent working.

"Thanks for riding with me," Rome had said the moment before he'd bent and placed a firm, moist kiss to her mouth.

"Thanks for letting me," she'd said in return once the kiss had ended.

"I'll see you later," he'd said. "But I'm going home to get some sleep now. You be sure you do the same, or you'll feel like hell in a couple of days."

Tierney had watched him drive away and then entered the house to find Alec had already showered and fallen into bed. He was snoring, and she decided not to wake him. She was glad to find out the next morning, however, that Alec had found the courage to kiss Celeste on the cheek when he'd dropped her off and thanked her for going with him that same morning.

"Where's Jessica?"

At the sound of Elias Potts's voice behind her, Tierney felt the hair on the back of her neck stand on end. Glancing up to the clock on the wall, Tierney realized that it was after five PM and that Jessica must've left over ten minutes before. Vaguely she remembered Jessica saying something about leaving, but Tierney had been so lost in her reveries of her time with Rome that she wasn't even sure if she'd acknowledged Jessica.

"She's around here somewhere, I think," Tierney lied. With the red flags unfurling like crazy in her mind, she figured it was better to fib than to admit to Elias that she was in the shop alone.

Quickly she rolled the cart and the arrangement she'd finished into the large floral refrigerator and then turned to face Elias. The sight of him affected her even more than the sound of his voice had. There was something not right about the man. She was sure of it.

Consequently, Tierney asked, "Do you happen to have your keys to the shop with you, Mr. Potts?"

"Of course," the man said, scowling. "But where's Jessica?" He took a step toward Tierney. Two more steps and she'd have to brush up against him to leave the back room.

"Nothing," Rome answered, winking at Tierney and causing butterflies to flutter about in her stomach.

"Oh my gosh!" Heidi Svensson exclaimed as she suddenly intruded. "Did you guys just hear that? On the news in the den—someone *else* just walked into a plane propeller! This time up in Bellingham!"

"No, it's gotta be rumors," Alec said, frowning. "That poor model that it happened to last year—"

"No, it's true!" Heidi interrupted.

Heidi Svensson—the girl that Rome thought Alec liked—the girl who Alec knew really liked Rome. She was the one person Tierney had met at the Novaks' Halloween party who kind of rubbed Tierney the wrong way. Tierney figured she was predisposed to dislike Heidi simply for the fact that Alec had revealed Heidi was after Rome. But when Celeste had introduced Heidi as her coworker at the Christmas Shoppe in town, for some inexplicable reason, Tierney's discomfort had increased.

"It was some old man or something, getting off a plane that had just come in from Seattle," Heidi continued. "He died."

Then, as quickly as she had arrived, Heidi flitted off to infiltrate another group of guests.

"She leaves such rays of joy and sunshine in her wake, doesn't she?" Alec muttered, frowning.

"I just don't get that," Celeste said.

"You mean how someone can be such a total Debbie Downer like Heidi and still get invited to parties?" Rome asked.

"No, you stupid," Celeste scolded. "I invited her because we work together and stuff. I'm talking about, like, how does someone just accidentally walk into an airplane propeller?"

Alec shrugged. "I don't know," he said. "But when I worked in Seattle, I used to fly from Seattle to Bellingham a couple of times a week, and there were always people on the runway that weren't paying attention to the planes, so I can see how—"

Celeste gasped, her mouth dropping open in astonishment as she stared at Alec with widened eyes. "You used to be a pilot?" she asked.

Rome, who had been drinking a cup of root beer, choked—overcome with amusement at his sister's misinterpretation of what Alec had said. No sooner had Rome begun to choke than Tierney hopped

"Oh…I'm not sure," Tierney said. Quickly grabbing her coat and purse from the nearby coat rack, she added, "But would you or Mrs. Potts lock up for me? I've got a…a date, and I'm running late already." Hurriedly pulling her phone from her purse, Tierney sent a text to Jessica explaining that she was just leaving but that Mr. Potts would lock up the shop.

She was thankful when Jessica sent a quick response text, saying, *Okay, thanks! Tell Elias I'm already home, please.*

Nearly racing past Elias and toward the front door of the shop, Tierney called over her shoulder, "She says to tell you she's already home, Mr. Potts. Thanks for locking up, and have a nice evening."

Without another word, Tierney stepped out of the shop and onto the busy sidewalks of Leavenworth. She turned right and started toward the Christmas Shoppe. It would be the busiest shop still open, and Celeste would be there. She and Celeste were meeting up after work. Celeste had called earlier in the day and invited Tierney to come over and enjoy the Novak family's hot tub when they were both finished working. Though Tierney had not been too thoroughly excited about going hot-tubbing—being that every hot tub party she'd ever been to had been nothing but a drunken grope-fest at which she always ended up playing bridge with the other wallflowers—now she couldn't wait to get to Celeste, couldn't wait to get to the Novaks' home and soak up the safe, happy feelings that permeated it. Elias Potts had rattled her, and Tierney figured that a hot tub and kind people were just the cure. And besides, she secretly hoped that Alec and Rome would finish their snow removal projects early so that she might get to see Rome before going home.

"Hey, Tierney!" she heard Celeste call. Looking ahead of her, she saw Celeste hurrying down the sidewalk toward her. It was like seeing an angel!

"Hi!" Tierney called. She found herself rushing toward Celeste and gratefully accepting the hug she offered in greeting.

"My heck!" Celeste exclaimed. "You're shaking like a leaf, Tierney. Are you that cold?"

Ever since she'd discovered that she and Celeste both had interests in old Hollywood at lunch several days before, Tierney had begun to really try to imagine that Celeste would be a true, faithful friend. And now—standing there not cold but rattled by the emotional red flags that had gone off in her head when Elias Potts had entered the shop—Tierney was more needful of a friend than ever, more willing to take a risk in confiding in one a little.

"No," Tierney answered. "Actually, Mrs. Potts's husband just came into the shop as I was getting ready to leave and kind of…you know…it kind of freaked me out."

Instantly Celeste ended their embrace, taking Tierney by the shoulders—a deep frown puckering her beautiful brow as she said, "Stay away from that jerk, Tierney." Tierney's eyes widened as Celeste repeated, "I mean it. You're right to be freaked out by him. He's…he's…freaky."

Tierney frowned. "You know him?"

Celeste nodded and exhaled a breath of what seemed to be sudden fatigue. "Yeah. I worked for Jessica the summer before I was a senior."

"And you felt kind of creepy and stuff whenever he was around too?"

"Oh yes," Celeste affirmed. "And for all her weirdness and pessimism, Heidi Svensson feels the same way. She worked there last summer and says she'll never work for Jessica again…because her husband is a perv."

Tierney sighed, feeling strangely relieved. "I don't know why, but that makes me feel better somehow."

Celeste's smile returned. "Affirmation always makes me feel better too." Linking arms with Tierney, she said, "Come on. Let's get home and claim the hot tub before anyone else does. I wore the wrong kind of shoes to work today, and my feet are killing me."

"Mine too," Tierney admitted, "even though I wore the right kind of shoes."

Celeste giggled and headed them toward where Tierney could see her car parked across the street. "Let's go then. And Mom promised she'd make us some homemade toffee! I love to sit in the hot tub and eat toffee this time of year."

Tierney giggled, feeling much better than she had even minutes before. Celeste was like a ray of sunshine breaking through a gray mass of winter clouds, and Tierney could understand why Alec was so in love with her—even if he couldn't find the courage to tell her.

"Homemade toffee, huh?" Tierney asked. "Sounds perfectly decadent!"

"I guess so. After all, the sugar and fat will probably stick right to our hips…to the very decadent of us keeping these girlish figures."

Tierney giggled. "You mean detriment?"

Celeste laughed, shrugging and saying, "Oh yeah, that's what I meant." She paused, however, frowning and adding, "I think that's what I meant anyway. Is that what I meant? What did you mean?"

As they reached the car and Celeste pushed the button on her key fob to unlock it, Tierney laughed as she slid into her seat. Celeste was a jewel—simply a jewel! She felt nearly all better and knew that once she was in the safe haven of the Novak home, all her red flags where Elias was concerned would disappear.

"Holy cow!" Tierney exclaimed in awe, for she had never imagined to find such a scene in the Novaks' back yard.

"I know, huh!" Celeste agreed. "Mom told Dad that if he wanted a hot tub, then it couldn't be some plain, old, ugly thing that just sat on the back porch," she explained. "So dad built the gazebo out here near the tree line, and Mom strung it with the white lights. She said she wanted it to be 'an experience,'" Celeste said, making the familiar quotation mark gesture with her fingers.

Tierney's eyebrows arched in further astonishment. "You mean she leaves the lights up all year long? They're not just for the holidays?"

Celeste nodded. "Oh yeah! It looks like this year round." Pausing to reconsider, however, she added, "Well, except it looks so much lovelier at Christmastime…when everything's all snowy like it's starting to be now." Celeste sighed with obvious pleasure. "It's a lot more relaxing too, being away from the house like this." She looked to Tierney and smiled. "It's why I invited you tonight. I thought we could both use some R&R. Leavenworth gets so crazy this time of year. It's quiet out here, and the hot tub is so nice and warm."

Tierney's smile broadened. "Well, I'm very grateful to have been invited. I really could use something to settle my nerves a bit…not to mention soothe my aching feet."

"Oh, I hear you there," Celeste said. "The Christmas Shoppe was nuts today! I didn't even take my lunch break."

"I wolfed down a sandwich while working on a bridal bouquet," Tierney offered. She sighed with the anticipation of relaxing as she studied the hot tub centered in the middle of the lovely gazebo, draped in twinkling white lights.

It was a tranquil, ethereal scene of serenity that lay before them. The tall pines, still flocked with snow from the storms of two nights before, stood tall and straight like dark sentinels behind the gazebo and outlined against the starry, moonlit sky. A path had been shoveled through the snow from the house to the gazebo and lay stretched out before Tierney and Celeste like some magical road beckoning to be followed.

Tierney could already imagine how good the warm water of the hot tub would feel on her sore and aching feet—on every sore and aching muscle in her sore and aching body.

"Are you ready?" Celeste asked, smiling.

"Of course!" Tierney assured her.

Then, linking arms, the two girls began to hurry down the path toward the gazebo, for they were only wearing their bathing suits with towels wrapped around their waists, and the night air was cold.

Once they'd discarded their towels onto the railing on one side of the gazebo, they tested the jet-bubbling hot water with their toes, both giggling with delight then as they settled into the soothing warmth of the hot tub.

"Oh my gosh," Tierney breathed as she laid her head back on the side of the hot tub and closed her eyes. "It's like a dream."

"I know," Celeste agreed. "And it's way better than some full-body massage by a stranger, right?"

Tierney smiled. "Absolutely!" she agreed.

They were silent for a long time, each enjoying the crisp, late autumn air that nipped at their noses, perfectly coupled with the warmth and comfort of the hot water. After a time, however, Tierney was so relaxed, she began to worry that she might indeed fall asleep.

Therefore, she was glad when Celeste asked, "So? What do you want to talk about?"

Tierney shrugged. "Anything," she sincerely answered. But thinking again, she added, "Anything but work, that is." She didn't want to talk about work; she didn't even want to *think* about it.

"Definitely," Celeste agreed. "Anything but that." Celeste paused a moment and then asked, "Wanna talk about old movie stars? Or boys?"

Tierney's eyes popped open as she raised her head from its resting position. She giggled as she saw the mischief in Celeste's expression.

"Of course! Though I'd rather talk about boys tonight for some reason," she openly admitted. "But...which boys do you want to talk about? After all, I don't know that many around here yet."

Celeste's beautiful smile broadened. "You know the only two that count."

"You mean Rome and Alec?" Tierney asked—though she already knew that Rome and Alec were exactly who Celeste meant.

"Yep," Celeste verified. "But more Alec than Rome...if you want me to be honest."

"Ooo! How intriguing!" Tierney said, sitting forward a bit. "What about Alec?" It was strange, but in that very moment—as she watched Celeste's eyes glowing with delight at the anticipation of talking about Alec—Tierney felt her fears of investing in a friendship with Celeste sifting away even further. Celeste was a kind, compassionate girl, with a fabulous zest for life and an incredible sense of humor, whether her sense of humor was intentional or not. Smiling at Celeste, she asked, "What do you want to know? Ask me anything about him, anything at all, and I'll tell you."

"Okay," Celeste sighed, her smile broadening with satisfaction. "When was the last steady girlfriend he had, and who was she? He hasn't dated anyone really seriously since he got to Leavenworth. So who was it...if you know, that is?"

"Oh, I know who it was, all right," Tierney said, heaving a heavy sigh of disgust. "And she really did a number on Alec too."

"You mean, like, broke his heart?" Celeste asked. The trepidation was obvious on Celeste's face.

But Tierney shook her head. "Nope. Just tried to rope him into getting her pregnant so he'd have to marry her."

Celeste gasped—looked so mortified that Tierney instantly regretted having spoken with such forthrightness.

"You're kidding me!" Celeste exclaimed. "You mean...he was sleeping with her and...and..."

Celeste looked so worried, pale, and nauseated suddenly that Tierney was actually worried for her and immediately interjected, "Oh no! No, no, no!" she assured Celeste, reaching out and placing a reassuring hand on the girl's forearm. "No. Alec doesn't…he doesn't do that."

Celeste frowned. "He doesn't do what? He doesn't get girls pregnant? Or he doesn't sleep around?"

Once again, Celeste's way of putting things was not only refreshing but also amusing, and Tierney struggled to suppress her desire to giggle.

"Both," she answered. "I mean, he doesn't sleep around…and therefore, it follows that he doesn't get girls pregnant."

With a heavy sigh of relief, and as the color returned to her face, Celeste said, "Oh, good. That's good. Whew! That's really good."

"Yes, it is," Tierney said as a small giggle managed to escape her throat even for all her efforts to prevent it.

Celeste frowned. "But I don't understand then," she began. "If Alec doesn't do that sort of thing, then why did this girl try to get him to…to do that sort of thing?"

"Because she's a spoiled brat," Tierney answered. "Valerie Gilland." Tierney shook her head. "Boy! Was she ever a nightmare! I don't think there's ever been a woman that walked the earth that was as determined to ruin a man's moral code as Valerie was to ruin Alec's."

"But surely…surely she knew Alec wasn't a…you know…a gigolo, right?" Celeste asked. "So why then did she even try to…to, you know…what's that word when you try to get a guy to…you know…"

"Seduce?" Tierney offered, smiling.

"Yeah! Why did she try to seduce him if he's not even the kind of guy who would…you know…"

"Honestly?" Tierney began. "Because he's handsome, and our parents are rich. She wanted him for his money…and for a trophy. I mean, you've heard of trophy wives, right?"

"Yeah," Celeste affirmed.

"I think she wanted Alec simply for the money she thought he would inherit and because he cleans up well for parties and events," Tierney finished answering.

Celeste's smile faded, the light that had been sparkling in her gorgeous eyes lessening its luminance for a moment. "I know how that goes…unfortunately. When someone wants you for something besides who you are…like, just because you look good on his arm and stuff." She paused a moment and then openly, and quite unexpectedly, confessed, "That's why I want Alec. That's why I'm so in love with him the way I am."

Tierney felt her eyes widen with astonishment at the unexpected, brutally honest revelation of Rome's sister.

"I think he likes me because I'm *me*…because I'm a total ditz and make him laugh…not because I can clean up well, as you put it."

"So…so you're admitting to me that you really do have strong feelings for Alec?" Tierney asked—just to be perfectly certain.

"Strong feelings? Strong feelings?" Celeste laughed. "I'm completely, unrecoverably in love with your brother, Tierney! I mean…do you want to know how in love with him I am?"

"Of course!" Tierney encouraged. Her heart was racing with gladness and joy. After all, Tierney knew just how much Alec was in love with Celeste—even if he was having difficulty letting himself charge ahead with winning her.

Leaning forward, Celeste's beautiful eyes widened as she lowered her voice and said, "I am *so* in love with your brother…that I want to marry him, live with him, laugh with him…forever! And I want to be the girl that he finally *does* get pregnant!" Celeste blushed, adding, "I-I mean…after I marry him, of course." Then exhaling another heavy sigh, Celeste leaned back against the hot tub, stretched her arms out on the rim on either side of her, and firmly stated, *"That's* how much I'm in love with Alec."

"Wow!" Tierney breathed.

"You think I'm crazy, don't you?" Celeste asked. "You think I'm just too…boring and dingbatty and young and for him and—"

"I think you're perfect for him," Tierney interrupted. "And I think you'll be perfect together."

Celeste smiled. "Really?"

"Really," Tierney assured her. "I mean, once Alec gets up the nerve to actually, you know, officially pursue you…then you guys will be perfect together."

But Celeste frowned. "What you mean…gets up the nerve to pursue me?"

Tierney laughed. Celeste was so much like her brother, Rome—somehow aware that she was attractive to others but unbelieving at the same time.

"Celeste," Tierney began, "you look like a freaking Victoria's Secret model! What guy isn't going to have to work up the courage to pursue a Victoria's Secret model?"

Celeste still frowned. "But I'm not a Victoria's Secret model," she grumbled unhappily.

Tierney smiled. "There's nothing wrong with *looking* like a Victoria's Secret model, Celeste. It's just rare and really intimidating to guys…especially good guys like Alec."

Celeste sighed, obviously unconvinced.

So Tierney ventured further with her encouragement and explanation. "Guys like my brother…they're trying to stay gentlemen in a world where being a gentleman is considered a weakness rather than a strength."

"You mean he's not promiscuous when everyone thinks promiscuity now equals manliness," Celeste offered. "I get it. Rome's the same way."

"Right," Tierney said. "Therefore, Alec is intimidated by you…because…he does want to…you now…you know…"

"Sleep with me?" Celeste finished. "I know. Guys are guys. They're made that way."

"Well, yeah…but that's not exactly what I mean," Tierney began to explain. "I *know* my brother, and I know he has so much respect for you…that even though he is a guy and all guys have that…you know…"

"Carnal desire," Celeste prodded.

"Yeah. But Alec…he would never hurt you or take advantage of you or anything like that. And yet he's having a hard time believing a beautiful Victoria's Secret, Carmen Miranda type like you could ever really find anything in him worthy of loving and committing to."

Celeste grinned. "You mean, kind of like the way you feel about Rome."

It was Tierney's turn to frown then. "What do you mean?" she asked—though she immediately understood the similarity.

"Oh, come on, Tierney!" Celeste giggled. "You don't really think I buy that act of confidence you put on with Rome, do you? When he's flirting with you and teasing you? Sure, you come right back at him—and bravo, by the way—but all the time, you're waiting for the dream to end. You think that he stepped out of a big box and played your Latin lover for that moment—for those moments when you guys are flirting and stuff. But then you wait for him to walk away…like you don't believe you could really hold his interest or something." Celeste leaned forward, "Even after the way he apparently nearly ate you alive the other night in his pickup." Tierney blushed, and Celeste nodded, saying, "Yeah, that's right. I know him well enough to recognize when he's—shall we say?—preoccupied."

"H-he told you we…that we…" Tierney stammered.

"That he nearly devoured you? Yeah, he told me. I *am* his sister," Celeste affirmed. "After all, you and Alec talk about stuff…obviously."

"He didn't nearly devour me," Tierney said, blushing at the thrill the memory of kissing Rome sent racing through her. "I-I don't think it could've been more than, like, maybe five minutes and—"

"My brother was born in Mexico City, Tierney," Celeste reminded her. "He's legitimately got Latin blood coursing through his veins. And being Latin myself, I can tell you we really do have the most passionate tendencies in the world!" She giggled as Tierney shook her head and continued to blush. "I know my brother as well as you know yours, and I'm telling you—East and South Leavenworth were probably lucky they got plowed out at *all* the other night!"

"Oh, he's such a good kisser, you know?" Tierney sighed, finally confiding in Celeste.

"Well, I wouldn't know, of course," Celeste giggled. "But I'm sure that he is."

"No, I mean…I mean he's like…when he kisses me, it's exactly like something out of a movie—only much, much better!" Tierney whispered. "I swear, every time he does it, I'm afraid I'll pass out, and I can't get over it afterward! I can't sleep. I can't think of anything else!"

"Oh, I want that with Alec so badly, Tierney!" Celeste whispered. Tierney studied her a moment, the expression of near agony on her face.

"Well…maybe you should take the initiative somehow, Celeste," Tierney suggested—although she well knew she'd never have the guts to take the initiative with Rome!

"What you mean? Like, throw myself at him or be pushy?" Celeste asked. "I'm not like that, and I don't think I could even fake that."

"No, I know," Tierney said. "But maybe there's something you can do to, like, encourage him more or something."

"You mean like flirt with him the way Rome does with you?" Celeste asked. "Does that encourage you toward him when he does that? Does it give you a bit more bravery to then pursue Rome?"

"I-I suppose so," Tierney admitted once she'd thought about it a moment. "I think that if Rome didn't flirt with me the way he did, I don't think I'd ever have the nerve to *talk* to him, let alone—"

"Maybe you're right," Celeste interrupted thoughtfully. "Maybe I'm not sending out the right vibes to Alec. Maybe he has no concept of how strongly I feel about him."

"Yeah. Maybe you need to give him a few more obvious hints that you're not going to scratch his eyes out or something if he, like, asks you on a date or plants a big, old passionate kiss on you."

"I think you've got something there," Celeste said. "So you're comparing me to Rome—telling me that if Rome weren't so drop-dead gorgeous, you'd be a lot more confident when it came to…um…stuff with him? Right?"

Tierney didn't answer, for she was still pondering the question in her own mind.

"And you think that, because I'm supposedly this really pretty girl, Alec might be a little—"

"Intimidated, yeah," Tierney finished. "Add to that a few bad experiences with women and voilà! You've hit the nail on the head as to why Alec is dragging his feet." Reaching out and taking Celeste's hands in hers, Tierney firmly told her, "I promise that if you can somehow break through Alec's terror barrier in all this…he is *not* going to hurt you or break your heart or anything like that. I promise."

"How can you be so sure?" Celeste asked as the expression of heartfelt agony returned to her face. "I mean, what if I reach out a little more bravely and Alec rejects me and—"

"Oh, ladies…"

Tierney and Celeste glanced toward the path leading from the house to the gazebo and hot tub to see none other than the subjects of their conversation sauntering toward them, donning nothing but board shorts and each carrying a towel.

Tierney's heart nearly stopped and then instantly seemed to jump into her throat as she realized Rome was sauntering toward her, intent on joining them in the hot tub. His bronze, broad, brawny chest and washboard abs caused her nerves to begin jittering. She couldn't sit in a hot tub with him! She couldn't! Almost painfully she wished she looked like Celeste did in her bathing suit—like a Latin goddess modeling for a Victoria's Secret photo shoot. But instead she suddenly knew just what Mrs. Novak had meant on Halloween when she'd said she and Mr. Novak were plain, white, and boring—for Tierney instantly felt the same way in comparison with Rome and Celeste.

"Oh my gosh! He's going to see me in a bathing suit!" Tierney whispered in a panic.

But Celeste smiled. "Yeah, and you look great!" Celeste's smile switched places with a frown suddenly as she said, "Now Alec is going to find out just how big my hips really are."

It wasn't fair! Tierney could tell by the way Rome and Alec were walking that they didn't have one shred of worry about what Tierney and Celeste would think about how they looked in their bathing suits. Women, however, had so many body issues—even perfectly shaped women like Celeste, obviously. It wasn't fair!

Determining she'd simply have to stay in the hot tub all night if she had to—or at least until Rome wasn't around to see her exit it and find out how plain, white, and boring her body really was—Tierney sat down on the lowest seat in the hot tub, even though it meant she had to tip her head back to keep her chin above the water. Celeste did the same, and Tierney figured that if Celeste was nervous about Alec seeing *her*, then every woman must feel like she looked hideous in a bathing suit.

As the men stepped up onto the gazebo, Rome tossed his towel to the railing, stretched his massively muscular arms out at his sides, and teased, "Ladies…your entertainment for the evening has arrived."

"Entertainment, eh?" Celeste asked. "What are you going to do to entertain us, boys? You're already half undressed."

Tierney smiled as Alec's eyes widened with astonishment. She looked to Celeste and offered a nod of approval. Celeste was apparently going to jump right in flirting to encourage Alec.

"Ha-ha, Celeste," Rome said dryly.

Tierney wished she could just disappear as she watched Rome ascend the steps leading to the lip of the hot tub, obviously intent on joining her and Celeste right away. Alec strode around to the other side of the tub and climbed the second set of steps.

"And how was your day, Miss Bootylicious?" Rome asked Tierney, sitting next to her in the hot tub. Before she could answer, he reached into the water, taking hold of her arm and pulling her up to sit on the higher bench he was sitting on.

"Um…it was fine," Tierney answered. "Long but fine."

"Oh, I hear you there," He sighed, closing his eyes as he stretched his arms out, resting them on the hot tub lip. "I do hear you there."

"Me too," Alec agreed. "I'm hoping we have awhile before the next big storm."

"Heidi asked about you again today, Romeo," Celeste said to Rome—a rather naughty twinkle sparkling in her eyes.

"Great," Rome mumbled. "Did you tell her I moved away or something?"

"No," Celeste answered. "I just changed the subject."

"Thanks," Rome mumbled again.

"Oh, your mom told me she'll bring the toffee out in a minute, Celeste, okay?" Alec said. "She was just finishing breaking it up."

"Oh, good! I was afraid I'd have to go back on my promise that this would be a decadent night!" Celeste sighed. Looking to Tierney, she asked, "Decadent, right? That's what you said, right?"

Rome opened his eyes, smiled at Tierney, and chuckled. "Wow! What exactly did you have in mind, sugar cookie? Whatever it is, I'm game."

Tierney blushed as she felt his arm move from the lip of the hot tub to encircle her shoulders. She could feel the muscle definition of his bicep and forearm against her skin but tried to ignore it.

"Decadent…as in the toffee sounded perfectly decadent," she explained.

"Oh, sure," Rome teased. Leaning toward her, however, she felt him tug at her earlobe with his teeth a moment before he whispered, "And like I said…whatever you had in mind, I'm game."

Tierney wanted to get up and get out of the hot tub so badly! First of all, she was already feeling overly warm because of the water—actually thankful that Rome had moved her up a bit so that at least her shoulders were out and in the cool air. But his flirting had raised her temperature to an almost feverish height, and she knew she'd begin to perspire if she didn't cool off. And yet she wasn't about to stand up and let Rome see her plain, white, boring-in-a-bathing-suit self.

"You better watch out, Romeo," Alec chuckled. "My sister ain't no shrinking violet. She's liable to come up with something you'd have to step up to one day."

"Well, I certainly hope so," Rome said. "And if you call me Romeo one more time, I'll bust out your pretty front teeth."

"Alec," Celeste began then, slowly moving from the bottom bench of the hot tub to sit higher and very close next to Alec. Tierney smiled as she saw Alec gulp with nervousness mingled with desire.

"Yeah?" he managed.

"How come you've never asked me out?" Celeste's expression was purely that of a pouty, alluring seductress, and Tierney smiled and bit her lip to keep from giggling as Alec's face flushed red as a beet.

"What the hell's going on?" Rome whispered into Tierney's ear. "She's never been so forward like that with him."

"I know," Tierney breathed with delight.

"Well...I-I...well, what do you mean?" Alec stammered.

"I mean, why haven't you ever asked me out...like on a date?" Celeste repeated, playfully resting one arm on Alec's shoulder.

"W-well...I-I didn't think you wanted me to," Alec managed.

"Well, I do," Celeste brazenly confessed. "So will you? Ask me out on a date sometime, I mean?"

"Sure," Alec answered. "Sure. Just let me...think of something to do with you, and I will."

But Celeste smiled. "Oh, I'm certain you can think of something to do with me, Alec," she flirted.

"Dude!" Rome exclaimed with amusement. "You gotta come back at that one, man! Go on. Do it."

Alec gulped again. Then, exhaling a sigh, he smiled at Celeste and said, "Oh, I can think of a lot of things to do with you, Celeste. But it's already too hot in the hot tub, so we'll need to wait until a bit later, all right?"

Celeste giggled with sheer and observable pleasure. Linking her arms around Alec's arms, she nestled against him and said, "All right. I'll wait."

Rome looked to Tierney, frowning and grinning at the same time. *Did you say something to her?* he mouthed.

But Tierney shook her head, feigning ignorance.

"It's ready!" Mrs. Novak called as she stepped up onto the gazebo seemingly out of nowhere. She was wearing an old-fashioned apron made from fabric smattered with vintage-style images of turkeys and pumpkins, cranberries and gravy boats.

"Thanks so much, Mom," Celeste greeted as Nikki offered the plate of toffee to each hot-tubber in turn. "There's nothing like eating Mom's toffee while relaxing in the hot tub."

Tierney took a piece of toffee from the plate and said, "Thank you, Mrs.—I mean Nikki." As she took a bite, every salivary gland in her mouth was suddenly alive with pure pleasure! It was the best piece of toffee Tierney had ever eaten, and she couldn't help but mumble, "Mmm!"

"You're welcome, Tierney," Nikki said. "I'll just set this plate right here and leave you kids to your visiting." She set the plate on the stairs near Celeste and waved good-bye, saying, "You kids have fun!" as she hurried back up the path toward the house.

"Mmmm!" Alec sort of moaned. "I swear, Celeste, your mom's toffee is the best in the world!"

"I know, right?" Celeste said, reaching back to take another piece from the plate.

"It's even better than Almond Roca," Tierney offered. "And I thought nothing could ever be better than Almond Roca."

"I'll show you something better than Almond Roca, my little candy cane," Rome said, taking hold of Tierney's chin, turning her face toward his, and blessing her with a rather short but very intensely passionate kiss.

As he released her, Tierney opened her eyes and tried to steady the blissful, dizzy sensation that threatened to entirely overwhelm her.

She blushed when Alec said, "Man! You Latin dudes really do have all the moves."

"Latin women have the moves too, you know," Celeste said then, and Tierney's mouth dropped open in astonishment as Celeste leaned up, pressing a very sultry kiss to Alec's lips with her own.

"Wow!" Alec breathed, looking just as dazzled and dazed as Tierney felt. "What did your mom put in that toffee anyway?" he asked Celeste, smiling at her.

Celeste shrugged and retrieved another piece of toffee from the plate her mother had left for them.

"You've got goose bumps," Rome said, rubbing Tierney's shoulder with one hand. "Are you cold?" Dipping his other hand in the water, Rome drizzled warm water over Tierney's shoulders—apparently unaware that the reason for her goose bumps was not the cool, late-autumn air but the lingering effects of his very public, very wanton, and perfectly wonderful kiss.

CHAPTER NINE

"You two have fun," Alec said, holding Celeste's hand as she descended the hot tub stairs to the gazebo floor.

Tierney inhaled a deep breath, exhaling with discouragement as she noted that Celeste looked even more like a model when she *out* of the hot tub than when she was in.

When Celeste mentioned her fingers were getting pruny from being in the hot tub for so long, Alec had oh-so-chivalrously volunteered to escort her to the house. Furthermore, Rome had said he'd be in shortly, but when Alec asked whether Tierney wanted to go inside as well, she knew she didn't want Rome watching her walk to the house from his seat in the hot tub. Towel or no towel, there was nothing glamorous or attractive about a woman holding a towel around her shoulders and scurrying away in a bathing suit. Unless that woman was Celeste Novak, of course.

Tierney shook her head with disbelief as she watched Alec and Celeste stroll toward the house. No model or movie star who had ever lived could've matched the perfect swing of Celeste's hips—her natural grace.

Yet the moment Alec and Celeste were in the house, Tierney realized that, one way or the other, she would have to exit the hot tub eventually—and one way or the other, Rome was going to witness it. There was no getting around it, and therefore, since Tierney had been overheated for nearly half an hour already, when Rome lifted himself out of the hot tub to sit on the lip of it to cool off a moment, Tierney did too.

"It gets a little too hot for me sometimes," he said.

"Yeah," Tierney agreed, thankful that Rome's attention seemed fixed on her face instead of studying how the rest of her looked in her bathing suit. "I can never decide if I really like being in one...or if I just think I'm supposed to like being in one."

Rome smiled and chuckled. "I know what you mean. And then there's the whole body image thing we all struggle with, right?"

Tierney's eyes widened. Was he kidding? Was he really trying to intimate that *he* struggled with body image? Or was he struggling with the image of *her* body and just trying to make her feel better?

Either way, she shook her head and puffed a sigh of disgust.

"What?" he asked.

Frowning at him, she answered, "Oh, like you've ever had to worry about body image, Rome Novak."

Rome's brow puckered. "I think everybody struggles with it."

"I mean," Tierney continued, however, "is this even real?" she asked, poking at his stomach with her index finger. Leaning over to study his pectoral muscles more closely, she poked one of them as well, flinching when Rome suddenly flexed them to the same hardness as granite.

"What do you mean, is it real?" he asked, still frowning. "Of course it's real. And it's hard work too."

He was miffed, and Tierney struggled to keep from smiling. She'd hit a nerve in Rome Novak—an obviously very sensitive one.

Tierney's eyes narrowed as she decided to keep teasing him. After all, what comes around goes around. She studied him a moment, almost smiling when he straightened his posture, flexing every muscle in his torso.

"Hmm. I wonder," she mumbled. "You look a little *too* perfectly sculpted, if you ask me. Maybe all this...maybe you have those abdominal implants for men. Or maybe you had that etching thing done...that thing plastic surgeons are doing on movie star guys nowadays," she teased.

"Nope," Rome grumbled, reaching out and taking her hand. Placing her palm to one firm pectoral muscle, he said, "I'm as natural and real as you are." He slid her hand down over his six-packed abs.

"Yeah, yeah, yeah," Tierney said, snatching her hand away. "You have a great six-pack. I get it."

But Rome smiled. "Actually, I've got an eight-pack," he corrected her with a mischievous grin. "You just didn't look close enough. Or maybe you didn't know guys have these extra muscles they can work on to—"

"Okay, okay!" Tierney said, blushing and holding up one hand to indicate he'd defeated her. "You win that round. Consider me embarrassed."

Rome smiled and slid back into the hot tub.

Tierney had grown far more nervous since Alec and Celeste had returned to the house, and Rome was loving it! He truly never enjoyed being in the hot tub too long, but when he'd seen the chance to sequester Tierney, he'd jumped at it. Besides, it looked as if Celeste was finding a little gumption to let Alec know she was really interested in him. Therefore, Rome figured he and his sister could have the best of both worlds. Celeste could lead Alec into seclusion in the house, and he could have Tierney all to himself in the gazebo.

"I can't believe you even implied my abs were fake," he playfully grumbled. "Implants and etching...sheesh."

"I was teasing, and you know it," Tierney said.

Rome reached under the water and tickled the bottom of her foot. She flinched and giggled, and he made a mental note of the fact her feet were ticklish.

"So Celeste was pretty brazen tonight, huh?" he began.

"Yeah, she was," Tierney agreed. "She needs to be if she ever wants Alec to have the guts to go for her." She giggled, lowered her voice, and asked, "What do you think they're doing in there?"

Rome couldn't help himself. After all, she always made it so easy.

Turning a bit in his seat, he took hold of one of Tierney's ankles, placing a kiss on her knee and saying, "Probably the same thing we're going to be doing out here in a minute."

He almost felt bad when Tierney visibly gulped, the color draining from her face completely. But he only *almost* felt bad—so he gripped both her ankles (and a little more tightly), pulling and moving her closer to the edge of the hot tub as he kissed her knee again.

Releasing Tierney's ankles, Rome reached, taking hold of her hands instead, and placed a lingering kiss to the inside of her left wrist. He tugged at her arms, beckoning her to slip back into the water with him. When she didn't, he simply pulled her arm down further, pressing a long, moist kiss to the bend of it. He felt her trembling and hoped it was a signal that she was pleased with his affections.

Quickly he let his hands encircle her waist, pulling her to sit in the hot tub once more as he knelt in front of her. Rome liked the way Tierney's attention immediately settled on his mouth—an indication she was not averse to the idea of kissing.

Taking hold of her chin with one hand, while his other arm embraced her to pull her against him, Rome begin placing slow, seductive kisses to Tierney's neck and throat. He grinned to himself when he heard her sigh and felt her relax a little. As he kissed Tierney's neck, her ear, and then her temple, he felt her hands move to his shoulders—felt them slowly travel to the back of his neck and up into his hair in a titillating caress.

Unable to keep his attention sequestered to just her neck and cheeks any longer, Rome captured Tierney's mouth in a deeply driven, hot, and moist kiss he hoped would please her. Her willing response was affirmation that he had.

One classic Latin lover, indeed! Tierney thought to herself as she slipped to her knees when Rome pulled her all the way into his arms as they kissed. Rome's skin was so smooth, his muscles so defined. Tierney silently admitted to herself that she liked kissing him in the hot tub, even if the moist heat of his mouth mingled with the hot water of the hot tub gave her a sensation similar to running a fever. He was so strong—so incredibly good at kissing her.

Rome's mouth left hers for a moment, and Tierney inhaled a deep breath of satisfaction. He kissed her neck, mumbling, "Ahhh…the taste of chlorine on your skin…delicious."

Tierney breathed a light giggle, resting her head against Rome's shoulder a moment as he continued to slowly place a spray of playful kisses on her neck and shoulder.

"Why do you kiss me?" she heard herself ask unexpectedly—unexpectedly even to herself. It was if her mouth were out of sync with her brain.

"What do you mean?" Rome mumbled against her neck.

But Tierney's senses were working together once more, and she repeated, "Why do you kiss me?" After all, it was a legitimate question. There were many reasons guys kissed girls—some purely physical, others emotional, or preferably a balance of both. And considering that, like Alec and Celeste, Rome had never taken Tierney out, she wanted to know why he kissed her—wanted to hear him explain why.

Rome's straightened and studied her through narrowed, curious, and very alluring eyes. A delightfully naughty grin curved his lips, and he answered, "Because I like you, Tierney."

Although she was encouraged, his answer hadn't been as revealing as she'd hoped. Did he like her just physically (which she actually found hard to believe)? Or did he like her physically and emotionally (also hard to believe)?

Tierney rolled her eyes with exasperation. "Then *why* do you like me?"

"Because you're a good kisser," he answered, still grinning.

Tierney blushed. After all, she figured a guy like Rome—a masterful kisser like Rome—wouldn't continue kissing her if his answer hadn't been sincere. But it was an answer that also made her nervous—a purely physical reason.

"Really?" she asked as anxiety churned in her stomach a little.

Rome's smile broadened. "Come here," he said, directing her to sit next to him comfortably on the highest inner seat of the hot tub. "Now, what's all this questioning about? Here I have you secluded, in a very romantic setting I might add, and all you want to know is why this and why that. Can't you just live in the moment, sweet little booty babe?"

Tierney was embarrassed now. Why had she even asked him anything? He was right. They'd been kissing, and it had been wonderful! So why had she ruined it by asking why?

"I-I guess…I guess it just doesn't make much sense, and I—" she stammered.

"That I like you?" he interrupted. "Of course it makes sense," he playfully argued. "I mean, not only are you a hot, bootylicious honey, but you're brave, funny, smart, talented…did I mention sexy?"

But Tierney rolled her eyes. "No. I'm serious, Rome," she said. "We met once before—and under very abnormal circumstances—and I just find it hard to believe that a guy like you would—"

"What is it with you and your brother?" he grumbled. "He says the same thing about Celeste—that he can't imagine that 'a girl like her' would go for 'a guy like him' sort of thing." Rome leaned over and kissed Tierney's shoulder. "I mean, Celeste and I may have that stereotypical Latin blood running through our veins, but it's not like we're mutants or something. We're just passionate about things—life, love, food. You name it; we're passionate about it. That's all. When we see something we like…we just don't hold back. At least maybe not the way we should. So…I like you, Tierney. I knew it the moment I stepped out of that damn box dressed up like an idiot. So why shouldn't I kiss you, huh? I like you. I like kissing you. And I think you like me and like kissing me too, right?"

He kissed her shoulder again, and Tierney smiled. When she didn't immediately answer, however, Rome kissed her shoulder again and asked, "You *do* like kissing me, don't you, Tierney?" He kissed her neck, and Tierney bit her lip to keep from squealing with delight at the goose bumps racing over her spine. "I mean, the way you kiss me back…well, that should be enough positive proof for me." He kissed her cheek. "But now I kind of want you to confess it…out loud. Do you like kissing me as much as I like kissing you?"

Rome kissed the corner of her mouth—temptingly—trying to coax her into kissing him in return.

"Do you, Tierney?" he mumbled against her cheek.

"Yes," Tierney managed to breathe.

"Yes, what?" he impishly teased.

"Yes, Rome. I like kissing you," Tierney whispered.

She heard a triumphant chuckle rumble in his throat as he said, "Good. Then I'll show you what the best amenity of this hot tub gazebo thing is." Reaching behind him to the hot tub platform, Rome retrieved a little black remote and turned off the lights.

"Yep," he said. "Now nobody in the house can see what we're doing out here," he said.

Even for as warm as she was, Tierney began to tremble as she felt Rome's strong hand grip her right shoulder, his left taking hold of her chin. Her mouth began to water—a Pavlovian response—for she knew what was coming next.

Tierney couldn't help it. She couldn't help sighing with surrender when Rome's mouth met and mingled with her very, very willing and wanting one—a searing, wet kiss that utterly claimed not only her body and mind but also her heart—and her soul.

"I thought maybe you two had hard-boiled yourselves out there," Nikki said as Rome and Tierney entered the kitchen of the Novak home.

"Nope. Only parboiled, Mom," Rome said, setting the plate of leftover toffee on the counter. He kissed his mother's cheek and then put his arm around the shoulders of a shivering Tierney.

"Come on, Tierney," Celeste said, hopping down from the bar stool she'd been sitting on at the high kitchen counter facing the sink. "I'll show you where you can change."

Rome, however, gathered Tierney in his arms and teased, "Or you can just stay here like this, and I'll warm you up."

Tierney blushed vermilion—embarrassed that Rome would be so brazen in front of his mother but simultaneously delighted at his flirting.

"She's liable to get pneumonia if she doesn't dry off and put on something warm, Rome," Nikki told her son.

"But she has on something warm," Rome mumbled, pulling Tierney tightly against his body.

"Let the girl get dressed, Rome," Celeste said, taking Tierney's hand and fairly ripping her from Rome's arms. "You can grope her when she's warmed up."

Tierney looked to Nikki to see if she was astonished. But she only winked at Tierney, offering an understanding smile of encouragement.

"Oh, and Tiers," Alec began, "I accepted the Novaks' invitation to Thanksgiving dinner, okay?"

Tierney felt her eyes widen, even though she stammered, "O-of course." She looked to Nikki, smiled, and said, "Thank you."

"Oh, it'll be so fun!" Nikki exclaimed. She sighed. "I love Thanksgiving."

"Me too, Mom," Celeste added, tugging on Tierney's arm. "Come on, Tierney. Let's get you changed and warmed up, and then we can play a game or something."

"I saw the lights go out over at the gazebo, Rome Novak," Tierney heard Nikki say as Tierney followed Celeste down the hall toward the bathroom. "I hope you behaved yourself, young man."

"Don't I always behave myself, Mom?" Rome chuckled.

"Tierney!" Celeste exclaimed in a whisper as she closed the bathroom door behind them. Tierney smiled, for Celeste's beautiful eyes were as wide as the moon. "He asked me out! Alec! He really asked me out, and I didn't even have to hint again!"

"Oh, good!" Tierney exclaimed, giggling. "I knew he would. He just needed some reassurance that you wouldn't turn him down, I think."

Celeste frowned. "Why in the world would he think I would turn him down?" she asked. But Tierney just laughed, knowing that if Celeste didn't get it after their talk in the hot tub, she probably never would.

"So? When are you guys going out?" Tierney asked, catching Celeste's excitement.

"Friday," Celeste answered with near giddiness. "Alec didn't say what we'd be doing...but I'm so glad he asked me out that I wouldn't care if we just sat and stared at the wall together."

"Wow! Does he know you're this easy to please?" Tierney teased.

Celeste shrugged. "I don't know...but I am. I just want to spend time alone with him, you know? Without Rome or anybody else around. You know what I mean, right?"

"I do," Tierney admitted—for there was nothing in all the world she'd ever enjoyed more than the times she'd spent alone in Rome's company.

Celeste sighed and retrieved a towel from the linen closet of the bathroom. "You can rinse off in the shower, and your clothes are still in here. Then come out and we'll play a game."

"Okay," Tierney said.

"I'm so excited!" Celeste whispered, grinning like a madwoman as she closed the door behind her.

Tierney laughed, knowing Celeste was referring to her date with Alec—not playing a game after Tierney finished changing.

She was proud of Alec. Tierney knew the depth of the courage he would've had to muster in order to ask Celeste out—regardless of the encouragement Celeste herself had offered. She began to wonder what Alec would plan as their date, and that led her back to a question that had begun to haunt her ever since Celeste had mentioned it when they were all in the hot tub. Why didn't Rome ask Tierney out? After all, they'd already kissed on several occasions—and yet he still hadn't asked her out.

And as it always does when fatigue, darkness, and separation from a loved one occurs, doubt about Rome's feelings toward her began to creep into Tierney's mind once more.

Still, she pushed her fears and doubts to the back of her mind as she quickly rinsed the hot tub water and chemicals from her body, dressed, and hurried back out to the kitchen to meet the others.

"So I was thinking," Rome began as he moved his Rudolph Monopoly token six spaces on the Rudolph the Red-Nosed Reindeer Monopoly board.

"Well, that would explain the smoke coming out of your ears," Alec teased. "And I own that Donner's Cave property, so you owe me rent. Pay up, buddy."

"Scrooge," Rome mumbled as he counted out fourteen dollars in Monopoly money and tossed it at Alec.

"Thanks, man," Alec said, adding the paper bills to his quickly growing hoard. "Now what were you saying?"

Rome sat back in his chair, grumbled, "I always lose this game," and then, looking to Tierney, continued, "I was thinking that if Alec here can find the guts to ask Celeste out on an official date, then I oughta be able to dig up enough courage to ask you out, right?"

Tierney's eyes widened. Was she dreaming? Maybe she'd fallen asleep at the table, waiting for everyone to take a turn at Rudolph the Red-Nosed Reindeer Monopoly, and was simply imagining that Rome was implying he was going to ask her out.

"Wh-why would you need courage for that?" she stammered (just in case she really was awake).

Rome shrugged. "Because you might turn me down."

Tierney frowned. Was he kidding? They'd spent half an hour making out in the hot tub earlier that same evening! Did he really think she wouldn't want to go out with him?

"I would never turn you down!" she exclaimed—still astonished, still wondering whether she were awake.

Rome's lips curved into a naughty yet wonderfully wonderful grin. "Never?" he teased.

Celeste giggled, and Tierney blushed.

"Never within reason. You know what I meant."

"Then you'll go out with me...on a real date thing?" Rome asked, leaning toward her.

Tierney shook the Rudolph the Red-Nosed Reindeer Monopoly dice in her hand and let them drop on the board before answering, "Of course."

"Okay," Rome said, rubbing his hands together as if he'd just won something. "How about Monday night? I'll pick you up at seven?"

"Monday night it is," Tierney said, moving her Hermey the Elf token six spaces.

She landed on the Misfit Island Guest Chambers property, rolling her eyes when Alec clapped his hands and said, "I own that, Tiers! You owe me rent. Pay up."

Looking to Celeste, Tierney said, "He never, ever wins Monopoly. That's why he's so excited."

Celeste giggled. "Well, he hasn't won yet!" Celeste rolled her dice and moved her Sam the Snowman token three spaces.

As Alec and Celeste began to barter over the sales of certain properties from one another, Rome leaned over and whispered in Tierney's ear. "I mean, I think we're ready for the next step, don't you? An actual date?"

Tierney shivered with delight at the feel of his warm breath on her neck. Giggling a little, she turned to him and whispered, "The *next* step? Usually a date is the *first* step, you know."

"Well, maybe...for most people," he breathed. "But we're not most people, right?"

"I guess not," Tierney said, shivering with delight again.

"Dude!" Alec exclaimed. "Get a room, man," he chuckled.

"Don't tempt me," Rome said, returning his attention to the game board as Alec rolled the dice and moved his Bumble the Abominable token five spaces.

Tierney felt herself blush as Celeste said, "Sorry, Tierney. Rome's filter thins out when he's tired."

Rome covered his mouth and yawned. "That's true, Tierney. Sorry," he said, leaning back in his chair. "And it's the only reason Alec is whipping my butt at this game too."

"I'm kicking your butt because you stink at this game, dude," Alec countered.

"Just wait, man. Rudolph gets the best of the Bumble in the end…and *I* have the Rudolph token, so watch out," Rome said.

"Dream on, Romeo…dream on," Alec teased.

Tierney smiled as Alec and Rome continued to talk trash about the game. But she wasn't smiling about their trash talk (though it was hysterical, listening to them argue over tokens based on an old TV Christmas special). She was smiling about the fact Rome had asked her out on an official date! Monday couldn't come quickly enough. She knew Celeste must feel the same way about her upcoming date with Alec—about Friday. It was all too wonderful to be true, and she bit the inside of her cheek a little—just to make sure that it was.

Late that night, as Tierney lay in bed, glad that Rome had pulled out the Rudolph the Red-Nosed Reindeer Monopoly win after all, she sighed as she thought about her time in the hot tub with Rome. She wondered if he knew how completely he owned her—all of her. She wondered if he enjoyed kissing her as much as she enjoyed kissing him.

Closing her eyes at last, she thought about nothing but Rome. No worries pricked at her mind—nothing. No worries about how in the world she would ever exist on just a part-time salary, about whether Celeste would break Alec's heart, or whether she would ever have to deal with Elias Potts alone again—none of it entered her mind. There was only Rome—handsome, gorgeous Rome Novak and his perfect lover's caresses—his perfect, stereotypical Latin lover's kiss.

CHAPTER TEN

"So how do you feel about going full time, Tierney?" Jessica asked.

Tierney could not hide her relief and delight. "I would love it! Thank you so much, Jessica!"

Working at the florist full time meant Tierney would gain the financial self-reliance she so desperately craved. Oh, she knew Alec was in no hurry for her to get her own place—knew he'd help her out financially for as long as she needed him to, and willingly. But Tierney needed to know for herself that she could make it on her own, and Jessica's offer of full-time employment was the beginning.

"You're just so talented, Tierney," Jessica remarked. "I can't believe the arrangements your mind conceives. It just amazes me. I feel so fortunate that you moved to Leavenworth—as if you were meant to come to work for me."

Even for the little nagging anxiety that was pulling at the back of Tierney's mind where Elias Potts was concerned—for certainly there would be a higher chance that she may indeed run into Elias more often now—Tierney was ecstatic about Jessica's offer.

Therefore, she pushed her discomfort regarding Jessica's husband to the very farthest corners of her mind and simply enjoyed the relief of knowing she would make money to survive on her own.

In fact, it seemed nothing could dampen her heightened spirits that lovely Monday in November. Still, as the snow began to fall on her way home, Tierney wondered if her ravenously anticipated first official date with Rome was going to have to be postponed.

The snow was piling up quickly, and as Tierney entered the house to see Alec decked out in his snowplowing gear, her heart sank to the pit of her stomach with a painful thud.

"You guys are going to be out all night again, aren't you?" she asked her brother.

Alec exhaled a heavy sigh of compassion as he nodded.

"It's not fair," Tierney grumbled. "You got to have your date with Celeste. Why is it my evening that has to be ruined? Stupid snow."

"I'm sorry, Tiers," Alec said, "really...but it can't be helped. I swear that if I could control the weather, I'd postpone this storm so you could have your scandalous evening with Rome. You know that, right?"

"I know," Tierney sighed as her shoulders began to droop. "And it wasn't going to be scandalous, for your information. Just...just fun."

Her cell rang. The caller ID said *Rome*, and she answered, "Hello?"

"Hey there, bootylicious booty babe," Rome greeted, causing a broad smile to spread across Tierney's face. Date or no date, the sound of Rome's voice always titillated her.

"Hi," Tierney giggled.

"Are you up for a little change of plans?" he asked. "Not a postponement or cancellation...just a little change in what I originally had in mind."

"I'm up for anything," Tierney answered as her hopes began to soar once more.

"Oooo! Anything?" Rome teased.

"Yep," Tierney ventured.

"Good! Then wrap yourself in one of those way-too-sexy sweaters of yours and those cute little snow boots and meet me in front of your house in thirty minutes, okay?"

"Okay," she answered.

Tierney's heart was hammering so hard the rhythm was echoing in her ears. Rome hadn't canceled their date after all! In fact, the idea of being with him all night again as he plowed sounded even better than a regular date with him. After all, a regular date lasted only a few hours. With any luck, Tierney would be with Rome all night long!

"All right then. See you in a while, my little pancake batter bubble," Rome flirted.

Tierney giggled, "Bye." She loved Rome's ridiculous terms of endearment.

"I take it by the crazed look in your eyes that your date with Rome is still on, huh?" Alec asked, smiling.

"Yep," Tierney said.

Alec shook his head with amusement. "If I had the guts, I'd call up Celeste and ask her to go with me too. But…I don't want to push my luck, you know?"

Tierney frowned. "Alec, ask her! If she can't go, she'll tell you why, and if she can, she will. You've got to reach out and take hold of her, Alec. She likes you!"

"It seems like she does," he mumbled, retrieving his cell from his pocket and staring at it.

"Do it, Alec," Tierney demanded. "Just call her."

Inhaling a deep breath of courage, he did call Celeste. And as Tierney listened to the conversation, as she watched a smile of relief and excitement spread across her brother's handsome face, she knew it would be a night to remember for Alec as well as herself.

"Are you ready for some action?" Rome asked as he reached over, assisting Tierney with her seatbelt.

"I was born ready," Tierney ventured.

"Ooo! Ho!" Rome laughed. "You're already frisky tonight, huh?"

"Frisky?" Tierney asked, her eyes widening.

Still smiling, Rome shook his head. "I didn't mean frisky in a…you know…*frisky* way. I meant *frisky*, like a kitten with a new catnip toy thing."

Tierney giggled. "Well then, yes, I am feeling frisky already…just like a kitten with a new catnip toy."

Rome's smile broadened. "Can I be the toy?"

Tierney blushed, rolled her eyes, and shook her head with disbelief. "You're unbelievable."

"No. But the date I had planned *was*," Rome grumbled with discouragement.

"Really?" Tierney couldn't help but ask.

"Yep," Rome assured her. "I had it all planned out—a romantic sleigh ride outside of town, complete with jingle bells, a warm blanket to snuggle up under, a thermos full of hot chocolate. I think you would've enjoyed it. And I was hoping to make it onto your 'top five best dates' list."

For some reason, Tierney found that she was feeling a bit more confident than usual in that moment. Perhaps it was the smile on Alec's face as he'd left to pick up Celeste. Or maybe it was the fact that she now had full-time employment. And though she suspected the reason was the fact Rome hadn't canceled their date altogether, it didn't matter. What mattered was she did feel a bit more frisky than usual.

And so she ventured a flirtatious compliment. "This is already on the top of my list, Rome…because, after all, I *am* with you."

"Frisky!" Rome chuckled. "And I like it."

Tierney blushed and looked forward, out into the blowing snow.

"But, since our romantic sleigh ride had to be postponed, I figured a guy has to make do with what he has," Rome began. "So I still brought the thermos of hot chocolate, a warm blanket to snuggle under—just in case we end up in a snowdrift or something—the soft music. And for a little added adventure, I figure I'll teach you how to drive the truck and operate the plow tonight…just in case you ever need to fill in for me if I'm sick one night or something."

Tierney laughed at the idea of herself operating a snowplow blade. "It sounds like the first date of a lifetime to me," she told him.

Rome winked at her and said, "Baby, I promise you it will be a first date you'll never forget."

Tierney shook her head, still smiling (and blushing a little) as Rome lowered the plow blade and drove them off into the dark, snowy night.

Eight hours later, Tierney didn't even care that she only had five hours to catch a little sleep and get ready before having to be at work—for her first official date with Rome had been magnificent! Hot chocolate, warm and entertaining conversation, even an adventure when the truck had gotten high-centered and Rome had had to get out and dig it out—it truly had been the greatest first date Tierney had ever experienced. The fact that it eventually came to an end only after a deliciously passionate hour of kissing made it all the more wonderful—so wonderful that the only thing that finally wiped the happy smile from Tierney's face was the sight that met Tierney when she walked into the floral shop at 8 AM.

Jessica was not in the front of the shop as she usually was. Instead, Tierney found Elias Potts there.

"Good morning, Tierney," Elias greeted as Tierney removed her coat and hung it on the coatrack in the back of the shop. "Jessica is home with the flu or something today. I told her I'd fill in this morning, but you'll be by yourself for the afternoon. Hope you don't mind."

Tierney certainly didn't mind being by herself in the afternoon, but she certainly *did* mind that Elias would be there all morning. The emotional red flags in her mind began to slowly unfurl—and she tried to keep them in check. After all, what could the man possibly do to harm her, there in the broad light of day, in a floral shop?

As it turned out, Elias was more annoying than anything else. He spent the whole morning following Tierney around the shop asking insipid questions. And although he drove her nearly batty, he didn't do or say anything inappropriate. By the time he'd left for the day at one PM, Tierney had convinced herself that perhaps she was just being paranoid where Elias was concerned. It seemed it was one of those instances where, though her red flags were keeping her on guard, Tierney was safe enough. And besides, what woman in her right mind would quit the only full-time job she'd ever had (and needed) over the fact that the boss's husband simply creeped her out?

The two weeks before Thanksgiving were fantastic for not only Tierney but Alec as well. Rome had begun to call, text, or drop by to see Tierney every day—and it was marvelous! He always kissed her good-bye, always sat with his arm around her shoulders whenever they were together, and even managed to find a night when he didn't have to plow to take her on the romantic sleigh ride he'd planned before.

Tierney was so in love with Rome, there were times she couldn't breathe—times she'd find herself weeping in bed with fear that he would lose interest in her and move on. She tried to convince herself to live in the moment—enjoy his attention, affections, and company while they were focused on her. But the truth was, her heart would begin to break every time she'd think of Rome not wanting her anymore—not liking her anymore—not kissing her anymore.

Alec was as torn up over Celeste as Tierney was over Rome, and it was many a night the siblings spent consoling and encouraging one another. For Alec's sake, Tierney knew that Celeste would marry Alec in a single heartbeat if he asked her. She never revealed the fact to Alec, being that she knew his relationship with Celeste needed to take its natural course. But the more she saw Alec and Celeste moving toward a serious commitment, the more Tierney began to think that it didn't make any sense for a brother and sister to end up marrying a brother and sister. Things just didn't work out that way in the world—where everybody had their happy ending. Percentages probably proved it.

Therefore, as much time as Tierney spent in the bliss of having Rome's attention, she spent nearly as much time waiting for it to end. It wasn't a healthy way to think, she knew—but she couldn't seem to help it. When added to her fears of Rome's growing bored with her, Tierney's anxieties over Elias Potts nearly overwhelmed her at times.

Elias had begun to spend more and more time at the floral shop each day—whether or not his wife was present—and Tierney's emotional red flags were full out flapping in the wind most of the time he was around. Still, she needed her job, and she loved the floral arranging. And so she endured—just tried to ignore her worries—made certain that she focused on thinking of Rome as much as possible. And in the end, everything seemed to be rolling along fine at work.

So, figuring that life was simply a rollercoaster of joys and worries, Tierney settled in to life in Leavenworth—to her job, to watching Alec and Celeste's romance erupt, and, most importantly, to falling more deeply in love with Rome at every turn.

And all at once, it was Thanksgiving Day. Tierney found herself wrapped in the warm and welcoming embrace of Nikki and Edward Novak's home.

Mrs. Novak had asked that Tierney arrive first thing in the morning to help her and Celeste with the pies, rolls, stuffing, and other delicious wonders that would embellish the turkey in making the Thanksgiving meal. Tierney had been more than willing—and not just because of Rome. Tierney and Celeste had become close, finding they had so much in common that it was uncanny at times. Furthermore, Rome and Celeste's parents were even more wonderful than Tierney had first imagined. Always welcoming, always friendly, Nikki Novak was a sharp contrast to Glynnis O'Brien. Loving, compassionate, and always putting others before herself it seemed, Nikki was someone Tierney wanted to emulate and enjoyed being around. Edward Novak was a jewel as well, and Tierney loved to observe him and Alec together. Edward was good for Alec. Someone to be emulated as well, it was obvious that Edward had a true admiration of Alec and what he'd accomplished in his young life, as well as for the kind of character Alec owned. The camaraderie with not only Rome but also his father was a great gift to Alec, and Tierney knew her brother recognized it.

And so it was that on Thanksgiving Day morning, Tierney, Celeste, and Nikki baked, cooked, and visited in the kitchen while Rome, Alec, and Mr. Novak prepared for the "after-dinner festivities," as Nikki referred to them.

"And then," Celeste began with a sigh, "then…Alec pressed his lips to mine for the very first time. I thought I was going to die because, seriously, I swear I couldn't breathe for a minute!" Celeste explained as her mother smiled and continued to knead the dinner roll dough.

"How romantic!" Nikki sighed. "I love hearing about a couple's first kiss…as long as it was a good kiss, that is."

Tierney smiled. "I guess it wouldn't be much fun if the first kiss were a bad kiss, right?"

"Eww, no!" Nikki mumbled.

"But my first kiss with Alec," Celeste began, "it was magical! And, Tierney, Alec is a *great* kisser, by the way."

Tierney laughed.

"Too much information?" Celeste asked.

But Tierney shook her head. "Not at all," she answered. "I'm just so glad he finally manned up and kissed you!"

"Me too," Nikki interjected.

"Mom!" Celeste exclaimed in a giggle.

But Nikki shrugged. "Well, it's true. If you want to know the truth of it, I've been wanting that boy to kiss you since the day I met him, Celeste."

"Mother!" Celeste scolded, although it was obvious she was wildly delighted. Gasping then, Celeste said, "Oh, Mom, you *have* to tell Tierney about your first kiss with Daddy. It was so romantic!"

"Oh, I'm sure Tierney doesn't want to hear about that, honey," Nikki mumbled.

"Of course she does!" Celeste assured her mother, however.

"Of course I do!" Tierney chirped with sincere excitement.

"You will love this story, Tiers," Celeste assured her friend. "It's, like, the best first kiss story ever!"

Tierney smiled as Celeste's contagious excitement overtook her as well.

"Well, I was sixteen," Nikki began, "and Eddie was the guy every girl was in love with, you know?"

"Oh yes," Tierney assured her, thinking instantly of Rome.

"Anyway, I had been admiring Eddie from afar, as it were…just like every other female on the face of the earth that had ever seen him," Nikki continued. "Well, it was Halloween…"

Tierney's smile broadened. She looked to Celeste, who winked at her with understanding. Tierney guessed she was about to find out why the Novak family did Halloween in such unmatched style.

"And a bunch of kids from high school had planned this Halloween party out at the old asylum north of town," Nikki explained.

"An *insane* asylum," Celeste whispered aside to Tierney.

"It was a really creepy place," Nikki continued. "You know the type. You see them all the time in movies and stuff. Turn of the century type thing…the last century, that is. It closed down in, like, 1927 because of 'strange happenings'…yadda yadda yadda. Anyway, to this day, I've never seen any place that was spookier. So naturally, the kids at school decided that was exactly the place to have a Halloween party." Nikki paused, smiling as she silently reminisced a moment.

"We spent all day decorating with fake cobwebs, making refreshments, root beer…the works," Nikki explained. "The guys set up this haunted house tour—really freaky, by the way—and everyone was stoked about the party. Some people had dates and stuff, but I just went with a bunch of my girlfriends." Nikki smiled at Tierney. "You know, the old safety in numbers thing. I was pretty freaked out about going to the old asylum at *all*, let alone on Halloween. Anyway, me and my friend arrived at the party." She laughed. "I was dressed as Princess Leia, of course."

"Of course," Celeste sighed. She looked to Tierney, adding, "Mom and Rome…they're, like, Star Wars freaks." She shook her head. "In fact, ask Rome anything about, like, life and stuff, and he finds a way to relate it to Star Wars." Celeste shrugged. "It's hereditary or something. I mean, I spent my first three Halloweens dressed in an Ewok costume."

"And so did Rome," Nikki laughed.

"Sorry, Mom. Keep going," Celeste mumbled as she fluted the edges of a piecrust.

"Well, I walked into the asylum, dressed as Princess Leia, and right away I noticed this guy dressed as Batman, right?" Nikki continued. "I didn't know who it was, of course—because Batman always wears a mask when he's Batman. Anyway, there was this Batman guy, and for some reason, I just couldn't take my eyes off him. Of course, nobody could, but there was something—I don't know—like, magnetic about him that night." Nikki sighed, smiling at the memory. "So the night wears on, people start dancing—which is kind of morbid, now that I think about it, dancing in an old insane asylum. But anyway, people are dancing when all of a sudden, Batman walks right up to me! Me—plain old Princess Leia! Batman walked right up to me and asked me to dance." Nikki smiled and sighed again. "I'll never forget that moment…or the song. Batman asked me to dance to—"

"'True' by Spandau Ballet," Celeste couldn't keep from interjecting.

"Ooo! I love that song!" Tierney exclaimed.

"I know, right?" Nikki added. "*This much is true-hoo…this much is true-hoo-hoo,*" she sang.

Looking at Celeste, Tierney joined in as Celeste and her mother repeated, "*This much is true-hoo, this much is true-hoo-hoo…I know, I know, I know this much is true!*"

"I love that song," Celeste giggled.

"Yeah, me too," Nikki sighed.

"So? You danced with him, and…" Tierney prodded.

Nikki sighed and smiled again. "I did. And I still had no idea who it was. I mean, in my innermost thoughts, I was wishing it was Edward Novak, but I knew it was probably just some other guy. Still, the longer we danced, the more I began to wonder if it really was Eddie. It was weird. It *felt* like Eddie Novak to me, even for as dark as it was and the fact I couldn't really see his eyes well because of the mask." She paused again, plopping the dinner roll dough into a greased bowl to rise.

"Well, when the song ended," Nikki continued, "the hot Batman didn't say a word to me. He just took my hand and began to lead me to the corner of the room, right? I wasn't sure what to do. I mean, I wasn't at all sure it was Eddie, but I didn't feel afraid or anything, so I just went where he led."

Elias Potts intruded on Tierney's thoughts for a moment—but she pushed him away, focusing on Nikki's story.

"So once we're out of pretty much everyone's line of vision, sexy Batman gently pushes me up against the wall, right?" Nikki explained.

Celeste giggled and whispered, "I *love* this part!"

"Then sexy Batman says to me, 'Nikki, I have been in love with you since you were a freshman, and I'm telling you right now that I'm going to marry you someday…no matter what I have to do!' And then, Batman reached up and pushed back his mask…and I nearly dropped dead when I saw that it really was Edward Novak!"

Tierney smiled as empathetic butterflies took flight in her stomach. It was a truly romantic story! She understood why Celeste loved it so much.

Nikki giggled. "Of course, I was standing there with my mouth gaping open like a hooked bass." She shook her head. "I must've looked like such an idiot. But the next thing I knew, Edward Novak was kissing me!"

"Closed or open mouths, Mom?" Celeste asked, winking at Tierney.

Nikki grinned. "Closed…at first. And then, wham! It was awesome!" she answered.

Tierney squealed in unison with Celeste, delighted by the story of Mr. and Mrs. Novak's first kiss. It was the stuff of old movies—of teenage romance novels—of dreams.

All three women laughed and blushed, gasping when Mr. Novak suddenly appeared from the adjoining family room, commenting, "And what are you girls up to? It sounds like a henhouse in here."

Tierney blushed, feeling as if she'd just been caught with her hand in the cookie jar. But Celeste simply rushed to her father, throwing her arms around his neck in an affectionate embrace.

"Oh, Daddy!" she giggled. "I can just see you…all dressed up as Batman and putting the moves on Princess Leia!"

Mr. Novak smiled. "Oh, that story again, huh?"

"We were just exchanging 'first kiss' stories," Nikki explained.

"Were you now?" Edward Novak asked. He kissed his daughter on the cheek and then stepped out of her embrace as he began to stride toward Nikki. "Hmmm. Maybe we should have a reenactment, huh?"

Nikki giggled as her husband pushed her up against the wall and kissed her, open-mouthed and very, very passionately.

"I see they're at it again," Rome mumbled as he entered the room. Tierney watched him walk to the refrigerator and open it up to begin scrounging around inside. Her heart fluttered and her stomach flip-flopped as she watched him. He was so handsome! He was so romantic! He was so, so, so the only man she wanted to spend forever with!

Retrieving two pieces of cold pizza from the refrigerator, Rome winked at Tierney before heading back into the family room. Just his glance would've set her heart on fire, but his wink nearly melted her. How could it be that a man could wink and send shivers running up and down her spine? Other men had winked at her, but there was something in Rome Novak's wink that was different. It was flirtatious, implicative, dazzlingly attractive.

Edward finished kissing his wife, snitched a piece of leftover piecrust pastry from the pile next to the pie Celeste was working on, and followed his son back into the family room.

"I can imagine it, you know," Tierney said as she returned to dicing the onions meant to be sautéed for the stuffing. "Batman and Princess Leia…a smoldering kiss shared in an old, abandoned insane asylum on Halloween night. It must've been *so* romantic."

"Oh, it was," Nikki sighed, still blushing from her husband's affectionate attention.

"I love that story, Mom," Celeste said. "Thanks for telling it again. I can never hear it too many times."

"It was your favorite when you were little," Nikki reminded, "though I always left out the part about the asylum being for the mentally ill…at least until you were old enough that I hoped it wouldn't give you nightmares."

All three women laughed, and Tierney moved to chopping celery stalks next.

"So?" Nikki asked then. "What about you and Rome, Tierney?"

Tierney looked up to see both Nikki and Celeste staring at her with expectant, knowing smiles.

"M-me and Rome?" Tierney stammered.

"Yeah," Celeste answered. "Tell us about your first kiss with Rome."

Tierney gulped and looked to Nikki. How could she possibly tell Rome's mother about their first kiss? His mother?

"Uh...um...you mean the one at my bridal shower or the first real one, after I moved here, I mean?" Tierney ventured.

"Oooo!" Nikki and Celeste exclaimed in unison.

"Definitely both!" Celeste giggled.

"Yes, definitely!" Nikki agreed.

Tierney felt herself blushing. How could she possibly recount two of the most wonderful moments of her entire life to the mother of the man who had created them?

"Don't be shy, Tierney," Celeste encouraged. "Mom and I both know Rome can't keep his lips off of you," she giggled.

Tierney blushed, and Nikki said, "Just pretend I'm one of your other friends...instead of Rome's mom."

Tierney smiled and laughed a little. "Well, that's easier said than done, I'm afraid."

"Just tell us the one at your bridal shower, Tiers," Celeste suggested. "We'll let you off the hook after that."

"Okay," Tierney agreed. Inhaling a deep breath—for it was a hard thing to discuss in front of Rome's mother—Tierney began, "Well, I was at my bridal shower...feeling sick to my stomach and like I was about to make the biggest mistake of my life."

"Mm hmmm," Celeste prodded.

"And someone—I don't even remember who—someone rolls in this giant box. It was wrapped in shiny red paper with a black velvet bow, and when I read the card, everyone was sure that a male stripper was going to pop out of it."

"Well, I wouldn't put it past Rome to strip down to his panties at least," Celeste giggled.

"I'm sure your brother does not wear *panties*, Celeste," Nikki corrected.

"You know what I mean," Celeste clarified. "His boxer briefs or whatever. That's what I meant."

"Anyway," Nikki urged Tierney to continue.

"Well, I read the card from Alec, telling me that he'd sent one classic Latin lover with a very special message," Tierney explained. "And then I pulled this handle thing to open the box, and there he was—Rome, all dressed up like some perfect lover that had stepped right out of my imagination."

Nikki and Celeste were both smiling at Tierney with grins as wide as the Amazon River.

"And?" Celeste asked.

"And…and I couldn't believe it," Tierney admitted. "Someone started some music, and Rome and I…well, we danced." She smiled at the memory, goose bumps breaking over her arms just as if it were happening all over again. "Rome assured me that he was not a stranger, at least to Alec, and then he told me what Alec had sent him to tell me."

"That you shouldn't marry that Dillon guy," Celeste couldn't keep from answering.

"Exactly," Tierney affirmed.

"And then?" Nikki prodded.

"Well," Tierney began again, "Rome told me what Alec wanted him to…added his own thoughts, as well. But I was afraid, afraid of making my mother angry, of running to a life that was so unfamiliar. Rome knew it—I know he knew it—because then he told me he thought I needed something more to convince me…something other than Alec's message. Rome kissed me slowly at first—you know, like he didn't want to freak me out…even though I was totally freaked out already. But all of a sudden…all of a sudden I was kissing him back, and we were…were like totally, you know…"

"Making out?" Celeste offered.

"Kind of…yeah," Tierney admitted. "And I realized that in all my life, I'd never felt anything like that. And I just wanted him to kiss me forever. I wanted to kiss him forever. And I knew that if a complete stranger could make me feel that way…then it would be so very thoroughly the wrong thing to do to marry Dillon. When the kiss ended, Rome said one last word to me, and I…I…"

"What was the word?" Celeste asked in desperation when Tierney failed to finish her sentence.

Tierney looked up to see both Nikki and Celeste staring at her with wide, wondering eyes. "Run," she answered. "He told me to run. And I did, thinking that would be the last time I ever laid eyes on that classic Latin lover who had changed my life...in more ways than he would ever know."

There was silence for a moment as Nikki and Celeste seemed to be taking it all in. But at last it was Nikki who spoke first.

Smiling, she exhaled a sigh of satisfaction and said, "That is the best first kiss story I have ever heard in my entire life!"

"Actually, me too," Celeste said. "I mean, don't get me wrong. I'm still reeling from the first time Alec kissed me. But *that* is such a crazy, wonderful story, Tierney. I love it!"

Rome smiled as he leaned up against the family room wall. Oh, there were certainly some benefits to knowing when to hang around and eavesdrop, even if it were a tacky invasion of privacy. Still, hearing Tierney tell the story of the first kiss she and Rome had shared—hearing the emotion evident in her voice—it gave Rome more courage and determination where she was concerned, even more than he'd owned a moment before.

Closing his eyes, Rome thought back to that first kiss—the one he'd nearly had to force on Tierney. Yet he hadn't had to press her for very long before she'd accepted and then reciprocated a kiss that usually only happened between a man and a woman who were seriously involved with one another.

Damn, he was glad he'd kissed her that day.

CHAPTER ELEVEN

Tierney had never enjoyed a Thanksgiving more—never. Helping to prepare dinner was not only educational where cooking was concerned but also wonderfully entertaining and fun. Nikki, Celeste, and Tierney had begun by sharing first kiss stories, and from there the conversation only became more engaging. Tierney couldn't remember a time when she'd giggled, laughed, and even wept so much. It was marvelous.

And Thanksgiving dinner? Well, Thanksgiving dinner was like nothing Tierney had ever tasted! There certainly was a vast difference between home-cooked food and catered or restaurant food—no matter how high-end the caterer or restaurant was. The turkey was moist and tender, and Nikki had seasoned it with butter, salt and pepper, and herbs. Tierney had watched with interest when Nikki had stuffed the turkey's body cavities with chopped onion, celery, apples, and fresh sprigs of thyme, rosemary, and sage. Nikki had explained that their family preferred the stuffing be served separately so as not to taste so much like turkey. The Novak family preferred the purity of the cornbread and seasonings, with only a little water added for moisture and consistency. And when Tierney tasted Nikki's stuffing, she understood why! The flavors of the fresh herbs Nikki Novak used were so comforting and delicious that Tierney nearly ate herself sick on just stuffing alone.

Then there was everything else that was so good to eat—deep-orange-colored yams covered in a sticky, sweet syrup made of butter, brown sugar, and cloves, homemade dinner rolls served warm and slathered in melting butter, and wonderfully lumpy mashed potatoes served with the most savory gravy Tierney had ever tasted. It truly, truly was the best meal Tierney had ever eaten, and she knew by the way Alec kept nodding at her that he felt exactly the same way.

After the massive meal, Tierney was surprised when, although Mr. and Mrs. Novak worked together to quickly put the food away and clear and rinse the dishes, everything else was left to sit. Apparently the Novak family preferred to spend the first few hours following their meal just sitting around and visiting. Sometimes Mr. Novak would doze off for a moment or two in his well-worn armchair, sending everyone into amused snickering when he'd begin to snore and then wake up with a, "I'm not sleeping. I'm just resting my eyes," comment.

Nikki sat in a comfortable slider rocker, smiling and laughing as Celeste and Rome told stories of Thanksgivings gone by—like the time Mr. Novak had purchased a very fresh turkey for Thanksgiving dinner, and after having helped to "pluck and gut" it (as Rome described), neither Rome nor Celeste had any appetite when the turkey was served.

Alec and Tierney even shared tales of some of their Thanksgivings, and Tierney found it to be almost therapeutic in a manner. What she had once looked back on as sad, disappointing, and sometimes nightmarish now seemed humorous. As she sat on the sofa with Rome's strong arm around her shoulder—as she watched Celeste cuddle up against Alec like a sleepy kitten—the atmosphere in the Novak home allowed her to not only enjoy the moment and appreciate that Thanksgiving she'd just experienced but also let go of the resentment she always felt when she looked back on the O'Briens' Thanksgivings.

One story in particular seemed so laughable as Alec recounted it. Before it had always been a painful memory for Tierney, but when Alec told it and the Novaks laughed so hard they could hardly contain themselves, Tierney too was able to see the humor in it.

"So there we are," Alec continued, "sitting at the senator's Thanksgiving table, right? All the servants milling around and everyone on their best behavior. It was awful, right, Tierney?"

Tierney nodded. "I'd never been so afraid I was going to use the wrong fork in all my life," she added.

"So there we are, the senator and his wife, all hoity-toity in their fancy clothes. And as everyone is served and ready to take their first bite...Tierney throws up all over herself!"

"Oh no!" Nikki said, frowning with sympathy even as she laughed.

"It was great!" Alec laughed. "Because it started a chain reaction, and the senator's daughter puked and then his son and then me."

Everyone was laughing so hard they could hardly breathe. And in that moment, Tierney (who had always thought of the incident as the most horrific and embarrassing of her life, especially since her mother had never let her forget it) saw the humor of it—realized just why her father had always smiled to himself when the incident had been mentioned.

"So what happened?" Edward asked when he finally caught a breath.

Alec wiped tears of mirth from his eyes and sighed, "Oh, well, we left posthaste, of course. Mom was mortified and chewed Tierney up one side and down the other for hours." He looked to Tierney then, adding, "But remember what Dad said?"

Tierney nodded, residual giggling still tickling her throat. "Yep. He told me it was okay…that a person couldn't keep from throwing up if their body needed to do it." She smiled at the memory of her father's comforting arms around her that night as she cried against his warm shirt. "Then he told me it was one of the greatest amusements of his life—the look on the senator's and his wife's faces when I barfed."

Still laughing, Rome kissed the top of Tierney's head, pulling her closer to him and tucking her snuggly under his arm. "You're so funny, Tierney," he chuckled "I can just see it now—you in your little black velvet dress, lacey socks, patent leather shoes…and blaaahhhh!" He laughed again, adding, "You're so cute that I almost can't take it sometimes."

"Oh yeah, that's a real cute vision," Tierney mumbled.

The visiting continued through the afternoon, through the overindulgences of pumpkin and pecan pie, through Edward building a fire in the fireplace, and into the night. Tierney had no desire to leave— ever—and began dreading the end of it all.

And then, early in the evening, Thanksgiving night began to outshine Thanksgiving day, when Nikki pulled a guitar case out from under one of the sofas in the family room and said, "Okay, Rome. Let's have it."

Rome exhaled a heavy sigh (of fatigue, not frustration), stood up from the sofa, leaving Tierney feeling cold, and accepted the guitar his mother removed from the case and handed to him. He retrieved an antique kitchen chair from one corner, spun it around, and sat down facing Tierney and the others.

"You play the guitar?" Tierney asked as she stared at Rome in utter astonishment.

Rome smiled and mumbled, "Mm-hmm," as he tuned the guitar a bit—by ear.

"Mm-hmm?" Celeste exclaimed then. "Rome…you haven't told Tierney that you play? What you play? How well you play?"

Rome shook his head and shrugged. "It hadn't come up yet."

Celeste shook her head and sighed, "Unbelievable." Then turning to Tierney, she began to explain, "Rome is an incredible flamenco guitarist—I mean really incredible. He performs professionally once in a while, when someone offers him enough money or can talk him into it."

"Shut up, Celeste," Rome grumbled, still tuning.

"No," Celeste argued, however. She continued, "When we were little and studying up on our biological backgrounds and culture, Rome decided he wanted to be in a mariachi band, so Mom and Dad bought him one of those big guitarron guitars for Christmas that year. The next year he'd, like, totally mastered that, so they bought him a flamenco guitar, and he began playing flamenco music. He's really good too."

"But when I was sixteen," Rome interjected, "I decided I wanted to be more like Richie Sambora."

Edward groaned, rolled his eyes, and exhaled a sigh that let everyone know he and Nikki had endured *something* over that. "Oh, don't remind us," he mumbled.

"Anyway," Rome continued, smiling with sympathy for his father, "I bought my first steel string guitar and my first electric guitar and went into that for a while."

"In other words, you're really a true, like, guitarist," Tierney noted.

But Rome shook his head. "I guess…maybe."

"He's incredible," Celeste offered once more.

"But today, I'm all about entertaining the family," Rome chuckled. "So, Mom…what will it be?"

Nikki giggled, rubbing her hands together like an excited child. "Well, warm up with my favorite, of course, honey." She looked to Tierney and explained, "Malagueña."

"You're kidding," Tierney said. Oh, she was all too familiar with "Malagueña." The sixth movement in composer Ernesto Lecuona's *Suite Andalucia*, "Malagueña" enjoyed fame and familiarity for at least fifty years.

"Not kidding," Nikki giggled. Then gesturing to Rome, she said, "Okay, go."

Rome smiled, shook his head with amusement, and then began to play.

Tierney's mouth dropped open in stunned awe as she watched Rome play—as she listened to the obvious expertise he owned for not only the instrument but also flamenco guitar. She almost couldn't believe it—couldn't believe she was sitting in the Novaks' family room, watching Rome play the way he was. Celeste was right; Rome's playing was incredible!

No one made a sound or moved as Rome rather humbly executed his mastery of the song—picking, strumming, drumming on the guitar's face. *"Malagueña," really?* Tierney thought. She thought of the way Rome had looked dressed in the tuxedo he'd been wearing the first time she'd ever seen him—though of how fantastically ideal he'd appeared. Now, as she watched him play, she wondered just how delicious he would look dressed in mariachi costume—and the thought made her mouth water for some reason.

When the song was over, Nikki burst into applause, and everyone joined in. Tierney was amused by the way Rome seemed to blush, even as he thanked his small audience for their accolades.

"Now what?" he asked his mother.

"Hmmm," Nikki mumbled as she appeared to think. "Let's have a sing-along. Do 'Chestnuts Roasting,' okay?"

"You bet," Rome said, winking at Tierney as he immediately dropped into a prelude of the familiar Mel Tormé favorite.

Leaning over closer to Tierney, Alec whispered, "Oh, and he sings well too. So try to keep from panting over him, okay?" He chuckled, and Tierney blushed. Was her astonishment and admiration as obvious to everyone as it had been to Alec?

Nikki, Edward, Alec, and Celeste joined Rome as he began singing "The Christmas Song," and in a moment more, Tierney managed to settle down enough to join in.

Oh, he had her now! Rome winked at Tierney as she continued to stare at him, her beautiful eyes fairly glistening with admiration. Had he known Tierney would be so impressed by his stupid guitar skills, he would've broken out one of his instruments a long time ago. Rome thought then that he was pretty stupid not to have figured it out before. After all, the girl *did* have a thing for Latin lovers. All of a sudden, Rome found himself being more grateful than ever for his biological background.

As his mother requested Christmas song after Christmas song, Rome continued to study Tierney's reaction to his playing—to him. Her eyes were so bright with approval and adoration that he just wanted to stop playing, take her in his arms, and kiss her all over! Still, he knew that the Thanksgiving night sing-along was one of his mother's favorite moments of the year, so he didn't stop. Plus, he figured Tierney might not quite be ready to be ravished in front of his parents.

Finally, after over an hour, Rome's mother sighed with contentment and asked his father if he'd help her with something in the kitchen. His mom winked at him, and Rome knew she really didn't need any help with anything. She was just trying to allow Rome some time alone with Tierney.

Celeste asked Alec if he wanted to have some hot chocolate and then go for a walk. Fresh frost was falling, and Celeste loved nothing more than walking through a clear winter's night when frost was drifting down. Alec and Celeste left the room to enjoy a mug of hot chocolate before venturing out, ensuring that Rome had Tierney all to himself. Rome smiled at Tierney, and she smiled back. She hadn't taken her eyes off him since he'd begun to play, and he liked the fact.

"Any requests, ma'am?" he asked, quietly.

But Tierney shrugged. "I don't know. Like what?"

"Anything," Rome said. "Do you have a favorite Christmas song?"

"'Silent Night,'" she answered without pause. "I love it so much. It's everything Christmas is to me, you know?"

"I do," Rome affirmed. "You know it was originally written for guitar, right?"

But she didn't answer him aloud—only nodded.

"'Silent Night' it is then, my little peanut butter cup," Rome said. He felt a sudden self-inflicted pressure he'd never felt before, for he wanted to play Tierney's favorite Christmas song for her like she'd never heard it played before—in a way that did the song justice, which no one ever did, in Rome's opinion.

Inhaling a deep breath and smiling as Tierney leaned forward on the sofa, closer to him, Rome began to tenderly play "Silent Night"—just for Tierney.

Tierney sat in quiet, marveling awe. In all her life, she'd never heard such a moving rendition of "Silent Night." Of course, she wondered whether it were simply Rome's performing it that made it so seem so perfect. Yet never before (not ever) had Tierney heard anyone play the song with such perfectly conveyed emotion.

She closed her eyes, and as she listened, she could almost imagine she was sitting in the St. Nicholas parish church in a little Austrian town in 1818—on the very night the young priest Josef Mohr's lyrics were performed with Franz Gruber's divinely inspired melody for the very first time.

Tierney's eyes burned with emotive tears, and she opened them in an attempt to regain her composure. Yet as she gazed at Rome sitting on a simple chair before the fire, playing "Silent Night" on his guitar, her tears spilled over onto her cheeks. She brushed at them as unnoticeably as possible.

Tierney thought there was no more perfect atmosphere of reflection on the reason for the very existence of Christmas than sitting there in that moment, listening to such a profound performance of the most beautiful carol ever written—the perfect remembrance of Christ's birth. She stared at Rome, savoring every note of the simple, elegant, deeply moving song, as the fire burned warm in the hearth—the soft crackle of wood lending a sense of comfort and relaxation. The fresh scent of the pine boughs Nikki had placed on the mantel mingled with the faint fragrance of vanilla emitted by the candles nestled among them. It was a rare and flawless moment—a moment Tierney knew would never be

Tierney was ravenous for Rome's affections! Her arms wrapped around his neck, her hands lost in his the smooth, soft hair at the back of his head. She was oblivious to anything but him. She didn't care what the future held in those moments; she only cared that for that very instant in time, she was in his arms where she wanted to be.

"Sheesh! Get a room," she heard Alec chuckle.

The sound of her brother's voice and the sudden realization that Alec was witnessing the passionate exchange was enough to reel Tierney out of the euphoric daze in which she'd been swimming and back to reality.

"Don't tempt me, man," Rome said, still gazing down at Tierney with a fire of desire in his eyes that took her breath away.

"No. I'm serious, dude," Alec added then. "Your parents could walk in here any minute and…"

"You're right," Rome said. And before Tierney could begin to imagine what Rome meant to do, he took hold of her arm and began rather marching out of the family room and toward the door that Tierney knew led to the garage.

"Where are we going?" she managed to ask as Rome pretty much kicked open the door leading to the garage, grabbed a set of keys off the hook hanging just inside it, and continued to pull her along after him.

"Getting a room," he mumbled. Rome opened the driver's side door of an older silver pickup and gestured that Tierney should get in. "Slide in, baby," he said. "We're getting out of here."

The pickup was an old enough model that it didn't have bucket seats, and Tierney didn't pause—just quickly slid across the driver's seat to the passenger's side of the pickup.

Rome was in the pickup and pressing the button on garage door opener clipped to the sun visor before Tierney had even settled. The garage door opened behind the pickup, and Rome shoved the key into the ignition, revved the engine as it roared to life, and peeled back out of the garage.

He didn't drive far—only two or three blocks—before pulling the vehicle up next to a curb and popping the gearshift into neutral as he stomped on the emergency brake. Leaving the engine running, he pushed the heat control on the dashboard to high.

"Come here," he mumbled, reaching out and taking hold of Tierney's arm, pulling her back across the seat. Taking her chin in one hand, Rome's mouth claimed Tierney's—somehow literally claimed it, as if he meant to kiss her forever!

He paused for a moment, staring down at her with eyes that conveyed want, desire, and an emotion Tierney hoped she recognized as love.

"Wanna *really* fog up these windows, sugar cube?" he asked without even the slightest grin.

Tierney couldn't speak; she was too overpowered by her attraction to him. So she simply smiled and nodded.

Rome sighed, as if he'd been expecting her to refuse. "All right then. Let's get to it," he said. Tierney smiled and leaned toward him once more, but his index finger pressed to her lips stopped her from kissing him.

She frowned, not understanding why he would whisk her away, ask if she wanted to make out, and then pause.

"But first," he began, "there's something I want to ask you."

"Yeah?" Tierney asked tentatively. What could he possible mean to ask her? Naturally, her wildest hopes and dreams screamed for want of a marriage proposal—but Tierney knew how ridiculous a hope and dream it was. In fact, he seemed so serious-minded in that moment that she began to fear whatever it was he meant to ask.

Rome smiled then and shook his head as if suddenly amused with himself. "It's just that I've had the damn song playing in my head constantly for more than a week."

Tierney frowned. "You mean…you mean 'Silent Night'?" After all, it was the most recent song Tierney had heard.

Rome did smile then—even laughed. "No…not 'Silent Night,'" he explained. "The other one." Pausing, he exhaled a long breath and then sang, "*If I was your boyfriend, I'd never let you go.*"

Tierney smiled, asking, "You mean 'Boyfriend'…by Justin Bieber?"

"Don't act so surprised," Rome said. "The little dude really kicks it."

Tierney giggled. "I know, but…I just never expected that you'd be a fan."

"I'm not a fan," Rome defended himself, frowning. "But I can appreciate his skills." He shook his head, adding, "But that's not the point. The point is…how about a full-on, *committal* make-out session, baby?"

As understanding slowly began to wash over her, Tierney breathed, "A *committal* make-out session? You mean…you mean like—"

"When are you gonna let me be your boyfriend?" Rome mumbled. "When are you gonna officially think of yourself as my girlfriend? You see what I'm getting at here?"

Tierney felt the tears beginning to brim in her eyes. "I-I think you're getting at the word *commitment*…in regard to you and me…unless I'm dreaming."

Rome's handsome grin reappeared then. "You ain't dreaming, baby," he said. "So? Can I officially be, you know, your boyfriend?"

Tierney smiled. Reaching up to take hold of Rome's whiskery, square chin, she answered, "Well, the truth of it is…you're hardly anywhere *close* to being a boy, Rome."

Rome smiled, kissed the corner of Tierney's mouth, and asked, "Then what am I?"

Tierney sighed as Rome gathered her into his arms. "How about…"

He laughed. "Let me guess…your classic Latin lover?"

Tierney giggled. "Can't you be both?"

Rome smiled—the naughty smile of mischief Tierney had come to adore so much. "Of course I can, bootylicious babe of mine. I can be anything you want." He chuckled, adding, "Girl…you know it's true."

Tierney laughed—but only for a moment—because it was only a moment before Rome said, "Now let's get busy and fog up these windows with a little committal making out," and then mingled the warm, moist flavor of his mouth with hers.

It may have been cold outside the pickup cab—new frost may have been falling through the starry night sky—but Tierney was entirely unaware of it. As her dream-borne classic Latin lover boyfriend endeavored to help her fog up the windows of the pickup, Tierney's mind was void of anything else. Nothing could dampen her bliss over Rome's revealing his desire they be an exclusive couple. Nothing—not the weather, not her worries over Alec's happiness, not even the emotional red flags Elias Potts stirred in her mind. Rome Novak wanted her—*her*—Tierney O'Brien! Unfathomable? Of course! But apparently very true. And that night, Tierney swore to herself that nothing would ever keep her from holding onto his Latin lover's heart. Nothing.

CHAPTER TWELVE

"Rome Novak's girlfriend," Tierney whispered to herself as she added more greens to the arrangement she was working on. Smiling, she whispered, "Me? Yes, I'm Rome Novak's girlfriend. Why do you ask?"

Tierney giggled, delighted at how good it still felt to say the words, even after almost three weeks—three glorious, wonderful, fabulous, magnificent weeks since she and Rome had become an official couple.

She'd thought nothing would ever be more romantic or make her more happy than the moment on Thanksgiving night when Rome had dragged her out to his father's old pickup, driven off to park in an isolated part of the neighborhood, and asked her when he could be her official boyfriend. But what she knew now, three weeks later, was that every minute spent in Rome's company since then was nothing short of magical! Tierney was so much more relaxed around him, more comfortable. She hadn't even realized how nervous and uptight she'd always been before, even when they were kissing. But after Rome had played "Silent Night" so beautifully—after Tierney had been able to shed every one of her inhibitions and allow him to know just how strong her feelings were—well, all she could think most of the time was, *Wow!*

"You and Rome doing anything fun tonight?" Jessica asked as she stepped out of the floral refrigerator carrying several roses.

Tierney's smile broadened. "Everything is always fun with Rome," she answered.

Jessica laughed. "Oh, I can imagine!" she said.

Tierney smiled, delighted by the obvious compliment to her boyfriend's good looks. "But we are going out to do a little Christmas shopping," Tierney added. "You know how guys are…always waiting until the final moments."

Jessica nodded. "Oh yeah! I'm lucky if Elias gets his shopping done anytime before noon on Christmas Eve."

Tierney's smile didn't fade, even for the mention of Elias, and she nodded. "My brother is the same way—always running around like a nutcase two days before Christmas, stressing himself out over trying to find the perfect gift for everyone." Glancing up to where Jessica was arranging the roses in a bud vase, she asked, "How about you? Any fun plans for tonight? Only six shopping days left, you know."

"Oh, I know," Jessica admitted. "But I'm all finished. And, nope, nothing exciting planned. Though I do have to leave early today to meet with a client and get an idea of how much she wants to spend on her daughter's wedding on Valentine's Day."

"Ooo! A Valentine's Day wedding—how romantic!" Tierney offered. Secretly she wished to herself that *she* could be having a Valentine's Day wedding. Actually, she'd marry Rome any day he asked her to—but she squelched the thought for the moment. She may be Rome Novak's girlfriend, but that was a far cry from being Rome Novak's wife. Still, the thought of one day being his wife gave her goose bumps all the same.

"Very romantic indeed," Jessica admitted. "Yeah…so I'm leaving about three. Don't worry though. Elias volunteered to come in and work the counter so that you can keep up with any new orders placed at the last minute."

Instantly the goose bumps thoughts of being Rome's wife had raised disappeared. In their place were the thoroughgoing sensations of trepidation and nausea. Tierney hadn't told anyone her feelings where Elias Potts was concerned—her anxiety, unease, apprehension, and constant sense of foreboding. The emotional red flags that unfurled in Tierney's mind and sixth sense had quadrupled in number over the past couple of weeks. Anytime Elias lingered in the shop—whether or not Jessica were there—Tierney was fearful. She always felt sick to her stomach and had to fight the urge to run out into the street and cry for help. There was definitely something not right about Elias, and Tierney often wondered why in the world Jessica didn't sense it—wondered how she could be married to him, live with him, be intimate with him.

But Tierney didn't just want her job; she needed it. Self-reliance was just over the horizon, and Tierney knew she couldn't up and quit because her boss's husband was a creeper. Anyway, every job had a downside. Alec and Rome had been sleep-deprived for over two weeks due to the constant snowstorms. Even if new snow didn't fall on any given day or night, the wind blew it into high drifts that had to be removed from parking lots, driveways, and school bus routes. It was the downside to their business—to their jobs. Snow was a steady little dickens in the winter months of Leavenworth. But it was what it was, and Tierney understood it. Besides, she liked to snuggle up next to Rome on his sofa and listen to his steady breathing as he snoozed through whatever movie they might be watching. Sometimes Tierney would drift to sleep too, waking up and finding herself wrapped in his arms—held protectively against his broad, muscular chest.

The point was that every job came with irritations and frustrations, and for Tierney, Elias was that part of her job—the yucky part. Therefore, what was to be done but to deal with it and try to avoid being isolated in the back room with him? So that's what she had learned to do. Anytime Elias Potts was in the shop, Tierney made sure she was in whatever room of the shop that he wasn't in.

"Whew!" Jessica breathed, drawing Tierney's attention back to her. "It's going to be good to have some time off, isn't it?"

"Absolutely," Tierney agreed.

"Are you doing Christmas Eve and Christmas with Rome's family? Or just Alec?" Jessica asked.

Tierney smiled, the thought of Christmas with the Novaks lightening her mood a little again. "Alec and I are going to the Novaks' Christmas Eve party and then spending the night over there with everyone. I guess Rome spends the night there too…and of course Celeste. So we'll all be together Christmas morning too."

"Sounds like so much fun!" Jessica said. "Makes me wish I knew the Novaks better so that Elias and I could make the guest list to one of their parties." She paused and then added, "Celeste Novak worked for me one summer—not for very long, though. And she was really young, so I never really got to know her parents very well. Mr. Novak comes in and picks up an arrangement or some stems now and then for his wife, but other than that, I guess we're just in totally different social circles."

"And they're very happy just staying home most of the time," Tierney offered. She wondered for a moment if Rome and Celeste's parents felt the same way about Elias that Tierney and Celeste did—just plain creeped out. If they did, it would explain why a friendly couple like Edward and Nikki hadn't made an effort to get to know Jessica and Elias better. Celeste had once mentioned that even Heidi Svensson steered clear of Elias Potts, so it made perfect sense that people like Rome's parents would do the same.

"Well, I really like Celeste," Jessica said. "She still says hi to me whenever we run into one another. She was a great employee. I would've liked to have kept her on part-time back then."

Celeste—Tierney adored her! The more she got to know her, the more she adored her. Alec was head-over-heels, irrevocably, desperately in love with Celeste. In fact, just after Thanksgiving, Alec had confessed to Tierney (during one of their late-night sibling chats) that he knew Celeste was the woman he wanted to spend his life with. Tierney giggled a little when Alec had mentioned that he thought he and Celeste would have cute kids too—her thoughts being drawn back to Celeste's confession that night in the hot tub, about wanting to have Alec's children (so to speak).

Tierney had instantly encouraged her brother not to drag his feet. Celeste was a go-getter and a very passionate woman who wouldn't fare well being dragged along for an extended period of time. Alec assured her that he knew it all too well and explained that he didn't plan to wait much longer before "stepping things up," as he put it. Tierney knew exactly what "stepping things up" meant too—a marriage proposal! She could just imagine it—Alec kneeling before Celeste on one knee, opening a little red or black velvet ring box, and asking Celeste to marry him. No doubt Celeste would accept Alec's proposal by nearly mauling him, no matter who might be around to witness it. Then there'd be the wedding, and Celeste would be the most beautiful bride the world had ever seen.

Tierney smiled, thinking then that she could create the arrangements and bouquets for Celeste, if Celeste would allow it. And if she did allow it, Tierney would create the arrangements of her life for her friend, and soon-to-be sister-in-law.

Imagining Celeste and Alec's wedding sent Tierney's thoughts streaming back to her own ill-fated (thankfully ill-fated) bridal shower. All over again, she felt the butterflies whirling in her stomach, the goose bumps rippling over her arms, just at the memory of the first time she'd ever seen Rome Novak. Oh, he'd been so gorgeous that day! Not that he wasn't gorgeous every day—he was—even more gorgeous with every passing hour. But it was that moment Tierney reflected on then—that moment when Rome stepped out of the box and blessedly changed her life forever.

"You're grinning like a Cheshire cat, Tierney," Jessica laughed, once more pulling Tierney's attention back to the present and the floral shop. "I'm guessing you're thinking about your handsome boyfriend, huh?"

"Always." Tierney sighed and then giggled.

"Well, I don't blame you," Jessica admitted. "That man is one tasty piece of beefcake."

Tierney laughed. "That's sure one way to put it."

Trying to keep her attention on the arrangement she was working on then, Tierney hummed "Boyfriend" for the rest of the morning. She didn't stop humming (or grinning either) until Jessica left at three PM.

But when Elias Potts walked through the front door of the floral shop, such a wave of emotional red flags unfurled inside Tierney, she actually began to tremble.

"Four thirty," Tierney mumbled to herself as she stared at the clock on the wall of the design room. "Only thirty more minutes." Surely she could endure thirty more minutes in the shop. In thirty minutes, Tierney would be finished for the day and could flee from Elias's presence.

Surprisingly, Elias hadn't bothered Tierney too much. He'd kept to the counter in the front of the shop, being that there'd been nearly a steady stream of customers since Jessica had left. Meanwhile, Tierney concentrated on her work—finished up existing orders for the next day and even completed a few smaller arrangements for the impulse case at the front of the store. But she still had thirty minutes before she could leave, so she kept busy cleaning up the back room and storage refrigerator.

She felt somewhat safe too—until four forty-five PM, that was. She happened to look up from where she stood dethorning a few roses to see Elias quietly move to the front door of the shop and turn the open sign on the front door to closed. Tierney's eyes widened as she watched him lock the deadbolt. Tierney always left by way of the front door—never through the back door or delivery entrance—and Elias Potts knew it.

Wave after wave of red flags began flapping in Tierney's mind and heart. Something was not right. Elias was not right. Quickly she retrieved her phone from her apron pocket, staring at it as a state of panic began to envelop her. She'd escape through the back door, but something told her to call for help first—an enormous, red, flapping flag. But who should she call? Fear was muddling her thoughts. Quickly she sent a universal text to every number in her phone—even though there weren't many anymore.

"*911 at the Floral Shop!*" she mumbled as she pressed send. Then quickly she headed for the back door.

Taking hold of the doorknob, however, she found that it was locked, and it required a key to unlock—a key that only Jessica and Elias owned copies of. Gasping with horror and sudden realization that she should've just left the shop at four thirty and taken the heat for leaving early instead of lingering until closing time, Tierney raced to the delivery entrance. But to her further horror, it was not only closed, of course, but also padlocked. She knew only Jessica and Elias had keys to the padlock as well, and as she turned around to see Elias Potts standing behind her, Tierney knew she'd waited too long to heed her instincts.

"What're you doing, Tierney?" Elias asked.

"Leaving," she spat. Knowing the front door was deadbolted from the inside and didn't require a key, Tierney determined to push past Elias and run to the front door. With any luck, she'd be able to scramble her way out of the peril she knew she was in.

"But it's only quarter to five," Elias said, reaching out and catching hold of Tierney's arm as she tried to move past him. "You can't leave early."

"I can leave whenever I want to. And let go of me," Tierney growled, wrenching her arm free of his grasp.

"You're not leaving until I say you can leave," Elias bellowed.

Tierney wasn't even sure how it had happened—how Elias had managed to get his hands around her throat before she'd had a chance to run. But he had, and he was squeezing.

"Let me go!" Tierney demanded as tears filled her eyes. She wouldn't pass out—not yet. So far, Elias was just strangling her enough to make breathing difficult—enough to hurt her and cause her body to stiffen with fear.

"I'll let you go…when we're finished here," he mumbled.

"Don't you dare touch me!" Tierney gasped.

But Elias simply laughed. "I'm already touching you, honey," he told her. "Now quit struggling, and let's just have a little fun. That's all I'm after…just some fooling around."

Tierney blinked, sending tears trickling over her cheeks. "Let me go," she breathed.

"Settle down and make yourself cooperative, and I will," Elias responded.

Tierney tried to think clearly—tried to think—tried to think. The thought then occurred to her that if she did settle down (or at least pretended to), Elias might loosen his grip enough on her throat to allow her to kick him in the crotch and render him momentarily weak. Maybe he'd even release her throat altogether, and then she could really hurt him and bolt for the front door. If she could make it to the front door before he took her down, Tierney knew the sidewalks and streets of Leavenworth were crowded with holiday shoppers, and surely she could scream or break a window in order to draw attention to the shop and get help.

"Okay, okay," she gasped. "Just let me go. I can't breathe. I'm going to pass out if you don't let me go."

Elias paused a moment, his eyes narrowing as he studied her. His grip actually tightened for a moment, and Tierney winced—but it was only an unspoken threat, and she felt his hold slacken a bit.

What Tierney hadn't expected, however, was how the slight strangling had already weakened her. As she drew in a deeper breath, she realized that she didn't have the strength to fight her attacker—not yet.

"Now," Elias said, "where were we?"

More tears escaped Tierney's eyes as Elias let go of her throat but took brutal hold of her forearms and pulled her body flush with his.

"Mmm...you do smell good, Tierney," he moaned as he kissed her cheek.

The feel of his disgusting lips to her flesh revitalized Tierney, however, and she landed a knee to his crotch as solidly as she could.

Elias swore under his breath as his hold on Tierney lessened, and he doubled over a bit. It was her chance, and Tierney broke away from him, turned, and raced through the shop toward the front door.

She was almost there—almost close enough to take hold of the deadbolt. But Elias was nearly there too, and she felt his hand at the back of her head. She cried out when he gripped her hair in his fist and pulled her backward, swiftly sweeping Tierney's legs out from under her with one of his.

Tierney felt the breath leave her lungs as she hit the floor hard on her back. She couldn't gasp—couldn't draw a breath—couldn't defend herself—and before she could stop the dizzying sensation in her head, Elias Potts was crouched over her, pinning her hands to the floor on either side of her and sitting down hard on her thighs.

"Well, aren't you a feisty little thing today, hmmm?" he asked. Tierney looked up to see Elias's head descending toward hers.

"I won't keep quiet about this," she growled in an effort to scare him into leaving her alone. "I'll tell everyone...including the police."

"Go ahead," Elias said. "My brother is a sergeant down at the precinct. I'm sure he'd love to hear your lies."

Tierney screamed and closed her eyes as she heard the glass on the front door shatter—heard it scatter on the floor nearby.

"What the hell are you doing?" Rome shouted as he stepped through the broken glass of the floral shop door. "What the hell are you doing?" he shouted again, taking hold of the back of Elias's shirt collar and dragging him off Tierney.

Tierney wept with joy and then gasped as she watched Rome land a powerful fist to Elias's face.

"Who the hell do you think you are?" Rome roared as he landed another punch to Elias's face, sending him reeling back against the register counter. "You touched her? You piece of sh—" he growled as he continued to beat Elias.

"Tierney!" Celeste cried as she stepped into the shop, rushing to Tierney and helping her to sit up. "Are you okay?" she cried. "I should've never let you work here. I should've—"

"Tierney!" Alec shouted then, stepping into the shop. "What did the bastard do to you?"

"I'm fine," Tierney wept. "Stop him. Stop Rome," she stammered through her tears. Elias Potts was lying on the floor, his entire face covered in blood, groaning as Rome continued to kick him in the stomach, shout, and swear at him.

"You filthy piece of sh—" Rome grumbled.

"Hey, man!" Alec said, taking hold of Rome's arm and pulling him away from Elias. "He's down, Rome. It's all right. She's safe, and the bastard is down."

Instantly, Rome's attention fell to Tierney. "Baby! Baby, baby, baby," he mumbled as he gathered Tierney into his arms. "Are you all right? What did the bastard do to you? Did he touch you? Did he hurt you?" Rome pulled back, studying Tierney's face and neck. "He hurt you, didn't he?"

"I'm fine," Tierney answered. "You came. I'm fine. He just choked me. You got here, and I…I…"

Burying her face against the warmth of Rome's sweater—against his strong chest as his powerful arms enveloped her—Tierney sobbed.

"Call the police, Celeste," Alec said. "Man, you're going to jail!" Tierney heard her brother growl. "And you're damn lucky Rome didn't kill you."

"He'll be the one going to jail," Tierney heard Elias panting. "For assault and battery…breaking and entering. I'll make sure that cocky little bastard pays for this."

Tierney looked up at Rome as fear overwhelmed her. Remembering that Elias had boasted about his brother, a sergeant at the precinct, terror overtook her rational thoughts.

"He means it, Rome!" she cried. "He'll try to have you charged and…and…and…"

"No, he won't," Celeste said, however. Tierney watched as Celeste turned to look to Elias. "You crawl home to Jessica like the dirty dog you are, Elias," she said. "You lick your wounds and man up to confessing to your wife about the real reasons none of us ever worked here for very long. You do it, and you leave Rome alone…or I'll be telling the police, Jessica, and everyone else what you tried to do to me when I worked here. Do you understand?"

"What do you mean what he tried to do to you?" Alec asked.

"Celeste?" Rome ventured. "What haven't you told me?"

Celeste looked to Rome, forced a comforting smile, and answered, "I've told you everything I ever needed to or wanted to tell you, Rome," she answered. "But until now, I never told anyone that this…this monster…that Elias Potts tried to…he tried to hurt me when I was working here that summer in high school." Celeste looked back to Elias. "Jessica returned from her lunch hour early that day—unexpectedly early—and this scumbag had to let me go. I walked up to Jessica the very next moment, quit, and I've never set foot in here again." Celeste paused. "I thought I was the only girl Elias had tried to…until Heidi Svensson and I got to talking a few months back. She told me how Elias was always grabbing her butt and stuff…and that's why she quit."

"Celeste," Rome breathed, "you should've told someone. You should've told me."

"I know," Celeste admitted. "But I was young and afraid…and kept thinking that I had done something wrong." She shook her head. "When I heard Tierney was going to go to work here, I almost told her…but I figured nobody had said anything about Elias being a pervert since me and Heidi. So I thought he'd learned his lesson." Celeste looked to Tierney, tears streaming down her face. "I'm so sorry, Tierney. I should've…I should've…"

"It's all right, Celeste," Tierney said. "It's not your fault."

Alec gathered Celeste into his arms as he glared at Elias. "You're lucky you're not dead, man. I swear I should do it myself."

"Call the police, Alec," Rome growled. "I'm not letting this bastard get away with all this. I don't care if they charge me or who his damn brother is. He's gonna pay for all this."

Alec nodded. "You're right."

"But, Rome—" Tierney began.

"Shhh," Rome interrupted her. "They won't put me in jail, baby," he soothed. "Not when they find out what this guy has been up to. You know that, right?"

But Tierney could only sob, fearful that Rome would be charged and end up paying a terrible price for simply saving her.

Tierney's cell began to ring. With one trembling hand, she reached into her apron pocket and retrieved it.

Rome took it from her, however, pressed the answer button, and said, "Hello?" Tierney watched him, her terrified heart swelling with love as he said, "Rome Novak, sir. I'm Tierney's boyfriend. Mmm-hmmm. Yes, she's fine. I'll have her call you in a few minutes. Of course, Mr. O'Brien. Okay. Good-bye."

Shoving the phone in his back pocket, Rome helped Tierney to her feet and told her, "It was your dad. He got your 911 text and was worried."

"My dad?" she asked.

"What is going on?" Mr. Novak asked as he and Nikki stepped into the shop.

"Yeah...Elias Potts assaulted my sister here at the florist's shop," Alec was telling the police on the phone.

"Are you all right, sweetie?" Nikki asked, brushing Tierney's hair from her face.

"She's okay, Mom," Rome said, pulling Tierney into his arms and kissing her forehead. "She's okay...thank God."

Tierney melted to Rome, weeping with relief in her own safety and for the fact she owned the heart of such a hero. She was tired, overwhelmed, and simultaneously miserable and happy.

"I...I guess I'm out of a job," she said. "What am I going to do?"

She heard a low chuckle rumble in Rome's chest. He took her face in his hands and forced her to look up at him.

"Baby, that's what you're worried about?" he asked, smiling with disbelief. "After all this...you're worried about your job?"

"I have to have a job, Rome," she explained through her tears. "I can't mooch off of Alec forever." Lowering her voice, she added, "And I think he's getting ready to ask Celeste—"

"Shhh," Rome said, pressing an index finger to her lips. "Don't worry about it, bootylicious bunny," he said. "You'll just have to become a kept woman...my kept woman." His embrace enveloped her again. "I'll pay for whatever you need, baby, and you'll find another job.

Hey, maybe you can become one of the Christmas Shoppe sales babes, hmmm? Either way, do not worry about that now."

Tierney relaxed a little, clinging to Rome and his protective strength. As the sirens of approaching police cars grew louder, she ventured a glance at Elias Potts. No flags unfurled in her mind as she looked at him, however. It was over. Should she have heeded the anxieties of her mind more thoroughly? Of course she should have—but that was in the past. All that was before Tierney now was a life after Elias Potts—a life perhaps to be spent with Rome—and a life where Tierney would never ignore or rationalize away those apprehensions in her mind ever again.

CHAPTER THIRTEEN

"The minute I heard that door slam, Tierney, I knew I had to get control of myself," Kiefer O'Brien explained as he sat on the sofa of Alec's front room explaining why he'd unexpectedly appeared at the front door that morning—Christmas Eve morning. "I-I sat there for a long time wondering when it had all gone so wrong...when I'd given up and just given into your mother's ridiculously controlling will. I sat there for hours, thinking back over my life." He looked up to Alec and Tierney, tears brimming in his eyes. "I sat there hating myself for hours, focusing on the weak fool I'd become...thinking how disappointed my parents would be." Kiefer paused, tears spilling from his eyes and over his cheeks. "And it was in that moment that I finally understood how thoroughly the deaths of my parents had destroyed me, destroyed to the point that I'd retreated to a dark place inside myself...destroyed me to a point that I'd failed my own children."

Tierney brushed the tears from her cheeks, sniffled, and tried not to sob.

When she'd opened the door an hour before, she had never expected to see her father standing on the other side of it. Certainly she'd been touched, deeply moved that her father had called her the day of Elias Potts's attack. Rome had answered the phone, of course, but an hour or so later, Tierney had returned her father's phone call, assuring him she was well. She'd still been too rattled for days afterward to fully appreciate the fact that her father had called, that he'd sounded different than he had in years, and that she hadn't heard a word from her mother. Still, as the week progressed—as the incident with Elias Potts fell further into the past and lovely, glorious Christmas edged closer and closer—Tierney did find her thoughts often lingered on the fact that her father had called, that he'd assured her several times of his love for her—something he hadn't spoken to her in years.

And now that Kiefer O'Brien sat in the same room as his children, explaining not only why he was there in Leavenworth with them but how, Tierney felt only compassion and love for her father—not resentment or anger.

"Dad, Tierney and I know that—" Alec began.

"Please, Alec," Kiefer interrupted, however. "I know I'll never be able to make up for the neglect and wrong I've done to you both, but let me tell you how I'm going to try to move ahead. Okay?"

Alec nodded and settled back in the sofa.

"Well," Kiefer continued, "that next morning—the morning after you left, Tierney—I dragged myself out of bed, packed a few things, and drove to a doctor's office. I needed help. I realized that somewhere along the way, I'd fallen into a deep, deep state of depression. Nothing else could've turned me into the gutless worm I'd become. I thought about the fact that there seemed to be no color in the world to me...none. Everything was some lifeless gray fog to me. The sky, the grass, flowers—nothing had color when I looked at it. Furthermore, whenever I thought of your mother, I found there was no feeling in me—nothing, not even disgust, impatience, or...just nothing. I'd lost myself when my parents were killed. And I don't think it was just that. I think that was simply the proverbial straw that broke the camel's back, you know?"

Tierney sniffled and nodded. Alec nodded as well, and their father continued. "Anyway, if you want the gory details of my treatment for severe depression, we can talk about that later," he said. "But I will say this. People never walk up to cancer patients and say, "Hey! Get over it! It's just cancer," right? But there's a real stigma that comes with depression, especially where your mother is concerned." He paused a moment, exhaled a heavy sigh, and then said, "I'm getting better. It's been almost eight weeks, and I'm a new man." He chuckled, and Tierney's heart leapt at the familiar but long-absent sound. "Well, actually, I'm an old man—the man I used to be. And I've divorced your mom."

"What?" Alec exclaimed.

"Oh, don't worry, son," Kiefer assured Alec. "Except for about a million in cash and one new car dealership in Seattle, I just gave her everything. I gave her everything because I knew if I did, she'd let me go without so much as a word. And I was right. Your mom didn't want me; she wanted my money. And I didn't want my money anymore."

Tierney's mouth was still gaping open in astonishment as her father said, "So I've moved to Seattle, tucked away my cash for a rainy day and old age, and I'm just helping to run the dealership—which I chose to keep simply because it ensured I could be closer to you two. You, Alec and Tierney, you were always the most important things to me—always…always what I loved more than anything. And I'm sorry that I let my personal tragedies, your mom's strong will, and weakness nearly destroy you." Kiefer cleared his throat and ventured, "And I hope…I hope that one day, you'll let me be a part of your lives again." He smiled. "It looks like you got a couple of pretty good lives going here, and I just pray you'll let me share in them sometimes."

Tierney was off the sofa and in her father's loving embrace before she'd even realized it—sobbing against him—sobbing with joy in having her father returned to her.

Alec was there soon too, embracing them both. "Dad…we've missed you."

Kiefer O'Brien was weeping as well, and Tierney could feel the way he desperately clung to her and Alec—as if he never meant to let go of them again. The family embraced for a long time, weeping and choking out endearments and thankfulness when their emotions would allow.

Finally, they let go of one another, and Tierney retrieved a box of tissue from the coffee table. As they all dried tears of heartache and joy, Kiefer said, "Now…I know your first impulse is going to be to try and get me to stay with you here. But please let me go back to Seattle tonight…just until I get things settled a little more and until you've both had a chance for this all to sink in."

"But, Daddy—" Tierney began.

Kiefer shook his head, however. "It's okay, Tierney. I'll come just after New Year's—maybe the second or third, okay? I'll come over for a visit, and we can plan more then. I'm sure you both have plans tonight anyway, right?"

"Plans can be changed, Dad," Alec offered. "And besides, I was planning to propose to Celeste tonight…but I'd rather wait until you can be there."

"Absolutely not," Kiefer grumbled. "This is just what I'm talking about, son. You and Tierney, you're both so brave, and you've found these lives here…normal, happy lives. Do not put them on pause for me…please. It would make me very unhappy."

But Tierney was still looking at Alec in awed astonishment. "You're proposing tonight?"

Alec sighed, smiled, and nodded. "I love her," he said. "I love her more than anything…more than anyone. And like you've told me a million times, Tiers, Celeste isn't one to be dragged along for a stretched-out amount of time."

New tears sprang to Tierney's eyes as she threw her arms around Alec's neck. "Oh, Alec! How wonderful! How wonderful! I'm so happy for you!"

"Thanks, Tiers," Alec said, kissing her cheek. Looking back to his father, he said, "Celeste is amazing, Dad. Are you sure you don't want to just stay tonight? You can come with us over to the Novaks' and be there when—"

"No, Alec," Kiefer answered kindly. He smiled, and Tierney felt warm inside. "I'll meet her next week. I mean, everything between us seems exciting and hopeful, and it is. But I don't want to press you…or smother something in this new life of yours. I want you to have time to mull this all over for a while. At some point, you're going to realize that I divorced your mother and—"

"Daddy…it's okay," Tierney interrupted. "Divorcing Mom, moving, getting yourself settled—we understand. You need your space as well…so no worries. When you feel like coming over, just let us know." Tierney smiled, adding, "Call me and let me know."

It felt wonderful to be able to talk to her father again—the father Tierney had known as a little girl. It felt wonderful to know that he had her cell phone number and was only a text message or phone call away. And as he smiled and nodded at her, she sighed, for she knew he would call—soon.

"So your dad's going to be around, huh?" Rome asked almost tentatively as he and Tierney slow danced to Ella Fitzgerald's version of "Laura." "How much of your time will he be expecting?"

Tierney smiled up at her handsome, handsome, oh-so-handsome Latin lover boyfriend. "Why?" she asked. "Are you worried that my time with my father will interfere with our time together? Our time together, which so far this week has consisted of the very few hours you *haven't* been plowing?"

Rome smiled and exhaled a heavy sigh. "Okay…maybe I am a little worried. I'm man enough to admit that I don't want to share you with anybody, not even your brother, let alone your dad."

"You're always my top priority, Romeo Novak," Tierney giggled. "You know that."

"Only because I follow you around like a lovesick puppy," Rome flirted. "And, boy oh boy, am I lovesick over you, baby."

Tierney bit her lip with delight, and Rome smiled, feeling warm and passionate all over. He couldn't believe Alec had chosen Christmas Eve to propose to Celeste! As happy as he was for his sister—not to mention his best friend—he hated that he'd instantly felt obligated to wait to propose to Tierney. After all, he'd been planning to propose to her on Christmas Eve ever since Thanksgiving! But he wanted Celeste to have her moment—and Alec. So when Celeste had suddenly burst into tears while she and Alec were dancing earlier that evening—when she'd thrown her arms around Alec next and squealed, "Yes! Yes, I'll marry you, Alec O'Brien!"—Rome had decided to leave the diamond engagement ring in his pocket instead of asking Tierney to marry him that night the way he'd been planning. After all, not only did he want Celeste to have her moment, but also he wanted Tierney to have hers.

And so, as much as it frustrated Rome to do so, he hadn't proposed to Tierney. But it didn't mean it wasn't the most awesome Christmas Eve he'd ever known. It still was—because Tierney was in his arms.

"You don't know what lovesick is," Tierney flirted with Rome in return. "I'm the one who's lovesick. I'm the one who is in love with you."

Rome grinned with satisfaction. "Only because I'm Latin and can fulfill all your classic Latin lover fantasies." Tierney giggled, and he continued, "At least I'm in love with you for a good reason."

"And what reason might that be?" she asked, delighted, as she was every time Rome said he loved her, no matter how he said it.

"Because you look good in this sexy little black dress you're wearing," he teased.

Tierney smiled, relishing his flirting. Then she remembered the stockings Celeste had given her and said, "Oh! And did you notice the stockings your sister found for me?"

Rome's brows puckered. He glanced down at her legs and asked, "What's so great about them? Other than the dead-sexy legs that are wearing them?"

Tierney giggled, "They have seams, silly boy!" she explained. Pausing their dance, she twisted one foot so Rome could see the vintage-style stocking seams running up the back of her calves. "I mean, do you know how hard it is to get these seams straight? Then you have to fasten the tops to the garter belt and—"

"Garter belt?" Rome interrupted.

Tierney looked up to seem him almost glaring down at her.

"Well…well, yeah," she stammered. "They're just like real vintage stockings, Rome—seams up the back, thigh high so that you have to wear a garter belt to—"

"Holy cow, Tierney!" Rome exclaimed in a whisper then. "Don't tell me things like that! Not on Christmas Eve when I was planning to…and then I couldn't…and then you show up wearing that dress and tell me your stockings have seams and hook up to a garter belt!"

Tierney was confused, for Rome seemed sincerely rattled. He stepped back from her as the music ended, raked a hand back through his hair, and then reached up to loosen the knot in his tie.

"So…so you don't like the seams in my stockings?" she ventured. "I don't understand why you—"

"Dammit, Tierney!" Rome grumbled, raking his hand through his hair again. "Just stop talking about it, okay? You *don't* understand."

"O-okay, Rome," Tierney mumbled. "Okay. I'm sorry I ever mentioned it."

Rome exhaled a heavy sigh, casting his gaze to the floor then. Shaking his head, he laughed almost nervously and said, "Oh, great…oh, great. Of course you're wearing black pumps too." He sounded almost angry.

Tierney looked down to her simple black pumps. "You…you know what pumps are?"

In a lowered voice, and with a frustrated frown still furrowing his brow, Rome leaned closer to her and nearly growled, "Of course I know what pumps are, Tierney. I'm a guy, aren't I?"

Tierney was more confused than ever, but if there were one thing she didn't want, it was for Rome to be unhappy with her on Christmas Eve. After all, with Alec having proposed to Celeste and the beauty of the Novak home all drenched in white lights, poinsettias, holly, and pinecones, she'd never thought anything could go wrong.

"Rome…I'm sorry," she began. "I-I don't understand. I thought you liked my dress and…the stockings…"

"Oh my hell, Tierney," Rome growled. Taking hold of her hand, he began pulling her from the now enclosed patio where a few of the Novak guests still lingered in dancing and into the house itself.

"Rome! What's wrong? I don't understand," Tierney asked as tears filled her eyes.

"Of course you don't, baby," he grumbled. "Because you're a girl."

Before she knew it, Rome had pulled her into what had once been his bedroom but now served as an extra bedroom for guests. Closing the door behind them, Tierney gasped when, unexpectedly, Rome was at her like a lion that had just taken down a gazelle.

His kiss was ravenous, demanding, and burning with desire! First he seemed to endeavor to feed his hungry passion with kissing Tierney's mouth, but as his fervor became somewhat more controlled, Rome's attention moved to Tierney's neck and throat, weakening her knees and causing her entire body to feel weightless—her mind to empty of anything but her own desire for him.

All of a sudden, Rome swept Tierney up into the cradle of his arms, mumbling, "Kick them off," against her mouth. "Kick your damn shoes off, Tierney."

Tierney smiled as she realized Rome was either knowingly or unknowingly fulfilling yet another one of her silly, Hollywood movie fantasies—and she did as he commanded. Wiggling her toes, she giggled as she felt her black pumps loosen, slip from her feet, and tumble to the floor.

She felt Rome exhale a heavy breath as he none too gently laid her down on what had once been his bed. Hovering over her like some handsome Hollywood vampire about to passionately bite her neck, Rome's smoldering gaze mesmerized her so thoroughly that Tierney couldn't move when she felt him reach down and take hold of her ankle—not that she wanted to move if she could have. Still holding her gaze with his, Rome's hand slowly slid up the back of Tierney's calf until it reached the back of her knee. There his hand stopped.

"I'm a gentleman, you know," Rome mumbled, still staring at her.

Tierney grinned at him and whispered, "I know."

"But if you keep talking about what you're wearing underneath this dress," he breathed, "I might have a difficult time staying one. Do you understand?"

"I do," Tierney answered.

It was Rome's undoing—her answer of, "I do." For it was what he so badly wanted to hear her answer when she was asked if she would take Rome Novak to be her lawfully wedded husband.

Celeste had had her moment, dammit! Alec had had his. Now it was time for Tierney and Rome to have theirs. Therefore, Rome kissed his lover softly—slowly at first—before claiming her mouth in the kind of kiss he knew she liked best from him—a fiery, demanding, moist kiss filled with desire and expressed passion.

There were no red flags unfurling in Tierney's mind as Rome kissed her. She was safe in his arms. And so she kissed him back—unreservedly—and as hungrily as he kissed her. It was why she didn't notice it at first—the fact that one of his hands was caressing one of hers—then fumbling with one of hers. She might not even have noticed he'd slipped the ring onto her finger if it hadn't been for the fact that the white gold of the band was cooler than his skin.

Gasping as Rome broke the seal of their mouths and stared at her hopefully, Tierney raised her hand to see the most beautiful set of diamonds arranged on a white gold band that she'd ever seen.

Looking back to him as tears filled her eyes, she watched Rome's mouth speak the words, "Please marry me, Tierney. Marry me and let me be your Latin lover forever…all right?"

"All right," Tierney breathed as tears escaped her eyes to trickle over her temples.

Taking hold of her shoulders and pulling her off the bed, onto her feet, and into his arms, Rome whispered into her hair, "I love you, Tierney. I started loving you the second I stepped out of that stupid box dressed like an idiot. From that moment on…you're all I wanted. Maybe it only seems like a few weeks to you…only a couple of months…but it felt like forever for me."

"It felt like forever to me too," Tierney confessed through her tears. "I love you, Rome! You have no idea how much I love you!"

"I love you, baby," he breathed. "Promise you won't make me wait too long to marry you." Pulling back from her a moment, he brushed the tears from her cheeks, smiled, and said, "And how about you just skip the whole bridal shower thing this time, okay? Just in case some other guy shows up looking better in a tux than me."

But Tierney shook her head. "Not possible…not ever."

Rome kissed her once more. Taking her hands in his then, he began to pull her back toward the door. "Okay then. Let's go tell Mom and Dad…before I rip that dress off you and—"

Tierney's giggle and hand over his mouth silenced Rome—but only for a moment before he added, "And don't mention again tonight the seams in your stockings or that other thing you're wearing that I can't see, okay?"

"Okay," Tierney agreed.

"Okay," Rome said with a nod. Then opening the door, he swept Tierney up in his arms and strode with her toward the kitchen.

"Oh, Mom?" he called as he carried her.

Sighing with unfathomable joy and contentment, Tierney rested her head on Rome's strong shoulder. She couldn't believe it. She couldn't believe Rome loved her—that he wanted to marry her. It was the stuff of dreams—of old Hollywood movies and Ella Fitzgerald songs—a poor little rich girl, swept away to a happily ever after in the arms of her Latin lover.

EPILOGUE

"This is still my favorite dress you own, you know?" Rome said, sweeping Tierney up into his arms as he stepped into their bedroom.

Tierney giggled. "You know it's not the same dress, Rome Novak. I only *wish* I could still wear that dress I wore that Christmas Eve when…"

"When I almost lost it and took you right there in my old bedroom of my parents' house?" Rome finished.

"You didn't almost *take* me," Tierney said.

But Rome puffed a short laugh. "That shows how much you know, baby."

Tierney laughed as she wiggled her toes to loosen her shoes. She heard her black pumps fall to the floor.

Rome chuckled and whispered, "You better be quiet, Mommy. If you wake up the baby, we'll be up all night." Letting Tierney's feet drop to the floor, he added, "Of course, then again…maybe we'll be up all night anyway."

Tierney blushed and turned her back to Rome. "Unzip me, please," she said.

"Oh, I'll unzip you all right," Rome teased. Tierney felt goose bumps envelop her body when she felt Rome's breath on the back of her neck—when she felt him take the pull tab of her zipper in his teeth and begin tugging it down. Once he'd unzipped her dress, she sighed when she felt him push open the back of her dress and place a moist and lingering kiss to her back.

"It's snowing, you know," Tierney needlessly reminded her husband.

"I know," Rome affirmed. "But I got your dad to fill in for me tonight…told him it was the anniversary of our engagement and that we had…you know…plans after my parents' party."

Tierney's smile broadened. Three years she and Rome had been married—well, three years on January 15—and every year, Rome made sure they could be together on Christmas Eve—all Christmas Eve. And though sleeping in Rome's arms was magical every night, there was something about sleeping in them on Christmas Eve that always made Tierney's heart race with heightened happiness and desire.

"And what if the baby wakes up?" Tierney asked her husband as he stripped his tie from his collar and began unbuttoning his shirt.

"She won't," Rome said. "Not for a while anyway. And if she does, we'll just snuggle her up with us like we always do…being that we're a couple of weenies when it comes to little Miss Avery Anne Novak."

"We'll be tougher on the next one, maybe," Tierney suggested as Rome's strong arms encircled her waist, his mouth trailing soft kisses over her shoulder.

"Maybe," he mumbled. Tierney heard him sigh as he rested his forehead against the back of her head. "I love you, Tierney," he mumbled. "More than ever. And I thanked Alec again today for sending me on that errand almost four years ago."

Tierney smiled. "So did I."

Rome chuckled and released her. Going to the nightstand, he picked up the remote for the iPod dock.

"Do you tango, Mrs. Novak?" he asked, taking her in dance position as "Assassin's Tango" began to play.

"Only with handsome strangers that step out of boxes pretending to be Latin lovers," Tierney answered.

Rome smiled and began to lead Tierney in a light tango. "It's a good thing I showed up tonight then, huh?"

Tierney rested her head on her husband's chest, smiled, and sighed, "Yes, it is."

"And by the way," Rome added, pausing their dance and taking Tierney's chin in one hand, "I never *pretend* to be anything, baby. I *am* a Latin lover…*your* Latin lover."

"I know," Tierney whispered. "I do know."

She trembled with overwhelming love and powerful desire when Rome kissed her then—when his mouth claimed hers with just as much passion as ever he had before.

AUTHOR'S NOTE

Okay, so here's the thing (as my friend Gina always says). The summer I turned twelve, I experienced an epoch in my life—Star Wars! Today Star Wars is old hat. Star Wars, its prequels, and multiple variations of the story have been around for over thirty years, and therefore, some folks may simply shrug their shoulders and think, "So what's the big deal about Star Wars?" But let me tell you this—if you were lucky enough to be in a theater the summer of 1977, you know what I'm talking about. And if you weren't that lucky but were lucky enough to have a mom or dad (or preferably both) who were there and then made sure you had the VHS version and DVD version while you were growing up, then you know what I'm talking about.

An epic and incredible telling of a hero's journey, George Lucas's masterpiece, *Star Wars*—its story, cutting-edge special effects (at the time), and characters that planted themselves in your heart instantly— was life-altering to one almost twelve-year-old girl the summer of 1977—moi! I was there for the real thing—the first release. I even stood in line at some big department store at the mall the Christmas following the movie release with my friend Amy for three hours, just to have Darth Vader sign my paperback copy of the book! (Okay, I know now that it wasn't really Dave Prowse signing books at the mall, but who cares! Amy and I had an adventure of a lifetime anyway. And if I remember correctly, there were some really cute boys—Justin Bieber types—in line near us!)

Now you may be wondering why I'm babbling on nonsensically about my original *Star Wars* experience. Well, there are a couple of reasons, and they will reveal themselves shortly. First, it's important to understand that when I was eleven years old (almost twelve), I saw *Star Wars* and thought Luke Skywalker (a.k.a. Mark Hamill) was the bomb! I couldn't figure out why in the world Leia didn't totally go for Luke. (Remember this important fact: in 1977, none of us had a clue that Luke and Leia were siblings. Not a clue. So I wasn't weird for wanting Leia to fall in love with Luke. Just wanted to make sure that was clear.)

Then, for three years, as I impatiently waited for the second installment (yes, I know, it's really the fifth) of Star Wars to arrive—*The Empire Strikes Back*—all I could do was hope that Leia would wise up and fall in love with Luke. But when *The Empire Strikes Back* finally did arrive and I sat in the theater watching Leia and Han banter back and forth, kiss, and then kiss again as Leia confessed her love for Han right before he's frozen in carbonite (and believe me, *that* was traumatizing), I began to understand. I was fourteen almost fifteen by then, after all, and could see how much more of a man Han was compared with Luke. Not that Luke wasn't a man—I mean, he did eventually become a Jedi, right? It was just that I could see Han as the far more desirable male hero—to women, anyway.

Now, I know you're still wondering what the whole Star Wars epoch in my life has to do with this book. Well, the second reason is that not only does Rome Novak draw life lessons from Star Wars, but my youngest son, Trent, does too. In fact, just the other day, my oldest son, Mitch, and Trent were sitting in the family room discussing guns, the military, policemen, and so forth when all of a sudden my attention was drawn more alertly to their conversation. The question posed by one or the other of them, or by someone else in the room, was, "What would you be willing to die for?"

The answers Mitch quickly gave were very serious: "My wife, my family, my freedom, my religious beliefs." And then Trent added, "Mine would be if the Empire killed my whole family. Then I would totally join the Rebel Alliance and fight against the Empire." As everyone laughed, Trent added, "No, I'm serious." (He then proceeded to tell me that when he was a very little boy, he used to be afraid he'd come home from school one day and walk in to find nothing left of his dad and I but smoldering skeletons. Poor little thing!)

But Rome's kinship with my son Trent regarding Star Wars metaphors is not the only reason I began this Author's Note with my Star Wars tale. Going back to the Han versus Luke as the romantic hero—the first reason Star Wars is pertinent to my inspiration for *One Classic Latin Lover, Please* is this: it was *Star Wars, The Empire Strikes Back*, and *Return of the Jedi* that really helped me consciously understand my lifelong adoration of one Ricardo Gonzalo Pedro Montalbán y Merino. For just as Han was far more manly than Luke, so Ricardo Montalbán was iconic to me as the ideal Latin lover.

Now, of course I've always loved Ricardo in everything—old movies, *Fantasy Island*, as Kahn in the original Star Trek series and in the Star Trek movie *The Wrath of Kahn*. And I loved the way he would always say, "Rich Corinthian leather," in old Chrysler commercials. I loved Ricardo's accent, his mannerisms, his smile, his dashing good looks, and the way he danced. For many years, my favorite Ricardo Montalbán movie was *Neptune's Daughter*. I loved Ricardo and Esther Williams singing "Baby, It's Cold Outside." But when the day came that I was lucky enough to catch *Two Weeks with Love* on TV somewhere— *wham*! *Two Weeks with Love* starring Ricardo and Jane Powell is still my favorite Hollywood musical of the 1950s. I love it! I *love* Ricardo's character in that movie—so suave, so romantic, so flirtatious. Yikes!

And obviously he continues to inspire me, even long after his death. It isn't only his movie personas that I admire. A devout Roman Catholic, Ricardo was married to his wife, Georgiana, for sixty-three years until her death in 2007. Not only was he married to her but also he was faithful to her, and that is a thing to be admired—especially in Hollywood during any era.

This next little ditty I'm going to tell you about isn't nearly as sunshiny as either Ricardo Montalbán or Star Wars, but it is a very big part of one of Tierney's thought processes. I'll begin by telling you this: Mom was always reading articles. A favorite impersonation for me, my sister, and my husband to do of my mom is to wag an index finger in the air and say, "You know, just the other day I was reading an article…" We always have to leave it open-ended, of course, because there could be a billion different endings to Mom's famous tagline. It could be, "Just the other day, I was reading an article about the methods used for amputating limbs during the Civil War, and did you know…"

Or it might be more like, "Just the other day, I was reading an article on cumulous cloud formations, and it said…" My mom was always reading articles—thus the inspiration for the "emotional red flags" article Tierney's thoughts reference in *One Classic Latin Lover, Please.* (I find that my mother always inspires something in every book!)

Though I've never read an article about it, I did watch a program once on warning instincts—how many mental warnings people experience before something bad happens to them and how many they ignore. One incident counted nearly forty red flags a woman identified having gone off in her mind before she was victimized. She said in the interview that she'd realized afterward if she'd listened to even one of those warnings and followed it, her victimization could've been avoided.

I found the program not only incredibly informative but also profoundly affirming to what I'd always believed—that if we listen to our feelings, our silent promptings, and act accordingly, we can save ourselves, our children, and our families from who knows what kind of disasters and possible harm. Of course, the hard part is listening to our "emotional red flags," following their instructions, and then—when nothing goes wrong—just accepting that it's always better to be safe than sorry.

One incident I experienced in college was a very good example to me of how important it really is to heed thoughts or feelings of pending danger. It was life-altering—literally. It changed the way I watched the world and paid attention to my instincts.

At the time, I was the female vocalist in several pop-rock "dance bands" while I was in college, and no matter what the weather was on any give day in good ol' Rexburg, Idaho, pop-rock dance band practice was never canceled and was always mandatory. Being that Rexburg during the winter months can be—um, how can I say this?—inclement, most students didn't even bother bringing cars to school back in the early 1980s, even if they did have one. Why not? Well, I remember in April of 1984, as the snow in one of our parking lots eventually began to melt, lo and behold, a car that had been parked there all winter was revealed. It had been completely buried by the deep snow and slowly began to emerge as the snow melted. Who knew? None of us did, that's for sure. That's how deep and consistent the snow was that year—deep enough to hide entire cars.

Anyway, as I said, most people didn't have cars up there, so everyone walked everywhere. Walking was good for my roommates and me (especially considering we ate nothing but Jell-O Cheesecakes, baked potatoes, Chinese noodles, and candy bars out of the vending machines most of the time). But on those cold afternoons and evenings when the temperature dropped to forty degrees below zero, those mandatory (and often nighttime) band rehearsals were tough.

On one such frigid Rexburg evening in 1984, I walked out of the rehearsal room to be met by a cold blast of wind that chilled me to the bone. The bass player for that particular band (Tom, whom I adored, of course—I always dug the bass players) had worn only a light jacket. I had a coat, but it wasn't my heavy one. Well, we both stood there freezing for a while, contemplating the idea of wrapping up in each other's arms for warmth as we walked home (an idea to which neither one of us was averse, by the way).

Fortunately and unfortunately, however, one of the guitar players in the band owned a car. (I've changed this particular guitar player's name in to Justin for the purpose of this little reminiscence.) Justin kindly offered me a ride home. The gentlemanly thing to do, right? However, he did not include Tom the Cute Bass Player in his offer, which I thought was rude. I had no desire to be alone in a car with Justin.

Justin had always creeped me out. I was a shallow-thinking eighteen-year-old and thought maybe it was because he was sort of short, round, and not very cute. But there were a lot of short, round, not very cute guys that I liked and was friends with and enjoyed being around. Therefore, it wasn't until this incident on that frigid day in Rexburg that I realized exactly why Justin creeped me out.

So Justin offers me a ride home—and I'm not going to lie, I wanted a ride home. It was freezing! The wind had picked up, and it was beginning to snow and probably would've taken me at least thirty minutes to walk back to our dorm apartment—uphill against the wind and snow all the way.

Yes, I wanted a ride home, but my feelings where Justin was concerned, mingled with the fact that I couldn't imagine Tom the Cute Bass Player having to walk all the way home, uphill and against the wind, wearing nothing but a light jacket carrying his bass in its case— well, all of it made me pause a moment before accepting.

Then, just as I was getting ready to ask Justin myself if Tom the Cute Bass Player could have a ride also, a shivering Tom the Cute Bass Player asked Justin, "Dude? Can you take me home too?" Rolling his eyes with distain, Justin unwillingly agreed.

Tom the Cute Bass Player was a tall, handsome, charismatic guy with a great sense of humor—a guy that all the girls loved and wanted to date. You know the type, right? Whether it's the '80s or the 2000s, it's always the same. Anyway, Justin's envy and animosity toward Tom the Cute Bass Player had always been unspoken, perhaps, but very obvious—no more so than when Justin barked at Tom to put his bass in the back seat with Justin's electric guitar.

Now, being that the guys had put their cased instruments in the backseat, and being that Justin's vintage hot rod had bucket seats in the front, there was no choice but for Tom the Cute Bass Player and I to share the front passenger's seat (to which neither of us was averse, of course). But thinking back on the situation as I am right now, I think this may have really ticked off Justin—and possibly added to what happened when...

Anyway, Tom the Cute Bass Player coolly slid into the passenger's seat, and I hopped in, too—onto his lap. (I was much thinner then and much more able to not only hop but also sit on someone's lap and not cause them any discomfort.) Tom the Cute Bass Player closed the car door, and Justin hit the gas, peeling out of the parking lot like a ruptured duck. I knew Justin was ticked off, but it wasn't far to my apartment, and Tom the Cute Bass Player and I were both very warm and safe from the elements (especially considering that his arms were around my waist, mine were around his neck, and we were snuggled close together).

Justin drove uphill against the wind and blowing snow, and it wasn't long before he pulled up next to the curb of the sidewalk outside Tom the Cute Bass Player's apartment. I let Tom the Cute Bass Player out, and he removed his bass from the back seat, thanked Justin, told me he'd see me later, and closed the door. And that was the moment—that was the moment the emotional red flags in my brain really began to unfurl! It was kind of like one of those scenes in a sci-fi movie. You know the ones I mean—someone falls into like a cave or something and she's standing there in complete and utter darkness. Then she finds a cell phone (or, in the movies I grew up with, a cigarette lighter or recaptured. And though she thought it impossible, Tierney felt herself falling even more deeply in love with Rome Novak.

Suddenly, she was overwhelmed—so full of joy and love and appreciation for Rome's talent that she could hardly contain herself. In fact, she couldn't! And as Rome finished the song and set his guitar on the floor next to his chair, Tierney reacted.

Fairly lunging from her place on the sofa, she reached out, gathering the front of Rome's shirt tightly in her fists, leaning forward and kissing him with such a pent-up passion that she felt she might detonate somehow as it began to surrender through her kiss. Over and over again she kissed him, until she could hardly draw a breath—until he could hardly draw a breath. She loved him! Oh, she loved him so thoroughly! And finally—finally Tierney ignored her fears, her self-doubt, and everything else that had been keeping her from effusively trying to capture Rome's heart for her own.

Still, Tierney knew if she didn't draw a full breath, she'd faint and not be able to kiss Rome at all. Therefore, she broke the seal of their lips, pulling away from him ever so slightly but still clutching his shirt. Rome's beautiful, smoldering eyes held hers in an impassioned gaze that sent goose bumps racing over Tierney's body.

She gasped then as she felt Rome's hands at the back of her knees— as he pulled them, inducing them to buckle and moving them to either side of his chair, thus causing her to sit down promptly on his lap.

Taking her face between his strong hands, he breathed, "If I'd known I was gonna get this reaction, I would've played for you a long time ago."

Rome's mouth captured Tierney's in a fierce, demanding kiss that provoked an uncontrollable trembling in her as her mouth met and melded with his.

Tierney's heart leapt in her chest; over and over and over it leapt with joy, unbridled love, and admiration for Rome. She felt unfamiliarly free—as if some invisible wall had been broken down, allowing her to wholly give her heart to the man she was so desperately in love with.

Tierney frowned a moment as Rome broke the seal of their lips, placing his hands firmly under her arms. Lifting her from his lap, he stood with her, drawing her body against his as they then lingered in the Novaks' family room, embroiled in delicious kissing.

flashlight), clicks it on, and sees that she's standing right in the midst of a nest of flesh-eating alien pupas or eggs. Naturally, the light produced by the cell phone has disturbed the nest of human-eating pupa alien things, and they begin to hatch or squirm around, and the person who fell into their nest has no way out. And then the cell phone, lighter, or flashlight suddenly goes out, and the audience hears screaming and munching noises. It was like that feeling when Tom the Cute Bass Player closed the passenger door and Justin peeled away from the curb. I experienced that same sort of feeling (only the light hadn't gone out and the screaming and munching noises hadn't begun yet).

Of course, I instantly thought what most eighteen-year-old girls going to college in a small town in Idaho think: "I'm just being paranoid." That's what I kept silently telling myself—until the moment that Justin hit the gas pedal and blew past my dorm building, that is!

"What are you doing?" I asked Justin as he hung a left at the main street up ahead, leaving the safety of my apartment and roommates farther behind.

"I'm taking you somewhere," Justin answered. Okay, *not* the response a girl wants to hear from a guy that creeps her out, right?

"I want to go home," I informed him. (A classic line—not unlike many lines uttered in slasher movies, right?)

"I'll take you home later," Justin said. "I'm taking you to my place first."

And the red flags began to unfurl by the thousands! Suddenly, my worried "inklings" erupted into full-fledged fear!

"Take me home now, Justin," I said as he hung a right, heading into a neighborhood that I never even knew was there before, let alone was familiar with.

"Oh, come on," he said. "Don't be such a prude. I'll take you home later…after we go to my place."

I am not exaggerating when I tell you that in that moment, my hand was on the handle of the passenger's side door. I had already determined that I would jump out of the car if I had to. Snow and wind no longer seemed very miserable. Everything in my body, mind, and soul was telling me to get myself out of this situation.

Therefore, I demanded, "I swear, Justin, if you don't turn around, I *will* jump out of your car…no matter how fast you're going."

"Oh, come on!" he laughed. "I just want to have a little fun. You're acting all weird. I'll take you home later. I promise."

"Turn around!" I demanded. "I'm serious. If you don't turn around now, I swear I will jump out!"

I had visions of opening the door and tucking myself into a little ball, rolling out of the car the way my little neighbor boy Josh had done once when I was driving him somewhere, made a left turn, and my car door suddenly flew open, sending him tumbling out into the street. He was a little dusty, his hair was mussed, and the flower he'd been holding to give to my mom didn't have any petals left on it, but he'd survived. Thus, I figured if Josh could survive, without big snow banks to break his fall, so could I.

My mind then determined that if I survived jumping out of a moving car, I would simply get up and run to the closest house and begin screaming and knocking on the door. This was my plan, and to this day I promise you I would've carried it out.

But as I started to open the door, Justin hollered, "Okay! Okay! Jeez! You're such a prude!"

He whipped his hot rod around and sped back to my dorm building, screeching to a stop in front of the parking lot of the building. And can you believe that as I got out of the car, Justin actually had the unmitigated gall to say, "See you tomorrow"?

I was rattled—I mean really rattled, wigged out, scared. I raced to my apartment, burst through the front door, and, weeping and trembling, told my best friend and roommate, Sandy, what had happened. We spent some time talking about what a jerk Justin was and how lucky I was. Tom the Cute Bass Player even called to make sure I'd gotten home okay, because he'd had some red flags of his own the instant he'd closed the door and trapped me in the car with Justin.

It wasn't like I hadn't had "emotional red flags" before. I'd had them my whole life; I think everyone does. I remember when I was about eight years old, a car began following me as I walked home from 7-Eleven one day. My instincts told me to turn and hurry into the backyard of a nearby house, which I did. The car that had been following me slowed down and, as I watched from my stealth position behind some bushes, even turned around and drove by the house a couple more times before finally speeding off.

So, really, I'd heeded warnings before. But this time, the cold weather, fatigue, and, to be honest, fear of hurting Justin's feelings by refusing his offer (in other words, "I'd rather freeze to death in a blizzard trying to walk home than ever get in a car with you" sort of implication)—coupled with the fact that Tom the Cute Bass Player was going to be with me up until we were a block or two from my building—had convinced me to ignore the silent warnings of my sixth sense.

What would've happened if I hadn't demanded to be taken home? What would've happened if I'd demanded to be taken home, he'd refused again, and then I'd chickened out and hadn't jumped out of the car? Honestly, I have no idea! It could be that Justin just wanted me to go to his apartment to see his guitar pick collection or to offer me a nice, warm cup of hot cocoa. And although I don't think Justin meant anything as innocent as all that—although I do not know what would've happened and never will—guess what? Better safe than sorry.

Now, perhaps the most profound emotional red flags story I've heard of late was from a dear friend of mine as we enjoyed a casual lunch one day. Several of my friends and I had met for lunch on a Thursday at noon. There we were, just chatting about how miserable bra shopping is (you know, the basic lunch conversation), when the subject turned to something else—the possible dangers we come in contact with throughout life and sometimes without ever knowing.

Anyway, my friend began to tell a story. One evening back when she was a teenager, she was attending a church dance. Now of course at church dances everyone knows you're not supposed to leave the building, right? Well, my friend was a little bored, and so she left the building to go to her car to retrieve something (I don't remember what—maybe gum). As she stepped off the sidewalk surrounding the building, a car pulled up in front of her—nothing unusual to happen at a church building. And it was just a plain old white Volkswagen bug.

A man rolled down the window and asked my friend, "So what's going on here?"

"Just a church dance," my friend replied as her emotional red flags began to unfurl.

The man tried to keep a conversation going with my friend, but she was listening to her emotional red flags that night, offered a polite good-bye to the man, turned, and hurried back into the church building.

Only a few days later, something hit the news that confirmed to my friend that she had been wise to listen to her promptings. The man driving the white VW bug—the man who'd spoken to her—was none other than Ted Bundy, the brutal serial killer of the 1970s who eventually confessed to murdering at least thirty women (though he is suspected of perhaps killing many, many more). When my friend saw Ted Bundy's photos and heard and read the description of his car in the newspaper and on the news, she knew she'd had a very narrow escape. Can you even imagine?

Yep, I'm a believer in listening to emotional red flags—always. People can say you're paranoid, overprotective of your children, or just plain chicken, but I don't care. And even though I've never had a Ted Bundy type near miss (that I know of), the times I haven't listened to my warning instincts—well, some turned out fine, and others did not. So when those flags start to unfurl in your mind, pay attention.

Tierney's experience with Elias Potts was indeed inspired by not only my own personal experience with those "sixth sense," "gut instinct," "spiritual promptings" we all have but also by stories I've heard from friends and family. It's an important lesson that we all learn at some point—either the hard way or, better and hopefully, the easy way.

Did the Milli Vanilli lip sync in the book make you go, "Where'd she come up with that?" at all? Well, if it did, here's the scoop: I *loved* "Girl, You Know Its True" by Milli Vanilli! Still love it! To me, it was one of the best songs of the late 1980s, and I don't care if Rob and Fab were lip-syncing to the voices of some lesser-attractive wannabes. They were awesome! And, yes, Rob was totally my favorite. Of course, the fact that my sons, Mitch and Trent, still plan to dress up as Milli Vanilli one Halloween in the future played a big part in my inspiration for that Halloween party too.

And now I think it's time to let you off the Author's Note hook. I've been rambling for hours about stuff that doesn't even matter, and you're probably tired and needing some sleep. So here's wishing you a

good night's sleep and hoping that handsome, dashing, 1950 *Two Weeks with Love* visits your dreams!
~ Marcia Lynn McClure

One Classic Latin Lover, Please Trivia Snippets

Snippet #1—As a freshman in high school, my best friend and I taught ourselves to play the guitar. Oh, sure, we had an official class, "Beginning Guitar," that appeared on our high school class schedule. But the class was instructed by the school's choral teacher; we'll call him Mr. Shots. Why is the fact that Mr. Shots taught the Beginning Guitar class even relevant? Well, it's relevant because Mr. Shots was always drunk. Oh, he was a nice old guy, in truth. He'd get up and lead the school in the fight song every assembly, and somehow our school choral groups always managed to pull off some sort of performance. But at eight AM every morning when "Beginning Guitar" was scheduled, Mr. Shots was either already drunk and sitting in his office or sitting in his office getting drunk. Therefore, my best friend and I spent the class time teaching ourselves to play guitar.

Anyway, I digress. So by the middle to end of our freshman year of high school, my BFF and I were pretty good little guitar players. I mean, we weren't proficient at like "Stairway to Heaven" or anything, but we could strum or pick a good tune. And since both of us sang as well, we performed here and there together.

My BFF was also a pianist, however, so as freshman year ended, I spent a lot more time playing my guitar in my room than she probably did. The result was that I began to take flamenco guitar lessons, having grown a little tired of pop songs and folk songs.

So the point of this snippet is purely for trivia's sake. Though I can't play it anymore (I gave up guitar in college—long story), I used to be pretty good at playing flamenco guitar, drumming my fingers on the wood of the guitar's face as I strummed and everything! YouTube a popular video of the song "Malagueña" (maybe cliché but still my favorite to play back then) or even of Charo playing—she's awesome!

Snippet #2—Yep, Tierney's name was inspired by one of my favorite "Golden Age of Hollywood" actresses, Gene Tierney. Loved her in

Laura and everything else I've ever seen her in. And, yes, Gene Tierney is why Rome and Tierney are dancing to Ella Fitzgerald's version (my favorite) of "Laura" on Christmas Eve.

Snippet #3—Absolutely! Rome's last name, Novak, was absolutely inspired by the beautiful Kim Novak (for whom one of my sister-in-laws is middle-named, by the way). I will admit to being a little worried when one of my dear friends asked me what the name of my hero for this book was. I answered, "Rome Novak!" and she smiled and said, "Hmmm. Sounds kind of like a little Polish apple or something."

Snippet #4—Not only is "Silent Night" my favorite Christmas carol, but over the years I've begun to realize that it is perhaps my very favorite song. I love "Silent Night"; it soothes me, calms my soul, and inspires me. And I do own a rendition done on guitar that will bring the listener to tears almost every time. I love it!

Snippet #5—Nikki! Ladies and gentlemen, I give you my inspiration for Nikki Novak's character and Halloween costume: my friend Nikki! Nikki is a fellow movie soundtrack lover and a dear, dear supportive friend. In fact, now that I think about it, I would term Nikki a movie soundtrack aficionado—a true expert on the subject of good, worthy, beautiful, inspirational movie soundtracks, and music overall. Furthermore, and most importantly, I find that any time I see Nikki's smile, I feel better through and through; Nikki's smile is medicinal to me. *And* the first time I saw this photo of Nikki dressed like Professor Trelawney from Harry Potter, I laughed out loud with amusement, happiness, and just plain cheerfulness! The mere sight of Nikki and her smile cheers me, and it was never more evident in a photograph than in this one. So thank you, Nikki Nikki Noo Noo! I love you!

Surprise! A gift from Marcia Lynn McClure to you!
Read on and enjoy another wonderful, holiday romance—
Marcia's romantic novella,
The Chimney Sweep Charm follows
—in its entirety!

CHAPTER ONE

"Okay. Let's get started," the tall, gray-haired man standing at the front of the room began.

"I don't like orientations," Baylee Cabot whispered aside to the friend sitting next to her. "They always make me nervous for some reason."

Baylee's friend Candice giggled. "They make you nervous? Why?"

"I think I'm always afraid they'll throw something unexpected at me," Baylee explained.

"Like what?" Candice asked quietly. "We already have our costumes and schedules. What could they possible throw at us now?"

Baylee shrugged. "I don't know."

"What?" Candice asked. "Do you think they're going to announce that there's a bathing suit competition or something?"

Baylee frowned. "Of course not."

"Then quit worrying and listen up. Maybe we'll get free hot cocoa whenever we want or something like that."

"Though I would like to see you two in a bathing suit competition," Tate Polanski said as he turned around and winked at Baylee and Candice.

"Shut up, Tate," Baylee groaned, rolling her eyes. Tate drove her nuts. Actually, Tate drove everyone nuts. Oh sure, he was a great vocalist and supreme handbell ringer, but he was a pain in the neck too. In fact, at that moment Tate Polanski was the only negative thing Baylee could think of when it came to being a member of the Hampton Handbell Ringers.

"At this point, everyone should have their schedules," the tall, gray-haired man said. "If you don't have your schedules, see me immediately following the orientation."

Baylee sighed and focused her attention on the man addressing the room full of people. His name was John O'Sullivan, the events coordinator for the Dickens Village theme square.

"I'd like to begin our meeting by offering a little background into the Dickens Village, for those who might not be familiar with it," Mr. O'Sullivan said.

Baylee sighed again and settled back in her chair. Working evenings at the Dickens Village would be hard, but she was very excited to be doing so. Not only would the extra moonlighting with her handbell ringing group leave her with some great cash, but it would be fun to linger in the atmosphere and ambiance the Dickens Village offered.

"The Dickens Village is the brainchild of a man named Malcolm McBride," Mr. O'Sullivan said. "Malcolm conceived the idea in the late 1970s, but it took him nearly thirty years to round up the investors, architects, and so forth needed to finance and construct such an undertaking as an entire recreation of an early 1800s English village here in the US. Still, Malcolm managed it somehow, and in the year 2000 construction began on the Dickens Village—a theme commons meant to transport visitors back to the time of Charles Dickens."

Baylee smiled. Oh, she already knew the history of the Dickens Village—but she loved hearing it all the same. She listened with interest as Mr. O'Sullivan began to read from a pamphlet he'd taken out of his pocket.

"The Dickens Village is composed of several square blocks of buildings that comprise retail establishments and dwellings, fashioned to emulate Camden Town in London, England, the way it may have appeared in 1843…the year Charles Dickens's *A Christmas Carol* was first published." Mr. O'Sullivan paused, looking out over the gathered conglomeration of retail workers, vendors, and security personnel that had congregated for the orientation. "I'm assuming all of you have visited the Dickens Village at one time or another." There was a general hum of yeses and nodding heads. "Then you know how truly magical a place it is." Again hums of yeses and other agreeing sounds. "Good," Mr. O'Sullivan continued, "because by accepting holiday employment or vending space with the Dickens Village, you have agreed to take on the responsibility of ensuring that each and every visitor this holiday season enjoys themselves to the fullest."

Baylee liked the warm, delighted sensation that was welling in her chest. She loved the Dickens Village—she always had. And to have the opportunity to perform with the Hampton Handbell Ringers and Carolers in the Dickens Village for two entire months during the holidays would be a dream come true! Baylee brushed a stray strand of caramel-highlighted brown hair from her cheek, thinking of how grateful she was she'd managed to pass the five auditions necessary to make it into the Hampton Handbell Ringers the year before. Sure, it was a lot of work—a ton of practicing was necessary—but whenever she was performing with the others, whether in public or just in practice, every one of Baylee's five senses was overjoyed.

Handbell ringing was a vanishing and somewhat magical novelty. Yet Baylee had loved the beautiful chimes of a handbell choir since the moment she'd first heard one at the age of three. She'd never forget it. She'd been watching television—something her mother was watching on PBS—and a handbell choir had performed "Carol of the Bells." Baylee had never heard anything so beautiful—not in all her long three years upon the earth! She'd been mesmerized by handbells ever since and had begun begging for her own set handbells the very next Christmas.

Though her parents had complied, gifting her a new handbell each year as one of her Christmas presents, it wasn't until she was in the sixth grade that Baylee had really begun to learn the skill and art of handbell ringing. When she had been able to finally audition for a local handbell choir in middle school, her love of handbells and handbell ringing had really begun to know a measure of satisfaction. She'd continued with the same handbell choir through high school, eventually leaving it for the opportunity to join the Randolph Handbell Ringers. It was while ringing with Randolph's that Baylee discovered she owned a pretty darn good soprano singing voice as well. In fact, during her first interview with the Hampton Handbell Ringers, the conductor had asked her why it was she hadn't been singing all her life—why it had taken her until she started college to earn her music degree to realize it. Baylee simply explained that she'd always focused on the music of the bells she'd heard in her head and had never really noticed she could sing until college.

And now, as she sat listening to Mr. O'Sullivan describe the new vendors and shops that had been added to the Dickens Village for the holidays, Baylee thought there could be no more beautiful thing on earth than to be dressed in Dickens's era clothing and wandering the cobblestone streets ringing or singing Christmas carols to all the world.

"We're really excited about having the Hampton Handbell Ringers and Carolers aboard for this season," Mr. O'Sullivan said. He smiled at the group of bell ringers sitting on the first two rows. "I've heard you all perform so many times, and as glorious as it was...I can't imagine how truly amazing it's going to be to see you roaming the streets of the Dickens Village this year."

Baylee smiled, thinking that Mr. O'Sullivan must indeed be a like-minded soul to her. She could tell he truly appreciated the beauty of handbells—and not just because of the price he'd agreed to pay the Hampton Handbell Ringers and Carolers to perform at the Dickens Village.

"He hasn't said anything about a bathing suit competition yet," Candice whispered.

"Thank goodness," Baylee quietly giggled.

"There's another new addition to this year's holiday festivities," Mr. O'Sullivan said. "And that's a larger security force than we've had before."

Baylee frowned a little. She didn't like to think of that fact that the Dickens Village needed security—though she knew it did. It seemed every inch of everywhere needed security any more.

She was a little relieved when Mr. Sullivan explained, "Of course, the visitors won't know they're there. Our security team will be incognito, as always."

Baylee was glad to know that at least it wouldn't look like the streets of old Camden Town at Christmas were operating under martial law.

"But we do want all of you to know who you can contact if you see anything amiss or have trouble yourself," Mr. O'Sullivan said. Nodding toward someone in the audience, he asked, "Brian? Would you like to give us a little update on exactly who we can to contact if the need should arise? For those of you who might not already know him, Brian is our new head of security."

"You bet," a man sitting about halfway back in the middle of the room said.

Baylee watched the man as he stood up, trying to memorize his face in case she ever needed the assistance of the security staff—though she couldn't imagine why she ever would. The head of security, Brian, was in truth a very handsome guy. He was the archetypal tall, dark, and handsome hero type—with brown eyes, black hair, and biceps the size of tree trunks.

"All of a sudden, I'm a little more excited about this particular bell-ringing gig," Candice whispered to Baylee as she too studied Brian, the head of security.

"Absolutely," Baylee agreed.

"I'm Brian Reagan, and my security teams are the best available," the handsome head of security began. "As John said, we're bringing in some extra guys for the holidays…so you'll be surrounded by multiple safety measures."

"Hmmm," Candice mumbled. "I'd be fine if it were just *him* who was surrounding me."

"Absolutely," Baylee giggled.

"If you need help," Brian continued, "just let one of us know. We will be positioned throughout the village and dressed up like all of you, of course. For example, the roasted chestnut vendor, the hot soup vendor, and an older guy who might look a lot to you like Ebenezer Scrooge—" He paused to allow for everyone's laughter to die down and then continued, "They'll be right in the center of town, near the fountain. Beyond that, all you need to do is find yourself a chimney sweep, and you've got one of us on the line. We figured chimney sweeps, with their smudged-up faces and black-ops uniforms, would be the stealth way to keep watch. With the chimney sweep thing, we can be wherever we want to without looking out of place—rooftops, streets, shops, dwellings…everywhere. So if you need something, just grab a chimney sweep."

"Well, there you go," Baylee whispered to Candice. "That's easy enough to remember. If we need help, we just look for Dick Van Dyke and sing 'Chim Chim Cher-ee.'"

"I'm totally down with that," Candice whispered in return. "I *love* Dick Van Dyke!"

"Me too," Baylee said quietly. "I always thought Mary Poppins was an idiot for not giving up the nanny gig to go for Bert."

"Worst mistake of her life," Candice agreed in a mumble.

"I'll have the guys stand up so you can see how many of us there are," Brian said. "And remember, half the staff is already on duty over at the village. Guys?"

There was the muffled sound of audience members standing up, and Baylee and Candice turned to look behind them.

"Holy smokes!" Baylee breathed.

"It's like a Navy SEAL convention or something," Candice added.

And it was! Baylee couldn't believe that over twenty-five of the people in the orientation audience were tall, dark, handsome, buff guys dressed all in black. Each man stood with his feet apart and hands held at his back—similar if not exactly like a military "at ease" stance.

"They're all packing heat too," Baylee whispered to Candice as she noted all the holstered sidearms.

"I guess Mr. O'Sullivan wants to be prepared," Candice said.

"I suppose you girls are all wowed now, right?" Tate said from the front row.

"Let's see," Candice began, looking to Tate and feigning an expression of thoughtfulness. "Let's say I'm being assaulted by some weirdo in the street…and who am I going to look to for protection? One of these guys?" she said, nodding toward the security staff. "Or you, Tate? You…who freaked out in June when we were in New York and you thought some guy was looking at you funny. You freaked out and slammed Megan's finger in the door and cut it off! Who do you think I'm going to trust?"

"It was an accident, and you know it," Tate grumbled.

Baylee did know it. Still, she found her eyes glancing down the row of chairs in front of her to Megan—to the missing first joint and fingertip on her right hand.

"Yeah, it was," Candice admitted. "But you still cared more about yourself than Megan. The guy was stalking Megan…not you. Real heroic, Tate. Way to go to instilling a sense of confidence in me that you would have my back."

"Whatever," Tate grumbled, turning around in his seat to pout.

"Thank you," Brian said to his men. Baylee watched as the security staff sat down in unison. "So there you have it…our extra security staff for the next two months. As I said, if you need assistance…just grab a chimney sweep."

Baylee giggled. "Grab a cab, grab a snack…grab a chimney sweep."

Candice giggled too. "And you know what? I just figured out what I want for Christmas."

"Absolutely," Baylee agreed. "I'll never ring 'Chim Chim Cher-ee' with the same mental pictures again."

They giggled together, biting their lips and binding their tongues when Mr. O'Sullivan's attention lingered rather scoldingly on them a moment.

Baylee knew their joking around might sound scandalous to anyone listening, but they were only kidding. Sure, the security guys were attractive—a striking group of militant-looking hero-types—but in truth they were probably a bunch of egotistical gun freaks. She wondered how they felt about being dressed up as chimney sweeps and skulking around in a reproduction of an old London town, which was no doubt already slathered in Christmas decor.

"Thank you, Brian," Mr. O'Sullivan said. "Next I'd like to make you all aware of some new vendors we have for this year's holiday season."

Baylee smiled, amused by their ridiculous comments concerning the security staff guys. Yet as she tried to focus once more on what Mr. O'Sullivan was saying—on the new ragdoll vendor he'd just introduced—a strange sensation began to travel up the back of her neck. It wasn't an unpleasant sensation at all—just strange. She felt as if an old electric heating pad had been pressed to the back of her neck— had the odd feeling that someone sitting behind her was significant to her somehow.

But she brushed the sensation aside. After all, twenty-five intimidating Navy SEAL types were sitting behind her, armed to the teeth. Who wouldn't feel weird?

"Well, I guess tomorrow night will find us dressed up like the Cratchit kids and ringing our little hearts out," Candice said as Baylee walked with her across the parking lot toward their cars. The parking lot of the

Dickens Village office headquarters was quickly emptying, but Baylee was in no hurry. She and Candice had discovered that one of the opinions they shared was that *not* racing to get out of a parking lot was far wiser, as well as safer, than rushing into a fender bender, or worse. Yep, they'd each discovered that the spring before when hurrying to meet some friends for dinner after handbell practice one night—and had found Candice's car T-boned and Candice in the hospital for three days.

And so, as others associated with the Dickens Village orientation hurried on, Baylee and Candice contentedly meandered toward their cars.

"Wanna know a secret?" Baylee asked her friend.

"Always," Candice answered.

"Do you think it's weird that I'm so excited about this? I mean, I can't wait to get there tomorrow night…to see people's faces when they hear the bells."

"I don't think you're weird at all," Candice said. "I know how you feel about the bells. There's something vintage about handbells. That's why we love them so much. That's why we do what we do. The bells are, like, totally magical. They make people feel things they don't feel very often anymore." Baylee nodded. "We've got the rest of our lives to teach music or whatever…but we might not always be able to have handbell ringing as our career."

"That's true," Baylee agreed. "Think of all the emotions you can see washing over people's faces when we perform. Things like true, tingly joy," Baylee suggested.

"And the sensation of a sincere smile," Candice added.

"And, of course, the most important emotion…" Baylee began.

Giggling, both girls sighed, "Love!"

"And there they are…the two little goody-goody girls."

At the sound of Tate's voice behind them, Baylee's heart sank to the pit of her stomach. Something about Tate Polanski just made her skin crawl. Though she'd never said a word about it out loud, she secretly hoped that Mr. Hampton would get fed up with Tate's irritating personality and drop-kick him out of the Hampton Handbell Ringers. But since it was a terrible thing to think toward someone, Baylee always just bit her tongue—even when Candice would rant her own disgust concerning Tate.

"Good-bye, Tate," Candice said as Tate stepped between her and Baylee. "We don't have time for your crap today."

"But wait," Tate said, taking hold of Baylee's arm with one hand and Candice's with the other and pulling them to a halt. "Don't you want to hear what I just found out about those beefy security guys you two were drooling over at the orientation meeting?"

"We were not drooling over them, Tate," Baylee countered.

"I was," Candice playfully interjected.

"Yes, you were, Candice…and so were you, Baylee," Tate mocked. "Anyway, I thought you two might just want to know where these guys came from before you go off trying to reel a couple of them into your boyfriend traps."

"I really don't care, Tate," Baylee said. "And let go of my arm." She tried to pull her arm free, but Tate held tight.

"All those black-clad, muscle-bound, jarheads types in there," he continued however. "That's exactly what they are—jarheads."

"What are you talking about?" Candice asked, the irritation growing in her voice as she too tried to disengage her arm from Tate's grasp.

"They're jarheads. They're exactly what they look like," he answered.

"You mean they're Marines?" Baylee asked. "Like, ex-Marines?"

Tate shrugged. "Maybe not all of them are Marines, but they're all ex-military somethings…Army, Marines, Navy…whatever. They're all ex-military."

"Well, good," Baylee said, wrenching her arm free at last. "I feel safer already." She glared at Tate. Oooo! He drove her nuts!

"Do you?" he asked, however, taking hold of her arm again. "You feel safer having a bunch of ex-military, discharged for medical reasons, chimney sweeps hopping over rooftops at the Dickens Village? I'm telling you, some of these guys are literally insane."

"And how do you know that?" Candice asked.

"I overheard Mr. O'Sullivan talking to buffed-up head of security," he explained. "Some of these guys were wounded in action, some of them just didn't reenlist when their time was up, and some of them were discharged for psychological reasons…and that makes you feel more safe?"

"Absolutely," Baylee said through gritted teeth.

Tate frowned at her a moment. "Who are you? Rocky Balboa or something?"

"Ex-military," Candice said. "Seems to me they'd make the best security force."

But Tate growled with disgust, shaking his head. "They're ex-soldiers, ladies. Damaged goods. It ain't like it's gonna be Dick Van Dyke leaping around on those rooftops while we're performing. It'll be jarheads and nut jobs."

"For your information, Tate," Baylee began, attempting to keep her temper reined in. "Dick Van Dyke is a military veteran himself. He was in the United States Army Air Corps during World War II…which apparently you did not know. So keep your opinions to yourself. I'm glad they're all ex-military…whether or not they're dressed like chimney sweeps."

A knowing grin spread across Tate's face, and he only egged Baylee on by saying, "Oooo! Those pretty brown eyes of yours are blazing now, aren't they, Baylee Cabot? You really do have a thing for those jarheads, don't you?"

"Excuse me."

"Holy smokes!" she heard Candice breathe.

Baylee glanced up to see two members of the new security staff standing behind them—and they were both more than merely striking. Though one man was far and away more handsome than the other, they were both attractive—as well as intimidating.

One of the men nodded to Tate and asked, "You're one of the handbell ringers, right?"

"Yeah," Tate managed to answer.

"I heard you guys are really good," the more handsome one said.

Baylee stared at him for a moment—because he was certainly a sight to behold. He was tall, with an unusual color of brown hair (that reminded her of Brazil nut shells), and green eyes that looked fabulous against his dark complexion.

"We've been told we're the best," Tate countered.

"Cool," the exceptionally good-looking chimney-sweep-to-be said. "I can't wait to see you guys do your thing."

"Me neither," the other agreed.

Baylee couldn't help but smile a little—for she knew exactly what the two security guys were doing. As the too-handsome-for-words guy stepped between her and Tate, gently disengaging Tate's hand from her arm, the other guy did the same thing as he stepped between Tate and Candice. They were intimidating Tate but under the guise of interest in the Hampton Handbell Ringers.

"Excuse me," the sinfully handsome guy said, still looking at Tate. "We've gotta get going. I guess we'll see you tomorrow night, right?"

"I guess so," Tate mumbled. He was mad—furious. And the expression of irritation on his face was fabulous!

"Ladies," the dazzlingly handsome guy said, looking quickly to Candice and then to Baylee.

"You all have a good evening," the other guy aded, nodding to Tate. And then they simply sauntered toward their vehicles.

"Well, that's nauseatingly predictable," Tate mumbled as Baylee watched each security guy climb into a pickup. The wickedly handsome guy was driving, and as the big black Dodge Ram drove away, Baylee noted the Silver Star license plate on the front bumper of the truck and the Purple Heart license plate on the back. Both were embellished with license plate frames that read *Iraq/Afganistan Veteran—US Army Ranger.*

"Wow!" Baylee heard herself whisper.

"Wow is right," Tate grumbled. "Egotistical jarheads."

But Baylee was the daughter of a Gulf War veteran—the granddaughter of a Vietnam veteran as well.

And as her irritation and disgust with Tate heightened, she turned to him and said, "You know what, Tate? You have no idea. What's the worst thing you've ever had to do? Have a cavity filled at the dentist's office? So shut up. The Silver Star?" she asked, pointing in the direction the two military veterans had driven off in. "The Purple Heart? That's wounded in combat…and the Silver Star is for valor in the face of the enemy. So go on and whine about the fact that these guys are working security for whatever reason. I'll tell you this—I'd rather have chimney sweeps with Purple Heart medals pinned to their chests keeping things in line wherever I'm working than to have to depend on you for anything! So shut up and go home!"

"Geez, Baylee," Tate whined. "Take a lozenge and calm down."

"And don't lay a hand on me again, okay?" she added, turning from him and storming off toward her car.

"I guess Tate didn't get the memo about your feelings where the military is concerned," Candice laughed as she hurriedly caught up to Baylee.

Baylee shook her head. "Tate Polanski makes me sick," she growled. "It's guys like him…people like that…they're what's wrong with this country. They've never had to suffer or do without or live in fear of having their freedom stripped away. I just can't tolerate him anymore today. I swear, half the time I want to take his bells and shove them down his throat!"

"I love when you lose your cool," Candice giggled. "You so seldom do. But when you do…*bam*! I love it!"

"I don't," Baylee admitted, exhaling a heavy sigh.

"Well, don't let it bother you…and don't let Tate bother you. Think about those handsome ex-whatever-they-ares and the fact that they'll be working at the Dickens Village with us for two whole months." Candice giggled. "Did you see the way they just so smoothly interceded between us and Tate? Smooth and cool like nothing I've ever seen."

Baylee smiled again too. "Yeah. And that made it official."

"Made what official?" Candice asked.

"I officially know exactly what I want for Christmas," Baylee answered, smiling at her friend.

"A chimney sweep?" Candice asked knowingly.

"Absolutely!" Baylee confirmed.

"What an idiot," Justice Kincaid mumbled as he drove out of the Dickens Village office parking lot.

"*Freaking* idiot," his friend Tristan embellished. "Guys like that just chap my—"

"I know," Justice agreed. He grinned however, glanced to Tristan, and added, "But that one little bell ringer girl was shweet, right?"

"Both of them were," Tristan answered.

Justice sighed as he turned onto the main road. "Did you ever think we'd be pulling security duty at some theme park dressed like chimney sweeps, dude?"

"Hell no!" Tristan laughed. He shook his head. "But maybe this gig will be more interesting than we think. Especially if the intel is correct."

"Roger that," Justice chuckled.

He raked a hand over his short dark hair. "I just hope that handbell choir group thing doesn't play 'Chim Chim Cher-ee.' I might be overcome by the urge to start leaping around over rooftops like Dick Van Dyke."

"Who?" Tristan asked.

"Dude!" Justice exclaimed, frowning at his friend. "Are you kidding me? Dick Van Dyke? *Mary Poppins?*" But Tristan just shrugged with an expression of ignorance on the subject. Justice shook his head and mumbled, "Man…growing up without sisters really must've jacked you up. You don't even know who Dick Van Dyke is."

"Maybe not," Tristan admitted. "But I know who that idiot who was just handling those bell ringer girls is…and I plan to keep him in my sights. I hate dudes like that."

"Absolutely," Justice agreed. "Abso-freakin'-lutely."

Justice turned on the satellite radio, tuned it to the classic rock station, and heightened the volume. He was trying to distract himself from the weird sensation he'd had when he'd stepped between the guy bell ringer moron and the pretty girl he'd been man-handling. He hadn't even looked at the girl more than once—and he hadn't because of the strange wave of warmth that had washed over him in simply knowing she was there. It was kind of creepy—the way her image was lingering in his mind even at that very moment—like he already knew her or had seen her somewhere before. He didn't even know the shweet honey's name, but somehow he felt like he should.

He shook his head in an effort to dispel the vision of the girl from his mind. Yet he thought twice about it and decided to keep her there. After all, why chase away something so pretty and sweet, when there were so many other things clicking around in his brain that were exactly the opposite?

"Chimney sweeps, dude," Tristan chuckled. "I like it."

Justice nodded. "Me too," he said, still thinking about the cute bell ringer girl. "Me too."

CHAPTER TWO

"It's so pretty I'm gonna die!" Baylee exclaimed as she and Candice stepped through the ornate iron gates leading from the Dickens Village parking lot to the village itself. "I mean, look at that! Can you even believe it?"

Baylee was truly awestruck. In all her life she'd never seen anything like the Dickens Village as it stood all dressed up for the holidays.

"Haven't you been here before?" Candice asked.

"Well, yeah," Baylee answered, "but never when it was all lit up for Christmas like this! I only moved here in January, remember?" She shook her head in awed wonder. "I cannot believe this!"

Baylee was experiencing something nearly magical. For just a moment, she actually felt like she'd stepped out of the modern world and into a beautiful, warm-lighted globe created by Charles Dickens. In truth, she knew the London Camden Town of 1843 would've appeared much differently than the electric-lighted reproduction she was walking into now—but the sensation of having stepped into the past washed over with such command that, even for the warm red velvet caroler costume she was wearing, her entire body rippled with goose bumps.

Everywhere she looked she saw only beauty—pure loveliness! The buildings loomed dark against the evening sky, but every old-fashioned paned window was lit golden with flickering candlelight. Pine boughs strewn with red berries were draped overhead across the main streets. Christmas wreaths made of more pine boughs, holly sprigs, and pinecones hung on every door. Mistletoe balls, adorned with red ribbon, hung from every lamppost. The buildings and vendor carts seemed drenched in winter greenery and red berry sprigs. The cheering scent of burning pine was in the air—of cinnamon and freshly baked bread.

Baylee inhaled deeply. "Do you smell that? It actually smells as good as it looks!"

Candice giggled. "Girl, you need to get out more."

Baylee smiled and countered, "Girl, you need to appreciate things more."

"Look!" Candice suddenly exclaimed. Pointing to a nearby shop, she said, "There goes one now."

"One what?" Baylee asked, turning her attention to the shop Candice was indicating.

Candice rolled her eyes. "A chimney sweep, you goof."

Baylee saw him then—a man dressed all in black, with soot smudging his face. She smiled when she noted the authenticity of his costume. He seriously looked as if he'd just leapt out of a Dickens novel! He wore black pants and boots, a tattered, soot-dusted white shirt and black vest, a tight-fitting tailed jacket with silver buttons, fingerless gloves, and a ragged top hat. He even had a chimney sweep brush propped on one shoulder.

"I totally want one," Baylee giggled.

"I know!" Taking hold of Baylee's sleeve, Candice tugged her arm. "Come on. We have a few minutes before we're supposed to meet the others. Let's get a closer look at that that guy."

"Absolutely," Baylee readily agreed. After all, she was just as curious about the chimney sweep security staff as Candice was. She did doubt, however, that she'd find any member of the security staff interesting at all after having had a look at the exceptionally gorgeous one who had stepped between she and Tate the day before. Even in that moment, she couldn't believe how handsome he'd been—how her skin had instantly warmed at just the sight of him.

As Baylee and Candice hurried toward the shop into which the chimney sweep had disappeared, a young boy with a wooden crutch tucked under one arm hobbled toward them.

He was dressed in Dickens period costume, and as he approached, he lifted his hat, nodded to Baylee and Candice, and said, "God bless us, every one!"

Baylee smiled and asked, "You're Tiny Tim then?"

"Yes, milady," the boy answered. He smiled at her, studied her from head to toe a moment, and said, "And you must be a couple of the handbell ringers Mr. O'Sullivan told us about today. Nice costumes."

"Thanks," Baylee said. She removed one of her hands from the white muff she'd had it tucked in and smoothed the red velvet of her dress.

"The matching cape is cool," the boy commented. "Do your shoes match too?"

"Well, they're not velvet, of course, but they match for the time period we're in," Baylee giggled. Hitching up the hem of her dress, she displayed the black Victorian lace-up boots she was wearing. The boy smiled.

"You guys look totally real. Good job," he complimented.

"How about this?" Baylee asked as she lifted the hood of her matching red velvet cape, trimmed in white fur, to cover the back of her neck and head. She tucked her hand back into the muff she held and asked, "Better?"

"Perfect!' the boy laughed. He looked to Candice and said, "Do all you guys match like this?"

"The guys were other stuff," Candice answered. "You know, top hats, black tailcoats…that kind of stuff."

"I can't wait to see them," the boy said. "My grandpa owns this place and let me be Tiny Tim some of the time this year." Removing his hat, he said, "Malcolm McBride the Third, ladies…in case you ever need to know."

Baylee smiled and nodded at the boy. "Thanks, Malcolm. I'm Baylee, and this is Candice. You should come listen to our bells tonight if you can."

"Oh, I will for sure. Happy holidays!" he chimed as he hurried off.

Baylee and Candice watched him bolt away—laughed when the boy seemed to realize he was supposed to be a sickly Tiny Tim and began limping once more.

"Well, he's just too adorable for words," Candice said as she opened the door to the shop before them and stepped in.

A bell sounded as the door opened, and both Baylee and Candice gasped as their eyes beheld the dreamlike glory within the tiny shop. China dolls were everywhere! Nestled in among beautiful Victorian-era dollhouses, vintage-looking china dolls waited in small rocking chairs or in handcrafted cradles to be purchased.

"It's a doll shop," Baylee mumbled.

"You've got it, Sherlock," Candice teased.

Baylee playfully rammed an elbow into Candice's ribcage as she continued to look around the room. "I could spend hours in here," she sighed.

"Me too," Candice agreed. "Only we don't have hours…and it looks like the chimney sweep has already ducked out." Candice frowned and grumbled, "Dang it! How could he disappear so fast?"

"Well, I guess we'll just have to find another one later," Baylee said. "We've got to go. I don't want to be late and catch it from Mr. Hampton."

"Chimney sweeps and dolls will just have to wait," Candice sighed with disappointment.

As the girls hurried from the shop and toward the fountain in the center of town, Baylee knew it was going to be nearly impossible for her to concentrate on handbell ringing when the Dickens Village offered so much beauty and nostalgic atmosphere to bathe in. Still, she loved ringing and singing Christmas carols. Her time at the Dickens Village would be wonderful! She knew it would, and the joy swelling in her bosom warmed her to the very core of her heart.

Justice rubbed at his eyes a moment. He should've gotten a better night's sleep. If he weren't at his best, he wouldn't do the team any good if or when the maniac they were looking for *did* decide to show up at the Dickens Village. He shook his head and exhaled a heavy sigh, knowing all too well that he would never be wholly at his best again—not after Afghanistan. Still, he was alive, and everything that had been broken, lacerated, or mashed had healed as well as it would. Changing the attitude of his train of thought, Justice reminded his sore shoulder how lucky it was to be in the shape it was in.

Inhaling a deep breath of the crisp, cool night air, he was surprised at how truly great it smelled. He could smell the bread baking in the bakery, already knowing he was near its chimney. It made his stomach growl with hunger—as the scent of freshly baked bread always did. His mouth began to water as the thought of warm bread slathered in butter flitted through his mind.

Gazing out over the little nostalgic village, Justice admitted that it was quite an amazing thing—a reproduction of mid-1800s Camden Town right there on the outskirts of the big city. Of course, he could look behind him and see the skyscrapers of the busy metropolises stretching up into the sky. But the visitors to the Dickens Village on the streets below him were completely unaware of them. He smiled, liking the fact that the people enjoying the shops and sight in the Dickens Village were able to escape their worries and fast-paced lives for a time. He just hoped his team could keep them all safe.

It was Justice's opinion that Malcolm McBride should've let John O'Sullivan in on the truth about the added security—that the FBI was on the trail of a notorious psychopath who believed he was the actual Jack the Ripper and that recent evidence implied that the Dickens Village might be his next focus in searching for victims. But Brian had agreed that only a few higher-ups would know about the operation.

And so, there he stood, perched on top of a reproduction Camden Town building, dressed as a chimney sweep. He smiled, chuckling with amusement as "Chim Chim Cher-ee" began echoing in his mind.

Justice's thoughts were suddenly scattered, however—by the most beautiful sound he could ever remember hearing. Stealthily altering his position, he looked down to see the handbell ringers gathered in the square and beginning to perform. As he recognized the opening of "Carol of the Bells," he held his breath a moment. "Carol of the Bells" was one of his favorite Christmas carols—and he knew how easily it could be butchered. It seemed most choirs or musicians either played it so fast that it felt like a horse race or so slow that it made him want to nod off.

Yet as the Hampton Handbell Ringers moved into the full cadence of the carol, Justice grinned. "Perfect," he whispered. And it was. He'd never heard anything like it—not in real life anyway. The perfect measure of the bells—the way their tinkling sounds rang out into the night—gave his heart a lift. For just an instant, he owned the same delight in knowing the holidays were at hand as he had when he was a little kid. The sensation only lasted an instant, but it was powerful—and welcomed.

Justice's grandmother had been a great fan of "Carol of the Bells" and had owned a set of chimes she played the song on each Christmas Eve. He wondered for a moment if she still owned the chimes—missed being a carefree child who believed in Santa Claus and that his parents could protect him from any and all harm in the world.

The impression of childlike joy was fleeting, but the beautiful ringing of the bells wasn't, and Justice stood mesmerized as he watched the handbell ringers perform—specifically the pretty little thing he'd attempted to champion the day before in the parking lot.

The young woman stood center front, holding a shiny brass handbell in each hand and playing each one in turn with the grace and countenance of any Christmas angel that ever sat atop any Christmas tree. She was dressed all in red velvet and white fur—of course, all the women were—but for some reason Justice thought her red velvet dress and hooded cape looked brighter than the others.

He focused on the girl for a long time—entirely fascinated by everything about her. And then, as "Carol of the Bells" ended, he was even more amazed when it began again—this time with the handbell ringers performing the carol vocally. The a cappella vocal rendition of the piece was nearly as stirring as the handbell rendition. And Justice smiled when he picked out the voice of his favorite handbell ringer—first soprano.

He sighed—awed at the peace and tranquility the handbell ringers caroling were sifting into the night. He felt in that moment that all *was* calm. He knew it wasn't, of course. He knew men, women, and children were lingering in misery in many places all over the world—that people were suffering with loss, desperation, pain, and agony. Yet something about the carolers—they'd soothed his soul for a time. He couldn't remember the last time he'd experienced a feeling of calm. Sure, it was brief—but it was wonderful.

Then, as his eyes darted to a man cloaked in black and wearing a tall top hat, he was all too aware of exactly why he was there on the rooftops of the Dickens Village. But as the man bent down and picked up a small boy to put him on his shoulders—and being that the boy's face was radiating with love and recognition—he figured it was safe to listen to the carolers for a moment again. It was a lovely sound, and

Justice wondered if the fact that he'd thought the word *lovely* meant he was getting too complacent.

Straightening his posture and refocusing his attention on why he was there, he pulled the small set of binoculars from his pocket and began studying the people gathered in the square.

"A Jack the Ripper copycat," he grumbled to himself. "What next?"

"Oh, but look at this one!" Candice exclaimed. "You so need it! It looks so much like us!"

Baylee smiled as Candice handed her the small sterling silver charm fashioned to look like a Victorian caroler. "It does look like us," she said, studying the charm. "It really does. She even has a muff."

"You totally need that for your good bracelet," Candice said.

Baylee turned over the little box housing the charm to look at the price. "Ouch! It's thirty bucks," she whispered to Candice.

"Oh, come on," Candice pleaded, however. "I'll go halves with you. It's too perfect not to be dangling from your wrist."

Baylee giggled, for she wholeheartedly agreed with Candice. The Victorian caroler charm *was* perfect for her charm bracelet! "It is perfect…and you don't have to go halves with me. I'll buy it." Handing the pretty charm in the red velvet box to the lady behind the jewelry shop counter, Baylee nodded and said, "I just have to have it."

"It looks just like you," the lady said. "I can see why you can't pass it up." The woman moved to the cash register and scanned the price sticker barcode on the bottom of the box. "Cash, debit, or charge?"

"Cash," Baylee said, reaching into her red velvet dress pocket and retrieving the small change purse in which she carried her cash and ID when performing.

"It's so cute, Baylee!" Candice chimed again. "Really it is. It's just too perfect for you."

"I know," Baylee agreed. The sterling Victorian caroler charm would look so pretty on her new bracelet. She couldn't wait to attach it!

Ever since she'd been a little girl, Baylee Cabot had wanted a charm bracelet—not a little kids' one, but a real charm bracelet with real charms. Once she was old enough and had some spending money here and there, she'd begun making her own charm bracelets, and they were pretty ones too. However, she'd still wanted a real one—sterling silver or gold. Thus, when she'd landed the job with the Hampton Handbell Ringers and moved away from home, the first luxury she'd allowed herself was the purchase of a sterling silver charm bracelet.

Baylee soon discovered, however, that the sort of charms she liked were pretty pricey, and so she'd promised herself she'd only buy a charm when one appeared that she fell in love with—literally loved and knew she'd never find another one like it. She'd also promised herself that each charm she did purchase would need to be significant—have a memory or some sort of favoritism attached. And the moment she'd seen the Victorian caroler charm, she'd known both requirements to validate a charm purchase were fulfilled—even without Candice's encouragement she'd known it.

The Victorian caroler charm was not only beautiful but far and away singular because it was a Victorian caroler (just as Baylee and Candice were) but also because she had purchased it at the Dickens Village. It would be so lastingly meaningful—the fact that she'd purchased the charm right there at the jewelry shop in the Dickens Village.

As she handed the price of the charm to the jewelry shop clerk, Baylee sighed. It was such a lovely little bracelet charm!

"Thank you," the clerk said, handing Baylee a small brown paper bag stamped with holly and berries. "It really is a very beautiful charm…just like the music you girls are providing the village this year. I can't believe how beautiful those handbells are!"

"Thank you," Baylee said. "And I'm sure we'll be back to browse around. It's only our first day on the job, and already we've spent every penny we earned today."

"Oh, believe me…if anybody knows how hard it is to work here and not spend money, it's me!" the woman laughed. "You girls enjoy the rest of your evening."

"Thanks," Candice called as she and Baylee turned to leave.

"Do we have time to run into the candy shop?" Baylee asked as they stepped out into the cool November night.

"Um," Candice hummed, taking her cell phone from her pocket to check the time. "Probably not…and I wanted to pop into that doll store again."

"Well, why don't I just run in to the candy shop for a minute and you run into the doll shop?" Baylee suggested.

Looking to one another, they smiled. "Two birds with one stone!" they chimed in unison.

"Perfect!" Candice exclaimed. "I'll see you back at the square in a few. You only have about fifteen minutes left, okay? I don't know how you could've forgotten your phone tonight."

"I know," Baylee sighed, rolling her eyes in exasperation at her own forgetfulness. "I'll see you back at the square." When Candice quirked one eyebrow in doubt, Baylee giggled, "And on time too! I've never been late to a performance before."

"You've never forgotten your phone before," Candice reminded as she hurried in the opposite direction of where Baylee was headed.

As Baylee hurried toward the Ye Old Candy Shoppe she'd noticed while she was performing earlier, she tucked the small brown paper bag back into her pocket, pushing it in as far as it would go. She already loved her new charm—*loved* it! She couldn't believe Candice had spotted it, because Candice was usually anything but observant of details. She tried to imagine how perfectly it would fit next to the beautiful Christmas tree charm she'd purchased that summer when the Hampton Handbell Ringers had done a stint of performing in Leavenworth, Washington.

"Hi!" she heard someone call. When she looked over to see Malcolm McBride the Third waving to her from across the square, she smiled and tossed a wave as she stepped up onto the steps of Ye Old Candy Shoppe. He was a cute little boy, and his cheeks were rosy with the cold and his own merriment.

"Oh! Excuse me," Baylee apologized as she bumped into someone who was just leaving the candy shop as she was arriving.

"No problem," a deep, masculine voice responded. The man's voice was so sensuously stirring that she immediately looked up.

When Baylee found herself staring into the simmering peacock-green eyes of the phenomenally handsome security guy who had stepped between her and Tate the day before, she could only sputter, "S-sorry."

The gorgeous, black-clad chimney sweep (whose soot-smeared face only served to emphasize the fascinating green of his eyes) smiled, displaying beautiful white teeth, also accentuated by the soot smears.

"Like I said, no problem," he repeated. Baylee blushed when the man rather brazenly studied her from head to toe for a moment. "And don't you look cute in your little Christmas caroler outfit," he said.

Baylee's shock and awe at standing so near the handsome chimney sweep was instantly replaced with humiliation as she realized how silly she must look to him—all dressed in her red velvet and gold trim. At least she wasn't carrying her bells or some stupid thing. Yet as she stood before the good-looking chimney sweep, complete with a chimney brush propped over one shoulder and a raggedy black top hat sitting on his head, she couldn't help but smile.

Furthermore, before she could stop herself, she said, "You too." He smiled again, his green eyes sparkling with amusement as she stammered, "I-I mean…you look good in your chimney sweep togs…because, of course, you're not wearing a caroler's dress…uh…costume and stuff."

He chuckled, and the sound of it caused the back of Baylee's neck to warm with pleasure.

"I'm Justice Kincaid, by the way," he said, offering a hand to her. Baylee smiled as she glanced at his hand to see he wore knitted, black, fingerless gloves.

"I'm Baylee Cabot," she countered as she accepted his hand. The moment the man's hand touched hers, however, she wished she'd been wearing her gloves—for such a wonderfully warming heat passed from his hand to melt into hers that she thought her knees might melt too.

He smiled again and kept hold of Baylee's hand as he asked, "Baylee the handbell ringer, huh?"

"Yeah," she managed. "And Justice the chimney sweep, right?"

"Absolutely," he confirmed. Baylee's breath caught in her throat a moment. Absolutely? *Absolutely* was Baylee's word of choice when it came to offering assurance. The fact that the way-better-looking-than-any-man-in-Hollywood faux chimney sweep would use her word—well, it startled her for some reason.

"You guys are awesome," he said, shaking Baylee out of her astonished stupor. She was bathing, shoulder-deep, in the fact that he still hadn't released her hand. "When you guys performed 'Carol of the Bells' a while ago…" He feigned a shiver and said, "Wow! It was seriously incredible."

"Thank you," she responded, managing to remember the way Mr. Hampton always insisted the members of his handbell ringers accept compliments as graciously as possible. "I-I'm glad you enjoyed it. It's my favorite Christmas carol…well, that and 'Silent Night.'"

"Really?" Justice Kincaid asked, arching one dark eyebrow. "Mine too. I mean…my favorites in the true-meaning-of-Christmas genre, that is. Otherwise I'm always down with 'White Christmas.'"

Baylee giggled, amused by his way of mixing proper speech with urban slang. "I love that one too," she offered, smiling so hard her cheeks hurt. She couldn't believe he was talking to her. She couldn't believe he was still holding her hand!

She wondered how many women had stood in front of this Justice Kincaid guy wishing he would turn out to be their own Mr. Right—just the way she was wishing it right then. *Probably a million*, was her final determination.

Justice grinned, and his eyes seemed to heat up their simmering to something closer to a boil. "We should do hot chocolate sometime, you and me," he suggested.

"The way they do lunch in L.A.?" she giggled.

"Absolutely," he laughed. "Is it a date then? Maybe one night this week? When do you take your dinner break tomorrow night?"

Was he really asking her out—sort of? Did he really mean it? Baylee was fearful that he didn't—that maybe he was just messing with her. But she decided to take a chance anyway—come humiliation or heavenly bliss.

"Um…eight o'clock," she answered. She held her breath, waiting for his response—for his rejection or acceptance.

"Cool. I'll just schedule my break for that same time," he said. "Wanna just meet right here tomorrow night at eight?"

"Sure. That'll be great."

Justice Kincaid's smile broadened again. "Yes…it will," he said. "I'll see you tomorrow night then." He paused a moment, still holding her hand in his and adding, "Well, I'll see you tonight too…all night until the place closes, in fact." He leaned forward, in a low voice, whispering, "You just won't see me. We chimney sweeps are sneaky that way."

"I bet," was all Baylee could think to say.

Releasing her hand, Justice touched the brim of his raggedy black top hat. "Until tomorrow night then, Miss Cabot." Then he stepped around her, disappearing into the pine bough-slathered, cobble-stoned street of Camden Town 1843.

CHAPTER THREE

Justice smiled as he watched the handbell ringers—as he listened to their incredible performance of "Jesu, Joy of Man's Desiring." It was incredible—the peace and calm that seeped into his skin as he listened. And, of course, his favorite little handbell ringer looked as radiant as starlight.

Maybe his asking her out for hot chocolate without even knowing her yet would seem hasty to most people—but he wasn't most people. Justice knew the importance of truly living every second of God-given life. His own life had almost been snuffed out—well, shot out, blown out, or whatever someone wanted to call it. And the moment he'd finally woken up in the hospital to find he hadn't been killed by the crash of the CH-47F Chinook or the IED that had exploded near the crash survivors, Justice swore to himself that he would never let one moment of life pass him by without living it to the fullest.

He nodded, assuring himself he'd done the right thing in already approaching Baylee Cabot, the pretty little red-velvet-draped handbell ringer. Everything about her lured him in—drew him like some awaiting destiny. He would've been an idiot to ignore the feelings she provoked in him. And so, tomorrow night, he'd have hot chocolate with her— treat her to dinner and get to know her better—see if she even wanted to get to know him better.

Raising his binoculars, he quickly scanned the crowds below for anything or anyone who might appear suspicious. It was going to be difficult to keep his mind on his work when the little handbell ringing caroler was always in his sights—but he could do it. It's what he'd done for a very long time.

As the Hampton Handbell Ringers and Carolers began a vocal performance of "God Rest Ye, Merry Gentlemen," Baylee found her attention drawn to the rooftops of the Dickens Village. Her performer's smile broadened as she saw the shadow-like silhouettes of chimney sweeps against the moon- and starlit sky. Some were standing near chimneys, some were sitting on rooftop ledges, and some were hunkered down. She could tell by their silhouetted stances that many of them were watching the handbell ringers, and she wondered if the dashing, flirtatious, seemingly confident Justice Kincaid was one of them.

She still couldn't believe he'd asked her out—well, asked her to *do hot chocolate* with him. For several minutes after their encounter at the candy shop, she'd wondered if she'd just imagined it all. But she knew she hadn't. He really had asked her out for hot chocolate—and she wondered why. Why her? She wasn't anything super extraordinary—nobody who really stood out in a crowd. Well, maybe at that moment she did—after all, she was dressed in red velvet and white fur, holding handbells, and singing "God Rest Ye, Merry Gentlemen"—but other than that, she was just an average Jane. Not that she had low self-esteem or anything like that—not any worse than any other woman her age, anyway. She knew she was smart and semi-talented—but wasn't everybody?

Baylee decided it didn't matter. For some reason, Justice Kincaid had noticed her and wanted to take her out. She wouldn't look a gift horse in the mouth then—she'd just go with it. In fact, her smile broadened as she thought that, more than go *with* it, she'd go *for* it! In her guts she felt that it wasn't just Justice's sinfully good looks that made the back of her neck tingle with excitement—made her skin warm and goose-bumpy at the same time. He would mean something to her, she was sure of it—and she wouldn't screw it up with self-doubt and fear. Nope. Tomorrow at eight she would just be herself in his company—get to know him and hope that he wanted to get to know her. Oh—and she'd try not to stare at him with her mouth gaping open in awed admiration.

As Mr. Hampton cued the handbell ringers to prepare to perform "Carol of the Birds" with their bells, Baylee wished he'd chosen something a bit livelier—something that might have found the silhouetted chimney sweeps linking their elbows to "step in time." A vision of Dick Van Dyke and Julie Andrews all soot-faced and sitting atop the rooftops of London flashed in her mind and she smiled—thinking she'd like nothing more in that moment than to be up on one of the rooftops of the Dickens Village beside Justice Kincaid, her own charming chimney sweep.

❧

"Just like that?" Candice asked. "He just bumped into you in the candy shop and asked you out for tomorrow night?"

"Can you believe it?" Baylee asked, beaming with delighted anticipation.

Candice sipped her warm apple cider and then shook her head. "Dang! And I had to go trotting off to the doll shop and miss everything."

"Maybe he wouldn't have had the nerve to ask me if you'd been with me, Candice. Think about it like that," Baylee offered.

But Candice rolled her eyes. "An Army Ranger, Baylee? Yeah…I'm sure he would've lacked the nerve to ask you out with someone else watching. Please."

Baylee giggled. "Good point," she admitted. She sighed then, sipped her own warm cider a moment, and then said, "He gets me all tingly and, like…you know…thinking stuff that's crazy."

"Like what?" Candice asked.

Baylee shrugged. "I don't know…like…like maybe he can actually really find me interesting and that maybe it could lead to…you know…"

"A house with a white picket fence?" Candice finished.

Baylee nodded a little. "It's crazy, I know. But even though I've only seen him twice…he really does something weird to me."

Candice smiled and whispered, "My guess is he does something weird to any woman who sees him twice…but that he doesn't ask every one of *them* out to do hot chocolate. So quit wondering why he asked you, and just go for it." Candice sipped her cider and added, "Stranger things have happened than a handbell ringer marrying a chimney sweep Army Ranger. I mean, look at Mrs. Graham at the instrument store."

Baylee laughed then, entirely amused by Candice's example. "I will admit that that might have been stranger."

"Of course it was stranger!' Candice said. "Mrs. Graham is, what, midfifties? And Colton Roberts was, what, *maybe* thirty when they got married? And they met at a scrapbooking store? Okay…a handbell ringer and an Army Ranger is nothing…believe me."

Baylee giggled again. It had been quite a scandal—the fact that Mrs. Graham, the uptight violin teacher (for all outward appearances) at the instrument store next to Mr. Hampton's bell shop, up and eloped with some twenty-something hottie whose mother owned the local scrapbooking store.

"You're talking about Mrs. Graham and her boy-toy again?" Tate interrupted, intruding on Candice and Baylee's conversation as usual. "Word on the street is he married her for her money."

"She's a violin teacher, Tate," Baylee sighed. "It's not like she's loaded."

But Tate shrugged and said, "I'm just saying…there's got to be some reason he married her."

"He married her because he loves her, you dork," Candice said.

Tate grimaced. "She's like fifty-five or something! Who could love that?"

"Oh my gosh…you are such a butt. I can't even talk to you," Candice grumbled.

"And what brought that up anyway?" Tate asked, ignoring Candice's cut down.

But Candice's temperament was piqued, and even though Baylee warned, "Candice…don't," Candice turned to Tate and said, "We were talking about how you never can tell who the one for you might be. It just so happens that one of the chimney sweeps has asked Baylee out."

Tate frowned at Baylee. "Don't tell me you're getting sucked into that 'fallen hero,' too much muscle and not enough brain thing. Come on, Baylee. I thought you were smarter than that. Those guys are nothing but warmongers. There's nothing to them but guns and testosterone."

"As opposed to the good fashion sense and cowardice that composes you, Tate?" Baylee countered. She couldn't stand Tate! He was so soft and mushy—like a Beanie Baby, only not as cute. And he was cocky, which made everything else she didn't like about him worse.

"Hey, a well-dressed man goes places," Tate argued.

"Then why don't you go somewhere right now?" Candice suggested. She frowned a moment, studying Tate from head to toe. "Why is it you're always in our business anyway, Tate? I've never been able to figure that out."

"Well, someone has to look out for you two," he answered. "I mean, look at you. We've been here one evening, and already Baylee has managed to get snagged by some GI who's only after one thing."

"And what's he after, Tate?" Baylee asked. Her temper was rising—just as her confidence where Justice Kincaid's reasons for asking her out was waning a little.

"Why don't you let me show you, Baylee?" Tate said, unexpectedly taking her waist between his hands and attempting to pull her against him.

But Baylee's knee to his groin region caused him to immediately release her and double over a little. "Don't ever touch me again, Tate," Baylee growled. "And maybe you better tell Mr. Hampton you'll be singing tenor for the rest of the night."

Justice chuckled quietly as he watched Baylee and her friend walk away from the same jerk who had been hassling them in the parking lot the day before.

"She's ain't shy, that's for sure," he chuckled to himself as he continued to peer through his binoculars—this time scanning the different gatherings of people below for any sign of the FBI's Jack the Ripper. "I guess you'll be singing tenor for the rest of the night, you idiot."

He paused in scanning the area below, his smile immediately fading as he watched a black-cloaked figure keeping to the shadows of a nearby alleyway. But when the man tossed something in a trash barrel and returned to the village square and to a vendor's cart selling Christmas puddings, he exhaled the breath he'd been holding. With all the period clothing running around in the Dickens Village, any man wearing a cloak and a top hat looked like Jack the Ripper to Justice.

Lowering his binoculars, he wondered for a minute if he still wanted to be a field agent. An office job wasn't any more boring than standing on a rooftop at night waiting for Jack the Ripper to show up. Still, at least he was outside in the fresh, crisp air.

Shaking his head, he thought to himself that he wasn't ready to give up fieldwork—not yet. He figured the day would come when maybe he wouldn't want to be in the line of fire at all—but it hadn't come yet.

Justice heard Brian's voice on his earpiece and hurried to follow his instructions to check out the alleyway between the bakery and the candy shop. As he stealthily hurried over the rooftops, he was certain that scaling buildings in the dark of night was preferable to working nine to five behind a desk. Yet he wondered how his favorite little caroler would feel about it. Of course, that thought was immediately followed by another. *What the heck does it matter and who is she to cause me to even worry about it?*

Still, as he lay down and adjusted his binoculars to recon the cloaked man in the top hat in the alley, he wondered again what Baylee Cabot would think if she knew what he really did for a living.

"I am *so* tired," Candice yawned as they walked toward the exit gates of the Dickens Village.

The village was closing for the night—finally—and Baylee felt like she could sleep for a week!

"I think this gig might be more taxing than I thought," she said.

"Me too," Candice agreed. "But at least tomorrow night it'll only be six hours. And we don't even have to be here until four, so that's good."

"Plus, I'm sure we'll adjust," Baylee added. It was her attempt to remotivate herself, but she was still more tired than she'd expected.

"You didn't lose your new charm, did you?" Candice asked.

Baylee shook her head but stuffed her hand in her pocket to make sure the little box in the brown paper bag was still there anyway. "Nope. It's safe and sound, and I'm going to put it on my bracelet the minute I get home."

Baylee and Candice were quiet for a moment as they stepped out of 1843 London and back into real life. Baylee inhaled a breath of the cool night air. The scent of wood smoke, cinnamon, and pine boughs still laced the night, and she smiled.

"It's such a dreamy place, isn't it?" she asked Candice.

"The Dickens Village? Totally! As tired as I am, I hate to leave it," Candice replied.

"And since it is such a dreamy place," Baylee began, "you don't think I only dreamed that Justice Kincaid asked me out, do you?"

Candice laughed. "No, stupid! He really did." But Candice's brows drew together in a frown as she added, "Though I wasn't there to see it happen. But just because I didn't see it doesn't mean you dreamed it." She grumbled and playfully slapped Baylee on one velvet-covered shoulder. "See? Now you've got me doing it. Of course he asked you out!"

Then, as if in answer to Baylee's doubts, she heard Justice's voice call out, "Hey, Baylee," from behind them.

Stopping in their tracks, both Baylee and Candice spun around to see a very handsome chimney sweep striding toward them.

"Holy cow! Maybe we *are* dreaming!" Candice whispered. "I swear I've never seen a guy that handsome in real life."

"Shhh," Baylee softly scolded as she watched Justice approach.

"Hi," he said as he stopped before them. He looked from Baylee to Candice, offered a strong hand, and said, "I'm Justice Kincaid."

Taking his hand, Candice smiled and said, "Candice Jones."

"It's nice to meet you," he said, smiling.

"You too," Candice managed to answer, though Baylee knew Candice well enough to know when her friend was entirely rattled.

"I just wanted to make sure you're still available to do hot chocolate tomorrow night," Justice said, addressing Baylee.

"Oh, yeah! Absolutely!" she answered, knowing she was way too exuberant.

"Good," he said. "I'll meet you by the fountain. But I think we should get something to eat too. I won't last the rest of the night on just hot chocolate, okay?"

"Absolutely!" Baylee exclaimed again. "I'm really looking forward to it."

"Me too," Justice confirmed. He looked up a moment then, beyond them. "Where are you girls parked? I don't feel right about you walking out into this dark parking lot alone like this."

"Just over there," Baylee said, gesturing to where her car and Candice's were parked.

"Well, I'll see you girls to your cars all the same," he said. "I'm old school, you see. I don't believe women should have to walk to their cars alone in the dark or change flat tires."

"How very chivalrous, Mr. Kincaid," Candice said.

"No. Just paranoid," he answered.

Baylee felt a shock of excitement travel up her spine as Justice placed a hand at her lower back and nodded toward the cars. "Come on, ladies. Let's get you safely to your cars and on your way home."

"Thank you," Baylee said, again grateful for all the nagging Mr. Hampton had given the handbell ringers about gracious acceptance.

Once they were to the cars, Baylee smiled when Justice opened her car door for her after she'd pushed the unlock button her key. "Wow! You *are* quite a charming chimney sweep, aren't you?"

"Not really," he said. Then, smiling, he added, "Have a good night, Baylee. See you tomorrow," and closed her door for her.

As she drove out of the Dickens Village parking lot, Baylee Cabot was on cloud nine! She wondered briefly what was so special about cloud number nine that everyone who was there was euphoric. But the trivial question quickly left her thoughts, for nothing would ever again hold her attention the way Justice Kincaid did. Of that she was sure!

Baylee's apartment was quiet—except for the soft, sweet sounds of Aureole's harps, dulcimers, and flutes playing via their *Christmas Wishes* CD. She snuffed out the flame of her pine- and peppermint-scented candle and turned off all the lights in her bedroom, save the strand of colored mini Christmas lights wound around the post of the lamp that stood by her bed.

Sitting down on her bed, she gently removed the beautiful silver Victorian caroler charm from its pretty velvet box and began to attach it to her special charm bracelet. She didn't have very many charms on her sterling charm bracelet yet—only the Leavenworth Christmas tree, a pretty silver-handled gold bell charm, and the pirate ship charm she'd fallen in love with in a shop in Boston.

Carefully Baylee attached the caroler charm to her bracelet and then held it up toward the mini Christmas lights and watched the colors they beamed sparkle on the pretty charms.

"Perfect!' she sighed with contentment. It was late, and she was tired, but there was always time for one more delight in life—at least to Baylee's way of thinking there was.

Still, fatigue did get the best of her, and she put the charm bracelet back in her jewelry box and snuggled down into her warm, comfortable bed. The CD would play a few more songs and then turn off on its own, and the Christmas lights were so soothing that Baylee decided to leave them on as well.

She was amazed that she was so relaxed. The date she had scheduled with Justice Kincaid normally would've found her wound up like top, but she was astonishingly calm. Oh, it wasn't like the image of Justice that kept swaying back and forth in her mind wasn't distracting, as well as exciting. It was just that it soothed her somehow too—as if he were right there in the room watching over and protecting her. It was weird, but the whole thing was weird anyway. Baylee had never accepted a date with a guy she hadn't known for at least a couple of weeks. Well, she'd never accepted one until Justice Kincaid had asked. But what woman in her right mind would've turned down a date with that piece of French silk pie, huh?

She thought then of how the soot on his face made his peacock-green eyes all the more alluring. And, yes, that's what they were—alluring. As she gazed at the small colored lights wrapped around her lamppost, she thought that maybe Justice's eyes were more the color of the warm-lit Christmas green bulbs on the string of lights. Either way, whether peacock-green or mini-Christmas-lights green, Justice's eyes were definitely something a girl could get lost in.

Smiling, Baylee thought that Justice Kincaid's arms were also something a girl could get lost in—and his smile—and his muscles—and his hair—and the sound of his voice…

CHAPTER FOUR

Baylee may have fallen asleep easily enough, but the next morning she was so stirred up she could hardly concentrate on anything! All day long she found herself fidgeting, impatient, and nervous. And when four o'clock finally rolled around and the Hampton Handbell Ringers began performing in the Dickens Village square, all Baylee could think about was whether Justice Kincaid was perched up on one of the rooftops watching her. She was so entirely distracted, wondering where Justice was stationed and why in the world it was taking eight p.m. so long to arrive, that she was constantly worried she'd make a mistake while ringing—but she didn't, and time ticked by as slowly as a sloth could swim through molasses. She watched the sun set while the group sang "Good King Wenceslas" and enjoyed a cup of mulled cider with Candice during a short break, and still all she could think of was seeing Justice—of being with him. She knew it was crazy to be so fixated— insane! But that didn't change the truth of it.

At long, long, *long* last, the big hand on the large clock in the Dickens Village clock tower began to inch toward twelve as the little hand settled on eight, and then—he was there! Baylee spied Justice Kincaid standing near the fountain in the square, smiling as he watched the troupe perform. He was there! He was there waiting for her! Her heart swelled with such raging anticipation she could hardly contain her delight. She knew her smile was way too big to be appropriate when the group was singing "Coventry Carol," but she couldn't help it. Justice was waiting for her—for *her*—Baylee Cabot!

As the carol ended and the onlookers began to applaud, Baylee barely managed to wait for Mr. Hampton to dismiss them before hurrying off to meet Justice.

"Hi," Justice greeted as she approached. Oh, his smile was simply over the moon!

"Hi," she greeted in return.

"Are you ready?" he asked.

"Absolutely," she answered (too enthusiastically, of course).

"I was thinking we'd go to the place that does the old-fashioned ham and potato thing," he suggested. "What do you think?"

Baylee shrugged. "I don't know anything about it…but I like ham, and I like potatoes."

"Should be good then," he chuckled.

As they walked toward the little restaurant near the bakery, Baylee tried to breathe evenly, but it was difficult. She wasn't only nervous and excited about being with Justice; she was nervous and unsettled by the way people looked at them and grinned—by the way women looked at Justice, their eyes lighting up like Christmas trees.

Baylee figured she and Justice probably did provide quite a sight— the Victorian Christmas caroler, all bedecked in red velvet and white fur, and the sooty, and outrageously handsome, chimney sweep with the peacock-green eyes and the tattered top hat.

They entered the restaurant (Baylee blushing with delight as Justice opened the door, allowing her to enter first), and in minutes, a waitress had seated them at a small table next to a window. The waitress, dressed in the perfect period clothing, handed them menus and left them.

"Mmm. I'm starving," Justice mumbled as he studied the menu. "You know, I never really realize how hungry I am until I start reading a list of good things to eat."

Baylee smiled. "Me neither," she agreed. "And, look, they do have hot chocolate. I was worried for a moment that they wouldn't have any and I'd start into chocolate withdrawal right here in front of you."

"It's that bad, huh?" he chuckled.

Baylee nodded. "You should've seen me scrounging around in my baking cabinet, hoping to find a stray chocolate chip or something last night before I went to bed."

Justice chuckled again, and she silently scolded herself for being so forthcoming about her passion for chocolate. He'd think she was an idiot for sure.

Smiling, however, he studied her a moment, his unsettling green gaze warming her from her insides out.

"I like hot chocolate too," he said, returning his attention to his menu. "And I'm not just saying that to try to impress you." He grinned, adding, "Though I'm not sure I need chocolate enough to recon a rogue chocolate chip from the cabinet."

Baylee giggled. "Well, now you know my worst secret," she sighed. "So I guess there's no reason for me to be nervous anymore."

Wow, Justice thought. If rooting around in a cabinet looking for chocolate chips were Baylee Cabot's worst secret, then he hoped opposites really did attract as strongly as the old cliché claimed. He grinned, thinking his worst secrets would probably set her hair on fire.

He looked up, smiling with amusement as he watched her considering her menu. Her pretty forehead was furrowed with a frown, her lips were pursed to one side, and one slender index finger rested at her rosy cheek.

"Looks pretty straightforward to me," she mumbled. Then, rather dramatically closing her menu with a contented sigh, she smiled at him and said, "Ham and fried potatoes for me." Her smile broadened, and her brown eyes twinkled warmly as she added, "With the dinner roll, of course! Maybe I'll ask for two." She frowned again, adding, "Do you think they'd get mad if I asked for two?"

Justice smiled and answered, "I'm sure they won't get mad." She was too funny! He'd already decided that this was the best, most enjoyable dinner date he'd ever been on, and it hadn't even been ten minutes yet.

"So," Baylee said, folding her arms and plopping them down on the top of the table. "Is it true that all you chimney sweep security guys are ex-military?"

And here it came—the moment when Justice would begin to determine what the pretty little bell ringer's opinion of certain things was.

"Yep," he answered with trepidation rising in his chest. "Every one of us."

She smiled at him, dispelling much of his anxiety over what she would think of his having been in the military. In fact, it subsided almost instantly. "And judging from your license plate…I'm guessing you were Army," she baited.

He chuckled. "Judging by the *vanity* plates my grandma had put on that truck before she gave it to me, you mean? Yes."

Her eyes widened, and she giggled. "Wow! Your grandma *gave* you a truck?"

"Yep. When I was discharged," he began to explain. He folded his menu and set it aside, having decided on the ham, fried potatoes, and two dinner rolls himself. "Grandma has always spoiled me rotten…and since my Grandpa died last year, I haven't had the heart to argue with her. The truck was actually my grandpa's, and when he died she ordered those stupid vanity license plates and gave his truck to me. It was only, like, maybe three months old when he died, and she was determined I should have it." He looked up to see Baylee smiling at him and couldn't help but smile himself. He shrugged and added, "What's a grandson to do, right? And besides…she gave me the payment too."

Baylee giggled. "Wow! That's a nice truck…so I'm sure the payment is nice as well."

"Absolutely," Justice chuckled.

"And as for the license plates, I think you *should* be proud of your service. Besides, people need to be reminded that conflicts and the soldiers who deal with them really do exist. That's half of what's wrong with this country today. Nobody has had to worry about their freedom being stripped away in far too long."

"Agreed," Justice said.

"My daddy is a Gulf War vet, and my grandpa did four tours in Vietnam, so I get it," she said. "Probably not as much as I would have seventy years or so ago, but I do get it." Her smile broadened, and the light in her eyes flashed with approval. "So I like the plates your grandma had put on your truck. And furthermore, thank you for your service to me and my country, Mr. Justice Kincaid."

Justice was far more than just merely impressed; he was touched emotionally. It wasn't very often that a young person thanked him for his service—especially a beautiful young bell-ringing caroler. He could see that she was thoroughly sincere in thanking him—that she truly meant what she said.

"Well, you're welcome," he mumbled, smiling at her and blushing a little with humility. "It's not very often a pretty young thing like you thanks a beat-up old Army Ranger like me for his service." He breathed a quiet laugh and added, "I think I love you already."

Sure—Baylee knew he was kidding. She knew Justice was only expressing how rare it was these days for a military veteran to be thanked for his service. But even though she knew he didn't *really* think he loved her, the sound of his voice saying the words sent a wave of butterflies whirling around in her stomach.

She didn't know how to respond—couldn't think of anything to say. Therefore, her mouth made the call and said, "I hope so."

The waitress returned, setting two small tankards of water on the table and rescuing Baylee from any further flustering. "Are you ready to order?" she asked.

Saved by the waitress, Baylee thought.

"I think so," Justice answered. Looking to Baylee, however, he asked, "Are you sticking with the ham and fried potatoes?" even though she'd told him before that she was.

"Yes," she assured him.

"She'll be having the ham and fried potatoes, but will you please add an extra dinner roll to that?" he began.

"Of course, sir," the waitress assured him. "And for you, sir?"

"I'll have the same…including two rolls instead of just one, okay?" Justice grinned and winked at Baylee, and again the butterflies in her stomach whirled around again.

"Of course," the waitress said. "Anything else? Would you like something to drink?"

"Actually, yes…two hot chocolates as well," Justice answered.

The waitress smiled. "Our hot chocolate is the best in the village," she said, "even if I do say so myself. Would you like the soft peppermint cocoa stirrers too?"

"Are they the ones with the little holes in the middle so you can suck your hot chocolate through them?" Justice asked.

Baylee smiled. He knew about soft peppermint sticks in hot chocolate? How adorable! Maybe he really did like hot chocolate as much as she did. Or nearly as much, anyway.

"Yes, they are," the waitress giggled.

"Then I definitely want one," Justice assured her. "Baylee?" he asked, looking to her.

"Absolutely," she answered.

"All right then," the waitress began, "that's two ham and fried potato dinners, with two dinner rolls each." She smiled and winked at Justice. "And two hot chocolates complete with peppermint stirrers."

"That's it, exactly," Justice affirmed.

"Well then, it shouldn't be too long on the dinners. Would you like your hot chocolate now or later?"

"Both," Justice answered.

Baylee giggled as he winked at her again. It was like he could read her mind where hot chocolate was concerned.

"I'll have the first round brought right out to you then," the waitress affirmed.

"Thank you."

Baylee watched as even their waitress, who she gauged to be in her late fifties, blushed under Justice's gaze. "You're welcome, and let me know if there's anything else I can do for you," she said before leaving them alone once more.

Baylee studied Justice a moment, arching one brow with suspicion. "Do you *really* like hot chocolate that much? Or are you just trying to make me feel better?"

He smiled his goose-bump-inducing smile. "I really do love hot chocolate," he insisted. He leaned forward, however, and in a lowered, very provocative voice added, "But I would do anything to make you feel better too."

Baylee giggled—blushed as well. "Are all you Army Rangers so charming?"

"You mean chimney sweeps?" he asked.

Again she giggled. "Yeah. Are all you chimney sweeps so charming?"

He shrugged. "You know what they say—chimney sweeps are good luck, right? Isn't good luck a sort of charm or spell?" He grinned.

"Here," he said, offering his hand to her across the table. "Shake my hand. It's supposed to be good luck, according to Dick Van Dyke anyway."

Baylee laughed and accepted his hand. He shook hers firmly and then released it. Smiling at her, he then asked, "Do you feel charmed with good luck now?"

While it was true her palm was still tingling with the delight of having touched him, she didn't know if she felt any luckier that she had a moment ago. She already felt lucky to be with him—lucky that he'd even taken notice of her, lucky that he'd asked her out, lucky all the way around where he was concerned. Therefore, she didn't know what feeling luckier would've felt like because she was already euphoric.

"Well? Do you?" Justice pressed, teasing her. She knew he was teasing, because his peacock-green eyes were flashing like burning emeralds.

"I don't know," she answered honestly. "I was already feeling pretty lucky today."

He wrinkled his handsome brow, feigning concern. "Well, what's next then?" He pretended to be thoughtful. "Ah, yes. Blow me a kiss. Blowing me a kiss is supposed to be lucky as well."

"According to Dick Van Dyke," Baylee giggled.

"Absolutely," he chuckled.

"So you want me to blow you a kiss now? Is that it?" she asked.

He shrugged broad shoulders. "Well, you can just lean over here and give me a kiss…but we've only known each other, what, a total of twenty minutes?"

Baylee blushed and glanced away. She saw the older couple sitting at a table near them, smiling at her with understanding—and delight.

"Come on," Justice urged. "Blow me a kiss and see if you feel luckier." He winked at her. "I've always wanted a kiss from a pretty bell-ringing caroler girl."

Quickly, Baylee kissed her fingers, bending her hand toward Justice and blowing the kiss to him. "Okay. There. Are you happy?"

"Yep," he said, grinning at her. "And do you feel good luck washing over you now?"

At that moment, a busboy arrived, carrying a tray with two tankards sitting on it. Each had a peppermint stick sticking out of it.

"Here you go, sir…ma'am," the young man said as he sat a tankard of hot cocoa on the table in front of Baylee and then another in front of Justice.

"Thank you," Justice said, though his gaze never deviated from Baylee.

"You're welcome," the young man said as he walked away.

"Well?" Justice asked. The arrival of the hot chocolate did nothing to distract him from his previous question. "Do you feel lucky now or not?"

Smiling, Baylee reached out and pulled the tankard of hot chocolate closer to her. Stirring the hot chocolate with the long peppermint stick protruding from it, she smiled and said, "The hot chocolate arrived, didn't it? How much more luck could I hope for?"

Justice's smile broadened. Yep—he'd known her all of twenty minutes, and already he liked her more than he'd liked anyone in a very, very long time. He watched her sip her hot chocolate through the peppermint stick, thinking that her lips probably tasted pretty sweet right about then.

"So," she began, looking up at him, slowly stirring her cocoa. "Why did you leave the military? Rangers…that's, like, a big commitment. Most of you guys just don't up and quit, right?"

Usually when people asked Justice about his military service, he was instantly overwhelmed with the need to put up his guard. He more often than not felt defensive and was always waiting for the negative shoe to drop. But none of the usual feelings welled up in him when Baylee asked him about it. It was a strange sensation—not feeling immediately self-protective.

"I…uh…I was wounded," he answered. He hadn't even taken pause to think about what to tell her and what not to. He'd simply answered.

"Thus the Purple Heart?" she inquired.

"One of them, yes," he admitted. When she didn't say anything else, he knew she was waiting for particulars. He figured it wouldn't hurt to give her a few—not too many and no grisly details. But if he wanted to get to know her better and wanted her to get to know him…

"We'd picked up some Navy SEALS that had gotten…that were backed into a corner, so to speak. The Chinook we were in was shot down, and when we crashed—once we'd gotten the survivors out and dragged from the wreckage—an IED exploded and blew us all to hell. I woke up in the base hospital with enough serious injuries to find me discharged and unemployed."

Justice was surprised when he glanced up to see excess moisture brimming in Baylee's eyes. The sight of her sympathy for him pricked his heart and caused a pinching sensation in his chest.

"How awful," she mumbled. She looked down to the hot chocolate she had once again begun stirring with the peppermint stick. "And I'm sure that's the Easy Reader version too. Isn't it?"

Justice shrugged. "Probably."

He watched as she studied him for a moment, knowing she was looking for signs of lingering injury.

"Well, you look robust enough," she said once she realized she'd been staring at him.

Justice smiled. "Well, you haven't seen me naked," he said in a lowered voice.

The entire surface of Baylee's body blushed. Of course she hadn't seen him naked! What did he mean by that? It only took her a moment to calm herself, however—only a moment to realize that, though Justice Kincaid obviously had all his limbs and a wickedly handsome face, there was a profound amount of flesh, bone, and other parts of the human body that weren't visible to the world—when he was fully clothed, anyway.

"And here we go," the waitress said as she arrived with two plates of steaming food. She placed one in front of Baylee, the other in front of Justice. "And two rolls each," she added, smiling.

"Thank you," Justice said.

"Let me know if you need anything else," the waitress offered.

"We will. Thank you," Baylee promised.

"Mmm. It smells good," Justice mumbled as he inhaled the steam coming off his plate.

But Baylee was still rattled. She knew Justice was giving her merely a drop in the bucket of whatever had gone on to injure him enough to find him discharged from the Army—from the Army Rangers. She tried to keep more tears from welling in her eyes, but her heart was aching at wondering what he'd truly endured.

"So they patched you up and sent you on your way?" she asked as she used her knife and fork to cut a piece of ham.

"Yep," he answered. He shrugged. "I had the option, of course…a desk job, so to speak. But if it was a desk job or discharge—"

"You chose discharge." He nodded. She wouldn't press him further. She knew that it was important to wait until someone like Justice was ready to offer details of their service of their own accord. At least that's how it had always been with her father and grandfather. If he wanted her to know more, he'd tell her—someday.

"And now you're a security guard," she stated. She frowned a moment, looking up at him. "What company do you guys work for anyway? I mean…why would the Dickens Village need security guards with the backgrounds you guys all have?"

Baylee thought for a moment that the bite of potatoes Justice had just taken had gotten stuck in his throat when he coughed a little. But he took a drink of water and answered, "Well, we're not just a security force. We're more specialized than that. I'm a field agent, actually…for a bureau that…you know…does special assignments like this sometimes."

"For a bureau?" she asked. "You mean like the Federal Bureau of Investigation…the FBI or MI6, the CIA, or something?"

Justice smiled. "You're thinking of James Bond and Tom Cruise stuff," he chuckled. "I'm more like…oh, you know…mall cop."

Baylee giggled. "Oh, you are not," she playfully argued. "Mall cops don't carry the kinds of weapons you guys were packing at the orientation."

"Packing?" Justice said, grinning.

Baylee shrugged. "Isn't that's what it's called?"

"Armed is what I usually call it…but I guess packing works too," he laughed. He paused to take a bite of ham and a sip of hot chocolate, and then he said, "Maybe I just like weaponry."

Baylee nodded. "Most guys usually do. When my brother was little, he'd always sneak into my mom's sewing room and get her hot glue gun out to play with. He could make anything into a gun. I suppose you relate to that."

"Mmm hmmm," Justice confirmed. "But I was into the sword thing too. I started out with the old paper towel roll things—you know, the cardboard tube left over when you've finished the roll?"

Baylee giggled at the thought of a cute little Justice Kincaid playing with empty paper towel rolls.

"Then I graduated to the big ones," he continued. "You know, Christmas wrapping paper size." He smiled and chuckled to himself. "Those were awesome!"

"I can imagine," Baylee teased.

"But then, the Christmas I was four…" he sighed.

He paused and didn't continue, so Baylee prodded, "Yeah? The Christmas you were four…"

"That was the Christmas I got my first *real* weapon," he answered, gazing off to one corner of the room, reminiscently.

"At four years old?" Baylee exclaimed. She was mortified! What parent would give their child a weapon at only four years old?

"Yep," Justice confirmed, however. "That Christmas I got my very first light saber."

Baylee nearly choked on the potatoes she'd been swallowing. Bursting into laughter, she squealed, "Light saber? So it was a toy weapon they gave you?"

"It was a light saber, and it was as real to me as any light saber any other Jedi Knight ever owned," Justice explained. He laughed for a moment, obviously entertained by Baylee's amusement. "It was one of those plastic ones, you know, with the collapsible light saber part? Only it had batteries in the grip, so it really did light up." He shook his head and sighed. "Man! That was an awesome weapon. I still have it somewhere." He drank some hot chocolate and then asked, "And what about you? Have you always been a singing bell ringer?"

Baylee giggled—giggled because of the irony of what she was about to say. "Well, it seems that you and I both enjoyed profound Christmas gifts at an early age…because I received my first bell when I was the same age you were when you got your first *weapon*."

"Seriously?" he asked, chuckling.

Baylee nodded. "Yep. I had seen handbell ringers on TV one year and immediately began begging for my own set of handbells. When I didn't let up on the begging, I guess my parents began to realize that I really did want to play the bells, so they began buying them for me." She paused, laughing for a moment at the memory of her father wearing earmuffs whenever he was working in his office at home. "I must've drove them nuts now that I think about it."

Justice laughed too. "I'm sure of it. Especially if you only received one at a time. Imagine…the same bell…the same note…over and over and over until you received another one."

Baylee giggled. "Yeah, I kind of feel bad for them now."

"You probably should," Justice agreed. He ate a couple of bites of ham and then asked, "And do you plan on ringing and singing forever? Is that something a person can really do as a career for their whole life?"

Baylee shrugged. "Yeah. But there's a lot of travel involved usually, especially around the holidays," she explained. "It's not so bad now, especially this year when we're sticking close to home most of the time. But when I, you know, have my own family and stuff…I hope then I can just teach music…maybe start a little handbell ringing club or something—you know, to make sure the art doesn't become extinct."

So she wanted a family of her own, did she? Justice liked that. In fact, the same weird sensation he'd had the day he first sort-of met her was washing over him again—the intense warmth at the back of his neck and the feeling like he should already know everything about her. The difference was that this time the weird sensation didn't creep him out the way it had before. It pleased him—made him feel satisfied or content or something.

"Baylee's Baby Handbell Ringers, huh?" he teased. He laughed, adding, "You know, you could recruit all the toddlers in your neighborhood, give them each one bell, and teach them to drive their parents nuts."

Baylee laughed too. "Absolutely!"

Once they'd both laughed a moment longer, Justice said, "But, really…I love to listen to you guys perform. It's awesome."

"Thank you," she said, graciously accepting his compliment. She blushed, however, and she wondered if she'd simply been taught to politely recognize compliments.

Something caught Justice's eye then as Baylee lifted her fork to her mouth—a bracelet at her wrist. "What's that?" he asked.

Baylee finished putting a bite of food in her mouth, chewed, swallowed, and then looked at her wrist. "You mean the bracelet?" she asked, setting her fork down.

"Yeah."

"I know," she said, shaking her head. "I forgot to take it off today before I came to work, and Mr. Hampton had a fit when he saw it…because it can interfere with ringing. But I don't want to put it in my pocket and lose it or something."

Reaching out and taking hold of her hand, Justice began to inspect the bracelet. It was obviously a charm bracelet, and it was loaded with charms.

"So each one means something?" he asked, taking hold of a silver snowflake charm and studying it.

"Well, kind of," she answered. "This is my Christmas charm bracelet. See? All the charms are kind of wintery and Christmassy?"

Justice touched another charm—a Christmas wreath.

"I've always loved charm bracelets…though I don't know why," she explained. "I have several of them made from these kinds of charms. But the feather in my cap will be the sterling silver one I'm slowly working on…very slowly working on. I only have a few charms for it. In fact, I bought one here yesterday."

When she paused, Justice looked up to see her smiling at him—her beautiful brown eyes entirely alight with excitement.

"It was a Victorian Christmas caroler that my friend came across in the little jewelry store here," she finished.

"Well, how appropriate is that, right?" Justice offered, studying another charm on her bracelet. In truth, he wasn't all that interested in each individual charm—but he liked the way it felt to hold her little hand in his—to touch her wrist. It made him wish he were a charm on her bracelet so that he could lie against her warm, soft skin for a while.

"If you're worried about it," he began, "I can keep it safe for you until you're finished tonight." He smiled, adding, "I *am* a security guard, after all."

"I wouldn't want to inconvenience you," Baylee lied. Of *course* she wanted to inconvenience him with taking care of her bracelet! Any excuse to see him again was wonderful. And besides, the idea of his having possession of something of hers for a while—of knowing he'd touched it and kept it safe for her—it was a sort of titillating feeling.

"It wouldn't be an inconvenience," he said as he began to fumble with the bracelet clasp. "I don't want you getting in trouble with your boss again. Then you might not be able to meet me for dinner tomorrow night during our break, right?"

"Tomorrow night?" Baylee squeaked as her heart leapt with delight in her bosom.

"Sure," Justice said as the clasp released the bracelet into his hand. She watched as he tucked it into the inside pocket of his tailcoat. "You wouldn't mind another hour in my company, would you? Another free meal?"

Would she mind? Was he nuts? Of course she wouldn't mind! It was like a dream come true, his asking her to dinner again in a roundabout way.

"Of course not," she managed to answer. The strangely blissful joy in her heart was fast spreading to her entire body. "But you can't pay tomorrow too. Let's at least go dutch."

"I'll think about it," he said, smiling at her again.

And, oh, that smile! Baylee was sure she was going to melt into a puddle right there in her seat. Why on earth was she there with him? Why had he asked her to go out? What could a man like Justice Kincaid possibly see in a simple girl like her? He'd been around the world, seen battle, been wounded. Terror, adventure, harm—all those things had been a part of his life. He was a hero—a real, live American hero! How in the world had she managed to capture his attention at all?

Baylee began to wonder if maybe there was something else at work—some sort of magical charm that existed within the gates and walls of the Dickens Village. She wondered if outside the village it would dissipate—leave Justice wondering why he'd wasted an hour in the company of someone as pathetically average as Baylee was in comparison to him. She hoped not—prayed not. And yet it was all so unbelievable!

"I need more hot chocolate already," Justice mumbled. "How about you?"

Baylee glanced into her tankard, noting that it was almost empty. "Yep. Mine's gone as well."

"Well then, I'll order round two," he said, smiling. "Maybe I can get the waitress to shake my chimney sweep hand and she'll give us each two peppermint straws this time, huh?"

Baylee giggled as Justice stood up from his chair and strode across the room to talk to the waitress.

"That's one handsome chimney sweep you've got there, love," the elderly woman sitting at the nearby table said.

"Yes, it is," Baylee giggled as the woman's elderly husband winked at her with understanding.

"They're supposed to be good luck, you know," the elderly woman added. "So how's your luck running so far this evening?"

"Astonishingly good," Baylee answered as she watched Justice sauntering back toward her.

Taking his seat again, Justice asked, "So what's your friend doing for dinner tonight since you're busy with me?"

Baylee shrugged. "She went to another place with some of the others in the group."

Justice grinned. "Well, how about this? If I hook your friend up with a chimney sweep dinner date every night next week, can I have you for dinner every night next week?"

Baylee blushed—giggled when the elderly lady at the table next to theirs answered, "Of course you can!"

"Thank you, ma'am," Justice laughed, winking at the old woman. "I'll take care of it then," he said to Baylee. "What's your friend's name again?"

"Candice," she answered.

"She seems like an adventurous young lady…so I think I'll start her out with Tristan," he said thoughtfully.

"You don't have to entertain my friends for me, you know," Baylee said. Lowering her voice, she bravely, and rather brazenly, added, "You can have me for dinner every night next week without going to all that trouble."

Justice chuckled. He liked that she'd found the nerve to say what she'd said. He could tell by her blush that it took a bit more courage than she was used to exerting when communicating with a man. He liked her all the more for her bravery.

"Well, how about I have you for dinner every night and ease your mind about whether or not your friend is having fun too? Okay?" he said.

"Okay," she said, blushing again.

Justice chuckled when he heard the elderly woman at the table next to them sigh with contentment. Baylee giggled a little too, and he realized the sound of it made his smile broaden.

"Here you go," the waitress said, setting two new tankards of hot chocolate on the table. "Enjoy."

"We will, thank you," Justice said, indicating with a nod to Baylee that she should note the two peppermint stick straws in each tankard.

Life was too short to waste even one moment. When a man found what he wanted, there was no reason to mess around with squandering time. Something was telling him that this girl was what he'd been looking for—something that caused the back of his neck to heat up, caused his insides to twist and churn and feel good all at the same time. Therefore, he wouldn't dillydally, as his grandmother would say. Justice Kincaid decided then and there that he wouldn't let any of the unpredictable IEDs that life could throw at a man keep him from pursuing the sweetest little bell-ringing caroler he could ever have dreamt of—keep him from winning her, from having her for dinner every night for the rest of his life.

CHAPTER FIVE

"Wow," Justice said as he closed the Veterans Day card and returned it to its envelope. "I-I…I don't know what to say," he stammered. "Thank you, Baylee."

Baylee smiled when Justice didn't look up to her right away—when he did and she saw the moisture of tender emotion in his eyes.

"Thank *you*, Justice," she countered. "Though I should've given every one of you guys a Veterans Day card." She sighed, wishing she'd had the time, the money, and the information to send every military veteran in the world a card. Still, Justice was special. Justice was *very* special!

For the past ten days, Justice had treated Baylee to dinner at one or the other of the various eating establishments in the Dickens Village. Sure, she was secretly disappointed that he hadn't asked her out on a real date—something other than their work lunch break. But still, ten days and ten dinners in the company of Justice Kincaid? It was fabulous! Furthermore, he'd stayed true to his word in making certain Candice didn't ever get stuck eating dinner in Tate's company again. In fact, after Candice enjoyed several evenings of dinner with different members of the security staff, Justice's friend Tristan revealed a bit of his possessive nature toward Candice and kindly told Justice to "butt out"—that he could "take it from here." Thus, Candice had begun to "really like" Tristan and had joined Baylee in hanging out on the mythical cloud nine the past few evenings.

"You know, you're a very thoughtful girl, Baylee Cabot," Justice said, tucking the card she'd given him into his coat pocket and returning his attention to the mug of hot chocolate sitting on the table before him.

"No," Baylee said, however. "I'm just sappy—and proud of it, by the way."

Justice was smiling at her when she looked at him again. "I think I already love you because of that too," he said.

This wasn't the first time Justice had teased her about loving her because of some part of her character or something she'd done. At first Baylee had found it flattering—sort of dreamily hopeful. But now, it kind of bothered her—made her wonder if he was the type of man that just tossed out the word *love* as casually as if it were the word *pickle*. But she decided not to be too suspicious or harsh in judging why Justice did it. She decided to enjoy it—the way she had the times before.

And so Baylee simply responded to his teasing the way she had every other time. "I hope so."

Justice chuckled and savored a few sips of hot chocolate. Baylee smiled, liking the way his Adam's apple moved when he swallowed. Geez! Even his Adam's apple was handsome.

Unexpectedly he asked, "Are you going to that thing they're having tomorrow?"

Baylee tried to keep her heart from leaping in her chest with hope—hope that Justice was about to ask if she would go with him. He might simply be asking to make casual conversation. But her heart leapt anyway.

"You mean the tenth anniversary party for the Dickens Village thing?" she asked. After all, she wanted to make sure she'd understood what he was referring to.

"Yeah," he affirmed. "Are you going?"

"Well, we're not performing tomorrow night, so I thought I would at least drop in," she said. "I hear they're having the bakery cater part of it, after all…and you know what a sucker I am for good bread. How about you?"

Baylee held her breath. Was he planning on going? Would she get to see him there? Would he make her dreams come true and ask her to go with him?

Justice shrugged. "I was considering it."

Baylee tried to mask her disappointment—tried to find the courage to urge him to go.

But before she could begin to speak, he asked, "Wanna go with me?"

"Absolutely!" she answered—far too enthusiastically, as usual.

Justice smiled. "Good. And maybe they'll have lots of butter to spread on the bakery's bread goods."

"And maybe the bread will be warm and the butter will melt all over it! Mmmm!" Baylee giggled.

"You know, Baylee…you melt *my* butter sometimes, you little bell ringer," Justice said, winking at her flirtatiously.

Baylee giggled. "I melt your butter? Where'd you dig up that line, Casanova?"

"But you do," he assured her. "When I'm having dinner with you, I feel just like one of those bakery rolls—all fresh and slathered in butter…and then you warm me up and melt it."

Baylee laughed, rolling her eyes with simultaneous delight and amusement. "Oh my gosh! You are hysterical…*and* completely full of beans."

"I'm full of a lot more than beans," he chuckled. "But not when it comes to flirting with you, sugar plum."

"Sugar plum?" Baylee giggled. "And you're actually going to sit there and tell me you're not full of beans?"

"Wanna just leave right from here tomorrow?" he asked, purposefully changing the line of conversation. "If we just go straight there, we'll be there by seven. That's plenty of time, don't you think?"

"Yes, pony boy, it is," she answered.

"Pony boy?" Justice exclaimed with a grimace. "I choose sugar plum for you, and I get pony boy?"

"Hey!" Baylee teasingly scolded, wagging an index finger at him. "I'll have you know that before I fell in love with handbells, I loved ponies…and there was a little song my grandmother used to sing to me called 'Pony Boy.' So don't knock my nicknames."

"Oh, okay," Justice said, smiling. "Sorry. I just had a high school flashback there for a moment…and it wasn't a good one."

Baylee smiled with sudden insight. "Oh yeah…*The Outsiders*. Required reading…with that character named Ponyboy."

"Absolutely," Justice confirmed. "I hated that book. The ending sucked."

Baylee giggled, sipped her hot chocolate, and then said, "I'll think of something else then, okay?"

"Thanks," he sighed, winking at her. "So leaving right from work is okay with you tomorrow night?"

"Absolutely," she said—far too eagerly.

"All right then," he said, standing up from his chair. "I've got to get back now. So you have a wonderful rest of the evening, sugar plum...and I'll see you after work at nineteen hundred hours tomorrow night, okay?"

"Okay," Baylee giggled.

Justice winked at her once more, returned the tattered black top hat to his head, and hurried out the front door of the restaurant. It had been a quick exit, Baylee noted. And as she watched Justice jog across the square, looking as though he were talking to himself, she immediately realized that something must be up. Someone must have said something to him through the earpiece in his right ear that urged him to leave her so quickly after dinner—especially when there were still fifteen minutes left of their lunch hour.

Baylee frowned—for the realization caused a more than slight anxiety to rise in her. Still, she figured it was probably something not too serious. After all, what could possibly happen in the Dickens Village?

"DNA evidence confirms it," Brian said. "It's our Jack the Ripper copycat."

Justice frowned. The news was bad—worse than he'd hoped to hear.

"But this victim...she wasn't even a prostitute," Tristan noted aloud as he scanned the memo Brian handed him.

"Neither was the last victim," Brian said. "Our perp is changing his MO...becoming more desperate...spiraling."

"Two victims in two weeks...and this one was here in this city," Justice mumbled. "He will target the Dickens Village. It's obvious. Look where this victim lived."

"Exactly," Brian confirmed. "Two miles from the Dickens Village—that's where she lived. And the body was found a mile and half from the village. He's prowling—hunting. He's probably already been to the village more than once."

Justice thought about suggesting the FBI close the Dickens Village, but he knew that wouldn't fly. He knew the best way to catch the serial copycat killer was to bait him with the tempting lure of the Dickens Village. Naturally, the Dickens Village wasn't the killer's perfect vision of a hunting ground—being that it was 1840s era and the original Jack the Ripper terrorized London in the late 1880s and early 1890s. But for a copycat psycho killer, the Dickens Village was the closest he could come to living out his fantasy of being the true Ripper.

The photos of the copycat killer's seventh victim were gruesome. Justice had seen some gruesome stuff in his time, but something about the nature of what the killer did to the bodies of his victims sickened him. He began to perspire a bit, feeling more agitated than usual when working a case, and he knew why—Baylee.

"This victim worked at a clothing store?" he mumbled as his anxiety increased.

"Yep," Brian affirmed. "An upstanding young woman. There's no reason he should've targeted her. He's spiraling. The bureau is sure of it, and so am I."

"Kincaid and Holloway are worrying about their caroling handbell ringers just now," one of the men chuckled. "Wondering if the Ripper has seen them and—"

"Hey, Nichols," Justice interrupted, still studying the information Brian had handed him, "if I were you, I'd be worried about finding an IED shoved up your—"

"That's enough," Brian interrupted. "We need to tighten it from now on. Fifteen minute breaks only…and at the most. And I might have to have some of you pull some double shifts."

"Roger that," Justice mumbled.

"Let's keep the schedule as it is today," Brian continued. "Keep to your times…strictly to your times. But tomorrow, let's double it up a bit…especially after eight p.m. Okay?"

Everyone agreed and, when Brian dismissed them, began to mill around and talk amongst themselves.

"I don't like this," Tristan said to Justice. "I thought it was a fluke when the bureau pegged the Dickens Village as a target for this scum."

"I know," Justin agreed. "So did I. And now he's changed his victim pattern. Any woman is at risk now. We better step it up and find this guy fast."

"And you had to go and get me all interested in Candice," Tristan said, jamming an elbow into Justice. "Damn! I've always dreaded the day when my job would impact my personal life. Thanks a lot, buddy."

"It always happens…sooner or later," Justice said, frowning as he looked to Tristan. "And you fell for Candice on your own, bra. I only introduced you. And besides, I'm in the stewpot with you, man. I don't like this at all." He looked back to the info sheet. "Brunette, early twenties, five foot five inches, a hundred and twenty pounds…dammit! This victim even had brown eyes. She fits Baylee's description to a tee, man!"

Tristan inhaled a deep breath—exhaled it slowly. "I hate this one, man," he growled. "And we'll just have to employ Eagle Eye on our shweeties. And that ain't a bad thing, after all, right?"

Justice grinned at Tristan as they bumped fists. "Nope. That ain't a bad thing at all."

"My shift starts in fifteen minutes, dude," Tristan said as he stood up from his chair. "I'll see you at the shindig tonight, all right?"

"Absolutely," Justice assured him.

But even as he sat considering his and Tristan's plan to employ Eagle Eye (their method of keep a tight watch on any possible victim they considered to be prime), he didn't feel any calmer about the fact that Jack the Ripper was roaming the streets of the city looking for his next victim. He turned the page on the info sheet and exhaled a heavy sigh of trepidation. Especially when his last two had fit Baylee's basic description almost perfectly.

Justice ran his hand back over the top of his head through his short dark hair. He sighed once more, thinking that there were times he really hated his job—times when special ops missions in the Middle East didn't seem half as nerve-racking as chasing down some psychopathic killer whose victims matched the description of the girl he was planning on getting serious with.

"Are you all right?" Baylee asked as she walked with Justice toward the Dickens Village main offices. He'd been frowning ever since she'd gotten out of her car in the parking lot to meet him.

He looked at her, and the frown puckering his movie-star brow softened as he grinned at her. "Yeah. Just a little tired," he answered.

But Baylee wasn't convinced that his frown had simply been borne of fatigue. She began to wonder if maybe he'd changed his mind about wanting her to go with him to the Dickens Village anniversary party.

Yet when his smile broadened and he said, "But now that I'm with you, I'm feeling my oats again," and laid one muscular arm across her shoulders, her worries about whether she were the cause of his frown dissipated.

"What exactly does that mean anyway?" she giggled, warmed by the feel of his body next to hers. "Feeling your oats? I've always wondered that. I mean…I know what sewing your oats means…but *feeling* your oats?"

"Ah! Finally," Justice said then, pulling her a little more snugly under his arm and against him. "At last I know something someone else doesn't. I've been waiting my whole life for this moment."

Baylee giggled. "Well, I'm glad I'm ignorant enough to oblige."

He chuckled and then began, "The term 'feeling my oats' or 'feeling your oats' or 'feeling his oats' or 'feeling her oats' or—"

"Okay…I get it already," she playfully sighed, jabbing an elbow in his side.

"The phrase actually finds its origins in horse racing," he explained. "A bucket of oats would be given to a racehorse on the day of, or just before, a race. The high-fiber carbs gave or give the horse a short burst of added energy."

"Like eating a candy bar in the middle of the afternoon makes you feel better for twenty minutes," Baylee noted.

"Absolutely," Justice confirmed. "So right now you're having the same effect on me that a bucket of oats before a race has on a racehorse."

Baylee shook her head with amusement. "Where do you come up with this stuff?" she giggled with delight. She loved the way he flirted—absolutely loved it!

"What stuff? I'm just telling it the way it is, that's all," he said as he opened the door to the Dickens Village office conference room.

As she preceded Justice into the conference room, a wave of awed delight washed over her—for everything before her was simply stunning! The large conference room had been decorated in the very same manner as the Dickens Village itself. Pine boughs, holly, pinecones, mistletoe, and so many miniature lights swathed the room at every wall, corner, table, and chair—it was simply enchanting! The warm aroma of fresh bread swirled through the room, mingled with the titillating scents of spices, sugars, chocolate, berries, and every other delicious smell.

Of course, nothing smelled as good as the fragrance of whatever brand and scent of deodorant, aftershave, or cologne that Justice was wearing. Baylee had committed the scent to memory the moment Justice had put his arm around her. It was a sporty, fresh sent, blended with the faint bouquet of soot, warm wool, and cool night breezes—and Baylee knew nothing would ever smell as good to her again as Justice Kincaid had the moment he'd put his arm around her.

"Mmmm!" Justice moaned, inhaling deeply. Glancing down at Baylee, he smiled and asked, "Do you smell that?"

Baylee giggled and nodded. "Bread and butter!"

"Absolutely!" he chuckled. "Come on, and let's eat something. I'm starving."

"Me too," Baylee said.

Justice dropped his arm from her shoulder and took her hand, leading her toward one of the tables so laden with food and beautiful greenery, decorations, and lights that Baylee wondered how it was even possible the table wasn't sagging in the middle.

Once Justice had piled two plates with good things to eat, he sought out a table for them, and they settled down.

Baylee grinned as she watched Justice dig into a huge slab of ham.

"What?" he asked, glancing up at her to see her amusement.

"Nothing," she replied. "I was just thinking what a pig you must think I am. Every time you see me, I'm eating."

"That's not true," he countered, however. "Sometimes you're singing, sometimes you're ringing your cute little bells, sometimes you're sitting at a table in that little cider place drinking cider with Candice…sometimes you're kneeing that Tate Polanski idiot in the chongs for touching you without your permission, and sometimes you're talking to that little kid who's always limping around with the crutch like he's Tiny Tim."

Baylee felt her mouth fall open a little with astonishment—stared at him with disbelief. He *had* been watching her from the rooftops of the Dickens Village! She was simultaneously elated and freaked out. She tried to think of how many times she'd adjusted her bra or stockings since she'd been performing at the Dickens Village. Had she done anything entirely embarrassing that he may have seen?

Yet to know he was watching her—that he was interested in her enough to keep such a close eye on her—it thrilled her!

"Wow...you're pretty observant," she said.

Justice paused in chewing a bite of ham, looked at her, and said, "Surveillance, Baylee...it's what I'm good at."

"Surveillance and seduction," she mumbled aloud to herself.

"What?" he asked.

"Nothing," she lied, pinching off a piece of a dinner roll and popping it in her mouth. "Mmm. I love this bread!"

In truth, Justice had heard exactly what Baylee had mumbled—that he was good at surveillance *and* seduction. He was pleased—more than pleased. For one thing, the flirting and attention he'd been casting at her seemed to be working a little. She liked it when he flirted with her; he could tell by the smiles and blushes that always leapt to her face. Furthermore, he figured if she found him somewhat seductive, then maybe his chances of reeling her in were better than he'd even hoped.

He did need to find a way to have her all to himself, however—alone—and outside the realm of the Dickens Village. Oh, dinner every night was all well and fine, but he needed to find out if she liked him when he wasn't dressed up like Dick Van Dyke and working. Moreover, he was ready—more than ready—ready to lay one on the little velvet-swathed bell ringer and see how she responded.

For a moment, the anxiety that wracks every teenage boy before kissing a girl washed over him—the fear of rejection, the fear that he might screw up the kiss and gross her out. But he reminded his stupid brain that he was a man now and far beyond that pimple-faced, awkward stage. Besides, it wasn't like it was his first time kissing a girl. What was there to screw up?

Still, as Justice watched Baylee butter another dinner roll, smiling as the butter began to melt, he frowned a little—annoyed at the little lingering doubt in himself that was still nagging him. Surely he could kiss her well enough to please her—couldn't he?

"So you're off tomorrow?" Baylee asked, rattling him from his flashback to adolescence.

"Oh…um…yeah," he managed. "It'll be my last day off for a while. We're stepping up security at the village, and we're all gonna be working some doubles."

The minute it was out of his mouth, Justice knew he'd messed up. He watched Baylee's brow pucker with concern.

"Why?" she asked. "Why do you need to beef up security?"

Justice had lost his focus and revealed too much about the situation. To compound his frustration, the descriptions of the copycat killer's victims flooded his thoughts, reminding him how closely they all resembled his favorite little Victorian caroler.

He shrugged, feigning indifference, and lied, "O'Sullivan thinks shoplifting will increase the closer we get to the holidays." He hated lying to her, but he had his orders. Furthermore, he didn't want to raise any red flags in her brain that might prey on her sense of safety.

"Well, that stinks," she mumbled.

"And it gets worse," he added. "No more hour breaks for lunch or dinner."

"What?" she exclaimed—and Justice was inwardly pleased by her obvious distress. "I-I mean…you have to eat sometime, don't you?" she added, trying to make it appear that her concern was for the well-being of his appetite and not because they wouldn't be able to have dinner together every evening anymore.

In fact, the disappointment apparent in her pretty brown eyes was so obvious that, before he could think it over more thoroughly, he asked, "Are you off tomorrow too?" even though he knew she was. He'd kept a tight watch on her work schedule all week.

"Yeah," she answered. "Finally."

"Well, since we'll be working double-shifts and all for a while, I'm gonna do some early Christmas shopping tomorrow. If you don't have plans, would you be willing to help me out?"

Baylee was struck silent for a moment. Christmas shopping with Justice Kincaid? There wasn't anything in all the world she'd rather do on her day off. Suddenly she felt as warm as the melting butter on her dinner roll.

"I would love it!" she answered—way too enthusiastically, as usual.

"Good," he chuckled, obviously amused by her exuberance. "And if you've got things you need to check off your list…let's make a day of it. And maybe you'll let me take you out to for a *real* dinner date afterward, huh?"

You can take me anywhere anytime, you gorgeous chimney sweep, you, Baylee thought to herself. Out loud, however, she said, "That sounds wonderful! I'm in."

"Great," he said, cutting another piece of ham from the quickly disappearing slab on his plate. "Slather some butter on one of those rolls for me, will you, please?"

"Of course," Baylee giggled.

As she buttered a warm dinner roll for Justice, she sighed. Christmas shopping and dinner? Could it be real? Was it truly possible that Justice Kincaid was as interested in her as he seemed to be? And why would a guy like him be interested in a girl like her—a simple, regular, everyday girl who had no reason to catch the eye of a man with his background, experience, charm, and lethal good looks?

Still, inhaling a breath of determination to be confident and not look a gift horse in the mouth, so to speak, Baylee offered the freshly buttered dinner roll to Justice.

As Justice said, "Thank you," and accepted the roll from Baylee, she noticed that the butter on the roll had already begun to melt and had dribbled down the side of her hand. Reaching for a napkin with her free hand with which to wipe the melted butter, she was startled when Justice took hold of her wrist.

"Let me get that for you," he said.

Baylee felt her mouth drop open in rapturous awe as she watched, and felt, Justice Kincaid lick the butter dripping from the side of her hand. Goose bumps erupted over her body like a wave of stacked dominoes tripping.

He smiled at her, winked, and said, "I don't waste butter…ever."

"Oh," she managed to breathe, still overwhelmed with the sense of intoxication his gesture had rinsed her in.

Justice nodded toward her plate. "You better eat something besides bread, sugar plum," he urged. "Get a little protein into your system there."

"Oh…oh, yes," Baylee stammered, still so affected by his having licked the butter from her hand that she could hardly speak or move—or even think clearly.

Almost robotically she watched as her hands used her utensils to cut a bite of ham—as her fork lifted the piece to her mouth and inserted it. The familiar feeling of doubt, of wondering if she were really sitting at a table with Justice Kincaid, lingered all around her. Yet when he began telling her a few of the things he needed to pick up on their shopping excursion the next day, the truth of it all began to settle in. Though she didn't know why—though she couldn't fathom why Justice had chosen her to spend his time with—the fact of the matter was that he had! And as her senses began to return, Baylee decided that the old adage of looking a gift horse in the mouth finally made sense to her. It didn't matter why Justice was interested in getting to know her. All that mattered was that he was. So she wouldn't waste any more energy on doubt and wondering why the gift horse had been gifted. She'd simply accept it and ride away into the sunset as far as the horse could carry her.

CHAPTER SIX

Baylee and Justice mingled with friends and acquaintances, ate too many sweet treats, laughed and talked, and did everything else everyone attending the Dickens Village anniversary soiree did. Yet all the while Baylee was distracted—distracted by her feral attraction to the ferociously handsome Justice Kincaid—distracted by the schoolgirl's, dreamlike nature of her thoughts concerning him. She had visions of him all decked out in a tuxedo and watching her as she approached him wearing a bridal gown. She had visions of being held in his arms and gazing up into the mesmerizing peacock-green of his eyes. She wondered if he were a good kisser—then scolded herself for such a ridiculous thought. Of course he was a good kisser! How could he not be? She imagined that kissing Justice Kincaid would be the experience of a lifetime—of an eternity! Just thinking about kissing him caused her to blush—caused her body to warm all over and her mouth to water.

In truth, Baylee couldn't think of anyone or anything in all her life to that point that made her feel the way she felt when she was in Justice's company—when she was simply looking at him from across the room. The thought entered her mind that she'd even toss her handbells into a melting pot if it meant she could win the affections and heart of Justice Kincaid.

How could she have such strong feelings for him already? she wondered as she sipped the last swig of hot chocolate from a mug Justice had handed her some time before. She'd only known him—what—less than two weeks? And yet she wanted him—she wanted him to be the mythical "Mr. Right" that every girl was always looking for—

that she was always looking for. She wanted Justice to be her Mr. Right more than she'd ever wanted anything! But was it too much to hope for? She knew it was. And yet he did seem genuinely pleased to be in her company—to be with her, to talk with her, to drink hot chocolate with her.

Baylee watched Justice as he stood some distance away talking to Candice and Tristan. He was so handsome! Truly! He couldn't be real, could he? Surely he hadn't just glanced over at *her* and winked—not at *her*! But when she saw him say something to Tristan and then turn and begin striding toward her, Baylee smiled, forgot her doubts and wonderings, and simply enjoyed the rhythm of his ultra cool manner of walking—bathed in the pure perfect beauty of his handsome face and dazzling smile.

"Are you getting tired yet?" he asked as he reached her.

Baylee shook her head. "No. Not at all," she fibbed. And it was a lie, for in truth she was really, really tired. But she wasn't going to miss a moment in Justice's company—not for anything—especially something stupid like fatigue.

"Well, you're a better man than me then," he chuckled. "I'm beat. I'm probably just anticipating working double shifts, but I'm tired all the same. Do you mind if we cut out in a little while?"

"Not at all," she answered truthfully.

"I mean, I guess you can stay if you like…since you have your car here and everything," he offered.

But Baylee shook her head. "Nope. I've eaten enough to feed a small country already, and now that you've mentioned it…I guess I am feeling a little worn around the edges."

"Okay," he said, smiling at her. "We'll go in a few minutes then. I'll make sure you get to your car okay and then…"

He paused a moment as the soft classical music that had been wafting through the room a moment before changed. Baylee recognized the music—the song. It was one of her favorites. In fact, normally whenever she heard Joss Stone's rendition of "I Put a Spell on You," she couldn't help but sing along with the jazzy blues number. However, this time—considering she was in a room full of Dickens Village employees—she bit her tongue.

"Man, I love this song," Justice said. "Especially this Joss Stone version."

Baylee's mouth dropped open in elated astonishment. "You're kidding," she said. "Me too…but I've really never met anybody else who is at all familiar with this version."

Justice frowned. "Seriously? Joss Stone? She's awesome."

Baylee smiled as she noted the way Justice's body began to move in time to the music. It was barely perceivable, but very, very, *very* cool.

Oh, no, she thought—because it looked as if Justice Kincaid were about to wow her even more than he already had, with a smooth, cool manner of dancing. He moved with a perfectly marvelous rhythm that caused Baylee's heart to race and her mouth to water.

As people around them began splitting into couples to slow dance, Justice said, "Hmmm. I guess we're not the only Joss Stone fans in Dickens Town after all."

"I guess not," Baylee agreed. "Though I like this song no matter who's singing it most of the time."

"Me too," he said as he hands went to her waist and pulled her body toward his. "Wanna dance with me?" he asked.

Was he kidding? Was he blind? Was he for real? Of *course* she wanted to dance with him! Furthermore, she loved the way he'd begun dancing with her before he'd even asked her.

"Are you asking or telling?" she teased him.

Justice chuckled, his eyes narrowing with a far too seductive expression. "Whichever you prefer," he answered.

Baylee giggled. "Do you ever stop?" she asked.

"Stop what?" he asked in return.

"Stop with the charming, sort of provocative one-liners."

He smiled at her—slowly slid his hands up her sides to the underside of her arms and then over the underside of her arms, lifting them and gently gripping her wrists a moment as he settled her hands on his shoulders.

Wrapping his arms around her body and pulling her against him, he mumbled, "Nope."

Baylee, now breathless in his embrace, whispered, "Oh, good."

As the song continued, Baylee wished someone would just hit the repeat button so that it would never end. Just as she'd suspected, being held by Justice Kincaid was the most euphoric sensation a woman could experience. She could feel the heat of his body, the solid, muscular contours of it—even for their costumes. She consciously felt safer—more protected than she ever had in her entire life. Likewise, she was aware of the potent desires welling in her—the desire to caress his whiskery, soot-smeared fact with her hands, the desire to kiss him, to feel his mouth pressed to hers.

I think I already love you, Justice's voice echoed in her mind.

I know I already love you, her own thoughts answered.

Everything, every sensation and romantic thought in her, became more powerful when Justice lowered his head to press his cheek against hers—began to mumble into her ear words similar to those Joss Stone was singing. "I'd put spell on *you* if I could," he breathed. The warmth of his breath on her neck—the heat of his skin next to hers—sent a rush of goose bumps surging over her body. "I'd put a spell on you and make you mine."

Baylee trembled a little—overcome with desire, hope, and disbelief. Surely he just didn't know the lyrics as well as she did. After all, it wasn't like Justice would really want her to be his.

"I thought you liked this song," she baited him, desperately hopeful that she was wrong—that he really did know the lyrics as well as she did and had intentionally changed them for her sake.

"I do," he said, raising his head to look at her. "Why?"

She was at his mercy—utterly at his mercy! As she gazed up into Justice's ridiculously handsome face, she ventured, "Well, the words to the song are actually—"

"I know the words to the song, Baylee," he said, grinning at her. "And I think you know that, don't you?"

She thought she might cry—burst into tears of perfect happiness! "M-maybe," she stammered, trying to keep tears from welling in her eyes.

Justice chuckled. "Maybe?" He laughed, amused by her response. His arms tightened around her then, and he rested his chin on her head a moment. "Maybe." He laughed again, and Baylee sighed—swept away in the blissful sound of his voice rumbling in his broad chest.

The song was nearing the end, and Baylee frowned. Their dance was almost over. She couldn't keep her body from reacting to the truth of it, and her arms rather involuntarily slid over his shoulders, her hands lacing at the back of his neck. She didn't want him to release her—ever!

But the song did end, and people at the party began talking and returning to the food tables as another, more upbeat selection started. Baylee felt herself blush with the realization that she was still clinging to Justice, even after the music had stopped. Unwillingly, but quickly, she released him as his embrace of her slackened.

"Do you want something to drink before we go?" Justice asked as he released Baylee altogether—leaving her feeling cold, nervous, and saddened.

"No…I'm okay," she answered.

"Good job, man!" another security guard dressed as a chimney sweep said, patting Justice on one strong shoulder. "You're slick, Kincaid. Real slick!"

"Thanks, man," Justice said, nodding at the man.

"I guess you've got more than just weapons expertise, huh?" the guy asked. "You're a tactical master too."

"You bet," Justice chuckled.

Baylee frowned with puzzlement as the guy smiled at her. "What?" she asked. "Am I missing something?"

Justice grinned, his grin slowly spreading into a full-fledged smile. "I've been waiting for a chance like this for quite a while now," he said.

"A chance like what?" she giggled.

"Mistletoe, shweety," the other chimney sweep said.

"What?" But when Bailey looked up to see she stood directly beneath a large mistletoe ball hanging from an overhead light, she understood.

Smiling with profound pleasure, she looked back to Justice. "Did you maneuver me here on purpose?"

"Of course," he answered. "Maneuvers, Baylee…it's what I'm good at."

She giggled and then gasped, breathless with anticipation, as Justice reached out, taking her face between his warm, powerful hands. "Come here, you little bell-ringer, you," he said in a low, provocative voice. "Let's see if I can ring your bell for a change, shall we?"

Baylee gulped. Would he really kiss her? And if he did, would he kiss her on the cheek or the…

Justice's kiss was confident and solidly applied. There was no timid, tender, practical kiss to Baylee's lips, but he didn't kiss her too forcefully either. He simply kissed her—and yet there was nothing whatsoever simple about it! In fact, it was the most perfect kiss Baylee could have ever dreamt of. Justice's lips weren't closed tight when he kissed her, but neither was his mouth wide open and excessively aggressive. His lips were parted, moist, and warm when they first met hers, and the feel of it all sent wave after wave of tingling, thrilling goose bumps streaming over Baylee's body. And yet, as if he knew she had been unprepared for such a perfect kiss the first time around, Justice kissed her again—allowing Baylee the opportunity to part her lips enough so that her returned kiss matched his as perfectly as if their mouths were made to be melded. Leaning forward so that his strong body was flush with her own, Justice kissed her a third and wildly exciting time. Three kisses—only three—and neither of the three lasting beyond a few seconds—and yet Baylee Cabot wanted nothing more than to throw her arms around Justice's neck and continuing kissing him for the rest of her life!

Baylee felt her eyes flutter open as their third kiss ended, not even having realized she'd closed them. She was suddenly aware of the catcalls echoing through the room and felt herself blush as she gazed up into the oh-so-breathlessly handsome, soot-smudged face of Justice Kincaid. His peacock-green eyes smoldered with a modest satisfaction in the low lighting. He grinned as Baylee attempted to appear unruffled.

"Well?" he asked.

"W-well, what?" Baylee stammered in a breathless whisper.

"Did my pathetic attempt to ring the little bell-ringer's bell…did it work?" he chuckled.

But Baylee couldn't verbally respond. She could only endure the deepening of the already rose-red blush on her cheeks.

"She looks like she's thinking 'ding-ding-ding' to me, Justice," Tristan chuckled as he approached. He reached out and playfully pinched Baylee's cheek as Justice released her. "Now *that's* the way it's done, people!" Tristan laughed. "Never let a good sprig of mistletoe go to waste." Tristan winked at Baylee, and she felt somewhat forgiving of his teasing.

"Come on," Justice said, taking Baylee's arm. "I'll walk you to your car."

"You don't have to do that," Baylee began to argue.

But Justice shook his head. "It's cold, late, and dark. What kind of a man would I be if I let a shweet little bell-ringer like you walk out to the parking lot all alone?"

"But…" she began to argue again. She was so dazed by the lingering bliss kissing him had caused that she couldn't even think straight at first.

But when he asked, "Are you gonna let me be a gentleman or not, sugar plum?" she remembered that they had come to the party together, so it only made sense they should leave together.

"I-I guess I'm just not used to there being any gentlemen around," she stammered, trying to mask how thoroughly discombobulated she was.

"Well, that's just wrong," he sighed. Placing one strong arm across her shoulders, he pulled her against him to tuck her securely under his arm.

Baylee didn't know how she managed to walk to the door with him. In fact, she wondered if she'd simply floated there with the help of the proverbial cloud nine.

As they exited the building Justice said, "Brrrr! It's cold out here."

But Baylee didn't think it was cold. In fact, she couldn't remember a time in her life when she'd been as warm as she was at that moment. She loved the feel of his arm around her—of his holding her protectively as they walked across the parking lot.

Again Baylee could smell the comforting aroma of the bakery wood smoke still clinging to Justice's chimney sweep jacket, of the soot on his clothes and face, and of the faint scent of his unidentified, masculine antiperspirant. Oooo! Justice Kincaid smelled *so* good!

"Do you girls wear long underwear under these dresses?" he asked, shivering again. "I hope you do, because I'm sure it's just going to get colder and colder as the season progresses."

"I'm warm enough," she answered. "But how about you?"

"I'm fine," he said. "Just being kind of a baby tonight because it was so warm inside, I guess. I'm not really a fan of really cold weather."

"But cold weather is the best way to be cozy," Baylee offered. "Evenings in front of the fire, drinking hot chocolate, and watching Christmas shows on TV aren't nearly as cozy and wonderful in the summertime."

He chuckled. "Good point…though I admit to not spending a whole lot of time watching Christmas shows on TV."

Baylee shrugged. "Actually, I don't either…but I wish I could."

"I like your little red car," he chuckled as they walked toward Baylee's Honda.

"Me too," she agreed. "It gets me where I need to go, and it's never let me down yet."

"Between your car and your cute little caroler dress…you're about as festive as they come," he teased.

"I try," Baylee giggled.

Reaching into the deep pocket of her red velvet caroler's cape, Baylee fumbled around for her keys.

"Thanks for walking me out," she said as she continued to fumble.

As she pulled the keys from her pocket at last, Justice said, "Thanks for letting me kiss you under the mistletoe back there."

Baylee blushed. "Well, I can just imagine what it must be like—you know, all your chimney sweep, Special Forces friends standing around and—"

"That's not why I did it," he interrupted. She looked up to see him staring at her with a somewhat perturbed expression on his face. "I've never kissed a girl I didn't want to kiss."

"Really?" she asked, more out of habit than doubt.

"Yeah, really," he affirmed. "I knew exactly where that mistletoe was in conjunction with your position in the room. Strategy, Baylee…it's what I'm…"

"It's what your good at, I know," Baylee giggled.

He nodded—chuckled at her wit. She gasped a little then as, in the next moment, he used his body to gently push hers back against her car.

Taking her face in his hands again, he mumbled, "And just to make sure you do…" the moment before he kissed her.

Again his kiss was confident without being too aggressive—just as it had been before. This time, however, it lingered. His mouth lingered against hers, warm and moist. Yet his manner of kissing her nearly frustrated her somehow, for it felt as if he were intentionally holding back, keeping a more passionate kiss in reserve. Her spinning senses managed to figure that he was probably being careful—not wanting her to think he was some kind of a creep who was out for only one thing.

Yet she wanted him to kiss her more deeply—more passionately—but he didn't.

Oh, it was absolutely true that Justice's kisses were the stuff of dreams—would be the winner of any MTV Best Kiss Award! Still, Baylee knew there was more, that what she was experiencing was the literal tip of the iceberg—that if he ever wanted to kiss her with no restraint, she would never recover from the ecstasy of it!

"Good night, Baylee," he said as he released her and stepped back. "I'll see you tomorrow. Ten a.m., okay?"

"Of course," she answered, far too breathlessly. "Let me give you my address."

But Justice shook his head. "No need. Reconnaissance, Baylee…"

"It's what you're good at," she finished for him with a giggle.

"Among other things," he said insinuatively, with a wink.

Baylee's insides were boiling with the warm, summer butterflies of delight.

Taking her keys, he opened her door for her, returning them once she'd slid into the driver's seat.

"Good night," he said.

"Good night," she said as he closed her door.

Her hand was trembling as she put the key in the ignition and turned it. Glancing at Justice once more, she smiled before pulling away.

As Baylee drove home through the dark November night, she sighed. She was emotionally compromised—too goofy-minded with the residual euphoria of kissing Justice to be a safe driver. She wondered if what she was feeling were similar to what intoxicated people felt just before they called a cab to drive them home. And when she glanced in her rearview mirror to see that her nose, cheeks, and the skin around her mouth were smudged with soot—a transference from Justice's chimney sweep's face to hers that had occurred when they'd kissed—she nearly ran a stop sign as she'd giggled with delight.

Shaking her head and attempting to capture her wits once more, Baylee drove on—smiling as the warm sense of Justice Kincaid's kissing lingered on her lips.

CHAPTER SEVEN

Christmas shopping with Justice was nothing if not an adventure. Baylee was awed by the consideration and time he'd put into making his list. Furthermore, he certainly wasn't a cheapskate or skinflint. Though Justice may have dressed like a Dickens-era chimney sweep to blend into the Dickens Village atmosphere at work, there was nothing Scrooge-ish about him. And that fact alone would've made the experience fun for Baylee. Shopping with a man who'd set his Christmas budget realistically high and considered the gifts he'd wanted to give before December 22? It was wonderful!

However, it wasn't the time in the jewelry store searching for the perfect set of opal earrings he wanted for his mother or in the sporting goods store as he chose just the right trench knife for his younger brother that was the most fun. It was the sheer fact that she was with him at all that caused Baylee's heart to beat double time.

Not only was Justice generous, but it was obvious he truly enjoyed giving to those he loved. Baylee's admiration of Justice only continued to grow as the day proceeded. He was adorable to watch—the way his handsome face would light up when he'd found exactly what he'd been looking for. Selfishly, and without any right to do so, Baylee secretly wondered what Justice would choose to give her, if she were someone fortunate enough to be cherished by him and therefore found her name on his Christmas gift-giving list. Of course, he didn't know her very well, she reminded herself. But still, she wondered what he'd give her—if the occasion ever presented itself for him to give her something.

Once they had grabbed a quick lunch at a sandwich shop, they were in Justice's truck and off and running once more.

"Now, Grandma is just about the hardest one on my list," he said as he drove them toward the high-end strip mall on the east side of town.

"Why don't you just buy her a new car and give her the payment along with it?" Baylee teased.

Justice laughed. "That would be funny, right?" he began. "I could buy her, like, a new Shelby Mustang or something and wrap up the payment book and put it under the tree." He shook his head. "You don't know what a little pill my grandma can be. But she's one of those ladies that you can't help but love…no matter what kind of crap she pulls."

Baylee smiled, warmly delighted by Justice's obvious affection for his grandmother. "So what *are* you planning on getting for her?" she asked.

Justice paused a moment. "Well, if you really want to know…this little subcompact Beretta nine-millimeter she's been hinting for all year," he answered.

Baylee frowned. "Um…a Beretta? As in a handgun?" She was astonished. Justice was planning on purchasing a handgun for his grandmother as a Christmas gift?

"Well, the one she carries now is just so heavy. And the Beretta Px4 Storm Subcompact pistol really is the best subcompact sidearm right now…in my opinion, anyway," he explained. "She's been carrying this big ol' Magnum for a couple of years, and though grandmas always seem to lug around heavy purses, I know the little Beretta will ease up her purse load a bit. So I had this gun shop order one in for me, and we just have to pick it up."

But Baylee giggled as she studied Justice for a moment as he drove. "You're serious, aren't you?"

"Absolutely," he assured her, glancing at her with not one hint of teasing in his eyes. "Grandma loves guns. She always has. She and Grandpa…well, let's just say they had—and she still has—quite an arsenal."

"Wow!" Baylee sighed. "It kind of makes me want to meet this Calamity Jane grandma of yours."

"Oh, you'll love her," he assured her—as if he fully expected her to meet his grandmother one day. "Like I said, she can be a handful, but she's hysterical at the same time. That's how she gets away with all the stuff she pulls on everybody."

Baylee kept smiling—sighed as she gazed out the truck window as they drove. It was wonderful, being with Justice. Absolutely wonderful! She wished the day would never end, but she knew it eventually would. Still, she hoped it would end with a good-bye kiss. She thought she'd do just about anything to experience another Justice Kincaid kiss.

"So I figure we'll do the gun store, then pick up that stuff at the mall you needed, and then…" He paused, looking over to her with a rather mischievous grin. "You know how I told you I'd take you out for a real dinner tonight?"

"Yeah?" she prodded as a warm, delightful sensation pressed the back of her neck.

"How about this? I set the DVR to record one of those girlie Christmas movies you chicks like so well last night. So how about I take you in for a real dinner instead, and we can watch a corny Christmas show while we eat? What do you say? I mean, we were talking about how we never get to watch stuff like that, right?"

"Absolutely," Baylee giggled. How adorable! How incredibly creative and thoughtful he was! She couldn't believe it. Surely it was just another thing about Justice that was too good to be true—wasn't it? Yet so far, everything that appeared too good to be true about him *was* true!

"Cool!" he said, smiling. "Then I hope you like French toast. It's what I'm good at," he said.

"French toast and seduction," Baylee mumbled to herself.

"What?" Justice asked.

"I said French toast…I love it," she answered.

"Oh, good," Justice said—though once again he'd heard exactly what Baylee had really said.

He smiled, proud of himself for having thought of the idea to take her *in* for dinner instead of out. He wanted this girl—wanted her to like him as much as he liked her—and if Brian was stepping up their shifts in order to better track the Jack the Ripper psycho, then Justice knew he needed to use the small windows of time he could grab with Baylee to the best advantage he could. Quality more than quantity—that's what he had to do. And he hoped a nice warm dinner of his special French toast, a corny, made-for-TV Christmas movie, and the opportunity to just spend more time with her would help his cause.

Yep. He had plans for the little handbell ringer sitting in the passenger's seat of his truck. But when the reality of why he and the others were posing as chimney sweeps at the Dickens Village in the first place polluted his thoughts, he wondered how he was going to stay on top of protecting all of humanity from a murderous and evil entity and still find time to woo and win Baylee Cabot.

The exquisite dinner of French toast and bacon Justice had whipped up at his house after they'd finished shopping had been sublime—mostly because Justice had cooked it, of course, but it had been delicious all the same. Still, nothing would ever be more blissful for Baylee than the hour she'd spent since, sitting next to Justice on his couch, watching *Miracle of the Mistletoe*—the corny, yet very romantic, made-for-TV movie he'd recorded the night before. An hour into the movie and Baylee was having a hard time keeping track of the simplistic plot of the show—for in that sweet, romantic hour, Justice had often put his arm around her shoulders, rested a hand on her knee, or fiddled with the ring on her right ring finger. It was heaven being there with Justice—pure heaven.

It's why Baylee frowned when there was a knock on Justice's front door. It interrupted not only their movie but Baylee's being tucked warm and cozy under Justice's arm—against him.

"Who can that be?" he mumbled as he pressed the pause button on the remote control. He glanced at his wristwatch and frowned as he released Baylee and stood up from the couch. "Hold on a second, okay?"

"Of course," Baylee answered. Of course she'd hold on a second. She'd hold on for hours and hours if it meant she'd have the chance to cuddle up next to Justice for a while longer.

From her seat on Justice's leather couch, Baylee watched as Justice opened the front door—a broad smile spreading over his handsome face.

"What are you doing here?" he asked, still smiling.

"I came over to make sure you were all right, honey," a woman's voice said. The voice sounded like music, and as the elderly white-haired lady stepped over the threshold and into Justice's embrace, Baylee understood why.

She knew at once that this must be Justice's grandmother—the one that wanted a Beretta for Christmas.

"I'm fine, Grandma," Justice said. "I was just—"

"Ahhh!" the older woman said as she glanced over, catching sight of Baylee. "You were just necking, eh?"

"No, Grandma. I wasn't necking," Justice chuckled, closing the door behind his grandmother. "This is Baylee," he said, gesturing toward Baylee. "She and I were out all day Christmas shopping and thought we'd watch some TV and—"

"Neck?" the woman finished for him. "So what you meant was you're not necking *yet*."

The woman's eyes—her peacock-green eyes—were intent on Baylee as Baylee rose from her seat and walked over to meet her.

"I'm Baylee Cabot," Baylee said, offering a hand to the woman.

The woman's smile broadened. "And I'm Francis Kincaid," she said, taking Baylee's hand, "Justice's grandmother."

"It's so nice to meet you, Mrs. Kincaid," Baylee said, noting the way the woman clung to her hand. Mrs. Kincaid's hand was warm and soft—just as a grandmother's hand should be.

"So you've been necking with Justice, is that it, honey?" Mrs. Kincaid asked.

Baylee couldn't help blushing—not because she had been necking with Justice but because she *wished* she had been.

"Come on, Grandma," Justice scolded. "You'll scare her off. Do you know how long it took me to lure her here? Now what did you need?"

"Like I said, sweetie," Mrs. Kincaid answered, though her attention never left Baylee, "I just wanted to make sure you were all right…since I hadn't heard from you today."

"Well, I'm fine," Justice said. "And now you know it, and you can go home and…and do whatever you were doing before."

Mrs. Kincaid smiled, leaned closer to Baylee, and whispered, "He wants me out of the way so he can neck with you."

Baylee giggled. "I hope so," she jested in return—though she wasn't really in jest at all.

"Come on, Grandma," Justice said, taking his grandmother's arm in an attempt to lead her toward the door. "Do the cops know you're out driving the streets this late? They oughta issue a warning."

"Oh, you hush, Justice," she scolded. "My driving is fine, and you know it." Aside to Baylee, she added, "He worries just because of my age, you know. But I'm only seventy-two years old. I've got at least twenty years of good driving ahead of me, right?"

Baylee smiled and nodded.

"Grandma," Justice urged.

"Have you seen his muscles, honey?" Mrs. Kincaid asked, however. When Baylee didn't answer right away—too stunned by the question to have a rational response come to mind—Mrs. Kincaid added, "Have you?"

"Um...I don't think I have," Baylee managed to stammer.

Then Mrs. Kincaid looked to Justice, put her hands on her hips in a scolding manner, and asked, "How do you ever expect to get to necking with this young woman if she hasn't seen your muscles, Justice?"

"Grandma...it's time to go," Justice said patiently.

But Mrs. Kincaid wasn't having any of it. "Take that sweater off, Justice. Right now."

Justice was wearing a red ribbed shirt. It was long-sleeved and tight-fitting and had made Baylee's head swim with admiration when he'd first picked her up that day.

"It's not a sweater, Grandma, and you need to be on your way," Justice countered.

"Take it off this minute and show that girl your muscles!" Mrs. Kincaid demanded, stomping one foot on the floor.

"She doesn't want to see my muscles, Grandma," Justice argued. Baylee could see his patience was wearing thin—yet the entire scene was so amusing that she couldn't help but giggle.

"Of course she does!" Mrs. Kincaid argued. Looking to Baylee, she asked, "Don't you, honey?"

"Of course I do," Baylee answered, joining ranks with the older woman. The expression of astonishment on Justice's face was wildly entertaining—an expression of disbelief and, for the first time since she'd met him, dumbfoundedness.

"See there, Justice," Mrs. Kincaid said. "She *does* want to see your muscles. I don't know how you ever expect her to start necking with you if she doesn't see how pretty you are." Taking hold of the bottom of Justice's shirt then, Mrs. Kincaid endeavored to strip it off him.

"Knock it off, Grandma!" Justice growled. "That's enough."

Baylee watched then as Justice pulled his shirt back down over his stomach—but not before she caught a glimpse of the sculpted washboard abs he owned.

"Take it off," Mrs. Kincaid ordered, attempting to remove his shirt a second time.

"Leave it alone," Justice told her.

"Just for a minute, Justice," Mrs. Kincaid argued. "Give that girl a show, and she'll do anything you want her to do." She looked to Baylee again and asked, "Isn't that right, honey?"

"Absolutely," Baylee giggled, entirely amused by what was going on between Justice and his grandmother.

What she didn't expect, however, was for Justice to daringly arch one eyebrow as he looked at Baylee and asked, "Is that so?"

"Of course it's so," Mrs. Kincaid answered for her.

Justice smiled then, and the warm sensation that rose to the back of Baylee's neck every time he did so returned with a fury.

"Be careful what you promise, sugar plum," he said. "Someone might just call you on it one day."

And without another word, Justice reached over one shoulder, taking hold of the back of his shirt and stripping it off right there, in front of the leftover French toast and everything.

Though Baylee's mouth dropped open and she began to blush at the sight of Adonis in the living flesh, Justice's grandmother clapped her hands and laughed.

"See?" she squealed. "I told you his muscles were something, didn't I?"

In truth, Baylee was astonished—thoroughly intimidated by the sight of Justice shirtless. He was as ripped as any guy to ever star in a workout video infomercial, and all Baylee could do was stand there in front of Justice and his grandmother and blush to the marrow of her bones.

"Okay, Grandma…now go home," Justice told his grandmother as he opened the front door once more, took hold of her arm, and pulled her over the threshold.

"All right, all right," Mrs. Kincaid whined. "I'm going." But a moment before Justice closed the door in her face, she looked at Baylee and added, "I'm sure he's as good at necking as he looks too!"

"Good night, Grandma," Justice said, closing the door. Raising his voice so that his grandmother could hear him through it, however, he added, "Text me when you're home safe, okay?"

"Okay!" Baylee heard Mrs. Kincaid call from the other side.

Baylee watched as Justice peered through a slit in the blinds at the window next to his front door. "I always worry when she's driving at night. I'm sure she can't see as well in dim conditions as she professes." Justice seemed intent on watching his grandmother to her car, but when Baylee heard the roar of an engine, he sighed and stepped back from the blinds.

"Sorry about that," he said, smiling at her. "But I told you she was a pill."

"Yes, you did," Baylee admitted.

"Here," he said, tossing the waded-up red shirt Baylee had loved on him behind the couch. "This is all stretched out now. Let me go get something else. Hang on, okay?"

Baylee wanted to say, *You don't have to put on a shirt on my account*—but instead she simply said, "Absolutely."

Justice wasn't gone long, and when he returned, he had a folded red T-shirt in hand. "I will say this," he said as he held the T-shirt by the shoulders, shaking it out. "That was the fastest I've ever seen Grandma leave any place." He chuckled. "She thinks I'm going to be making out with you all night and is so desperate to see me settled down and happy that she was willing to hightail it."

Baylee giggled, and Justice paused in putting on the T-shirt. "What?" he asked.

"Necking," she giggled again. "It's just such a funny term."

"I know," Justice agreed. "It brings to mind visions of people rubbing their necks together like giraffes or something."

"Yeah," Baylee laughed as she watched Justice put on the T-shirt. His torso had been bare long enough, however, for Baylee to notice not only the rippling muscles Justice owned but also several severe scars. There was one at his left shoulder—a brutal scar that looked to be left from some sort of intensive shoulder surgery. There were also several scars along his ribcage on the left side of his body, almost as if there were one for each rib. It was all she had time to notice, but it was enough to make her ponder a little more on what he'd said the night he'd told her she'd never seen him naked. His body was marked by the injuries he'd sustained during the helicopter crash and ensuing IED explosion. The scars she'd so briefly seen must've been what he'd been referencing that night.

"But she's off on her way now, so we can finish our epic movie," he said, smiling. "I'm riveted. I've just got to see how this all works out."

"Now don't be sarcastic," Baylee scolded as he sat down on the couch, took her hand, and pulled her to sit next to him. "It's a cute little holiday movie."

"I wasn't being sarcastic," he said, slipping an arm across her shoulders and picking up the remote. "But if Bianca doesn't end up with Paul, I'll be ticked off."

Baylee giggled and more than willingly cuddled up to him as he pulled her close.

"Ready?" he asked.

"Yeah," she answered.

As the movie resumed, Baylee wondered how a man could endure all that Justice had obviously endured during his time in the military and then just settle down on the couch and watch a corny Christmas movie. But then again, what else was a person supposed to do? She felt saddened—disturbed by the excruciating pain she knew he must've endured. And yet he seemed healthy and happy now. She'd just concentrate on the Justice Kincaid of now and not let her heart break by nesting on thoughts of him as a wounded soldier.

He chuckled a moment, and Baylee looked up at him. "What?" she asked, wondering if she'd missed something in the movie.

"Necking," he mumbled, however. "It is a weird thing to call it, isn't it?"

"Yeah," Baylee agreed, though she thought she'd love to be *necking* with Justice Kincaid just then. She quivered with delight at the mere thought of it, and Justice pulled her more tightly against him. He was so warm! It was intoxicating, the feel of him holding her.

And so, euphoric with the Justice-intoxication, Baylee sighed with contentment and pleasure and tried to focus on the comedic drama playing out on the TV.

"That's it?" Justice exclaimed with disappointment. "That's how they're going to end this stupid movie?"

Baylee giggled. "What? You don't like happy endings?" she teased.

"Of course I like happy endings," he grumbled. He clicked the off button on the TV remote. "But you call that a happy ending?"

"Well, they both discovered they loved each other…and managed to leave their significant others at the altar and race into each other's arms in the middle of New York City and kiss. What more do you want?"

"Kiss?" he asked, a grimace of disgust puckering his brow. He picked up a smaller remote that was lying on the floor, pointed it toward the iPod dock on his wall unit, and pushed a button. Music began to waft from the dock at a low volume, and Justice said, "We waited an hour and a half for that pathetic little peck at the end?"

"Well, at least he kissed her on the lips," Baylee pointed out, giggling with amusement at his obvious disapproval of the final kiss of the movie.

Justice rolled his eyes, however. "That was pathetic. I can't believe you women are content with a movie like that. Where's the romance? Where's the passion? Where's the good kissing? I thought you girls were all about good kissing."

"Well…it is what it is," Baylee said, shrugging. "What do you want me to do about it?"

The moment she looked at Justice, however, Baylee somehow knew exactly what he wanted her to do about it. Even before he said "satisfy me" and gathered her in his arms, she knew.

"I'm feeling dissatisfied, so satisfy me. That was the most pathetic movie kiss I've ever seen," he said, brushing a strand of hair from her face. "How about I show you how it should've ended, all right?"

Baylee couldn't speak. She could only gaze up at him—somehow hypnotized by the gorgeous peacock-green eyes that had been haunting her dreams every night for almost two weeks. She could only gaze up at him and nod.

"Now this, Baylee Cabot…you little bell-ringer, you…this is how it should've ended," he mumbled as his mouth pressed to hers. "Maybe a soft one like that at first," he whispered. "But then…" In one smooth motion, he left his seat on the couch, pulling her up to stand with him and wrapping her in his arms. "Then it should've gone more like this."

Driven, commanding—hot, moist, and intimate—that's what his next kiss was. It was mind-blowing and sent such a wave of heat and desire coursing through her body that she truly thought she might faint! But the kiss was too short, and she recovered fairly quickly. Too short it may have been, but it was life-altering all the same.

"See?" he said, still holding her against him. "*That's* how it should've ended."

Baylee swallowed the desire that was only expanding in her throat and said, "I see what you mean."

And then the music changed on the iPod dock. Baylee felt goose bumps racing over her arms and legs as she recognized the Jeff Beck guitar intro.

"Hey," Justice said, pulling her more snugly against him instead of releasing her. "It's our song."

"Our s-song?" Baylee stammered. It was hitting her full force then—the fact that she'd fallen irrevocably in love with Justice in the tight span and space of a mere eleven days.

"Yeah," he said, smiling down at her. "Remember last night at the party?"

Did she remember last night at the party? Was he kidding? Of course she remembered it.

"Of course," she breathed.

"Yeah…well, it's our song," he told her as if it were something everyone in the entire world knew except her. He smiled at her then, and his deep-green eyes began to smolder with such an expression of intent to seduce that it frightened Baylee a little. Furthermore, she couldn't believe what he asked her next.

"You wanna *neck* with me while it's playing?" he asked. "Just for my grandma's sake?" When she didn't answer—for she figured he'd probably read the "yes" in her eyes—he began to slow dance with her just a little, singing "I Put a Spell on You" with Joss Stone and wooing her into submission.

Baylee began to wonder if maybe Justice really did own some sort of strange power of bewitchment, for she truly felt as if she were under a sort of fairy tale enchantment, spell, or charm. In truth, Justice's natural charm—the powerful charisma and irresistible allure that literally oozed from every inch of his being—was enough to beguile her on its own. But add to it the way his deep voice provocatively sang the song to her as they swayed to the music—as his hands at her waist directed her as effectively as the slightest tug of the reins at a horse's bit directed it— and Baylee was no longer entirely convinced that there wasn't something supernatural about Justice Kincaid.

As he continued to provocatively sing about putting a "spell on you," Baylee felt herself begin to relax against him. His gaze held hers with such a mesmerizing grip that she could not look away from him. Moreover, she felt her own hands at his chest begin to slide upward to his shoulders, then around to the back of his neck. She trembled, still hypnotized by the simmering invitation in his peacock-green eyes, yet so powerfully overcome, with not only the physical desire to taste his kiss again but the nearly painful swelling of something akin to recognition in her heart, that she nearly quit breathing.

And then, without any further notice, Justice wrapped his arms around her, binding her against him as his mouth pressed firmly and confidently to hers, drawing her into joining him in a long, slow, rhythmic kiss. Baylee's knees began to buckle, but Justice held her unyieldingly, and she stiffened her stance, her hands softly caressing the back of his neck and head. Goose bumps broke over her body as the feel of his short hair tickled her palms. She quivered as his mouth ground against hers, demanding reciprocation—which she all too willingly gave.

As Joss Stone's raspy blues voice continued to weave a spell of heated desire throughout the room, Justice Kincaid continued to cast his own bewitching charm over Baylee. She was in trouble! She was entirely in trouble! She felt tears springing to her eyes, for the feel of his kiss melded to hers, of the moisture and flavor of their blended mouths, affirmed everything to her—that she wanted him—that she wanted Justice Kincaid to be her Mr. Right!

Wild, spontaneous thoughts began to crash around in her head—the thought that she'd give anything to be with him—that she'd give *up* anything to be with him. In that moment, she didn't care about her place in the Hampton Handbell Ringers. She didn't care about money or making a living. She didn't even care if she ever saw another loved one again in all her life! All she wanted was to be with Justice—to love him and win his love for her own somehow.

The crazy thoughts ripping through her only heightened Baylee's desire, and she kissed Justice hard, aggressively, and for a long, long time in response to his coaxing kisses. She loved him. She truly did love him! Baylee was so in love with Justice it hurt—caused her heart to feel as if it were tearing in two. She loved him, not just because he was the most handsome, physically attractive, and desirable man she'd ever seen in all her life but because her soul seemed to recognize his. She loved him. She loved him!

Justice could not satisfy his craving for her. No matter how hard he kissed Baylee, he still wanted more! The thirst he had for her mouth was insane. The thirst he had for *her* was insane!

Had he lost his mind? he wondered. A man couldn't really fall in love with a woman over the course of just a few days, could he? But he knew he had. In fact, he'd known he would nearly from the moment he'd first set eyes on her after the orientation at the Dickens Village offices. He'd known he wanted her—wanted to win her over, keep her as the one woman he'd spend his life with. But now that the reality that he was already insanely in love with her was washing over him, Justice began to doubt himself—and his worthiness to own her.

He'd lied to her, after all—flat out lied to her about what his job was at the village. And he suspected that Baylee Cabot wasn't one to have any patience with liars. But what else could he do? It was his job, and it was the nature of his job to keep secrets—to protect people, not only physically but psychologically and emotionally. What would Baylee do if she knew how close the Jack the Ripper killer was to her? Would she sleep better at night? Would she worry less about the dangers of the world? Hell no! And that's what he did—protected people from harm as well as worry.

"Baylee?" he mumbled against her cheek once he'd broken the seal of their lips.

"Yes," she breathed against his neck.

"You know how I told you I work for a bureau?" he tentatively began.

"Yes," she breathed again, causing the flesh at his neck to warm and goose bumps to break out over his body.

"Well, I think you should know that it's kind of, like…*the* bureau," he ventured.

She looked up at him then, frowning a little. "What do you mean?" she asked. Her eyebrows arched, and she asked, "Do you mean, like, literally the FBI or something?"

Justice called on his courage and said, "Not 'or something.' The actual FBI."

He watched her eyes widen as understanding washed over her. "But…but why would the FBI have chimney sweep security guards posted at the Dickens Village?"

Again Justice mustered his courage. "If I say that I can't tell you yet…what will you do?"

Baylee studied his expression for a moment—entirely awed by what she saw there. Did he actually think the fact that he worked for the FBI would change the way she was reacting to him—the way she was feeling about him? But he did. She could see it in his eyes.

"If you say you can't tell me why you're at the Dickens Village every day dressed up like a sexy chimney sweep," she began. Slipping her arms under his to embrace him and pull him more tightly against her once more, she smiled and said, "I'd say, 'Okay. So let's get back to what we were doing.' That's what I'd do."

Baylee saw the relief wash over him as he smiled. "Okay then, my little bell-ringer," he mumbled. "Pucker up and hold on tight. I'm about to ring your bell like it's never been rung."

Baylee giggled as Justice bent, kissing her neck a moment before his mouth returned to owning hers. Briefly the thought flittered through her mind that something big must be up concerning the Dickens

Village, but it was fleeting. After all, what woman in her right mind would want to worry about something so inconsequential when she had Justice Kincaid in her arms?

CHAPTER EIGHT

"Three more victims since Thanksgiving," Brian said as he handed case files to the men. "This guy is really stepping it up. We've got to find him."

"Well, why are we wasting our time?" Tristan growled. "We should be out hunting this guy down, not dressed up like a bunch of idiots and hanging around at some stupid theme park!"

"If you'll refer to the new information on the last three victims, Holloway," Brain said, "you'll see that every one of them had visited the Dickens Village more than twice in the past two weeks. One woman even worked there for a day. She filled in at one of the vendor carts for a sick employee. The Dickens Village has definitely become this bastard's hunting ground." Slamming a file on the table in front of Tristan, Brian shouted, "So why the hell haven't we got him yet? We're the ones screwing up, Holloway! He's right under our noses, and we haven't seen him! So quit whining about the fact that we're here, step up to the plate, and catch the son of a—"

"Okay, okay," Tristan interrupted. "Sorry. I'm just sick of this guy. He's entirely eluding us. It doesn't make any sense."

"Maybe we're not profiling this correctly," Justice mumbled. He flipped through the file, again sickened by the fact that each and every Jack the Ripper copycat victim was a pretty brunette between the ages of eighteen and twenty-five. He was starting to have nightmares about the fact that Baylee fit the killer's victim profile so flawlessly. The FBI had to catch him—or he did.

"What do you mean?" Brian asked.

"I don't know. Something just doesn't fit," he mumbled. He thought for a moment. "I mean, sure, this guy started out in New York, then moved to Atlanta, then Dallas…but what if those were places outside his territory? What if he's a local boy? What if the Dickens Village is what set him off in the first place?" Justice flipped through the file he held. "Look—twenty-one victims…and the last thirteen have been killed or found within a five-mile radius of the Dickens Village. And as far as dates are concerned, all thirteen of the local murders occurred since November first…the day the Dickens Village launched its holiday season." Justice nodded, suddenly more positive than ever that his suspicions were correct. "We're looking for a local perp. The first eight murders…I think he was just waiting for the Dickens Village's holiday season to begin…practicing his methods before he started shooting fish in a barrel, so to speak."

Brian frowned for a moment. Then taking his cell phone from the holster at his belt, he nodded and mumbled, "I'm gonna call D.C.…have them rework the profile a bit. I think you're right, Kincaid. This guy is feeding out of a homemade trough."

Tristan looked to Justice, arching one inquisitive eyebrow. "So you've gone all psychological profiler on me now?"

Justice shook his head. "No. I just want this guy out of commission. He's whipping up on us, and women are dying because of it."

"Not just dying, man," Tristan sighed as he studied the police photos of the most recent victim. "They're being tortured, mutilated, and *then* dying."

"Thanks for pointing out the obvious, Tristan," Justice grumbled.

"Come on, man. What's with you?" Tristan asked. "Candice and I never see you and Baylee anymore. What? Do you guys just spend every free moment together?"

"Absolutely," Justice said. "And yet, *you* know how few free moments this team gets." He sighed with frustration. "I want this over. I want this guy dead so I can…"

"So you can what?" Tristan prodded when Justice paused.

"So I can move on to something else," Justice said, rising from his chair.

Tristan stood up as well. "Yeah. The chimney sweep gig is getting old." Tristan looked to Justice, his expression serious. "And though I put on the idiot clown, joking and laughing and complaining, it's because this guy gets under my skin…and he scares me where certain cute little carolers are concerned."

"Yeah," Justice agreed. "We need to put this bastard six feet under."

Tristan nodded, and Justice tried to calm the anxiety that had taken root in his gut. Christmas was only two weeks away, and he'd hoped to be able to give Baylee a gift she'd never see coming. But with all the time and energy the team was spending on surveillance, briefings, and research, Justice wasn't sure he should even travel down the road he wanted to travel with Baylee—at least, not yet. He was too tired, angry, and busy working all the time to have a moment to really consider his own future—and hers.

Justice approached Brian and in a whisper asked, "Are we done for now?"

Brian was still on the phone with Washington, but he nodded and made a gesture indicating the briefing was indeed over.

"Where're you off to, bra?" Tristan asked.

But Justice only grinned. "Where do you think?"

"Geez, man!" Tristan chuckled. "Don't you think about anything but Baylee these days?"

"Nope," Justice answered as he hurried out of the briefing room of the FBI field office. And it was true. Justice found that, of late, he only ever had one of two things on his mind—Baylee Cabot and catching the Jack the Ripper copycat, in that order.

Climbing into his truck, he roared out of the field office parking lot and onto the main road. He'd made plans to meet Baylee during her fifteen-minute break at the Dickens Village before his next shift began. If he hurried, he'd make it—and since even one moment with Baylee was worth anything, he'd meet her or die trying!

Baylee smiled as she watched the ethereally handsome chimney sweep saunter toward her. Most of the time she still couldn't believe Justice Kincaid was hers—her boyfriend anyway. But it was true! Since the night more than a month before—the night they'd watched the corny Christmas movie on TV at his house—she and Justice had been nearly inseparable during what little free time he had. It was crazy how many hours he was working, and Baylee hated it. Yet she knew that a lot of jobs and careers escalated in demands of time and stress when the holidays were approaching, and so she tried to be as patient as she could—to simply savor every moment she could spend with Justice, instead of resenting all the ones she couldn't.

Naturally, Baylee spent a lot of time wondering where her relationship with Justice would lead. The truth was that if he asked her that minute to marry him, she'd fling her arms around his neck and beg him to carry her off to the justice of the peace right that minute. But she wasn't sure his feelings were as deeply solidified as hers. Certainly he appeared to be as in love with her as any man could be in love with a woman, but the little nagging doubt that keeps everyone from being perfectly positive about something was always at the back of her mind.

And yet, as Justice advanced and reached her, gathering her into his arms and forcing her into the little alleyway nearby, Baylee sighed with renewed hope when she saw the affection and desire so profoundly visible in his beautiful green eyes.

"Hey, pretty baby," he mumbled against her mouth. His face was cold, chilled from having been walking in the cold air. But his lips and mouth were as warm as a radiator.

Over and over Justice kissed her—passionately, demandingly, thirstily—and Baylee wished he would never, never stop!

"I missed you," he mumbled against her mouth when he allowed a pause in their exchange for her to catch her breath.

"I missed you more," she breathed, tightening her embrace around his neck.

"Three weeks and you're done with this gig, right?" he said. "I can't wait until you're finished and only have your day ring-a-ding dinging to do."

"But what about you?" Baylee asked. "Won't you be finished here then too?"

"It depends," he said, brushing a hair from her face with the back of his hand.

"On what?" she asked. She knew the FBI was at the Dickens Village for a reason, but since she also knew that Justice couldn't tell her what the reason was, she hadn't pressed him. But now—knowing that the Hampton Handbell Ringers and Carolers would be finished with their engagement at the Dickens Village, she'd hoped Justice's shifts would go back to normal as well.

"On some…stuff," Justice answered, and Baylee knew she couldn't press him about it. He grinned. "But…I'm only working one shift tomorrow," he informed her. "So that means, since you're off tomorrow too, we can hang out all night long. What do you say? Maybe there's a corny Christmas flick on we could watch, huh?"

"I say yes," Baylee giggled. "Don't I always say yes to you, Mr. Chimney Sweep?"

"Let's hope so," Justice chuckled. "Oh, I certainly hope so."

He kissed her again—long, deep, and hungrily. Then, releasing her and taking only her hand, he asked, "So how was your day, sugar plum?"

Baylee smiled. "Just fine," she answered. "Rather uneventful, in fact. How about you?"

Justice sighed. Oh, what he wouldn't give for the day to have been eventful—his team might have tagged and captured the Jack the Ripper killer. But unfortunately, everything had been as mundane as usual.

"Pretty uneventful as well, I'm afraid," he told her.

Baylee laughed and grasped his arm as they walked along the alleyway. "Well, how about you come over tomorrow before we watch our next wonderfully romantic made-for-TV Christmas show and help me decorate the rest of the gingerbread people cookies I made today?"

Justice laughed. "Yes!" he exclaimed with added dramatics. "That's exactly what I wanted to do on my only single-shift day." He looked at her and winked. "Provided there'll be cookie frosting available to lick off your lips."

"I'm sure I can arrange something," Baylee giggled.

Justice studied her a moment, wondering what he'd ever done in life to earn or deserve the love of a woman like Baylee. She was so beautiful—and not just her face and body. Everything about her was beautiful. From the way she rang her little handbells, to her voice, to the kindness she always, always displayed, to her witty sense of humor. All of her—that's what Justice loved—every inch and characteristic of Baylee Cabot.

"Oh, you guys are adorable!" an older woman exclaimed, rushing up to Baylee and Justice unexpectedly. "Would you mind if I took your picture?"

"Um…of course not," Justice stammered, uncertain as to whether he'd responded correctly. Looking to Baylee, he asked, "Do you mind, baby?"

"Of course I don't mind," Baylee giggled.

"Oh, thank you so much!" the woman gushed. "You guys are just too charming for words! The chimney sweep and the Christmas caroler—it's like a fairy tale!"

"Here, baby," Justice chuckled, brushing soot from Baylee's face. Leaning close to her, he whispered, "You better wipe that soot off your face. It looks like you've been necking with a chimney sweep or something."

Baylee giggled, allowing him to brush the soot from her face with his glove. Justice put his arm around her shoulders then, pulling her close to him so that the woman could take their photograph. Baylee was warm and smelled like apple cider and frosted snow, and Justice wished he could keep her there next to him, safe in his arms forever. He wished the Jack the Ripper killer would curl up and die somewhere so that at least one anxiety for Baylee's well-being would evaporate.

"Say cheese!" the enthusiastic lady said as she pressed the shutter button of her digital camera. "One more!" she begged, not waiting for permission. She studied them a moment after she'd taken their photo, sighed with contentment, and said, "Thank you so much, you guys. You really are too perfect together."

"Thank you, ma'am," Justice said. He nodded politely to the woman as she hurried off.

Looking down to Baylee, he smiled. "We do make a perfect couple, don't we?"

"Absolutely!" Baylee giggled.

Lowering his voice then, Justice suggested, "Maybe we oughta think about making it permanent, huh?"

"What?" Baylee asked. Had she heard him correctly? And if she had, had she understood his insinuation?'

Justice bent, pressing a quick kiss to her mouth. "You heard me," he said. "Now, you have a good evening, my little bell-ringer," he chuckled. "I'll be watching you from the rooftops…while I'm dancing around like ol' Dick Van Dyke up there."

But Baylee could only nod. She was still stunned by what he'd said. Make it permanent? Surely there could be only one thing he meant, right? He'd implied they should get married, hadn't he?

As Baylee walked back to the Dickens Village square, she was numb all over—numb with disbelief, numb with bliss, numb with utter, complete, and overwhelming euphoria! She was in love with Justice Kincaid—oh, so thoroughly, supremely, and eternally in love with him. And she was beginning to believe that he was nearly as in love with her.

"Maybe we oughta think about making it permanent?" she repeated in a breathy whisper as she took her place in the handbell choir.

"What did you say?" Candice asked. But Mr. Hampton cleared his voice, indicating that all eyes should be on him.

"Later," Baylee mumbled to Candice.

As the Hampton Handbell Ringers and Carolers began to perform "Carol of the Bells," Baylee Cabot silently hoped that maybe her dreams of owning Justice Kincaid's heart forever would come true in time for Christmas. After all, there was nothing in all the world she wanted more than Justice.

"Mmmm," Justice moaned as he kissed the cookie frosting from Baylee's lips the next afternoon. "You know," he began, pulling her against him, "you taste just like frosted gingerbread cookies today."

Baylee giggled—tried to keep the spoon in her left hand and the spatula in her right hand from getting frosting on Justice's clothes as he bound her to him, drinking in the warm passion her mouth willingly offered.

"I'm never going to get these cookies finished with you here. You do realize that," she teased him when their mouths separated for a moment.

"So you're saying you want me to leave you alone?" he flirted. "You'd rather ice cookies than neck with your boyfriend?"

Baylee's smile broadened. She tossed the spoon and spatula she'd been using to mix more frosting onto the nearby kitchen table, wrapped her arms tightly around Justice's neck, and breathed, "Absolutely not!" a moment before she applied a coaxing, playful kiss to his mouth.

Kissing, kissing, and more kissing! It's almost all they'd done all day. For some reason, Baylee was unable to find any explanation for why she and Justice seemed to be so driven to do nothing but kiss that day—but they were! It was as if something had escalated, but she didn't quite know what. All she knew was that she had to be in his arms, had to feel his lips pressed to hers almost constantly for the five hours they'd been attempting to ice gingerbread people cookies and watch a corny Christmas movie on TV.

They'd somehow managed to make it through the animated version of "How the Grinch Stole Christmas" without locking lips once. But that brief half an hour was the longest span of time they'd managed to not be somehow interlaced since Justice had arrived!

All at once something Justice had said flittered through Baylee's mind, and she giggled, even for the playful passion raging between them.

"What's so funny?" he asked, smiling at her.

She smiled up at him—ran her fingers over his head and through his short hair. "I just can't believe your grandma's verbiage has settled into our vernacular."

"You mean the term 'necking'?" he asked, grinning.

"Yeah," she affirmed. "It doesn't seem that long ago that we were joking about how archaic and weird it was…and yet—"

"Here we are," Justice interrupted. "Just standing in your kitchen, necking."

Baylee laughed. "Exactly!"

"Well, it just so happens…that I like your neck," Justice mumbled as he began placing soft, moist kisses along Baylee's throat.

"Well, it just so happens that I like that you like my neck," she whispered.

"Then it all works out…all the necking that goes on between the chimney sweep and the caroler, right?" he said, kissing her cheek.

"Absolutely," she sighed.

The sound of Candice's assigned ringtone startled Baylee from her bliss, however.

Justice released Baylee with a sigh of disappointment and said, "Cyndi Lauper and 'Girls Just Wanna Have Fun'—I guess Candice and Tristan aren't necking if she's calling you right now."

"I'm sorry, Justice," Baylee said, picking up her cell phone from the table. "Tristan is working, and she's a little rattled. It seems like some guy from the Dickens Village has a thing for her or something, and today she—"

A wave of nausea washed over Justice as he watched Baylee answer her phone—heard her say, "Hey, girl. What's going on?"

Baylee held up one index finger indicating she'd only be a minute. But as the ominous sense of dread continued to seep into his soul, Justice glanced out the window. It was already dark outside. According to the coroner's times of death on the Jack the Ripper copycat victims, the psychopathic murderer killed just after sundown.

"At your window? Are you sure, Candice?" Baylee exclaimed. "Well, have you called Tristan?"

Snatching the phone from Baylee's hand, Justice demanded, "Give me your address, Candice…now!"

Baylee was astonished by Justice's behavior—not angry or offended, just astonished. She watched as he listened to Candice a moment, obviously receiving the information he'd demanded from her.

"Make sure every window is locked, Candice…every door. And do not go outside until someone gets there, do you hear me?" Justice nearly growled. "Stay put…and stay on the phone with Baylee." Handing her cell phone back to Baylee, he ordered, "Do not hang up on her…no matter what she says or what you hear."

"O-okay," Baylee stammered.

She watched then as Justice pulled his own cell from the holster at his belt. He pressed one button and then said, "This is federal agent SSA Justice Kincaid. I have a line on our Jack the Ripper. Send federal agents and local police to 6181 Prairie Sunset Lane. The perp's possible target is Candice Jones, resident of that address. She reports seeing a man dressed in period clothing, looking at her through her window. A second possible target is Baylee Cabot, address 2984 Mystic Falls. I am with that possible target now, but send backup here as well. Notify Unit Chief Brian Reagan."

"Candice?" Baylee managed to breathe into her cell. "Are you all right?"

"Stay here, Baylee," Justice ordered.

Baylee watched as he reached down, drawing a small handgun from a holster built into his boot. "I'm just going to check your windows…make sure they're secured."

Baylee nodded and tried to listen as Candice asked her what was going on. "What was all that? Did I hear Justice say he was sending police over here?" Candice sobbed on the phone.

"Um…yes," Baylee managed. "Apparently this guy you told me you saw last night following you…well, maybe the fact that he was following you isn't as benign as we thought, Candice."

"Baylee! What should I do?" Candice cried.

"J-just do what Justice told you to do. Make sure the windows and doors are locked…and wait for the police to arrive. I'm sure they're close," Baylee answered as tears began to stream down her face.

"Who is this guy, Baylee?" Candice sobbed. "I'm scared! Justice sounded so…so…did I hear him say he's a federal agent? Is he, like, with like some—"

"He's FBI, Candice," Baylee interrupted. "I'm pretty sure all the chimney sweeps are FBI."

Justice returned then and began dimming all the lights in the kitchen and front rooms of Baylee's rental house.

He gestured to her that she should give him her cell again, and she complied. "Candice?" he began. "I want you to remain as calm as you possibly can. Federal agents and police are on their way, though you might not hear any sirens. Now, is there anywhere in your house you can…*wait* for them? Maybe a crawl space or attic? Somewhere someone couldn't find you easily?"

Baylee brushed tears from her face and listened as Candice began to fall apart on the phone.

"Candice!" Justice growled. "Do not melt! Not now. Just get to a more secure location and wait. You'll hear the agents identify themselves when they enter your house. Only then do you come out. Do you understand?"

Baylee watched as Justice nodded. "That sounds fine, Candice. That sounds perfect, in fact. Now you go in there, and stay quiet. I'll stay on the phone with you until the FBI or police arrive. Okay? Don't talk or make a sound. Just stay quiet."

"Justice?" Baylee cried in a whisper.

Reaching out, Justice pulled her into his embrace, even for her cell phone in one hand and his gun in the other. "Shhh. It'll be fine. It'll only take a few minutes for them to get there…and here." He kissed the top of her head and then led her into the kitchen. "Come on. Sit down here," he said, indicating she should sit down behind the small island between the sink counter and the front room. "Just sit here and wait with me," he said as he slid down to sit beside her. "It's going to be fine." He spoke into the phone next, "You okay, Candice? Good…good. Just wait. It'll be fine. They're almost to you. I'm sure they are almost to you."

"It'll be fine, baby," Justice whispered to Baylee. "I won't let anything happen to you. I love you. You know that, right? And you know I'd never let anything happen to you, don't you?" Baylee looked up into the now blazing green of his eyes and nodded. "Okay then," he said as he pulled her closer to him. "Candice…try not to gasp so loudly," he said quietly into the cell phone. "That's right. Just breathe deep…a deep breath and a slow exhale. They'll be there in a minute…a million cops and FBI guys, okay? You'll be fine. Just breathe…nice and slow. That's it."

Baylee closed her eyes—clung desperately to Justice, vowing she'd never let him go again. She didn't know all of what was going on, but she had heard enough buzzwords and terms to figure out that Candice might have been targeted by a serial killer that had been all over the news the past couple of months. It seemed impossible—not merely improbable, but entirely impossible!

But as all the pieces began to fit together in her mind—the ex-military security forces at the Dickens Village, Justice telling her weeks ago that he worked for the FBI but couldn't reveal details of his current assignment, and the fact that Justice had referred to the serial killer as Jack the Ripper when he'd called in about Candice—it all made sense in that moment.

"You're FB*I* FBI aren't you, Justice?" she whispered to him.

"Yeah," he answered, pulling her closer to him.

There was a noise then—like someone was messing with the doorknob of the front door.

"Hold this," Justice whispered, handing Baylee her cell once more.

Baylee stopped breathing as she watched Justice shift the safety on his gun—watched him take hold of it with two hands and look around the kitchen island toward the front door.

"SSA Kincaid?" a voice from the other side of the door called. "This is federal agent Javiar Morales informing you that the perimeter is secure."

Justice exhaled a relieved sigh and looked to Baylee.

"Everything is okay, baby. Breathe!" was the last thing she heard him say.

CHAPTER NINE

The Jack the Ripper copycat killer had chosen "death by cop." When police and federal agents arrived at Candice's house, they indeed did find a man, dressed in the period clothing common to the employees of the Dickens Village, lurking nearby. Yet when he was approached and told to surrender, he drew a pistol from somewhere within the folds of his black cape and began firing at police. Thus one of the most prolific serial killers of the new century was shot and killed.

Candice was found hiding in her kitchen pantry, in a state of shock. And even though she'd recovered by the time the ambulance arrived, she was taken to the hospital for observation and evaluation.

Baylee awoke from the short fainting spell that holding her breath had caused to find herself safely in Justice's arms and surrounded by police and FBI agents. The Hampton Handbell Ringers and Carolers missed their scheduled performance times at the Dickens Village that night, for it was closed to visitors while the FBI interviewed every employee and vendor and went over the village with a fine-tooth comb.

Justice had stayed the night with Baylee and slept on the couch so that she'd feel safe and secure and be able to sleep. Yet by morning, Baylee was ready to leave the terrifying, though brief, experience behind her. Though it was terrifying to know Candice had been targeted by a serial killer—though Baylee knew she may have been a target as well— she also knew that no good would come from her hiding away and trembling in fear for the rest of her life. One thing was still true the day after the Jack the Ripper copycat was found—Baylee loved Justice more than anything, and all she wanted was to be with him.

Yet the next evening, as she performed with the Hampton Handbell Ringers (minus Candice, who still needed some time to emotionally heal), she thought the village felt lonesome and bare without the silhouettes of the chimney sweeps on the rooftops. Baylee knew no one else felt the emptiness she did—at least not the way she did. She wondered if all the employees might have felt a little more secure had the FBI had allowed the team of chimney sweep agents to stay on for a few days. But they hadn't, and Justice has returned to the FBI field office to work on the details and follow-ups of the Jack the Ripper copycat case.

The only good thing about Justice's not being at the Dickens Village every day was that on the evenings the Handbell Ringers weren't performing he and Baylee could spend their time together.

Baylee was relieved to discover that nothing had changed between them because of the drama or his not being at the Dickens Village with her. If anything, they seemed even more comfortable together, and she figured it was because Jack the Ripper wasn't always lurking in the back of his mind.

Thus, one week before Christmas found Justice at Baylee's house—both of them watching *A Christmas Story* as they wrapped gifts together.

"So you're just going to wrap up that Beretta and stick it under your grandma's tree? Just like that?" Baylee asked as she watched Justice awkwardly try to tie a decent wire ribbon bow around the gift he'd just wrapped.

"Well, sure," he said. "What else would I do?"

Baylee giggled. "I guess you're right. It's a Christmas gift, after all."

"Absolutely," Justice agreed.

He sighed as he finished tying a pathetic bow. "I do need to tell you something, baby," he began. By the sound in his voice, Baylee knew it wasn't good news he was about to reveal. Every shred of apprehension that was wafting around in her body seemed to fuse together into one giant ball of anxiety. What was he about to say? For a moment she worried that he was going to break up with her. It was the worst thing she could conceive, and she began to tremble a little.

"Yeah?" she prodded, though she wished she didn't have to hear whatever it was that was coming.

"I've got to report to DC," he said. "I'll be gone until New Year's Eve."

Baylee exhaled a breath of relief and mumbled, "Oh, good!"

"What?" Justice asked, looking at her with a hurt frown puckering his brow.

"I mean...I thought it was going to be something else...something really, really bad," she explained.

"Like what?" he asked. "I thought you'd be upset that I wouldn't be here for Christmas."

"I am!" she assured him, taking hold of his arm. "I just thought...I thought..."

"You thought what?" he urged, still looking at her as if he were a hurt puppy.

"I thought you were going to break up with me," she confessed.

"What?" he exclaimed. "You're kidding, right?"

Baylee shrugged. "I tried to think of the worst thing you could say to me...and that's what I thought of."

"Baylee," he breathed, taking her face between his hands. He smiled and chuckled a little. "But you know what's kind of funny about this?"

"What?" she asked, gazing into his dreamy peacock-green eyes.

"I was afraid you'd dump me last week when I had to shed the chimney sweep outfit for good," he told her.

"What?" it was her turn to ask.

Justice shrugged. "I was kind of afraid that whatever spell I'd managed to cast over you would disappear or something...that the chimney sweep charm would be gone and you'd dropkick me to the curb."

Baylee put her arms around his neck and stared into his preposterously handsome face. "Dropkick you to the curb?" she asked. "The chimney sweep charm gone? Your charm goes far, far beyond your cute little chimney sweep costume, Justice Kincaid."

"Really?" he asked as his lips pressed a warm kiss to hers.

"Absolutely!" she assured him as she kissed him in return.

"Well, just in case it did...I got you this for Christmas," he said. Reaching over to where his leather jacket lay on the sofa, he reached into his pocket and removed a tiny plastic bag. As he handed the small bag to her, he said, "I'll need to take your bracelet to the jeweler's before I leave. He said they have to solder it onto your bracelet or something."

Opening the small plastic back, Baylee giggled with delight when she dumped the contents into her hand and saw the beautiful silver chimney sweep charm tumble onto her palm.

Gasping with delight, she exclaimed, "A chimney sweep charm? Oh, Justice! I love it!" She threw her arms around his neck again, hugging him tightly and kissing his cheek. "It's perfect! It's so, so, *so* perfect!"

Justice chuckled and said, "I figure the jeweler can put it right next to that little Victorian caroler one you bought at the Dickens Village, and then your caroler and my chimney sweep can neck forever on your wrist."

Baylee laughed, hugged him again, brushed the tears of joy from the corners of her eyes, and sighed. "Justice…it's so perfect! Look at his little top hat and chimney sweep brush! Where did you find this?"

"The jeweler had to order it from somewhere in England," he answered. "I was afraid it wouldn't get here before I had to leave, and I wanted to give it to you before I did."

"And why is it that I can't just attach it?" Baylee mumbled to herself as she studied the charm. "Oh, I see. They need to still make a hole for the charm ring. Is that it?"

"Yeah, I guess," Justice said. "All I know is he told me to bring it in with whatever bracelet you want it attached to. Do you trust me enough to take it in? He says he can have it done by the time I get back if I take it in tomorrow morning before I leave."

"Tomorrow morning?" Baylee exclaimed, suddenly so disheartened she felt depressed.

Justice smiled and caressed her soft cheek with the back of his hand. A man could drown in the brown of Baylee Cabot's eyes—in the warmth of her embrace and the flavor of her mouth. Justice thought it would be a good way to go—drowning in the arms of the woman he loved.

Her pretty eyes filled with tears, and it made his heart ache, but he had to report to DC. It was unavoidable. "I'll be back as soon as I can. And that leads me to my next question. What are you doing New Year's Eve, you little bell-ringer, you?"

She smiled at him and answered, "Making out with my handsome FBI lover."

"You mean *necking* with your charming chimney sweep lover?" he corrected.

"Either or," she giggled.

He had to taste her then. Enough with wrapping gifts and talking about chimney sweep charms. Gathering Baylee into his arms, Justice ground his mouth to hers in a loving, wanting, impassioned kiss. Goose bumps rippled over his arms and legs as she kissed him with just as much love, wanting, and passion.

Suddenly, however, she pushed at his chest, broke the seal of their lips, and gasped.

"What's the matter?" he asked, concerned.

"All I got you is a new boot knife for your collection," she confessed.

Justice laughed and pulled her against him again. "I love you, Baylee Cabot," he mumbled against her mouth.

"I love you more," she breathed a moment before she took his breath away with her ambrosial kiss.

CHAPTER TEN

It was the longest twelve days of Baylee's life—the miserable twelve days that Justice was in Washington DC. The entire time he'd been gone, she'd done nothing but worry and fret, miss him, and long for New Year's Eve and his return. No amount of handbell ringing and caroling had served to distract her. None of the Christmas parties she'd attended felt fun, and no other gift she'd opened on Christmas morning with her parents seemed nearly as wonderful as the chimney sweep charm she knew was waiting with her bracelet at the jeweler's. She'd even lost four pounds in the time Justice had been gone for missing him so badly.

But now he was nearly back with her. He'd called when his plane had landed—nearly an hour before—and said he'd pick up her bracelet on his way to spend New Year's Eve with her at her place. Baylee had spent all day cooking—making snacks for her and Justice to enjoy—and roasting a ham to go with the potato dish she'd made for their dinner together.

She and Justice had been planning their New Year's Eve since the day he left, having both agreed they'd rather stay in together all alone than attend the big to-do at the Dickens Village with everyone else. After all, they loved each other—liked each other's company more than anything else. Thus, they'd figured, why bother with socializing on such a crazy night as New Year's Eve tended to be?

Baylee heard his truck pull into her driveway, and a wave of emotion broke over her, causing tears of joy to spring to her eyes and goose bumps to race over every inch of her flesh. She heard the sound of his boots and opened the front door to be met by not only the sight of the most handsome man ever born but also an embrace and kiss that put any *The Princess Bride* kiss to shame!

Lifting Baylee off her feet as they kissed, Justice stepped into the house, kicking the door shut with his foot as he continued to nearly maul her with the mouth-to-mouth release of his pent-up desire.

"I missed you, I missed you, I missed you!" Baylee squealed as Justice kissed her cheeks, her forehead, her mouth, her neck, and the tip of her nose.

"I missed you more," he claimed, taking her mouth again. "Oh, you taste *so* good, Baylee Cabot!"

He was back! He was there in her arms, and Baylee felt her body breathe easier and relax a little for the first time in nearly two weeks. She couldn't seem to hug him tightly enough—couldn't seem to kiss him long enough. They paused in their affectionate exchange long enough for Justice to remove his coat, and then Baylee giggled as he pushed her back against the wall and ravished her with hot, moist kisses of desire.

"Mmm," he moaned at last. "You smell so good."

Baylee giggled, "That's not me. That's the ham and potatoes."

"Nope…I'm pretty sure it's you," Justice teased. "It's making me hungry."

Again Baylee laughed. Playfully slapping him on one shoulder, she disengaged herself from his arms and started toward the kitchen.

"That's because of the ham and potatoes," she giggled as she began to take the ham out of the oven. "I figured you'd be way hungry, so I made a ton of dinner for us…and some snacks and stuff for later."

"Did you get the movie?" he asked, following her into the kitchen.

"Of course," she said as he took hold of her elbow, turned her to face him, pushed her back against the counter, and kissed her again.

"And you didn't change your mind about me while I was gone?" he asked, his expression going serious for a moment.

"Why? Did you change your mind about me while you were gone?" Baylee asked, suddenly anxious.

"Am I acting like I changed my mind about you, sugar plum?" he asked, kissing her.

Baylee smiled. He loved her. She could see it in the smoldering green of his beautiful eyes.

"Am I acting like *I* changed my mind about *you*?" she countered.

Justice smiled. "So the chimney sweep charm didn't wear off then?"

"Never," she breathed. Suddenly remembering the bracelet charm Justice had given her for Christmas, she asked, "Did you have a chance to stop and pick up my bracelet?"

"Absolutely," Justice said. He released her and went to where he'd discarded his leather jacket. He picked it up, rummaging around in one pocket.

"Here you go," he said as he returned to her. Holding the clasp of the bracelet clutched in his fist, he held it above her head and teased, "What'll you give me for it?"

Baylee smiled, delighted by his teasing. "What do you want for it?" she flirted.

"Only your heart," he said. "And everything else that comes with it," he added as Baylee saw that more than the chimney sweep charm had been added to her bracelet.

Tears sprung to her eyes, and she couldn't breathe as she stared at the chocolate diamond solitaire ring that had been threaded onto the bracelet's chain.

"It's a…it's a ring," she whispered.

"It's an engagement ring, to be exact…and you better breathe, baby," he chuckled. "Remember what happened last time you held your breath too long."

"Justice," was all Baylee could say. Only his name. It was all that would come out of her mouth as she stood in stunned, yet euphoric, astonishment.

"Here," he said, unlatching the bracelet's clasp and removing the ring from its chain. "Maybe I better try it this way."

Dropping to one knee, Justice took Baylee's left hand in his, slipped her charm bracelet onto her wrist and the chocolate diamond onto her left ring finger, and asked, "Baylee Cabot, you little bell-ringer, you…will you marry me?"

As tears streamed down her cheeks, Baylee whispered, "Absolutely!" with just the perfect amount of blissful enthusiasm.

"Then feed me your ham and potatoes, wife-to be," Justice said, standing and gathering a sobbing Baylee into his arms. "Before my barely bridled desire consumes *you* first." Justice kissed her then—once again ravishing her mouth with passionate exchanges of love and desperate wanting.

As they continued to kiss, Baylee was somewhat aware of the charm bracelet at her wrist, very aware of the chocolate diamond on her finger, and thoroughly aware of how lucky she was to own the love of the handsome federal agent who had cast his chimney sweep charm and captured her heart.

AUTHOR'S NOTE

Yes, I love handbells and "Carol of the Bells" performed on them. Yes, I love Dick Van Dyke as the chimney sweep Bert in *Mary Poppins*—and I was totally disappointed when Mary Poppins drifted off at the end of the movie instead of staying to enjoy a mad, passionate love affair with Bert. Yes, I love hot chocolate—and with a soft peppermint stick to stir it with. Yes, I love and adore our military veterans and think they deserve more respect and adulation. Yes, I love Christmas and everything about it. And yes, I hope I've written something just easy and fun—romantic and kissy—something that enabled you to find a moment of respite this holiday season. Yes, I always wanted a charm bracelet of my own. (Thank you, Lisa J., for making that dream come true!) And yes, I could babble on and on about what inspired me while writing this little novella, *The Chimney Sweep Charm*.

But since I did intend for this book to be a little lighthearted holiday escape, I thought I'd skew off onto something a little different in this Author's Note: that being the incredible venue of amusement the cover artist and I enjoyed during our collaboration on the cover for *The Chimney Sweep Charm*—i.e., the Golden Man image.

As Sheri (the brilliant and singular graphics designer for my book covers) and I were searching through hundreds, then thousands, of images to be submitted as possibilities for the cover of *The Chimney Sweep Charm*, we began to experience a frustration we hadn't ever encountered before. We tried searching everywhere for just the right images! Every chimney sweep graphic anybody could find, we considered it. Every Old London-looking rooftop scene, every brick chimney photo—basically anything that could have had something to do with the book—we considered it.

"How about a brass handbell?" one of us suggested. "How about just this sooty-looking chimney sweep's hand?" The possibilities were endless, but the available graphics were few, and I couldn't like anything that was being presented.

With immense discouragement washing over me, I finally *settled* on a couple of images and asked Sheri, "Can you do something with *these*?" She agreed to try. However, her guts were churning with dissatisfaction as well. Nothing made Sheri feel positive, and nothing said "Justice Kincaid, the FBI chimney sweep," to me.

And so, one night as I was swathed in thinking I really would just have to settle when it came to a cover for *The Chimney Sweep Charm*, I sat down at my computer and began searching through more photographs—looking for anything that might spark my imagination or Sheri's.

Well, I must've blown a kiss to a chimney sweep myself sometime last summer because that night the first image that came up on my computer was of a guy who looked as if he might have potential for something someday where book covers were concerned. I wasn't all that excited about it, but I began to think (knowing Sheri's mad graphic design skill and creative majesty) that maybe she could fuse two images somehow the way she'd done with the new *Divine Deception* cover. Maybe the cover didn't need to be *just* a chimney sweep or *just* a rooftop scene. Maybe it could be made up of both.

Now, naturally, I knew we were never going to find an image of a handsome chimney sweep, stationed on an old Camden Town rooftop, peering through a pair of FBI-issued binoculars, but maybe (between Sheri and me and our common creative juices) we could create something similar.

So I e-mailed the guy's image to Sheri and began clicking around on other images while I waited for her response. I decided to see what other images this particular photographer might have to offer. I clicked on another image, and voilà! Holy better image, Batman! It was the same model the photographer had used in the first image, but this time he was kind of banged up, shirtless, and holding a sword, and the photo was entitled "Warrior."

Hmmm, I thought. *Maybe Sheri could use this one somehow…only not the shirtless part.* So I e-mailed the image to Sheri and continued to click around on the same photographer's images as I waited for her to respond to the second image I found.

However, the next image I clicked nearly reached out and slapped me in the face. Not only was it a great angle but the guy's face was smudged up just like a chimney sweep's!

"This is it!" I said aloud and instantly sent Sheri an e-mail with a subject line of something like *Hold the phone! Here it is!*

Sheri called me the second she opened the e-mail with Justice Kincaid's picture and agreed. We had found one of the images for the cover of *The Chimney Sweep Charm*!

So what's the big deal? you may be thinking. Well, I'll tell you: in truth, there were several big deals. First, I had to decide if I were really going to allow a significant portion of a person's face to dominate a cover. (You know how I like to leave things to the imagination, right?) Second, there were a couple of challenges with the image regarding Sheri's designing process. The photograph, in its entirety, is not only a shirtless one but the lighting was all orange and warm. Plus, the guy's skin was sort of glittery, and his elbow looked like it was jammed up against a glass wall or something.

However, Sheri and I both agreed—the Golden Man (as we affectionately nicknamed him) was perfect for the cover of *The Chimney Sweep Charm*. Glittery skin, neked shoulder, and orange lighting or not, the Golden Man won us over!

The challenge then fell to Sheri to perform miracles with the Golden Man while I tried to approve of a Christmassy rooftops image.

Covers are important to me—paramount! I've been so very disappointed in the past when things were beyond my decision or control that now that I'm able to accept or veto the covers for my books once again, I'm nearly obsessed with needing them to convey not only what the book is about but what I'm feeling as well. Furthermore, I cannot tell you what it meant to me to finally be able to have an artist like Sheri Brady creating my covers. And as you can see, her cover of *The Chimney Sweep Charm* was a dream come true (at least for me).

I wish I'd kept all the e-mail exchanges during the cover process for this book—the hysterical comments about the Golden Man and "getting his lips just right" in the blended image. Sheri knew that if I were going to take an uncomfortable leap and put a face on one of my covers, I needed the constant reassurance that the guy in the image was worthy of being there. Consequently, her hysterical remarks in e-mails and on the phone kept me in stitches through the entire process of not only her creating the cover but also my getting over the anxiety of having a real face on it!

Sheri's witty comments—such as "I spent hours with the Golden Man. His lips drew me in," or "I tried rubbing the glitter off his shoulder and running my fingers through his hair to straighten it"— made me giggle and enjoy moments of the same sort of worry-free escapism I hope the book offers to you. And *that's* why I even bothered telling you this little "behind-the-scenes" story—because I hope that reading *The Chimney Sweep Charm* is for you exactly what the cover collaboration between me and Sheri was for me—an easy, lighthearted, fun, "everything is okay," "Christmastime is wonderful" escape. I know that the Golden Man and all of Sheri's hilarious remarks and work on the cover don't really mean anything to you out of context, but it's the way I felt when she and I were collaborating on it that I want to convey. So I hope that in some way, this little novella—though it's no profound work of fiction that will sit on the shelf next to *Jane Eyre* in years to come—gave you a little lift and let you escape the craziness of life, the worries, the stress. It's what I always hope when I write a book—that you'll smile and feel rested for a time because of it.

And finally—just so you can have a better idea of what Sheri started with and why she stayed up all night with the Golden Man working on his lips—here he is in glorious, old 1940s movie-star black-and-white.

Merry Christmas!
~Marcia Lynn McClure

My everlasting admiration, gratitude, and love...
To my husband, Kevin...
My inspiration...
My heart's desire...
The man of my every dream!

ABOUT THE AUTHOR

Marcia Lynn McClure's intoxicating succession of novels, novellas, and e-books—including *The Visions of Ransom Lake*, *A Crimson Frost*, *Untethered*, and *The Pirate Ruse*—has established her as one of the most favored and engaging authors of true romance. Her unprecedented forte in weaving captivating stories of western, medieval, regency, and contemporary amour void of brusque intimacy has earned her the title "The Queen of Kissing."

Marcia, who was born in Albuquerque, New Mexico, has spent her life intrigued with people, history, love, and romance. A wife, mother, grandmother, family historian, poet, and author, Marcia Lynn McClure spins her tales of splendor for the sake of offering respite through the beauty, mirth, and delight of a worthwhile and wonderful story.

BIBLIOGRAPHY

Beneath the Honeysuckle Vine
A Better Reason to Fall in Love
The Bewitching of Amoretta Ipswich
Born for Thorton's Sake
The Chimney Sweep Charm
A Crimson Frost
Daydreams
Desert Fire
Divine Deception
Dusty Britches
The Fragrance of her Name
The Haunting of Autumn Lake
The Heavenly Surrender
The Highwayman of Tanglewood
Kiss in the Dark
Kissing Cousins
The Light of the Lovers' Moon
Love Me
The McCall Trilogy
Midnight Masquerade
An Old-Fashioned Romance
One Classic Latin Lover, Please
The Pirate Ruse
The Prairie Prince
The Rogue Knight
Romantic Vignettes-The Anthology of Premiere Novellas
Saphyre Snow
Shackles of Honor
Sudden Storms
Sweet Cherry Ray
Take a Walk With Me
The Tide of the Mermaid Tears
The Time of Aspen Falls
To Echo the Past
The Touch of Sage

The Trove of the Passion Room
Untethered
The Visions of Ransom Lake
Weathered Too Young
The Whispered Kiss
The Windswept Flame

www.ingramcontent.com/pod-product-compliance
Lightning Source LLC
Chambersburg PA
CBHW070627260626
47161CB00007B/2614